THE OBEDIENT BOW

SAMIRAH ZAMAN

To all the women imprisoned in a dreamless cage —
I see you. I hear you. I hope you break free.

But most importantly, for Bushra.
Who became what everybody else needed. Whose unwavering belief
upholds us, and whose determination never falters.
May the fruits of your labour transpire into happiness until you are
dreaming with your eyes wide open.

Playlist

Labour – **Paris Paloma**

This Is Me Trying – **Taylor Swift**

Million Reasons – **Lady Gaga**

Born To Be Somebody – **Justin Bieber**

Heartbeat – **James Arthur**

Alive – **Sia**

Like That – **Bea Miller**

Heal Me – **Grace Carter**

Easy On Me – **Adele**

Castles (Acoustic) – **Freya Ridings**

Hope Ur Ok – **Olivia Rodrigo**

Saajan Saajan – **Alka Yagnik**

Roke Na Ruke Naina – **Arjit Singh**

Khoobsurat - **Vishal Mishra**

Jaan Ban Gaye – **Mithoon**

Ik Lamha – **Azaan Sami Khan**

Char Ghar Chalen – **Mithoon**

Apna Bana Le – **Arjit Singh**

Channa Ve – **Akhil Sachdeva**

Adhura Lafz – **Sohail Sen**

CHAPTER ONE

IT WOULD BE UNFAIR to say my parents were *unhappy* when the doctor announced they were blessed with another daughter. My mother wept, but that was probably because her labour was exhausting and extended, as she always liked to remind me. She said I was stubborn, even in her womb, refusing to move during her scans so the midwife could complete all her checks.

My Dadi, *paternal grandmother,* was my mum's birth partner because she, and my father, believed a man should not witness such a womanly affair. The men should come after the woman has been neatly stitched back together.

When my father entered the room, he crouched down and fulfilled his Islamic duties by whispering the call to prayer in my ear.

I'm sure if someone snapped a picture of that moment, they would have called it *wholesome.* But they couldn't have possibly known the fear my parents felt at the prospect of raising yet another daughter.

My mother wondered if my stubbornness would follow me into the real world. Her first two daughters were easily malleable, but something told my mum that her luck had run out with me. As she stared into my innocent brown eyes, she made a silent prayer that I remained that way. Her arms held onto me tight, almost as if the world was already trying to snatch me away. Perhaps it was because she knew her time with me was limited. With so little time to teach me all a woman needs to survive, she knew love would have to wait.

My father had other worries because another daughter meant more responsibility. It was on him to make sure I didn't dishonour the good family name. It was on him to find me a suitable husband. It was on him to pay for a wedding because *women don't work.* And without a son to share the household responsibility with, it was solely on him to protect and provide for us.

So, no. My parents weren't unhappy at the birth of their third daughter. But it's fair to say they were *disappointed.*

My sisters were not. They bound into the room with wide grins and giggles. They stood over my glass carrier in awe and wonder.

"Ammi," *mum,* "what's her name?" Asma asked.

She had a name in mind, but she turned to her husband. "Have you decided yet?"

My dad shook his head, unwilling to admit he only thought of boy names because he was so sure God would finally give him a true heir. "There's still time."

And that was that.

My father's word was final. After all, he was the man of the house. There was no arguing with him. There was no reasoning with him. There was simply obeying him.

He made my mother wait two days before confirming my name. "Zoya Iqbal," he said.

She didn't like the name. She wanted a more traditional name, like her other daughters. But she still smiled at him. "What does it mean?"

"Loving, caring, joyous and alive."

She stared down at her sleeping baby. Her throat tightened as she said, "Alhamdulilah." *Praise be to God.*

There was an emptiness in my dad. Within the private confines of his home, he could no longer maintain the false smile. "Allah will give us a son next time."

My mother didn't want anymore children, but she stayed silent because she understood her role well. She was an excellent cook. She kept the house tidy. She carried and raised her children. She was the perfect host. She understood her place in the home. She took good care of her mother-in-law. She made sure her husband was always content. She never spoke back. She never asked for more than she was offered. She never complained. She was everything my father could have wanted because, more than anything else, she was *obedient.*

Chapter Two

"Give it back!" Maliha shouted as she chased me around the bedroom. "That's mine!"

I couldn't breathe from simultaneously running and laughing. When I tripped over the unfolded laundry, I barely stopped myself from face-planting the floor. Even that didn't stop me from taunting her. "If you want it, come and get it!" I screamed as I ran down the stairs.

"Zoya! Get back here!" Her heavy footsteps thudded close behind me.

My mother's yell halted us both. "Kia ho raha he?" *What is going on?*

With a devilish grin at my sister, I held up her treasured lip gloss. "Aapi," *sister,* "has makeup!"

The clear lip gloss was snatched out of my hold. She stared at Maliha in disgust. "Where did you get this?"

Her gaze dropped to the floor. "My school friend gave it."

Anger swirled in her brown eyes. "Wait until I tell your dad about this."

My smile faded as a single tear streaked down her face. My mother's rage was tolerable; *my father's was not.* Guilt ate at me and I stepped forward. "It's only lip gloss. It's basically the same as Vaseline."

"Thum khamosh raho." *You shut up.* "Why are you running around like a boy? Have you folded those clothes?"

I let out a groan. "I *hate* folding clothes. It's so boring," I whined.

"And my life is so interesting?" she asked sarcastically. "I have enough to do without you hassling me. Fold those clothes and then come down and dust the living room properly."

Zain screamed in the adjacent room; probably from losing his stupid game. My dad was finally granted a son two years after my birth. To say he was ecstatic would be an understatement. He went around gifting mithai, *Pakistani sweets,* to everyone, including the strangers on our street. Our White neighbours looked startled when they opened their front door to his wide grin and chant of *"I have son. God gave me son."*

"How come he doesn't have to help?" I snapped.

She pointed at the stairs. "Do as I asked!"

"That's not fair," I muttered as Maliha and I trudged up the stairs.

"He's *six.* How much help is he going to be?"

"When I was his age, I was wiping the dishes away."

Asma had already made the beds and wiped all the surfaces down when we joined her in our bedroom. "Hand or sandal?"

I grinned. "Neither."

She shook her head. "One of these days, you're really going to get it."

Waving off her concerns, I half-heartedly folded the clothes. "She's harmless."

"Dad's not." Maliha still wore a solemn expression. "He's going to kill me. You know how much he hates makeup."

Asma arched her brow at me. "Are you going to fold those properly?"

I sighed. It was a Saturday morning. I didn't want to be folding laundry. I wanted to sleep until midday and then lounge around doing nothing. I threw the trousers onto the floor and flopped onto the bed my sister just made. "*Nope.* If dad and Zain want their clothes washed, ironed and folded, they can do it themselves."

My eldest sister sighed and took over for me. "You're never going to learn if you make everyone do the work for you."

For an eight-year-old, I definitely had too much sass and attitude. Still, I clung to a dream I never wished to give up. "One day I'm going to own a business where I have people doing the work for me."

Maliha snickered. "And what business is that?"

I shrugged, not having the faintest idea how to get one up and running. I had ample time to figure that out.

Asma, who was the living embodiment of worry, studied me. "Uneducated people don't get to own businesses."

Once again, I shrugged. "I'm going to school, aren't I?"

She frowned. "GCSEs aren't enough."

Irritation settled in my chest. "You sound just like *them*." I didn't need to clarify who I was talking about, because we had heard the speech from our parents enough times to understand. If my father could have had it his way, he wouldn't have sent us to school. He would have much rather we stayed home and perfected my mother's daily routine.

She abandoned the clothes and took a seat next to me. There was something motherly about Asma. Not the harsh type our own mother was, but a gentle kind. Her hand rested on my knee and she squeezed tight. "Having dreams is a beautiful thing, Zoya. But don't hurt yourself by setting yourself up for disappointment. You know how Baba," *dad*, "is. You know what our lives are going to be."

Asma turned fifteen only a few months ago, but talk about what was to happen after she turned sixteen had already begun. While still a child, she would be expected to care for her husband and his family. Within a few years, she would become a mother herself.

I hated that at my young age, I understood everything. I hated that I could see the fear in my sister's eyes. I hated that we couldn't ask for a better life. But more than anything, I hated my life. At eight, I should have spent my weekends enjoying my childhood, not being trained to become a dutiful housewife.

I stared at my sister with determination flowing through my veins. "Why can't we say no?"

"That word does not exist in a Pakistani woman's vocabulary."

$$\text{❀❀❀❀}$$

I carried the last of the roti to the table, where my dad and Zain were already eating. With no other seat remaining, I was stuck sitting opposite my dad. I didn't want to be caught in his line of fire, so I kept my head down and silently ate.

"There's not enough salt," he complained while scoffing his face.

Automatically, my mum stopped eating to grab him the salt. Once she was back in her seat, she peered up at him and cleared her throat.

Even then, her voice came out mousey. "Could you give me two pounds?"

"What for?"

She swallowed hard. "I need to buy thread to fix Maliha's trousers." When his narrowed eyes landed on her, she bowed her head in fear.

I wished I had money of my own to give her, so she never had to belittle herself like that again. From the look on his face, one would have suspected she was asking for a million pounds. It was two measly pounds of whatever he earned. No one around the table knew what that true value was because it was *his* money, therefore none of our business. I jumped when his palm came down on the table.

"What are you looking at?" he snapped in my direction.

I hadn't realised I was still blankly staring at them. I shook my head. "Kuch naheen." *Nothing.*

"I better not get any more calls from your school to complain about your behaviour."

I wanted to explain I only pushed that boy because he tried to yank my trousers down in the playground. Even though Halima and Sumayyah backed my version of events, the teachers still punished me by taking away my playtime for an entire week. But that wasn't as bad as the two slaps I got across my face from my dad when I returned home.

"Okay," I whispered.

"Any more trouble and I will take you to Pakistan and leave you there with your uncle."

We all received that threat when he was angry. He never actually followed through.

We ate mostly in silence after that. I was helping Maliha clear the table when my dad called for my mother's attention. By the door, hidden from their sight, I listened in.

"Malik called me again. He wants to get the families together."

"What did you say?"

He sighed. "Malik is my good friend. He is an established man. Saying no would shame him."

"And the boy?"

"Saad is nearly twenty. He is a good boy."

My mum's voice carried the fear I saw in Asma's eyes. "She hasn't finished her exams."

"I said we would have to wait until next summer."

"So you have already agreed to giving our daughter away?"

He didn't like the tone of her voice. His icy glare landed on her. "Will you find a better family for her?" He stared past her. "We have three of them, Zainab. Three duties we must fulfil. Why should we delay the inevitable? The older they get, the less they understand. They will go out there and find boys who will ruin them. Then what will we do? How will we marry them off?"

Her head bowed, and she nodded. "When are you going to ask her?"

"There is no need to ask. When the time comes, we will introduce her to him. She is a good girl who understands. She will not disobey her father."

CHAPTER THREE

SUMAYYAH BID HER DAD goodbye and hung up before turning towards me. "He's happy to drop you off."

It was Friday afternoon, and we were all gathered in Rani's house. It took me an entire week to convince my parents to let me come. The only reason they agreed was because I said it was to revise for our upcoming final exams.

"Why does your dad call you Maya?" I asked.

Rani looked at me like I was missing something obvious. "It's a nickname. Her name is Sumayyah," she said, emphasizing the last two syllables of her name.

Halima looked up from her chemistry textbook. "It's more than that. In Bangla, *Maya* means love or kiss, depending what context you use it in. It's a term of endearment."

I pinched her cheek with a laugh. "Must be nice. My dad forgets my name half the time and the other half he's swearing at me."

Unknowing what to say, Sumayyah held up her textbook. "I was thinking we should start with module one."

I snatched her book away. "We should start with some music and food."

Her brow arched. "I only came because you *promised* to actually study. You might not care to pass your GCSEs, but I do."

Most people would have found her tone condescending, but I had known Sumayyah since we were three years old. Her head was always stuck in a book because getting anything less than top marks was unacceptable to her. In year two, when the teacher went around the class and asked what we aspired to be, everyone shouted out ridiculous dreams ranging from a clown to prime minister. Not Sumayyah, though. She quietly, yet confidently, stated she was going to be a doctor. And that dream never wavered or changed.

Halima was the first friend I ever made. When I approached her with a baby doll, she looked terrified. She hardly said two words to me as we played *mommy and baby*. The next day, we did finger-painting together, and she told me her name. We formed a friendship that was mostly silent on her part. That sufficed; I spoke enough for both of us. It was week two when Sumayyah was forced out of the reading corner by the teachers to make friends. From that moment, we became inseparable.

Rani was the last addition to our friendship group almost five years ago when we started secondary school. We were all the new kids, but she was the new kid from a different city. When a boy tripped in our first form class and she was the only other person to laugh with me, I knew she was going to be my partner in crime. Over the years, we had gotten up to our fair share of mischief. Rani laughed as loud as I did. Rani also dreamed of living as loud as me. She added the perfect balance to our friendship group. We were the chaos to Sumayyah and Halima's calm; and no matter how much trouble we'd land ourselves in, they didn't tire of our plans and abandon us.

"Ravi told me to tell you that Adeel said he misses you," Rani said.

A ridiculous smile took over my face. Adeel was my first actual *boyfriend*. There was something different about him and I put it down to his maturity because of the year age gap between us. Unlike the boys in my year, he could hold a proper conversation. He had career aspirations and since we met five months ago, he'd made a place for me in his future. He was handsome, smart and funny. Just one glance at him and my stomach was filled with butterflies.

"Tell Ravi to tell Adeel I miss him, too." I let out a long sigh. "I need my phone back."

Sumayyah, who had dug out her physics textbook since I still had her chemistry one, shot a parental look my way. "Maybe you shouldn't have been texting all night, so your parents didn't take it off you."

"Just wait until you fall in love because then you'll understand how hard it is to stop speaking to them."

Halima looked unconvinced. "Was it worth losing your phone over?"

No, it wasn't. Now, the only opportunity to speak to him was during school; even that was limited because he was in sixth form and I wasn't.

"What are they doing?" I asked Rani.

"They're going to play football and then get food."

"Why is a seventeen-year-old hanging around with a sixteen-year-old?" Halima asked.

Rani shrugged. "They're friends from playing on the school football team."

I wrapped my arm around Rani. "I can't believe we're dating two friends. Imagine all the cute double-date things we can do together."

She snapped her fingers at our other friends. "You two need to find yourselves a boyfriend, so we can plan all this stuff together."

Halima gagged. "Where does your dad fit into all these plans you've made?"

My dad was going to have to accept that I would not follow his plans. Asma had done that and got married the summer she finished school. Fifteen months later, she gave birth to a baby boy. Zayaan was cute, but it was impossible to turn a blind eye to her struggle. Two years later, she gave birth to her daughter, Mehnoor. Aryan, her second son, was born three years later. Only a few weeks ago, she announced she was expecting with her fourth child in seven years. My brother-in-law was a nice person. He treated my sister well, but to him, she was just a wife and mother. Nothing else. She stopped being a daughter and sister when she signed her life away to him.

Four years ago, while we were on a family holiday to Pakistan, my father was presented with a proposal for sixteen-year-old Maliha that was too good to pass up. Her in-laws adored her and spoiled her rotten. She was their only daughter-in-law, so that came with its own trials and tribulations. After her wedding, her husband travelled back to the UK because of work, while she remained there for four months without him. She said it wasn't that bad and her mother-in-law would take her shopping. Husnain, her husband, said she was to split her time between here and there, as his parents had no one to take care of them. Now that she was due to give birth to her firstborn in six months, I wondered if that would end.

The lives of my sisters were my biggest nightmare, and I was determined to live a dream. I would date Adeel in secret for a few years and after college, his father would approach mine to ask for my hand in marriage. I knew my dad would be furious about it, but he would rather get me married than bring shame upon the family. After marriage, Adeel would support me while I get my degree and open up my business. *I had it all planned out.*

"My dad will eventually have to learn he can't get everything his way. And anyway, Adeel is a good guy from a good family."

"My mum always says a good guy wouldn't date. He would do it the proper, halal way," Sumayyah added.

I rolled my eyes. "Well, your mum is as traditional as my dad. There is nothing wrong with falling in love. I want to marry someone I'm in love with. Not a stranger whose name I barely know."

Rani gave me a high-five. "My parents are a Bollywood movie come to life. I want that, and anything less isn't good enough. My dad raised me to know how much I am worth. No man can ever take that from me."

Halima startled us all with a cheer. "That's the spirit! If only it was easy to find a man who understands a woman's worth."

"There are good men out there," Sumayyah said. "One day we're all going to be happily married. We'll host dinner parties in our homes while our children laugh and play together. We'll get to witness them build friendships like the ones between us. Life is going to be perfect."

"I won't be having any children," Rani corrected, "But agreed! We're all going to be so happy it's ridiculous."

I held up my water bottle. "To marriages and friendships filled with love."

Rani pulled herself off the sofa and over to the hi-fi system. She played her favorite CD at high volume. "Who wants to dance with me?"

Sumayyah's groan was muffled by her hand covering her face. "You guys always dance to the same songs."

I was on my feet and clapping along to the beat of *Sajan Ke Ghar Jana Hain*. We had nailed the routine to where it was muscle memory. We treated her living room as our personal dance floor. Halima was cheering us and Sumayyah had given up trying to revise. Amid the loud music, neither of us noticed Rani's family coming in to watch us. Her dad's laugh boomed when her brother, Veer, jumped in when the male singer came in. I couldn't contain my laughter as he took my hand and danced with me.

Vihaan clapped and hugged his daughter tight. "Very beautiful dancing."

"This *has* to be one of our dances at your wedding," Rani said.

I closed my eyes and could envision it all. My parents would be appalled at me dancing at my wedding because a good Pakistani woman wouldn't be so shameless. But at that point, I wouldn't be their concern. If Adeel, as my husband, was okay with me dancing, there was nothing they could do because in my culture, a husband's needs and desires always take priority.

I winked at Rani. "Nothing will stop us."

ॐॐॐॐॐ

My sisters being married left me with no one to clean up after me. My bedroom was in the same state of untidy I left it in this morning. My mum was giving me the silent treatment because I *selfishly* went to Rani's house. Without directly saying it to me, she prattled on about how she had to clean the house and cook dinner on her own because nobody in the house cared about her.

Zain never got that treatment when he would go out. Despite being younger than me, he never made it home before his curfew. He could also be on his phone into stupid hours of the night and it was never confiscated as mine was. They also never invaded his privacy by going through his phone as they did to me.

It was completely unfair.

I knew they loved him more simply because he was a son. In their eyes, he could do no wrong. Their belief was that he should be out exploring the world, as is customary for a man. It is only a woman who should be trapped in her home.

I was sick and tired of it. So, while they ate dinner together, I remained upstairs and cleaned my room. I told myself it was because I wanted to, but truthfully, I hoped it would make my mum stop being angry with me and proud that I did it on my initiative. I wished they could love me as they did Zain.

Nightfall painted the sky a deep black. A puff of smoke appeared as I deeply exhaled. The joy I felt only an hour ago was nowhere to be seen. I was back to feeling lonely and unloved. I closed my eyes and embraced the chilly breeze. For a moment, I felt alive. I was flying somewhere far from here. I found happiness and freedom of self-expression there. I could love whoever I wanted openly and without shame. I wasn't weighed down by their expectations of what a good daughter is.

When I opened my eyes, a shooting star flew across the sky. I smiled, hoping the universe saw my dream and would make my wish come true.

Chapter Four

Rani patiently waited for me to add a little more blush to my cheeks. "How are you going to explain that to your dad when he comes to pick you up?"

I tapped my bag that hid the makeup wipes. "This isn't my first time scheming behind his back."

Perhaps I should have felt guilty about lying to my parents, but the glee I felt at experiencing prom with Adeel trumped everything. The summer holiday meant I was uncertain about the next time I would see him. If I wanted to leave the house, I'd need to come up with clever excuses.

When my parents started talking about finding me a suitable groom, I knew I had to put a stop to it. Adeel would have happily married me over the summer, but his parents wanted him to finish studying before settling down. But we knew we couldn't hold my parents off for another five years. We agreed to wait two years because by then he would be nineteen and halfway through his degree.

So, I begged them for two years to complete my further studies. The first time I brought it up, I was certain my dad's eyes were going to pop out of his head. His anger that night scared me, but the life he was trying to orchestrate for me terrified me. So, I pushed. And pushed.

And when that didn't work, I told my mum I would run away if they tried to get me married.

That scared them.

Not the thought of losing their daughter; that was something they had prepared for since my birth.

The shame. The dishonour. *That* was their Achilles' heel.

I promised them I would marry straight after my a-levels and they agreed on the grounds that I stay in my school sixth form. Unbeknownst to them, Adeel had one more year left here. Plus, I wouldn't be alone as Sumayyah was staying here, too.

"I can't imagine having a dad like that," she frowned. "My dad would set the world on fire for me."

I envied Rani. She was the only daughter of five children. Her parents never expected more from her because she was a woman. If anything, they never let her feet touch the ground and taught her brothers to treat her the same. Her family gave her the status her name represented.

Unable to respond, I huffed. It was a sweet gesture for the four of us to tie silk ribbons to our wrists, but mine didn't want to listen. No matter how many tight knots I did, it seemed to come undone. "This thing is so annoying."

Rani admired her simple knot. "I think it's cute."

"Yours is hardly a bow," I retaliated. Smiling at my reflection, I said, "Let's wow our boys."

Ravi swept a giggling Rani into his arms. They recently celebrated their six-month anniversary, and he bought her a beautiful pair of earrings she was proudly showing off. He whispered something in her ear that had a coy smile playing on her lips. I couldn't ask what it was because Adeel stepped into view.

"You look beautiful," he whispered.

My heart hammered in my chest. "Thank you."

"May I have your first dance?"

"Yes." I placed my hand in his and a calm came over me.

🎀🎀🎀🎀

The evening was passing like a dream. I didn't care that we were swaying to cheesy music in my school gym. The streamers and fairy lights could have been garbage, and it wouldn't have mattered because Adeel looked at me like there was nothing around us.

"I wish I could see you over the holidays."

My arms wrapped tighter around his neck. "We can see each other. I'll tell my mum I'm going to Sumayyah's house or something."

"How many times will she let you do that?"

"We can call and text every day."

When Rani upgraded her phone, she gave me her old one. It was another secret I was keeping from my parents because the thought of being in my house with no other human contact was enough to drive me crazy.

"But only when you're able to hide out in your room long enough." He sounded annoyed, which only made me feel guilty.

"I'm sorry. I know my parents are difficult."

He pulled me closer. "I wish you could stand up to them. You're *sixteen*. Why can't they know you have a phone? Your brother has one."

It was hard being a woman in my culture. It was even harder explaining the rules of being a woman, especially to a man, because they were not bound by them.

Unable to provide a reasonable explanation, I dropped my arms from his shoulders. "I'm going to see what my friends are doing."

Rani caught my disheartened gaze and walked alongside me. "You okay?"

I nodded my head and forced a smile onto my face. "Yeah."

Her attention went to our two friends, who were acting as if their asses were glued to their seats. "Why don't you come and dance with us?"

Sumayyah looked horrified at the suggestion. "I don't dance."

"Even if I say please?"

She shook her head. "Sorry." She smiled at us to soften the blow. "You guys look beautiful."

Halima's red dress made her the star of the night. Her curvy figure was made to be shown off, but she hid from the limelight. Sumayyah's deep green dress was covered in gold embroidered work. When she moved, she held us in a trance like a starry night. And as ever, Rani's dress was nothing short of glamourous. She spent weeks shopping for the perfect dress before settling on an orange mermaid style.

"I feel like a princess," Rani gushed. "Ravi said I look *sexy* in this dress."

Adeel called me sexy once. It was after our first kiss. We both wore stupid grins, and it was almost as if he didn't mean to say it out loud. My cheeks warmed, but all I could do was laugh.

A shadow of sadness came across Sumayyah's face. "Where did five years go? I can't believe this is the end."

"We're still going to be best friends."

"And talk *all* the time," I added to Halima's reassurance.

In a rare moment of emotion, Rani pulled us into a group hug. "Nothing will change."

$$\text{🎀🎀🎀🎀}$$

"I don't think we're allowed to walk around the school," Sumayyah hissed.

"What are they going to do? Kick us out?" Rani asked sarcastically. "After tonight, we're never coming back."

"Me and Zoya are!" She looked over her shoulder. "Let's go back."

Halima pushed the doors to the cafeteria open. She led the way to the lunch table we sat at on our first day. We sat in the same seats and smiled at one another.

"Where it all started," Halima said. "You guys have made this the best five years of my life."

"I'm so glad I met you girls that first day! I can't imagine my life without you guys."

I laughed. "Thanks to me! If I never met you in form, you would have walked past us as a stranger and remained that way."

With her worries about getting caught out the window, Sumayyah said, "I had a few classes with Rani. I'm sure we would have become friends eventually."

Rani's face blanked. "You would have had to take your eyes off the teacher long enough to notice me to become my friend."

"You're so loud, she would have heard you," Halima joked.

Her mouth dropped open. "You were so quiet in the beginning. I thought you hated me."

My palm slammed down on the table. "I remember that! You would constantly ask me if Halima had a problem with you."

We all fell into a soft laugh before it mellowed into a comfortable silence. We looked at one another with glossy eyes and hearts full of love. We were the lucky few to find sisterly bonds with one another. My friends had put their neck on their line for me one too many times. But no matter how close they came to the edge, they never turned their backs on me.

I cleared my throat. "Someone snap a picture of these stupid ribbons." I was going for light-hearted, but there was too much emotion in my voice.

"Hands in!" Rani ordered. She lowered her phone and stared at my undone ribbon. "Fix it."

It was the millionth time I had redone the damn thing. "My one must be broken because it doesn't want to listen."

"It's fabric. How is it supposed to listen to you?" Sumayyah asked with an amused glint in her eyes.

"Maybe you should take some more textile lessons from your mum."

"Ha-ha," I retorted sarcastically at Halima. "Someone thinks they're a comedian tonight."

Rani tied the bow for me a little too tight. "Maybe that should be your business idea. Bows that obey your command." She snapped the picture of our wrists.

Sumayyah was looking at us like we had lost our minds. "You know bows can't hear you, right?"

Rani winked at me. "But how cool would that be? You'd make millions if you could command bows to tie themselves. You could make gift bows, bow ties... the opportunities are endless."

Halima shook her head at us. "Mad. You're absolutely bonkers."

Rani kept working on the idea. She gasped. "Your business could be called The Obedient Bow! One bow that does it all!" Her hands pushed outwards as if the words were before her.

Knowing she was just trying to garner a reaction from Sumayyah, I laughed. "What a brilliant idea."

Sumayyah scoffed. "You, *Zoya Iqbal,* are going to start a business about something being *obedient*? Your face should replace the definition for *disobedient* in the dictionary."

I wrapped my arm around her. "And that is the beauty in it. An oxymoron, if you will. A rebel woman conforming to an easier way of living. Zoya Iqbal: the face and name behind The Obedient Bow."

CHAPTER FIVE

I CURLED UP UNDER my blanket. Despite the heating being on and the three layers I was wearing, the frosty December air attacked me. I pressed the phone against my ear as I tried to stop my teeth from chattering. It was only day two of our school holiday and I missed Adeel more than I could explain.

"What do you want for your birthday?" Adeel sounded as tired as I felt, but neither of us were ready to hang up.

My smile was involuntary. "There's still two months until my birthday."

"I know, but I want to take you somewhere nice."

For a moment, I let myself live out my dream date. I was wearing a beautiful dress and sculpted my face to perfection with makeup. Now that Adeel had his driver's license, he would pick me up and spend the drive showering me in compliments. After a fancy dinner, filled with laughter and love, we would drive around the city before stopping at a cliff to admire the starry sky.

In reality, I would tell my mum I was going out with the girls and she would tell me to be back no later than four o'clock. I'd go to Rani's house and get ready. After a rushed lunch, I would remove my makeup before running home to spend the rest of my birthday helping my mum around the house.

It wasn't ideal, but I had to suck it up for only six more months. Adeel and I just celebrated our two-year anniversary. Three months ago, he started university while I was still in my school's sixth form. It meant I couldn't see him as often, but at least I still had Sumayyah.

"I can't believe I'm going to be eighteen. I can't wait."

Eighteen marked my freedom's start. By summer, I would be happily married to Adeel. I'd enjoy my first year of marriage while working part time. My focus was going to be securing a place at university to study Business. He had already promised that we would move into our own home within six months of marriage. *Life was going to be bliss.*

"I can't wait until I marry you," he said dreamily.

"I can't wait to be your wife."

"I love you so much."

My heart skipped a beat. "I love you too. We are lucky to have found each other so young. I can't wait to grow old with you. I can't wait to share my body with you. I can't wait to have a million of your babies."

His grin was infectious, even over the phone. "I can't wait to *make* babies with you."

"After I finish my degree, though."

"That's fine with me. It gives us more time to practice."

My giggle abruptly stopped when my bedroom door swung open. I cut the call and hid the phone under my pillow. My heart felt like it was going to fall out of my chest. My wide eyes didn't waver from my father's accusatory gaze.

"Thum kia kerr rahe ho?" *What are you doing?* He stood frozen in my bedroom doorway. His eyes darkened to an impossible shade of black. His lips quivered in rage while his fingers trembled by his side.

"Nothing," I said. But I knew it was a futile lie. *He heard me talking on the phone.*

He took three large steps and was standing over me. "Don't lie! Who were you talking to?"

I shook my head. "Baba, I was reading."

His palm met my cheek. "Do you think I'm stupid? What were you reading? Where is the book?" He grabbed my arm and pulled me off the bed. "Watch what I do to you today!"

It would only take him seconds to find the phone he didn't know about. My tears poured out of my eyes. "Ammi!"

He threw my blanket to the floor before turning to face me. "Your mother can't save you today."

"What's happened?" She asked as she joined us, with Zain behind her. She took in my red cheek and his frenzied searching and knew this would not end well.

He held the phone in her face. "*This* is what your daughter has been doing."

She didn't dare to step closer to me. "Where did you get this?"

Telling them Rani gave it to me would cause them killing my friendship with her. But I was struggling to think of a lie. *Because there wasn't one good enough.*

"It must have been that boy she was talking to," my dad said.

I attempted to blink my tears away, but panic forced them to pour out. "There is no boy! I use it to talk to my friends."

My focus went on trying to remember what evidence was on that phone. Adeel's number was saved under a girl's name, but there was one picture of us. I always had a backup plan in case they found out, so I kept nothing that could be used against me. But I saved one because I knew how much I was going to miss him over the next two weeks.

My father grabbed my jaw and hurled every insult he could at me. "I'm going to kill you." He released me and held the phone up. "I heard you talking about disgusting things." Unable to navigate it, he handed the phone to Zain. "Show me everything on this."

My brother looked at me with despair. He clearly knew there was stuff on there I was hiding. He met my pleading gaze with a conflicted one of his own. "It's just a phone, Baba. I have one..." His words trailed off as a threatening look was directed at him. He glanced at me once again and I could almost hear his whisper of *I'm sorry*.

I stood frozen in my spot as Zain went through every app on the phone. There was nothing sexual or explicit, but it wouldn't matter. To my parents, having a boyfriend was just as bad as having a sex tape. It was shameful. It was wrong and punishable.

"Why would you do this to us?" my mum asked. "Why would you bring such dishonour on our name?"

"Ammi." I tried everything to control my sobs. "It's not like that."

My dad stormed over to me and grabbed a fistful of my hair. I let out a scream as he yanked my head back. He shoved the phone in front of my face. "Badtameez!" *Disrespectful.* "What is this?"

Through my blurred vision, I saw the picture of me and Adeel. I'm in the safe protection of his arms and my lips are pressed against his cheeks. The happiness I felt in that moment felt like a lifetime away.

"I'm sorry!" I gripped his fingers, trying to pull them out of my hair. "He's a good guy."

His eyes bulged with rage. He pinned me against the wall and grabbed my throat, strangling me.

I couldn't hear his abuse as I begged him to stop. My throat was burning as I was starved of oxygen. My nails scraped his arms as I tried to fight him off, but he was too strong. My breaths came out as gasps and the corners of my vision blurred.

"Baba!" Zain called. "You're going to kill her."

I looked at my mother, silently begging her to save me. But she stood immobile as he slammed me against the wall.

"Stop it!" Zain shouted.

Another cry broke out of me. My arms stretched out to catch my fall as he threw me to the ground. Gasping for breath, I doubled over in a coughing fit. The room spun endlessly, as my throat tightened in a silent scream. Each cough scraped my throat and set my lungs on fire.

"I'm sorry!" I sobbed. "Please, stop. Baba, please!"

"Don't call me that! My daughter would never commit such a sin! She wouldn't parade with a man who is not her husband! You are not my blood!"

I couldn't cower away fast enough before his palm came down on my cheek. I curled up in a ball on my floor, but that didn't stop him. Every slap felt like a belt or whip. It felt like I was being stoned to death. When his arms grew tired, I felt the first kick and howled in pain. I could hear Zain begging him to stop, but it fell on deaf ears.

One slur after another slipped off his tongue. He screamed I was filthy and used. He asked God how he was supposed to marry me to a good man when I had already been defiled by a dishonorable one.

Zain only pulled him off me when a blow landed on my head. "Look at her! If anyone sees this, they're going to call the police!"

"Let them!" he screamed. "I would rather go to prison for killing her than face the *shame* she has brought upon us."

I laid motionless on the floor as I accepted this was the end of my life. I refused to die with this thought, so I closed my eyes and recalled a happy memory. My heart broke as I saw myself laughing with the girls. Sumayyah's scolding blurred with Rani's loud voice and Halima's gentle giggle. I tried to scream for them to help me, but they vanished.

"Get up," he ordered.

I swallowed the blood in my mouth. Every bone in my body was aching, and it took everything in me to not scream when I moved.

"The day you were born, I knew in my heart I was cursed. You are nothing but a failure." He walked out of the room without sparing me another glance.

My head didn't lift from the ground as my mother and brother left behind him. Once I was all alone in my room, I closed my eyes. I took a deep breath in, but instead of exhaling, I fell to the floor and let out the loudest cry.

I didn't know what hurt the most: my broken bones or my shattered dream.

A sheen of sweat layered my skin. Pulling on pyjamas when it hurt to breathe felt impossible. Giving up, I stared at my almost-naked body in the mirror. Only a few hours had passed, but the bruises were already

29

a deep purple-black colour. There were only a few patches of my skin that remained of my usual porcelain tone.

Thinking it was my brother opening the door, I shouted, "I'm changing!"

My mum closed the door behind her. Without saying a word, she gathered my bloodied clothes and remade my bed. "Why?" It was barely a whisper.

"He's a good boy," I cried.

Her eyebrows shot up. "What decent boy would behave like this with a woman he is not married to?"

"Ammi, I did nothing like that. We want to get married in a few months."

"Married? Do you think your father would accept him?"

"Why not? He comes from a good family."

"He has no respect."

There was a foolish part of me that hoped they would force us to marry each other soon to save face with the Pakistani community. I wanted them to believe that marrying me to someone else would be impossible, so Adeel was my only option. But the disgust on her face made my hope fade away.

My heartache took a backseat, and I stared her down. "Then he is the perfect match for me. I too am shameless and disrespectful."

She dabbed her tears away. "I tried so hard to lead you on the right path. Your sisters never gave me any trouble, but you ... even when you were in my womb, you gave me a hard time. Why, Zoya? Why would you do this to us?"

"To *you*?" I opened my arms. "Look at me, Ammi! Look at what he did to me!"

She lacked the courage to face his abuse. "We only wanted to protect you. This world is unkind to women. That boy will find a woman to marry. But the mark of shame never abandons a woman. It hangs over her like a dark cloud, warning everyone that something unwanted is coming."

"This isn't protection. This is prison! And I *hate* it here!"

"Do you think life out there is easier? Here you are protected by your father's love."

"*Love*?" I cried. "If this is love, then please let me become loveless. Love shouldn't hurt. How can this be love? How does a father do this to his child? How could you, as my mother, stand there and watch him beat me within an inch of my life?"

She stared at me in disappointment. "One day, if you are unfortunate enough to have a daughter, you will understand the lengths a mother would go to protect her child." When my dad called her name, she silently exited the room.

I creeped over to the door and strained to listen in on their conversation.

"She may as well have dug my grave and left me to die in it."

"Nobody knows about it," she consoled. "Maybe everything will be okay."

I could imagine him shaking his head. "This time nobody found out, but what happens next time? That girl is not ours. She is borrowed property and if we don't do something, we'll never be able to give her away."

My heartbeat pounded in my ears. I gripped the door tight as I waited to hear what he was planning.

"My sister said she had a groom in mind."

"No. A boy from here can easily find out her past."

"Then what?"

"I spoke to Ali. He will book the tickets tonight."

No.

No.

No.

Whatever remained of my heart, hope, and dream obliterated.

My mother, still not understanding, asked, "Tickets?"

"Pack our bags. We're going to Pakistan in two days."

CHAPTER SIX

THE SOUND OF THE rain falling and muffled chatter faded into the distance as I stared at my open luggage. Any traces of my UK life were left behind, my mum having only packed my Pakistani clothes. I knelt on the ground and took out my toiletry bag, looking for my razor. I clenched it tight in my fist and took a deep breath.

We arrived in Pakistan almost two weeks ago and the search for my husband began on day two. I tried to plead my case with my mum, even though I knew she would never disobey her husband. I wanted to call my friends and beg one of them to save me, but I had no way of contacting them. It was Christmas break so school wouldn't notice my absence and it was normal for no one to hear from me during this time. When we got to the airport, I was tempted to beg an employee to save me from this hell, but I was too scared. What if they never believed me? *What if they arrested my dad?*

On the plane, I devised a plan. I would make sure every family and groom rejected me. So far, it had worked. All four men that saw me rejected me shortly after leaving our home. But nothing made my dad's determination waver. He would appear the next day with a new suitor.

There was another one coming today and I just couldn't do it anymore. I would rather have been dead than married to a man from here. How would my parents react upon entering this room and finding me lifeless? Would they try to stop my wrists from bleeding? Would my dad blame himself? Or would he thank me for solving this problem for him?

"Why aren't you ready yet?" Maliha walked into the room and watched me.

She was in Pakistan visiting her in-laws. When she heard of our arrival, she knew something was wrong. While my dad told everyone I was ready to get married, my mum was quick to cry her sorrows to Maliha. My sister said nothing in front of her, but when we were alone, she berated me for being stupid. And then she held me as I cried.

"I need to shower," I explained.

Her gaze fixed upon the razor. She paced over and took a seat next to me. "Marriage isn't so bad. Look at me. I'm happy."

"You're the one-in-a-million. Our lives aren't a luck of the draw. You love your husband. I love Adeel."

"I never loved him in the beginning, but as you learn who he is, the love will come naturally. Marriage is understanding and patience. Everything else is secondary. If you understand one another, you can get through anything."

"How can I understand these men? They can't even speak a word of English! They're all older and backward-minded. They want a slave, not a wife." I rolled my eyes. "To them, they are the same."

"He won't stop," she whispered. "He knows you're doing this on purpose. He's only going to let this family see you for a few minutes, so you don't ruin this proposal."

I clenched the blade tighter. "I can't do this. I would rather be dead than marry like this. Is that what he wants? Does he want me to kill myself? How can they not see they are killing me by doing this?" I wiped my tears away.

She sighed. "Killing yourself won't punish them. It will be only you who loses. Sometimes we must make happiness with what we have."

"But why? Why is it that men don't play by the same rules? A man can fuck a hundred women before marriage, and nobody says anything. But a woman falls in love, and she is beaten and broken. Why?"

Her arms wrapped around me. "Because being a woman is the hardest job one can do. At times, it feels impossible, but we are strong."

I shook my head. "No. We are tolerant. We are confined. We are obedient."

$$\approx \approx \approx \approx$$

The multitude of cousins that normally surrounded me had all scampered to get a good look at this groom and his family. I sat alone on the hard mattress and watched the clock tick by. His mother, Shazia, and sisters, Sadaf and Iram, had come in to see me. His mum was a stocky lady who jiggled when she walked. She asked me a few questions before my grandmother practically dragged her away under the pretense that her tea was getting cold. His sisters never spoke a word. They stood behind their mother and offered a polite smile.

I caught my reflection in the mirror and cringed. In just two weeks, I had lost weight from a combination of stress and no appetite. My sage kameez hung off my body. I wanted to yank off the dupatta draped across my head and chest. My mum allowed small amounts of concealer to hide the few yellow bruises that remained, but I still looked ghastly.

Outside my door, there was a hushed conversation in Urdu between my potential husband and his parents.

"I want to meet her," he demanded in a deep and authoritative voice.

"Her dad said no," his father replied.

"Is he the one marrying her?"

Shazia gasped. "Don't speak so crudely."

Her scolding went unheard, and he presented them with an ultimatum. "I either meet her or I leave."

I hoped that his family weren't all that impressed and agreed to walk away without meeting me.

There was a sigh. "Let me see what I can do," his father promised, and they walked away.

My heart went into overdrive, as I wasn't expecting to meet him. That conversation told me all I needed to know. He was a man who always got his way. Once he wanted something, he wouldn't take no for an answer. *And that was going to make my job of repelling him harder.*

Moments later, a knock sounded at the door. I didn't get the chance to welcome them in because the door opened. Expecting to see my mum or sister to introduce him, I was surprised when it was he himself.

His striking green eyes immediately caught my attention. Even with the distance between us, they were bright and unashamedly staring at me. I could hear my mother telling me to lower my gaze and only did so when he closed the door, leaving the two of us alone in the bedroom.

My parents were probably having a heart attack right now.

Determined to make sure nothing came from this, I ignored him and kept my mouth shut. If he believed I was disrespectful, he would certainly reject me.

He stayed pressed against the door, but his heavy stare could be felt. "Aapna sar oper athayein." *Lift your head.*

I followed his command and met his gaze with defiance. He was nothing like Adeel in build. This man was tall and broad. His sharp features and narrowed eyes gave nothing away as he scrutinized me. Every strand of his hair and beard were perfectly placed. He pulled the sleeves of his traditional Pakistani clothes up, leaving his expensive watch on display.

He stepped closer. "Aapka naam?" *Your name?*

"Zoya." I didn't care what his name was, so I didn't ask. He was a stranger and was going to remain that way.

He still introduced himself. "Idris Qadir. Aap kitnay saal kay hain?" *How old are you?*

Had his parents not told him anything about me? Why was he as clueless as me?

"Satrah. Taqriban atharah." *Seventeen. Nearly eighteen.*

At my answer, my heart clenched, and I remembered the plans I made with Adeel. Had he bought me a present he would never get the chance to give me? Instead of a day filled with loving memories, I was going to be stuck sweltering in Pakistan's heat.

"Saat saal. Bahat bra naheen." *Seven years. Not too bad,* he muttered to himself.

I quickly did the math in my head. That meant he was twenty-five years old. My heart plummeted.

"Kia up khana pakana jante haine?" *Do you know how to cook?*

Time to give him the first reason to reject me. "Naheen." *No,* I lied.

He turned around when the door opened. He gave an unimpressed look at his sister.

"They're calling you," she said.

His eyes were on me again. "I'm not done in here."

He can speak English? Why the hell was he speaking to me in Urdu then? He closed the door in her face, uncaring she was just about to say something. Perhaps it was the irritation etched onto my face, but he smiled for the first time. "You look surprised." The amusement doused over him made it clear he was testing me.

I scoffed. "I'm surprised anyone from this country knows how to speak English. That is all."

"And I'm surprised a girl from London knows how to speak Urdu. Not the best, but it will do." He tilted his head and eyed me from head to toe. "I live between Pakistan and the UK. I have businesses here that I come and tend to, but I am predominantly settled in London."

The mention of London had hope blooming in my chest, but it quickly withered when I realised he probably would have me remain here.

His arms crossed over his chest. "What brings a girl like you to Pakistan to get married?"

"Have you met my father?" I asked with too much sarcasm. Realising this was my chance to sabotage this once and for all, I smiled at him. "He found out about my boyfriend."

"What did he find?"

"Pictures." I kept my answer vague, hoping it would leave his imagination to run wild.

Idris surprised me by bluntly asking, "Did you have sex with him?"

The lack of makeup displayed my warm cheeks. I opened my mouth to say yes, but surprise rendered me silent. His question hung in the air until I cleared my throat. "I don't have to answer that question."

"I'm entitled to a wife that is chaste."

"As if you haven't already messed around before marriage."

"I have not."

I shrugged. "Good for you."

After a few more minutes of uncomfortable silence, he said, "You have not had sex with this boy."

"How do you know that?"

"Because if you had, you would have done everything to stop yourself from ending up here." He shook his head. "While rebellious, you are still a daughter bound by her father's moral code. You would not commit such a grave sin."

I bravely stood up and locked eyes with him. "My father can impose all the rules he wants. I will not marry a man of his choosing. He can bring every suitor in this entire country and I will make them reject me as I have done with you."

His eyebrows shot up. "You sound fairly certain of that, Zoya."

I laughed. "I know what type of man you are because you are all the same. You walked into this room and observed me as you probably did the outfit you are wearing. You made sure it was exactly what you wanted. You made sure it fit perfectly. That is why you demanded to meet me yourself. You had to make sure there wasn't a stitch undone.

But that doubt is there, and the thought of marrying a used woman isn't good enough for a man."

He closed the distance between us. "Used?"

"Filthy. Used. Immoral. Shameless. Disrespectful. *That* is the title my own father bestowed upon me when he beat me, so I was too afraid to not get on the plane." I mocked a bow. "So, kindly take your leave, Mr Qadir. This woman is not for you."

He grabbed my arm. "Nobody makes my decisions for me. And on our wedding night, I will discover if you are *used* or not." He let go of me and stepped back.

My plan didn't work.

Despite everything I said, he wanted to marry me. I could already see the life I would live with him. I would play the role of a part-time wife while he returned to where my true life existed. He would return to get me pregnant before going back to his freedom.

Desperation choked me. "You are setting yourself up for disappointment. I've had sex with him," I lied.

Idris never looked away from my face. "I wouldn't make it a habit to lie to me."

"I'm not lying! Ask my father and he will tell you that is why he is forcing me to marry a man from here. Our community back in London knows what I've done."

His amusement pissed me off. "I have the means to make you forget about this boy."

What was wrong with him? No sane Pakistani man would want to marry a woman who admitted to having sex before marriage. It was the biggest shame she could commit. Yet, he seemed even more determined to marry me and it enraged me.

"I won't ever love you," I spat at him.

"I don't need love. I need a wife."

I wanted to ask why he would choose me when he could easily find a woman who would bend over backwards for him. But he gave me one last lingering look before exiting the room.

The heartbreak was overtaken by the panic swarming me. I felt like I couldn't breathe and I wanted to run out there and beg his family to leave.

But Idris had commanded the attention of everyone. His deep voice was assured and definitive. "Begin making preparations. Zoya and I will marry in two weeks."

CHAPTER SEVEN

MY DREAM WEDDING DRESS had always been red. Growing up with Bollywood movies made me obsessed with the traditional bridal look. So, you can imagine my disappointment when my outfit, gifted by Idris, arrived the day before my wedding.

It was *green*.

A deep green lengha that was so heavily embroidered, it took three of us to lift it up. I stared at the bedazzled fabric in disgust. It was as ugly as the rest of my wedding outfits. My dark hair was in loose waves, with most of it covered by the equally heavy dupatta. My makeup was done in a salon. The thick layer of foundation and heavy-handed blush made me feel like a clown.

The past two weeks had passed in a frenzied blur. Nobody questioned why Idris was on such a tight deadline. My father was ecstatic he found someone willing to marry me. It was easy to plan and host a wedding in Pakistan on short notice when you had money. And per Idris' demand, all the events were joint. Once again, my father was overjoyed because it meant our side only paid for half the costs. The only event we incurred the full cost for was today, the *baraat*.

The celebration kicked off with our Islamic marriage, the *Nikkah*. It should come as no surprise that this was yet another, one of Idris' orders. The only thing I remembered was being squashed by so many bodies and wanting to vomit from my nerves. Everyone waited with bated breath for my consent, but it wouldn't come so easily. I ignored Idris' watchful eye across the room and focused on trying to breathe. It was the threat my father muttered that had the whisper passing through my lips. The room broke out into cheers. My parents sighed in relief and nobody saw the bride that felt like she was dying.

I took part in none of the events' festivities. Our families stuffed their faces with *mithai* and paraded the venues with glee. Idris and I sat on the stage without uttering a word to each other. He hardly paid attention to anything, including me. Occasionally, I would feel him watching me, but I didn't dare to meet his gaze. I had no doubt today was going to be the same, except he was taking me home at the end of the night.

Emotions were running high. I'm pretty sure my dad's tears were ones of relief that he had finally done it: *he was free from the burden of having daughters.* After today, I was no longer his problem.

I sat on the stage, with my head bowed, silently crying to myself. I could hear Rani whispering in my ear; *you've got this!* If anybody had told me my best friends wouldn't be by my side at my wedding, I would have called them a foolish moron. But there I was, in Pakistan, wishing they would appear by my side and tell me about the plan they had to get me out of this.

My mum returned to give me a final once over. "It's time."

Could she see the pain in my eyes? Was she turning a blind eye to my silent plea to get me out of this?

"I can't marry him. *Please.* Free me from this life."

Careful to not trample on my dress, she took the seat beside me. "He is an established man who can give you a good life. Do not ruin this, Zoya. Do not tell him about your past because, though he will never forget, he will also never let you free. It will become a knife he lodges in your chest when he is angry. A man's tongue is as dangerous as a sword."

If she was right, it was too late.

"Is that why you haven't told him you aren't happy with this marriage for me? I can see it in your eyes. They don't hold the same happiness you held for Asma and Maliha. You know what my life is to become."

"It is not my decision."

I grabbed her hands. "You're my mother!"

Her eyes reflected loss. "A girl belongs to her father. A woman belongs to her husband. It is our duty to take care of them. Do as he asks and you will see life can be easy."

"That's exactly what you did. Has your life been easy?"

She continued as if she hadn't heard me. "Don't wait for his mother to ask you to cook and clean. A man has needs only his wife should fill. Don't give him a reason to seek it elsewhere. Speak respectfully and gently. No more running around the house shouting at the top of your lungs. You are a daughter-in-law now and the eldest one. You must shoulder the responsibility well." She let go of my hand. "It's time to walk to your new life."

My dad replaced my mum as he walked me down the aisle. The guests in the vast hall all stood to get a peek at me. My head remained bowed as I focused on breathing. Idris stood on the stage, waiting for me.

"You will see, I was right," my dad whispered when we were a few steps away.

Uncaring that I would hurt him before he gave me away, I shook my head. "He is not Adeel and for that reason, I will *never* forgive you."

He was stunned into silence as he placed my hand in Idris'. The unshed tears did nothing to soften the hard shell encased around my heart.

I stood beside my husband and never looked at the camera or crowd once. I gripped my bouquet tight and remained silent.

"We will go to my home after this," Idris whispered to me. "You will smile and partake in the traditions."

I said nothing.

"We will stay in one of my hotels until the guests leave after the *Walima*."

I closed my eyes and held back my sobs.

"Then we will live in my family's home." He waited until the photo was taken before looking at me. "Did you hear me?"

"Yes," I muttered.

We were told to take our seat on the stage and I winced when a flower fell from my bouquet. Without realising, Idris trampled on it and squashed its petals. And somehow, I understood how that flower felt.

$$\text{🎀🎀🎀🎀}$$

Our room was on the top floor of his hotel. The space felt more like an apartment. I stood in the middle of the room and stared at myself. I looked as exhausted as I felt. All the crying had taken it out of me. I held onto my mum and sister, hoping they would tell me this was all a nightmare.

His home was enormous and adorned with lights. Idris never showed me around. I sat in the living room and played all the games that are a norm in my culture. I took pictures with a smile so forced it ached my cheeks. His extended family was as large as mine, but faces were all a blur. The minutes stretched to hours, and we left the celebrations behind at almost two in the morning. When the guests asked why we weren't spending the night in the family home, Shazia simply explained that her son didn't want to. Nobody asked any further questions.

Idris showed me up to the room before disappearing somewhere without an explanation. My plan was to fall asleep before he returned so I could avoid the sex part of tonight. But I couldn't move.

This wasn't how my wedding night was supposed to go. Adeel was meant to help me unpin my hair and outfit. He was going to stand back and admire me. He was going to tell me how much he loved me. We would undress and just hold each other. With him, I would have been ready to give that part of myself because I knew him. *I loved him.*

I couldn't even recite three facts about Idris. I didn't want to know anything about him. I wanted him to divorce me. Or at least, sleep in a different bed tonight.

"Why are you standing there?" he asked, as he joined me.

"I couldn't get the pins..." I was crying again.

His eyes narrowed. "Stop that crying. Nobody has died."

My bangles jingled as I wiped my tears. "I'm sorry."

He began removing the safety pins from my outfit, and the heavy fabric fell to the floor. "Did you take the medication I sent?"

By medication, he meant the contraceptive pill.

If I said no, would that stop him from having sex with me tonight?

He didn't wait for my answer. "You will only take that while I am in Pakistan. Until I have made arrangements, we won't be having a baby."

Relief flooded me. "Okay."

"I don't want you messing around with your body, so you will not use contraception."

I caught his eye in the mirror. "Will we be using ... will you..." I couldn't get the word out.

His fingers halted. "A man does not use condoms with his wife. That is for the filthy people fucking multiple partners."

The vulgar word coming from him made me recoil. "Okay."

Instead of stopping once my wedding dress was on the floor, he unclasped my bra and dragged the straps down my arms. His eyes hardened when I covered my breasts. "A woman does not hide away from her husband."

I stepped forward and turned to face him. "Idris..." *What was I supposed to say? I know it is your right, but I can't bring myself to have sex with you.*

"Were you this hesitant when you undressed for that boy?"

I shook my head. "I never..."

He closed the distance, and his fingers hooked into the waistband of my underwear. "I thought you had sex with him?"

I grabbed his hands. "I can't do this tonight."

"It is our wedding night. My wife will let me undress her."

One arm rested across my breasts and the other hand covered my womanhood. "I'm tired. Can't we..."

He was already removing his clothes. "Lay on the bed." His demand left no room for negotiation.

My knees felt like jelly as I padded over to the kingsize bed. My fingers trembled as I pulled the sheets off and climbed under them. Goosebumps rose all over me, and I couldn't stop the single tear that swam into my ears.

Idris climbed into the bed in just his underwear. He laid next to me, his head propped up on his hand. "Look at me." He stared at me. "Did you kiss that boy?"

What was he going to do to me?

I swallowed the lump in my throat and nodded. Before I could move, he grabbed my face and kissed me so hard it hurt. His beard scratched my skin as he forced the kiss to deepen. One hand was on my lower back and he pulled me closer to him. The saltiness of my tears mixed with the taste of him. Grabbing one leg, he wrapped it around his waist, and I could feel just how much he wanted tonight to happen.

"What else?" he breathed against my lips. "Where did he touch you?" His cold fingers brushed over my nipples. "Did you let his mouth touch these?"

I pressed my hand against his chest, needing some space away from him. "No."

He closed the distance again. "Then what else, Zoya? How did he *use* you? Tell me why your father labelled you as such."

I shook my head. "I only ever kissed him."

His hand found mine, and he forced me to palm him. "You never touched him? Tasted him?"

Trying to remove my hand, I truthfully answered. "No."

"Good." He let go of my hand and removed the blanket from us as he sat up. He spread my legs and kneeled before me.

I clamped my legs shut. "Idris, please," I begged. "Can you wait until I'm more comfortable? We don't know each other and..." My legs were pried open again.

"I am your husband. That is all I need to know." His fingers were spreading me open, and exploring parts of my body even I wasn't comfortable with.

On instinct, my legs slammed shut when he tried to insert his finger inside me. "It hurts. And I'm not..."

He climbed off the bed, and my heart stopped racing. But when he returned with a bottle of lube, she was back to overworking. "I have waited for this night with you. We will become one tonight." The finality of his words made me stop resisting.

I laid on my back, legs spread for him. I was looking at him, but I couldn't truly see him. All I saw were the dreams I once held close fading into darkness. I barely flinched when the cold lubricant was spread over my most intimate parts. I still felt the intrusion of his finger, and it only intensified when he added another.

Idris let out a satisfied groan. "Relax your body. This will only hurt for a moment."

Swallowing the lump in my throat, I nodded. I told myself that this was inevitable. If it wasn't tonight, it would be another, and I wanted to get it over with.

"Look at me." He was touching himself. "What are you thinking about?"

"Nothing."

His body pressed against mine as he lined himself against my opening. "Are you thinking about him?"

Adeel was nothing but a distant, stolen memory.

"No."

"Good."

And then he took away the last part of me that was mine.

A loud screech bubbled out of me at the intrusion. My mouth hung open while my eyes screwed shut. My back arched off the bed as the stinging grew worse. I gripped my bedsheets with a tight fist as a scream begged to be released.

Idris stilled and relished the feeling of being encased by a woman. His eyes closed as he let out a satisfied sigh. He withdrew, and I knew what he was checking for. *Blood.* He was content with the view that greeted him.

When he pushed back in, I let out another cry. My hands rested on his chest. "Stop. Please, just..." I knew my tears weren't just from the physical pain. The hurt my heart felt was much greater.

Idris stilled. "What's wrong?"

"I need a minute."

His solution was to add more lube before finding his rhythm. He was too busy enjoying the pleasure that he believed was rightfully his to notice I had frozen.

The muscles in my legs tightened. Nothing about it was enjoyable. It was an odd feeling to have something inside me *there*. As he thrust in and out, all I could focus on was the irony of a wedding night.

Our whole lives we are told that, as women, sex is not our place. Women shouldn't even utter the word sex. Women must avoid talking to men. Women are to hide their beauty. But then we are expected to lie naked in bed with a man we barely know and let him ravish us.

I turned my head, unable to look at him any longer. The pillow was stained with the mascara that had run with my tears. Luckily, I only had to endure another ten minutes of it before he was spilling inside me. I was grateful I hadn't already showered because it gave me an excuse to scrub his existence off me.

Finally satisfied, he dropped onto the pillow next to me. His chest was rising and falling. He turned to look at me. "That boy no longer exists. I have removed every trace of him from you. We are one. I am yours, as you are mine. Is that understood, Zoya?"

I pulled the blanket around me. "Yes."

When I tried to turn around, he stopped me. "Don't turn your back on me when I am speaking."

My lip quivered. "Okay."

"As your husband, I will provide for you. If you want anything, you ask me."

I want a divorce.

"In return, you will help around the house. You will not sleep till late. You will not work. You will carry our children and raise them to be good people. You will lie with me in bed when I say." He held my face. "Because that is what husband and wife do. Do you understand?"

One word summarised his desires. *Obedient.*

"Yes."

"I know this is not what you wanted, but I will take care of you."

"I'm tired," I whispered. "Can I go to sleep?"

He nodded his head towards a closed door. "Go and shower first."

My womanhood stung when I tried to walk. There was an ache so deep it reached my broken heart.

"Zoya?" he called. "Your father was unable to control you. You disobeyed and dishonoured him. I will not tolerate such behaviour in my marriage. My wife is *mine*. I took a vow of forever and I intend to honour that. So rid yourself of any plans to escape."

CHAPTER EIGHT

I DIDN'T THINK I could feel so relieved at the sight of my period. But I almost cried from joy. I was still taking the pill, but Idris was leaving his DNA in me every night. *And now I had a break from it.* The sex was tolerable, but I still wasn't bursting with excitement. Idris would huff every time he had to pull out the bottle of lube, because I wasn't aroused enough for him. I mostly positioned myself however he wanted and hoped it was over fast.

Three weeks of marriage had passed in a blur. The *Walima* party was as nerve-wracking as the *Baraat*. Once again, we sat on the stage without speaking to one another. Idris returned to work soon after we moved in with his family. And I found myself wishing he was by my side. I didn't feel the need to speak when it was just the two of us. He grew accustom to my silence.

But his family was another battle altogether. My mother-in-law would constantly shove different people in front of me. She would chatter non-stop while I helped her cook. They had an in-house paid cook, but she was adamant to show her relatives that her eldest daughter-in-law wasn't a dud. I served food. I cleaned up. I made small talk. At the end of the night, I would lie in bed with my husband.

The only lights in the dark tunnel were his sisters. Talking to them was the only thing that made me feel normal. Amal was married to Idris' younger brother, Bilal. She wasn't as chatty as his sisters, but was welcoming enough. When I asked Sadaf, the eldest of his siblings, why he married before Idris, she explained Idris was focused on building his businesses and didn't care for marriage at the time.

Bilal, like his other brother, Hamza, were freeloaders. They hung onto Idris' words because he provided for their lives. It seemed the two younger sons were settled in Pakistan, while the rest lived in London. My parent-in-laws split their time between the UK and their homeland. Their daughters were both married with children and their husbands barely spared me a glance. At first I thought they had a problem with me, but one evening when Idris told his cousin to divert his gaze from me, explained it all.

There was a knock at the door. "Zoya, are you okay in there?" Iram asked.

"I'm okay."

Her voice lowered. "Bhaiya," *brother*, "is home. He's looking for you."

I wasn't expecting him to be home this early. My parents were coming to visit before their flight home, but Idris said he was too busy to join us.

Now rushing, I washed my hands and opened the door. With my hair properly covered, I offered her a smile and made my way to my bedroom. "You were looking for me?"

He didn't even glance up from his laptop. "Where were you? I've been home for five minutes."

I closed our bedroom door. "I was in the bathroom."

"Which one?"

"The main one," I said, my voice wavering at the end. *Was I in trouble for using the wrong bathroom?*

"We have an ensuite. Next time use that one, so I don't have to ask around for my wife."

I nodded, even though he still wasn't looking at me. "What did you need?"

"I'm going to shower. Take some clean clothes out and iron them for me before I finish."

"Okay."

Finally looking at me, his lips settled into a straight line. His eyes raked up and down my body. "What are you wearing?"

I looked down at my clothes and wondered what was wrong with it. Since being married, I only wore traditional outfits. "Is something wrong?"

"It is too fitted. Your figure and breasts are on show. Get rid of it."

It was a stupid request, but I nodded and started pulling his clothes out for him.

"You're upset," he stated.

"I'm not. It's just clothes."

"It's not just clothes. It's your modesty, and that is my duty to protect. When you are dressed like that, men will have indecent thoughts."

"Nobody is thinking that about me," I argued.

Idris closed his laptop and came to stand behind me. His knuckles ran down the length of my spine. "I am," he stated. He pulled me so our bodies were pressed together. "The things I want to do to you." If it weren't for his husky tone, I would have taken that as a threat.

"The men in this house are your blood relatives and too scared of you to think of me like that."

Pulling my hair to one side, the tip of his nose glided along my neck. He pulled the skin between his teeth before soothing the pain with a kiss. "Do you feel what you do to me? Even when I'm at work, I can't concentrate knowing you're at home waiting for me."

Sex was the real reason Idris needed me. It was the only part of this marriage that mattered to him.

His hands were on my hips. "Have you finished cooking?"

I stilled. "Yes."

"And the cleaning is done?"

"Yes."

He moved his palms across my lower back and rested them on my ass. "Then you have time to shower before the guests arrive."

It took everything in me to suppress my groan until I realised I had a valid excuse to get out of it. I stood taller. "I started my period." Walking past him, I plugged the iron in and waited for it to heat. With my back turned to him, he couldn't see my smile.

His hands ran down the length of my arm. "How long must I wait until I can have you again?"

I could have laughed at him. He knew how to check if I was a virgin. He knew to bring lube. He knew where to shove his dick. *But he didn't know how long a period lasted?*

I shrugged, determined to milk this for as long as I could. "It depends. Sometimes my periods last for ten or twelve days."

He stopped breathing. "You bleed for half the month?"

"Yeah."

His fingers intertwined with mine. He pressed up against me so I could feel the bulge tucked into his pants. "We'll have to find other ways to be with one another. I do rather think you have pretty hands ... and feet."

Idris made a joke. *He was joking with me.* His smile could be felt in my hair as he chuckled.

And I laughed too.

It was my first laugh in almost two months. And it was so unexpected, it came out louder than I intended. My head fell back against him, and I allowed myself to pretend that I was happy.

His arms wrapped around my waist, and his lips pressed against my ear. "You have a wonderful laugh."

I wasn't sure he meant to say it. My laugh subsided, and I stared blankly out the window. Without warning, my chest felt heavy, and I wanted to cry again.

"Zoya?" he muttered.

I tried to step out of his arms, but he held on tight. It felt like someone was choking me. A cry broke out of me as my body shook. My fingers gripped his hands that rested on my stomach as I struggled to explain my sudden outburst.

"What do you want?" he asked.

Many desires filled me, yet I uttered only one. "I want to go home." I didn't know how to explain home wasn't my father's house. Home was London. Home was Sumayyah, Rani, and Halima. Home was anywhere but here in his arms.

Without warning, our bedroom door swung open. "The guests will be..." My mother-in-law stopped dead in her tracks.

"Get out!" he yelled at her.

Her eyes abruptly darted away from our embrace. "I didn't know you were in here."

Idris shielded me from her view. "Why did you come into our room without knocking?"

She stuttered. "I was looking for Zoya."

"My wife is busy. She'll come out when I say so."

❦❦❦❦

I topped Idris' glass with water. My father-in-law, Abbas, shook his head when I asked if he wanted a refill. I went back to the wall where I stayed on standby for any requests. From the living room, my mum gave me a proud smile.

"How is business?" my dad asked.

"Fine."

Idris' dislike for my dad was certain. He was always cold with him and gave one-worded answers wherever he could. And while part of me felt bad for him, another was smug.

He nodded at me. "Zoya, will you give your Baba some more roti?"

I pushed off the wall, but halted when Idris held his hand up. "Iram, give him what he's asking for."

That touched a nerve with my dad. "A father was hoping to have his daughter serve him before he left her in Pakistan for the foreseeable future."

Idris looked up from his plate. He sat tall in his seat at the head of the table. And then, with the driest tone, said, "You shouldn't have married her off then." He ignored his dad's pleas to keep quiet. "*My* wife serves no one but me."

58

An uncle broke through the tension with a cackle. "These young-sters and their romance."

But neither my dad nor Idris laughed. They locked eyes until my dad broke the stare and ate the food Iram handed him.

I hung my head low, but didn't miss the look Idris shot my way. A slight flutter touched my chest. Not because I agreed with him, but because no one had ever fought for me against my father. The conversation continued and nobody dared to ask me for anything except Idris.

"I heard you're leaving soon. When will you be back in Pakistan?" another uncle asked him.

My head shot up at that. He never told me he was leaving for London. *Why would he?* It's not like he was planning to take me with him.

He waved him off. "Let the time come."

My dad found his voice again. "Will your mum remain here with Zoya?"

His eyebrows creased. "Why would I leave my wife here?"

That flutter turned into a swarm, and I almost jumped in joy. A smile threatened to break free. I wanted to run and hug him so tight he would suffocate.

But my father didn't hold the same joy as me. Worry plagued him as he looked at me. He was scared I would return to London and pick up where I left off. His eyes hardened with rage as if I was to blame for Idris' decision. When I didn't back down from his stare, his nostrils flared. "It would be good for her to stay here."

"Don't tell me what to do with my wife. A husband and wife do not live separately."

"What will she do in London? Here she can take care of your parents."

A dark, menacing chuckle escaped Idris. "She is my responsibility. You don't need to fret over who she takes care of." He stood. "And if you ever look at my wife like that again, you will have *me* to answer to."

❀❀❀❀

My mum shook her head in disbelief as my dad recounted the conversation at the table. He kept calling Idris disrespectful and blamed his father for not controlling him. But it had only taken me a few days to learn that Idris called the shots in his family.

I climbed into bed, my body aching from another long day of hosting. Knowing there was no sex on the table, I got comfortable and closed my eyes with a smile on my lips.

"Are you awake?" Idris was looking down at me.

I sat up. "Did you need something?"

He handed me a piece of paper. "I cannot leave Pakistan for another two weeks because of some work commitments."

I read the confirmation email for our plane tickets. "You booked these today?"

"You said you wanted to go home," he explained.

I grabbed his hand before he could walk away. "Thank you. Not only for the ticket, but for standing up for me against him. Nobody has ever done that before."

"I said I would take care of you, no?"

Releasing him, I tucked my knees to my chest. "Yes."

"I am not your father. I will never raise my hand on you." If he was trying to be soothing, it wasn't working. His tone was abrupt and direct. When he spoke again, it was with warning. "*But* if you ever make me raise my voice, you will feel the same wrath. I can tolerate many things, but disobedience is not one of them."

I lowered my gaze. "I understand."

"I'm taking you home, Zoya. But remember, this is not your father's home. This is my home. Our home. If you contact that boy, I will bring you back to Pakistan and visit you every few months when I direly need your affection."

"I won't ever speak to him."

"Good." He got ready for bed and climbed in next to me. "Happy birthday."

I didn't ask how he knew it was my birthday. His wishes only reminded me of the plans I had originally made with Adeel. My reality was so far from my dream, I was struggling to see it. My chest felt heavy as I accepted my new life. That day, Idris showed me a glimpse of what life could be if I abided by his rules.

For the first time in my marriage, I hugged my husband, closed my eyes and dreamed of better days to come.

CHAPTER NINE

We had been back in London for three days. It was just the two of us, as his parents wanted a proper break now that the buzz of our wedding had died. When we arrived home, I realised how successful Idris really was. His home in Pakistan was grand and beautiful. There, wealth proved simpler to obtain.

The three-floor home I walked into screamed the money Idris never mentioned to me. Fitted with two living rooms, a dining room, a conservatory, an American-style kitchen, five bedrooms and four bathrooms, it was a surprise to walk through.

Idris', now *our* bedroom was the largest; and like our room in Pakistan, we had an ensuite. The furnishing was simple and sleek. I spent the first day unpacking and making space for my belongings. I cooked a simple dinner and fell asleep before he could come out of the shower.

The clean air felt amazing against my skin. Just being back made me feel alive again. I smiled for absolutely no reason whenever I looked out the window. I hadn't left the house since we returned and I was eager to get out to see my friends. Telling Idris I needed to withdraw from sixth form, I took the opportunity to send an email to Rani. I didn't offer any details but asked them to meet up with me tomorrow at our usual park. Her reply was almost instant, and she promised they would all be there.

I had one problem: *Idris*. It would have been smart to ask him before making arrangements, but in my excitement to see my friends, I forgot about him. He mentioned he had businesses here, but had spent the last three days at home with me. Everywhere I turned, there he was. We never spoke to one another unless he was asking me for something.

As we ate, I mentally pushed myself to ask about tomorrow, but I was too much of a coward. I jumped when he spoke up.

"Iron clothes for me after you finish eating. I'll be going to work for a few hours tomorrow."

I nodded and bit the bullet. "I was hoping to see my friends tomorrow."

He looked up from his food. "What friends?"

"School friends. All girls," I quickly threw in.

He shoved a mouthful of food into his mouth and chewed slowly. "Be back before I return from work. Clean the house and cook before you go."

I barely heard anything after his agreement. My eyes lit up with excitement and relief. I couldn't wait to hold my friends and tell them everything that happened. How would they react? How much of their lives had I missed?

Forcing myself to make an effort, I asked, "What do you do for work here?"

"I have a few businesses, but my focus is my restaurant, *Balti*. Hashim is my business partner in that."

I didn't have the faintest clue who Hashim was, but assumed it was his friend. "Do you have many friends?"

"Three good friends."

"I have three best friends, too." It was the first thing we had in common. "They're more like sisters to me, though. I've missed being able to speak to them."

Idris was studying me as if he thought I was lying. "Call me once you've reached them and once you're home. I want to make sure you are safe."

"I don't have a phone," I reminded him.

He hummed under his breath and we went back to eating in silence.

🎀🎀🎀🎀🎀

In the far distance, I saw a small huddle of three girls. My smile broke free as did I. I ran towards them and when they spotted me, they raced me to the middle. We became a tangle of arms as we engulfed one another. I didn't realise I was crying until Sumayyah wiped my tears away.

Rani inspected me. "It's so fucking good to see you! You're back and alive."

"I missed you guys. So much." I pulled them in for another hug. "How are you guys? What have I missed?"

Halima's mouth dropped open in shock. "Forget about us! What happened to you? It's been two months since you ghosted."

We sat in a circle on the damp grass. I told them everything from my dad finding out about Adeel to my marriage with Idris. They fished for every detail about him, and I shared as much as I knew. They needed a few minutes to take in my new life.

"I can't believe you're married," Sumayyah said.

"I can't believe it's not to Adeel!" Rani screeched.

"What is Idris like?"

I shrugged. "He's okay. I could have married worse." And that was true. The men that had visited me before him were proof of that.

"How are you?" Sumayyah appeared teary-eyed.

It was the first time someone had asked me that in two months and the question formed a lodge in my throat. "I'm getting through it. It's different, but also the same. He's strict like my dad, but in a different way. I don't know how to explain it."

Rani arched her brow. "Well, you better find the words because Adeel has been blowing up our phones since you've been gone."

Idris' warning blared loud and clear. I shook my head. "I can't see him."

"You've got to at least tell him you're married. This guy is still waiting for you."

I looked at the others for some advice. Sumayyah looked hesitant. "I feel bad for him, but you are married. It would be wrong for you to meet with him without Idris knowing. And from the sounds of it, he would flip out if he knew. One of us will tell Adeel and he will have to move on."

It was wrong of me to flinch at the thought of him *moving on*. Especially as I was the one with a husband. But it wasn't a choice for me. Adeel would meet someone he loved more than me. He would be genuinely happy with her. He would make love to her the way we had planned. She would get the dream I co-created.

Halima nibbled on her bottom lip. "I don't know. I think the least he's owed is the truth from you. It's going to be hard, but at least it will be done. You'll never speak to him again, and Idris wouldn't have to know. But you need to close that chapter of your life. You stopped writing mid-sentence and if you don't complete it, you'll spend the rest of your life wondering what would have come next."

Rani stared at our friend in wonder. "That was beautifully poetic. I'm impressed." Her playful manner broke the tension and moved the conversation along.

It was nice to listen to their rambles about their lives. None of them had gone through the trauma I had, but the mindless chatter eased my heart. *I could do this*, I thought. With my friends to remind me who I was, I could find a middle ground. I could be the wife Idris needed while holding onto some part of me.

"What time is it?" I asked, interrupting Sumayyah.

"Nealy four-thirty."

I jumped up. "Crap. I need to get home before he does." I hugged each of them. "Now that I'm back, we'll see each other more often."

They echoed my sentiment and promised to do just that.

༄ ༄ ༄ ༄

"Let's go to bed." It was an order, and I knew there was no getting out of having sex tonight.

I finished putting the dishes away and turned the lights off. In our bedroom, Idris was already waiting for me in bed. I stared at the box placed on my pillow. "What's that?"

"I bought you a phone."

66

Walking across the room, I picked it up. It wasn't any shabby phone. It was a latest model with all the features. "Thank you."

"I've already set it up for you and saved my number. You may use the phone to keep in contact with your friends. But I don't expect to see you on it while I am home."

It was tempting to remind him he was always on his phone and laptop, but I didn't want to ruin the nice thing he did for me. At least I could text the girls whenever I wanted.

"Have you stopped taking the pill?"

"Yes," I lied.

"Good. Now that we are here, there is no reason to prevent having a baby."

I brushed through my hair. "What if we waited a few years?" While my voice was strong, I lacked the courage to look at him.

"What are you waiting for?"

"Nothing. I just ... I thought you would want it to be just us for..." My voice trailed off.

His voice was harder as he repeated his question. When I failed to answer, he called my name. "You are a wife. Your job is to provide me with children and raise them."

Maybe it was being back in the UK. Or perhaps it was seeing the girls. But I scowled at him. "And where do you lie in that scenario? Do you plan to be a father or a sperm donor?"

It was the first time I had spoken back and his surprise was clear. "I will keep a roof over their head. I will put clothes on their back. I will bring food to the table. That is what a father does."

"So, you want me to have all these babies and drown in their nappies and cries on my own? How is that fair?"

"That is what a mother does!" he snapped.

I threw my hairbrush onto the table in frustration. "I'm eighteen! How can you expect me to become a mother?"

"Many generations of women before you had children at much younger ages. If it wasn't meant to be that way, God wouldn't have made it a possibility."

Taking a softer approach, I faced him. "Please, Idris? I'm asking for some time. I barely even know you."

He showed no empathy. If anything, he looked enraged at my tearful gaze. "Have you tried to know me? You've spent our entire marriage crying."

"Because I *hate* you!" The words were out before I could stop them. "I told you I would never love you and you forced me to marry you!"

His eyes turned cold. "Are you waiting for that boy?"

I knew a life with Adeel was unrealistic. Yet, a tiny ember of hope remained. Perhaps we could have the life we dreamed of and Idris' child wouldn't fit into that.

"I'm just asking for some time to settle down."

"Perhaps your father was right and I should have left you in Pakistan."

Dread filled me. "Idris—"

"Turn the lights off and get into bed." His tone made it clear the conversation was over.

Under the pretense of needing the bathroom, I scurried out of there. I locked the door and leaned against it. My hands covered my mouth to stop my sobs from spilling out. The last thing I needed was for him to hear me crying again. He was right; I hadn't made it through a full day without crying.

But I deserved to cry. Instead of marriage being the key to my freedom, I simply moved from my father's chains to his. Every nice thing he had done for me was to serve him. He married me because I was young, impressionable and malleable. He brought me to London because he needed a vice for his sexual release. He bought me a phone to keep tags on me.

But I would not give him the baby he wanted.

For no other reason than I wanted him to lose one of these battles. I had lost enough. And maybe if he thought I had a defect, he would divorce me.

Searching through my half-unpacked toiletry bag, I found the pill. I swallowed one down and hid the rest in my opened packet of sanitary towels. *He would never find them there.*

The consequence of my tantrum was rough sex. He was brash and forceful with his movements. As always, I laid there and took it. My arms rested alongside my body, and I blankly stared up at the ceiling.

Idris tried to kiss me and when I didn't reciprocate, he bit down on my lip. "Look at me."

I dragged my gaze down to his face.

"You're *mine*, Zoya," he grunted. "When will you understand that? You will be forced to love half of me when you bring our children into the world."

I couldn't look at him. I didn't want him. "Are you done? My legs are hurting."

"When are you going to forget about him?"

"I'm not thinking about him." It was true. I wasn't thinking about anything. My mind was as empty as my heart felt.

He grabbed my jaw. "You will not speak to me like that again."

"Okay."

Once he was done, he fell onto his pillow and caught his breath. "Did you see him today?"

I turned the other way and closed my eyes. "No."

Grabbing my shoulder, he said. "Do not turn your back on me while I am speaking. Do you love him?"

My silence said what I could not.

"If he loved you, he would have married you."

"He wanted to," I defended.

He scoffed. "And what could he have possibly provided that I have not?"

Happiness. Love. Dreams. *Freedom.*

Chapter Ten

A RATTLING CAME FROM the door handle. I slipped the sleeve of tablets back into my pack of pads and shut the cabinet.

"Zoya," Idris called with impatience. "What are you doing in there?"

One week had passed, but I was already itching to see the girls again. Now that he was back in the swing of his normal routine, I understood how little I would actually see Idris because he worked *a lot*. After breakfast, he would do the household shopping. Upon his return, he would get dressed and leave for work, only returning hours after dinner. He expected me to be awake so I could plate his food and warm the bed while he showered.

I enjoyed being home alone most of the day. It gave me the chance to talk to the girls on the phone between my cooking and cleaning. It was a freedom I never had at my parent's house and I *loved* it.

Idris disliked our separation because it empowered my defiance. Running away wasn't an option, but nothing was stopping him from kicking me out.

Taking a deep breath, I opened the door and almost walked straight into him. When he didn't move, I looked up at him. "Do I need permission to relieve myself now?"

He held his hand out. "Phone."

"Why?"

"Why did you need to take it with you to the bathroom?"

Having nothing to hide, I handed him the damn thing. It was only filled with messages to the girls about their days. If he wanted to read about Sumayyah's heavy period, he was more than welcome to. I began making the bed while he stood in that same spot and invaded my privacy.

Once he was reassured that I wasn't messaging Adeel, he placed the phone on the dresser. "I'm leaving for work."

I rolled my eyes, even though he couldn't see me. Was he expecting me to walk him to the door and kiss him goodbye?

"I'm talking to you. Look at me." He didn't give me a chance to react because he grabbed my shoulders and forcefully turned me around. "Don't turn your back on me when I'm speaking to you."

"My back was already turned to you."

"Don't get smart with me." He let go of me. "Why did you leave our bed in the middle of the night?"

I hoped he hadn't felt me creep downstairs. I needed to get away from him after having *another* dream about Adeel. Almost every single night he haunted me, begging me to give him another chance. With his number engrained in my brain, I was tempted to message him. I wanted one conversation to explain it was all out of my control; one chance to ask him to wait for me. Without a baby in his arms within a year, Idris would certainly believe that I was useless as a woman. He would divorce me, and with that label hanging over my head, my parents would accept any man who showed an interest in me.

"I was feeling hot."

"You were dreaming about him again."

I stilled.

"Do you deny it?"

"I can't remember what I dreamt about."

"You called his name." He wasn't angry. He wasn't upset. He was stating a fact. "Marriage is not a game. It is a vow before God. You are married, Zoya. *Married*. It would be good for you to remember that. And if you forget, I have plenty of ways to remind you."

It was a threat. One I didn't want to understand the consequences of.

"If you believe you can marry him, think again. His family would never accept you now."

Is he right?

"I don't..." I couldn't get the lie past my lips.

"Next time you utter that boy's name in our bed, I will find him. Is that understood?"

"Yes."

I waited for him to leave before I let the first tear fall. *What would he do to Adeel?* Is Idris the type of person to be violent? I didn't know him well enough to be reassured, but knew I had to do my best to protect Adeel. The only way to kill the dream was by taking Halima's advice and closing the chapter.

🎀🎀🎀🎀

I didn't ask Idris if I could go out. I didn't even tell him I was leaving the house. I knew the questions that would follow and I wasn't prepared to lie to him. My plan was simple: meet Adeel, give us closure, and return home before Idris did.

Except Adeel was sat silently on the bench next to me for minutes on end. I twisted my fingers nervously into a knot. I couldn't face the heartbreak on his face, so I stared straight ahead and waited for his hatred.

"Why didn't you run away? You could have come to me or your friends and we would have protected you."

I wiped my tears. "It all happened so fast. I was on lockdown and was scared. I've never seen him like that. I either got on that plane or into a coffin."

He grabbed my hand. "But you're here now and we can get you out. We can report him to the police."

Feeling panic, I shook my head. "No! I can't do that. Do you understand the consequences of that? My family would disown me."

"Who cares?" he shouted. "Look at what they've done to you! This is forced marriage, and that is illegal. I can talk to my parents. We can get married." The hope in him killed whatever part of me remained.

"A woman cannot have two husbands and Idris won't divorce me. And this culture won't let your parents accept me. Not as a divorcee. Not as a disowned daughter."

He stood up. "Then we'll run away."

"I can't ask you to do that."

"You're not asking. I'm offering."

"You will spend the rest of your life hating me."

He took a step away. "You want to stay with him."

Matching his stature, I stood too and stared at him in disbelief. "How could you say that?"

"You're rejecting every solution I'm offering. Do you love him?"

"No! I hate him. But because I love you, I can't let you do this. You have the chance to be happy with your family beside you."

"I love you too," he whispered. "So what do we do? How do we keep us a secret?"

I had two options before me. I could live a secret life with Adeel, where I was showered with the love I'd never receive from Idris. It would be just like before I was taken to Pakistan. But eventually he would also have to marry and then we would both be disgracing the sanctity of marriage.

And then there was the fact I was married. No matter how much I detested him, I couldn't break my vows. I couldn't commit adultery. Maybe Idris would leave me one day, and if the time was right, I could reconnect with Adeel. Maybe one day my life would become the dream I'd held on to. But until then, I needed to let go of it.

"I came today to give you the truth. I came to release you, Adeel. You need to move on and find someone else. I'm married."

"There's no one else for me."

"There has to be, because I won't cheat on my husband. He is far from ideal, but I can't do that to him or me. If we started an affair, we would both become someone we're not."

"That's what he is trying to do to you. He is breaking you to his will and command."

I smiled. "Then you know how much I love you to be here. The start of any journey indicates what is to come and how it will end. If we both cross that line, happiness will never find us because we would need to pay for our sins."

"And whose sins are you paying for now?"

"I'm paying for the sin of being a woman in this culture."

❦ ❦ ❦ ❦

"I won't be going to work tomorrow." He waited until I had finished ironing his clothes to tell me that.

Irritation burned in me. I hung his clothes up and nodded. "Okay. What would you like me to cook for lunch?"

"I want you to tell me what you did today." There was an undercurrent to his demand. His green eyes darkened as they fixated on me.

He couldn't know I was gone; I returned well before him. I erased the messages with Adeel from my phone. By the time he reached home, I had cooked, cleaned, and had a shower. When I voiced that, his expression hardened.

"Did you have everything you needed to cook?"

"Yes."

He hummed. "So where did you go between two and three-thirty?"

How does he know that?

"I went to see my friend." It was the first lie that slipped out.

"Which one?"

"Halima."

"Who else was there?"

"Nobody."

"Why did you go out?"

I sighed. "This is ridiculous, Idris. I was gone for less than two hours. I did everything you expect from me at home. What is the problem if I saw my friend? I just wanted some fresh air."

"Did you ask me?"

"For what?" Feeling frustrated, I pulled at my hair. "I can't do anything without you questioning me. I can't even go to the fucking toilet without you banging on the door!"

"Watch your mouth! Don't swear at me!"

"Or what?" I snapped. "I should tolerate all the foul words that come out of your mouth when you pin me to your mattress, but I say one word and you're screaming at me?"

He calmly stood. "You raised your voice first."

"Because I am sick and tired of you! At this rate, I would rather be in Pakistan than here with you. How did you even know I left the house? Are you tracking my phone?"

"I have CCTV at the front of the house."

I snorted. "Of course you do. After all, this is a prison."

His eyebrows shot up, and he smiled. "Prison? Okay, Zoya. Tell me what your punishment should be for lying to me."

I mocked a smile at him. "Divorce. But it would be a rather joyful punishment."

"Okay. I divorce you, and then what? How long before your father takes you back to Pakistan? As a divorcee, you'll only be worthy of old divorced men that have no means to bring you to the UK. He beat you when he learned you had a boyfriend. Imagine the consequences when he learns you continued your relationship with the boy after marriage. Maybe you won't make it to a second marriage. Maybe you'll be killed before then."

Refusing to feel intimidated by him, I stood taller and braced my shoulders back. "I would rather die than stay married to you. It's the same thing to me! This is hell on a limbo! So, go! Tell my dad about this alleged affair I'm having."

"You deny messaging the boy? You deny meeting with him today?"

I would have asked how he knows, but I didn't care. "No. I did message him and asked him to meet with me. I left the house without telling you. And I won't apologise for it."

He closed the distance between us. "I won't tolerate your disobedience."

"You're so small-minded I could laugh."

His fingers grabbed my jaw. "And you're treading on thin ice with me."

The anger in his eyes terrified me. All alone in this house, I wondered what he would do to me. He promised to never raise his hand on me, but the rage in his eyes proved he had forgotten about that.

"What did you do with him? Why did you shower before I returned?"

I should have run away with Adeel. Maybe it wouldn't have been perfect, but anything had to be better than this. I hated myself at that moment. I hated that I never selfishly chose myself.

"I told him I was married. He asked me to run away with him, and I told him he needs to move on because I have a husband. I had the chance to commit the very thing you're accusing me of. I had the chance of being *happy*. Yet, I came back."

Stunned by my honesty, Idris released me and stepped back. "After I strictly forbade you from speaking to him, you went behind my back and lied to me."

"Because I knew you would never understand."

"Understand *what*?" he snarled. "You are *my* wife. That is all that matters!"

"Understand that I love him!"

His nostrils flared. "Don't ever say that in my presence again."

"I can't turn it off, Idris! A piece of paper doesn't make it all go away. I thought I was going to marry him. I had plans for myself; a future that I wanted more than anything. That doesn't go away because you made me your wife!"

"What is so terrible about being married to me?"

"It's stifling! I can't breathe! I'm trapped in your home under your dictatorship!"

"And it seems even that isn't enough to control you." He nodded his head. "I warned you I don't tolerate such behaviour. I told you what would happen if you ever spoke to that boy."

He was sending me back to Pakistan.

"Take this as my permission for you to have a second wife," I remarked. "You can send me to Pakistan, but don't think when you come crawling to me, I'm going to spread my legs for you. Find another unfortunate woman to fulfil your urges."

He grabbed my hand when I tried to walk away. "I'm not sending you to Pakistan, Zoya. You are going to stay right next to me, under my watchful eye. I have no desire for another wife when I have one that will learn to meet my commands." He cupped my face. "Whether or not she likes it," he whispered against my lips.

"Idris—"

"I didn't give you permission to speak." His eyes were emotionless as he watched me. "You refuse to make this marriage work. I have given you what you have asked for. I brought you back to London. I bought you a phone. I haven't stopped you from speaking to your friends. But today has proved it is not enough. Your heart stupidly yearns for a boy that can't give you half of what I can."

"Idris—"

"You will not do or say anything unless I say you can. Only when I give you permission will you sit, stand, and serve. Unless I say you can speak, I expect silence. You are to not leave this house unless I have explicitly said you can. When I ask for something, you will give it without arguing back. You called this a prison? You called me a dictator? Then, that is what life will become. And only when you learn to *respect* this marriage and *me* will I loosen my chains."

CHAPTER ELEVEN

SHAZIA PEERED OVER HER rimless glasses as I wiped the dining table. "You should learn how to make these small alterations," she remarked with a huff. "A woman should learn these things. My mother taught me to sew from when I was a little girl. You've been married for two years. I can't keep fixing his clothes."

I wanted to tell her they had enough money to send it to a tailor if it was that much of a chore to fix. In fact, Idris had enough money to wear his clothes once and replace it with new ones.

I forced a smile and said, "Next time I'll do it."

"Come and watch me so you can learn."

There were still a million things left for me to do before the guests arrived. But the last thing I needed was her telling her son that I refused to do as she asked. So, I took a seat next to her and watched her thread the needle. She slowed down the process for me and explained which direction to thread and pull.

A soft *oh* passed my lips. "That was quick."

She tied a small loop at the end and tugged on the secured button. "Don't forget that bit or else the thread will come undone. What's next?" She turned the kurta inside out and laid it on the table. Her hands were steady as she worked the needle through the two pieces and fixed the tear. Every stitch was equal in size and spacing. "There's one left. Do you want to try?"

My mum had tried to teach me to sew, hoping to emulate the success she had with my sisters. But I had no patience or interest in it, so I was utterly useless. I didn't want to embarrass myself further in front of her. She was already amused at my state of awe in her skills.

I shook my head. "I don't want to ruin your work."

Waving me off, she forced the needle into my hand. "You won't learn if you don't try."

With my shaky, inexperienced hands, I tried my best. When I snagged the thread, she showed me how to restart the process. At that point, my mother would have called me useless and told me to piss off. But my mother-in-law showed a level of patience she never had on a day-to-day basis. And while I winced at the shabby job, she smiled.

"With some practice it will be perfect." She practically jumped out of her seat when the front door opened and ran towards her son.

I stayed put and packed away her materials. I ignored Idris upon his entrance. There was no part of me that was happy he had returned from Pakistan, and I couldn't bring myself to even pretend to be excited to see him. I folded the clothes into neat piles and ignored his heavy stare. Careful not to drop them, I stalked past him and headed to our bedroom.

The heavy footsteps got louder as they climbed the stairs. They abruptly stopped outside my bedroom door before it swung open. Even with my back turned, I knew it was Idris because nobody dared to enter our room.

I eyed his longer hair and thicker beard. He had gained a little weight from his aunts overfeeding him. Other than that, he looked the same as he wore his usual scowl when looking at me.

Two years of our marriage had passed. Some moments blurred; others felt endless. Marital life proved monotonous. My mother-in-law liked to cook every day. She liked to host and attend dinner parties. And I was her little lackey for every event. When she returned from Pakistan, she was displeased with my cooking. So, she took it upon herself to teach me. She also corrected everything else I did and never failed to tell her son all she had taught me.

I understood where Idris got his mannerisms from as I got to know his father. Abbas was also a man of few words, but when he spoke, he commanded everyone's attention. He saw the world in Idris and to him, his son could do no wrong. My relationship with him was barely there because he didn't speak to me unless he had to. By no means was he rude. He just didn't believe there was much to talk about with his daughter-in-law. And I was okay with that.

The only times I felt happiness is when my sister-in-laws would visit. It wasn't as often as I liked because my parent-in-laws believed a married daughter shouldn't return so often. It's why I rarely visited my family. Sadaf and Iram felt like my friends. Except, they were to be treated as guests when they came, so I would serve them. They'd always try to refuse, but I knew my mother-in-law would complain to her son and I'd have to face his wrath.

I liked it best when my mother-in-law visited Pakistan. It meant I could see my friends a little more often. Idris' imposed curfew was still standing, but I made use of what he offered. Our coffee and lunch dates were the only thing that sustained me. With my in-laws living with us, gone were the days of endlessly talking to them on the phone. While I couldn't relate to the lives they were living, I enjoyed listening to them talk about it.

They were all in their first year of university. Rani and Ravi were still going strong. Her days were filled with studying all day and partying all night. If Sumayyah was a study addict before, there were no words for it now. She was one step closer to becoming a doctor. We all hoped that she would finish her Medicine degree with more than a certificate when she told us about Ibrahim, a fellow student in her class. But she quashed that because studying was her sole focus. The biggest surprise was Halima's new *boyfriend*. We were all stunned when she told us about Nazir because she always swore off men. But Nazir had somehow broken her walls because she was smitten with him.

While their lives had moved on, mine remained stagnant. Idris remained firm in his threat and kept his reigns tight. While he could see his friends and return in the middle of the night, I was stuck in his home. It wasn't a reprieve when he went to Pakistan because his mother would be here to babysit me. And he would call me multiple times throughout the day. It was no different whether he was here or not.

He was already in a bad mood. "Did you decide to get off your ass today because I was returning home?"

I crossed my arms over my chest. "What are you talking about?"

"Why did I have to hear about you being lazy while I was gone? You were sleeping late, letting the laundry build up, not cleaning the kitchen properly, and disappearing to our room in the middle of the day for hours."

If I wanted to piss him off more, I would have rolled my eyes. Today was already going to be long without having to argue with him. "The only day I did that was when I was unwell. That was the day I didn't answer your call because I was sleeping. I'm not a robot; I get sick."

"What excuse do you have for making her put the dishes away? Why is she mopping with her bad back?"

That was the key problem I had with his mum. She could have easily asked me to do those things. We lived in the same house. Yet, she called her son, who was in a different country, to complain about me knowing how short his fuse was.

"She mopped while I went to buy groceries. How was I supposed to stop that?"

"You returned two hours later with only half of what was on the list. So, tell me where you really went."

My eyes narrowed. "I had to get the bus, Idris! And if I couldn't find everything in the shops, what was I supposed to do?"

"If I knew how fucking useless you were, I never would have paid your father so much money for you." His disgust made me recoil.

I felt like dirt beneath his shoe. I bit down on my lip to stop them from quivering. My gaze lowered, and I nodded my head. "I need to dust."

He locked the door, signaling that I wasn't going anywhere. "Did you bleed?"

"Yes."

Angry disappointment filled him. "Are you still bleeding?"

Not wanting to have sex with him, I lied. "Yes."

He sat on the bed. "Come here."

Please don't check.

He pulled me onto his lap, and his mouth was on mine in an instant. The kiss was feverish and desperate. His hands roamed my back before his nails dug into my hips. His arousal pressed into me and he rocked me against it.

"How much longer do I have to wait?" he asked, his head resting in the crook of my shoulder.

"A few more days."

He fingered the ends of my hair and his features settled into a sharp look. "What the hell have you done to your hair?"

"I cut it." I wasn't sure how it took him so long to notice because it went from waist-length to just above my shoulders.

"Why?"

I shrugged. "I felt like it."

"Did you ask me before you did that?"

Certain his irritation was a joke, I snickered. "It's *hair*. It grows back."

He gathered the shorter strands in his fist and his jaw clenched. "Don't ever cut your hair like this again."

His anger was irrational, and I didn't have the energy to understand why he was making a big deal out of it. Instead, I promised to ask his permission next time.

❀❀❀❀

My back and legs were aching from being on my feet all day. I leaned against the wall and smiled at aunty Jahan, who was approaching me. Of all my in-laws, her family was my favourite.

"You look tired," she said, stroking my cheek.

Her sister eyed me with a grin. "After two years, do we have good news?"

My nails dug into my palm at the rude, invasive question. This question came up at every family gathering. Not only did it irritate me, it burned my mother-in-law, too. She wasn't shy about wanting a grandchild. Amal had given birth last year to a boy, but it wasn't her beloved Idris' child, so it didn't count. Bilal's child wasn't the heir to the throne. That spot was rightfully reserved for the son my husband and mother-in-law were so desperate for me to have.

It wasn't just his family, but mine too; especially when Asma gave birth to her fifth child and Maliha welcomed her second daughter last year. My mother took it upon herself to share home remedies that boosted fertility every time she saw me, worried Idris would leave me unless I gave him a baby.

No matter how much pressure they put on me, I would not have a baby until I was ready. It was difficult picking up the pill, so I told Idris I had a doctor's appointment and got the IUD put in. I had five years' coverage, and Idris would never know. When my period came every month, I could see his frustrations. It only made him try harder the following month.

Ignoring the question, I turned to aunty Jahan. "How is Farrah doing? I haven't seen her in ages."

Her face shone with pride. "I don't even see her because she's always revising. That's why she didn't come today. She's picked Biology, Chemistry, and Math for college. She wants to be a doctor."

My chest felt heavy at the joy in her voice. I envied Farrah; her life wasn't going to be just marriage, housework, and children. "She's so smart she can do it with her eyes closed. My friend Sumayyah is studying to be a doctor. I'm sure she will happily give Farrah some advice." I fought the eye roll when Idris called for me.

She gave me a knowing smile. "The hardest job is being a wife. We have to be everything rolled into one. When they're sick, we become a doctor. When they're hungry, we become a chef. When they can't find something, we become a detective," she laughed.

"Zoya!" The sharp tone had eyes on me.

I pushed off the wall and scurried towards the dining room. The boisterous laughter of the men echoed the space. I kept my head down as I made my way to Idris' side. "Ji?" *Yes?*

He blindly handed me his glass. "Mujhe pani doh." *Get me water.*

"Bhabhi! I haven't seen you in ages. Where has Bhaiya been hiding you?" Rizwan grinned at me. It took a while to get used to the title of *Bhabhi* — the endearing, respectful way to address an elder brother's wife — especially as Rizwan and a few of his other cousins were older than me.

"I've been here. You haven't made the time to come and see me. I was just telling your mum I haven't seen Farrah in forever."

He laughed. "I've been so busy."

"Well, I miss you guys. Why don't you come over next week and I'll make that lasagne I promised?" Something pinched my leg, and I stared down into Idris' warning eyes. My heart pounded in my chest because I knew I had overstepped his boundaries.

With his filled, he gestured to the other empty glasses on the table. It was his way of giving me permission to offer them my service.

"Mamu, more water?"

Uncle Farhan shook his head. "No, I'm okay. I've eaten enough. Your cooking was extra delicious today. Must be because your husband was coming home after so long," he teased.

His wife appeared next to me and hugged me. "You must have missed him."

Absolutely not.

Uncle Farhan was the only one who dared to joke with Idris. He would relentlessly make, *mostly inappropriate*, comments he knew would rile him up. That's why he said, "You shouldn't leave such a young wife behind. Someone might try to steal her."

Everyone laughed. Not Idris. His lips thinned into a straight line and his eyes narrowed. He looked at me as if he wanted me to declare publicly that I was solely his possession.

"I almost didn't recognise you with your new hair," Rizwan quipped.

The aunt who had asked if I was pregnant, scrunched her nose. "Girls shouldn't have such short hair."

Uncle Farhan grinned at me. "Does your husband like it?"

I looked down at Idris, who was clenching his fists. "You'll have to ask him."

The knowing smile on his face made me smile, too. "Your hair looks very nice. He's just angry because now you look even younger than him."

Aunty Jahan laughed at her husband and pinched my cheek. "Our daughter-in-law *is* young. Young and beautiful."

Uncle Farhan nodded in agreement. "That is why I told Idris to not leave her behind in case someone steals her. Next time, I might take her for our Rizwan."

Laughter burst out of me when Rizwan looked disgusted until I remembered that a daughter-in-law doesn't laugh so freely. I pursed my lips and shook my head.

Sadaf wrapped her arm around me. "Stop teasing our Zoya. You're embarrassing the poor girl."

I leaned into her embrace. "I don't mind."

Uncle Farhan jutted his chin towards Idris. "Your husband does, though. Why is your face so sour?" he asked with a chuckle.

"I've had a long flight and am tired."

Aunty Jahan gripped his shoulder. "I'm sure you're eager to go to bed tonight."

Pushing his plate away, he stood up and stormed out of the room. The laughter subsided, and I awkwardly grabbed his plate and carried it to the kitchen.

Idris was aggressively washing his hands. "Tell me it's not true," he muttered when I was standing by his side.

My eyebrows furrowed. "What's not true?"

He moved to the side to let me wash up, but stood close behind me. "There's no one else," he whispered in a desperate plea. "Tell me there is no one else."

"You know there's no one else."

Adeel was a dream that had faded a long time ago. There had been moments when I wondered what he was doing. *Was he married yet? Was he happy?* I cut all contact with him. I told the girls I didn't want to hear any updates and soon enough they cut any ties with him, too.

He stared at his cousin, who was lingering too close until she scampered away. "Come upstairs. I need you."

My core tightened. "There is a house full of people."

"Zoya," he muttered.

I shut the water off. "I'm bleeding."

He swore under his breath. "Cover your hair properly," he snapped and stomped away like a child.

❀❀❀❀

The sweet relief of getting into bed after hosting was unparalleled. The guests had finally retreated to their homes. Dishes were cleaned and stored. I had vacuumed and wiped down all the surfaces. I was ready to sleep, but Idris had other plans.

His hands were already inside my top and stroking my stomach. He shuffled until he was spooning me. "You said you're still bleeding?"

I clenched my legs tight. "Yes."

His chin rested on my neck. "Then why is the bathroom bin empty?" He held me in place when I tried to skim away. "Why did you lie?"

I'd been caught in enough white lies to know the best thing was to remain silent. Anything I said would be used against me.

"Are you fucking Rizwan?"

Removing his hands from me, I gawked at him. "You did not just ask me that. That is disgusting."

"You complained he doesn't come to see you. You offer to cook for him. You said you missed him. But I never even got a hello. You didn't even have the decency to *look* at me."

"That doesn't give you the right to accuse me of screwing around. Rizwan is like a brother to me."

"I don't give a shit. You are not *their* Zoya." Without warning, his hand slipped into my underwear and he inserted two digits into me.

His soft moan rested between us. "Why did you lie to me? You don't crave your husband after being away from him?"

If I didn't stop him, he would feel the strings to my IUD and know I lied about the contraception too. "I was bleeding in the morning. Then it just stopped."

"Has there been someone else while I've been gone?"

"You know there hasn't."

His other hand lifted my chin, so I was forced to look at him. "Say it."

"There's no one else."

His lips were on mine. "Tell me you're mine."

"I'm yours."

"Nobody else has had you."

"Nobody else has had me."

He was hovering over me, stripping us naked from the waist down. "*Mine*, Zoya. You are mine. Only mine. Forever mine. Say you understand."

"I understand." And with my confirmation, he joined our bodies. I gripped his arms at the abrasive intrusion.

With every thrust, he repeated a single word. *Mine.*

Because I was his belonging. He bought me off my father. That was how my culture viewed us women. We had a numerical value attached to us. We were disposable. We could never be enough on our own.

CHAPTER TWELVE

I FELT SICK AS Idris parked the car outside of the GP clinic. After four years of failing to get me pregnant, he had enough and booked an appointment for me. A year ago he also made an appointment, but luckily he wasn't able to come with me so I got away with feeding him lies. I knew that wouldn't be the case today. Idris was certain there was something wrong with me and was determined to fix the problem.

I should have admitted to getting the coil and faced the consequences because after today the truth would be out. And I knew it wouldn't end well for anyone.

My body refused to get out of the car. I watched as he slammed his door shut and impatiently waited for me to move. Swallowing my fear, I walked alongside him into the clinic. He checked me in and I took a seat in the waiting area.

Just say it. He can't lose his temper in front of these strangers.

But the words wouldn't come. Four years into marriage with him, I became who he desired. Never wanting to deal with his angry side, I kept my head bowed and did what I needed to get through each day. It wasn't all bad, and there were times it was nice when we were alone. But those were fleeting moments. When he was having a bad day, everything pushed him over the edge. Those days and nights were the worst.

"Zoya Iqbal?"

I nodded at the doctor and followed him to the private room. Any hope that Idris would wait outside faded when his heavy footsteps trailed behind me.

The doctor nodded at the empty seats opposite him. "What seems to be the problem?"

"She can't get pregnant," he answered for me.

I imagined how exhausting being a doctor must be. I'd witnessed through Sumayyah how much time and effort goes into it. And in the end, you spend the rest of your life listening and fixing everyone else's problems.

That's probably why the man had no visible reaction to the statement. "Let me have a look through your records to see what tests have been done before."

I tried catching his gaze, silently begging him to stop. He would see I had the coil implanted, but never removed. He would look at us like we were crazy before forcing me to admit to Idris that I had lied all this time.

"When did you have your IUD removed?"

Idris froze. "What?"

The doctor was still scanning through my notes. "I can see we fit it May 2010. Your historic notes don't show a removal date."

I felt it; the equally burning and icy stare directed at me. His nostrils flared and his fingers curled into a fist. I couldn't breathe. I couldn't speak. I remained seated, head bowed.

Idris was trembling. "Let's go."

The doctor looked at us in surprise. "Pardon?"

He was already standing. "Zoya."

I followed him out of the clinic, into the car. He said nothing on the short drive home, but his foot was heavy on the pedal. I turned my head and stared out the window, trying to wipe my tears inconspicuously before he could see them. When we arrived home, he stormed up the stairs, and I debated whether I should follow him. But then he screamed my name so loud, my mother-in-law came running.

"What happened?"

I forced a smile. "Nothing." The last thing I needed was her knowing what I had done. Plucking non-existent courage, I joined him in our bedroom. I closed the door and kept the distance between us.

His menacing eyes were on me. "Get rid of those tears before I give you something to really cry about."

I was scared and no matter how hard I tried, they wouldn't stop falling. I let out a whimper when he came closer. "I'm sorry."

"You're always crying and I'm sick of it!" His knuckles turned white from how hard he was clenching his hands.

"I won't cry. Please..." I tried to back away, but the wall stopped me from going anywhere.

His voice shook, as did his hands. "I'm going to kill you."

"I—"

"The lying never stops! Four *years*? For four years you've kept a barrier between us?" He stepped closer. "For four years, you lied to me. Tell me why."

I had learned to distinguish when he wanted an answer or not. This was one of those times he wanted me to dig my grave with my own words. "I wasn't ready. I was only eighteen, and I barely knew you. I was scared and—"

"Of *what*? Scared to fulfil your duties as a wife and woman? Why did I marry you then?"

Something about his tone made me snap. He was acting as though *I* forced *him* to marry me. "You had the choice to marry anyone else. Yet, you chose a *child*. I was seventeen, Idris! You were a stranger to me. No normal person would expect me to have a baby!"

He stalked towards me. "I don't care about anyone else. This is *my* marriage!"

"Ours! A marriage works on a two-way basis. You don't get to call all the shots. I did everything else you wanted. I cooked. I cleaned. I laid in your bed. I took care of your parents."

Nothing I said registered. He stood at his full height and towered over me. "This is about him."

A groan of frustration filled the room. "No! I haven't even *heard* his name in years."

"What, Zoya? He'll accept you as a divorcee. He'll accept that I had your body first. But he won't accept you with a child?"

My mother was right; a man never forgets. When our arguments got bad, Idris was quick to throw Adeel in my face. It was the one thing that angered him like none other. He always mocked the idea of Adeel ever having me, like it was supposed to hurt me. But time healed that wound and if I ever thought of him, I only wished he were happy.

I rubbed my face and let out another cry. "I'm not doing this!"

His laugh was bitter. "Is he still waiting for you?"

"No!"

"Do you still want him?"

"No!" I screamed in his face.

He grabbed my cheeks and squeezed so tight my gums hurt. "So, why did you lie to me?"

It wasn't Idris standing before me. I was instantly reminded of that night when my dad grabbed me the same way. Panic was filling my lungs and I couldn't breathe.

I grabbed his hands, trying to pull them off me. "You're hurting me!"

He only held tighter as he pressed me against the wall. "Tomorrow you're going to get that *thing* taken out. And then you're going to offer yourself to me every night."

I gazed into the eyes of a man who vowed to never lay a hand on me. His green eyes housed the same anger my father's did that night. I was too scared to fight then and look at what my life became. I'd spent the last four years slaving for a man and family that never appreciated it.

I was going to fight today.

"No," I spat.

His eyes darkened. "What did you say to me?"

He wasn't going to threaten me into having a baby. "I said *no*. I'm not going to do that."

When his hands wrapped around my neck, it felt like someone had pressed rewind on my life and I was reliving the same moment. I gasped as he squeezed tight. A sob broke out, followed by a scream.

Idris was a solid wall that wouldn't budge, no matter how hard I pushed. "Then I'm going to *tear* it out of you."

"You do that, and I swear I will run out of here as fast as I can. I don't care what I lose. I don't care what my parents say. I will go and never come back." Just to hurt him as much as he'd hurt me, I twisted my knife in. "With nowhere else to go, I'll just go back to *him*."

The vein in his neck throbbed. "Do you want to die?"

I tightened his hold around my neck. My screams only made my throat burn more. "Do it! Kill me, Idris! You've already taken every other part of me! So do it! Kill me!" I could barely see his anger through my blur of tears.

With a push, he let go. "You disrespectful, disobedient liar! You are *disgusting*! How dare you talk about laying with another man to your husband?"

Idris was many things, but more than anything, he was a man of his word. And in just one moment, he broke the one promise I needed most from him.

This man wasn't my husband. He was a mirror image of my father, and that broke my heart.

"I hate you!" I cried. "How could you ever think I would want to carry half of you inside me? When you touch me, I feel sick! Every time you're on top of me, I wish it was anybody but you!" I cowered and turned my head when his arm raised.

But the impact never came.

The door swung open, and his mum stood there with a horrified expression. "Idris!"

He glared at her. "This is between me and her. Get out!"

I slid down the wall and let my head fall to my knees. My cries were so loud I couldn't make out what they were saying.

"Get up!" Idris grabbed me by my arm and dragged me up. "Stop crying!"

There was no stopping it because I knew how this would end. My hands rested on my chest as I tried to calm my racing heart.

He gripped my jaw again. "Zoya, stop fucking crying before I..."

Shazia grabbed my hand and pulled me away from him. "Don't you dare raise your hand on her again."

I leaned all my weight on her as I sobbed. "I can't do this. Let him kill me. Please, just let me die."

"Let go of my wife," he warned.

Her strength wavered for a moment. As my fingers gripped onto her, she met my pleading gaze and made her decision. "Look at what you've done to her," she said, sounding on the verge of tears herself.

He stepped closer. "Nobody comes between me and my wife. Give her back."

I was certain she would follow in my mother's footsteps and let him have his way with me. But she held my hand tight. "Once you've both calmed down, you can sort this out." She rubbed my back. "Come with me."

But Idris was unwilling to lose. "I'm not asking for your permission."

When he grabbed me, I let out another scream.

Abbas appeared in the doorway. "*Enough*. Let the girl leave with your mother."

"She's my wife!" he roared. "Nobody is taking her from me."

"Nobody is taking her," he snapped back. "She's going downstairs so you can control your temper."

When Idris spoke, his tone brought a chill over me. "Zoya, don't you dare walk out of here."

The threatening undercurrent made my feet halt. *What would he do when I was eventually forced to be alone with him?* I knew I couldn't hide behind Shazia for the rest of my life.

"Do you dare to disobey your husband?"

This wasn't my husband. I didn't know what I was going to do, but I took my escape when Abbas blocked Idris from us and let his wife take me away from this mess.

I sat in a daze as the tea brewed on the stove. The wave of heartbreak was building inside me, and it took all my strength to keep it at bay.

Her heavy eyes watched me. "One day, that temper of his is going to get him into trouble."

"I'm sorry you and Baba had to argue with him." I could barely recognise my hoarse voice.

She waved me off. "He'll see sense soon. He'll realise he was in the wrong and apologise." *Idris never apologised for anything.* "You two will be fine by tomorrow. There's no need to worry your parents by telling them about this. As his wife, you will forgive him. But the ones who love us hold our anger for us."

I almost smiled because if anything could get my dad to like Idris, it would be the way he handled me today. It was a leaf right out of his book.

"I don't talk to anyone about my marriage."

"That's good."

I wondered whether that was her intention when she entered our room. Was she scared Idris would cross a line, and I'd scream to the world about it? Or were her intentions as pure as I needed them to be?

As we made small talk, I realised it didn't matter because she saved me. She stood up for me, which was something my own mother couldn't do.

When I stood to wash the cups, she stopped me. "Go and get ready. You don't want to be late for your friend's party."

After the events of the day, I had forgotten about Halima's surprise birthday party. My chest tightened as I remembered, not only was Idris dropping me off, but attending with me. He didn't care to celebrate her birthday, but when he realised many of our school friends were invited, he couldn't risk me being alone with Adeel should he turn up.

ৼৼৼৼ

The air in the car was thick and stifling. I expected Idris to tell me I couldn't go, or at least refuse to drop me off. Despite that, I started getting ready and picked out a dress that hid the faint bruise on my neck. He caught my eye when I applied a second layer of foundation to hide the one on my jaw.

The weight on my chest remained even when I entered the small venue and hugged Rani and Sumayyah.

Ravi pushed his long hair back and pulled me into a side hug. "How are you? It's been ages."

I was hypervigilant about everything I did, scared something was going to send Idris off the rails again. Stepping away from Ravi, I said, "I'm good. I don't believe you've met Idris before." I couldn't call him my husband. I couldn't speak to him. I couldn't even look at him.

Idris shook Ravi's hand as they exchanged introductions.

Ravi wrapped his arm around Rani. "How is our Zoya married? I can't imagine you as a wife. You were so boisterous."

I gave him a pointed stare. "Rani was the loudest."

With a grin, Rani said, "Agreed, but you were definitely the naughtiest. Sumayyah will vouch for me on that."

Sumayyah shook her head at us. "You two were a terrible duo; always up to something," she chided.

She winked at me. "Some things never change."

Ravi asked Sumayyah about university and that started a conversation about how stressful a dissertation is. Sumayyah spoke about her recent exams and how she had two more years before she graduated. Rani and Ravi expressed their excitement about their upcoming graduation ceremony. I smiled politely at my friends, having nothing to offer to the conversation. Their lives were light years away from mine and it just added to the heartache I was already wearing that night.

We all hushed our chatter when it was announced the birthday girl had arrived. I watched in a daze as Halima jumped when we all yelled *happy birthday*. Nazir's boyish looks transformed into self-pride at pulling off the surprise. She stared at him with love before hugging him.

Idris was always one step behind me like a shadow. I didn't speak a word to him the entire night. I barely spoke to anyone. It didn't feel like I was really there. It was as if something in me died earlier today and it was my ghost here.

I only snapped back to reality when Nazir got on one knee and proposed to Halima. She was stunned into silence. For just a moment, she looked apprehensive and an awkward smile was directed at her guests. While his speech was heartwarming, he should have known Halima would have preferred a private, intimate proposal.

When Idris excused himself to answer a work call, I finally got a moment alone with my friends.

"That's not a ring. That's a rock!" Rani gawked. "Well done, Nazir!"

Sumayyah smiled. "I'm so happy for you."

But unlike my friends, I sensed something weighing on her mind. "You don't look excited considering you just became a fiancée."

Halima hesitated. "No, I am. It's just..." She looked around to make sure nobody could hear us. "My family still isn't on board with me and him."

"Why? He's a good guy," Rani argued.

She looked at Sumayyah. "You know how us Bangladeshis are. We dig into someone's entire family tree and history. His uncles have a bit of a past and my dad believes the apple doesn't fall far from the tree. But Nazir said he was marrying me whether or not they agreed. I think this proposal was just to reinforce that."

"Well, stick to your guns. They will come around."

"And ultimately your parents want you to be happy and Nazir clearly makes you happy," Sumayyah added.

All eyes were on me. "Yeah, I agree," I added lamely.

Sumayyah's eyebrows furrowed. "Are you okay? You've been a little off today."

Perhaps if Idris wasn't coming my way, I would have told them because I needed to get it out of me. But he gave me a look that said it was time to go.

"I need to go. Happy birthday and congratulations again." I wanted to cry. I wanted someone to tell me I wasn't a horrible person for not wanting a baby. I wanted someone to tell me it was okay to lie to him, considering the situation. But all I got was another silent drive home.

Removing my makeup and dress, I winced at my reflection. The bruises were taking proper form and more visible against my pale skin. My fingers lightly trailed over them. Unable to stomach the sight, I turned around at the same time Idris walked in.

He shut the door and stared at the consequence of our argument. Something similar to guilt was intertwined with anger in his eyes. "Zoya."

I didn't want to hear it. By no means was I innocent in our argument, but nothing gave him the right to do that to me. I lowered my gaze and grabbed my pyjamas. When he reached for me, I let out a whimper and flinched.

He retreated like I had electrocuted him. "Zoya," he pleaded. "Come here."

The tears that begged to be released all evening brimmed in my eyes. "I don't want to."

"I'm not going to hurt you. Let me—"

"Let you what, Idris?" I gestured to my bruises with a silent cry. "Let you do more of this to me? Let you have sex with me so rough I'll be unable to walk tomorrow?"

His throat tightened. "*No*. I just want to..." He never finished his sentence.

I had no escape. So, I turned my back to him and unclasped my bra. I let it fall to the floor the way I wished I could. "Stop it," I begged when his knuckles ran down my arm.

"He called you theirs. He said *our* Zoya like you're not mine."

I shrugged him off me. "Don't worry, Idris. This Zoya is all yours. The one they knew doesn't exist anymore." I finished getting dressed while he stood immobile behind me. "Your mother already advised me against telling anyone what happened today. I'm not going anywhere. Your chains are still holding me hostage." Without sparing him a glance, I got into bed.

I pulled my blanket tight around me despite the clammy August heat. I closed my eyes and tuned out the sounds of him getting ready for bed. When the mattress dipped under his weight, I pretended he wasn't there.

His voice was desperate. "Look at me."

My pillow soaked my tears. "Just stop it."

He sat up. "Zoya, look at me."

"No."

"I don't want to use force."

"Why not? That's all you've done since I married you."

His hands rested on my back. "Please, just look at me once. You haven't looked at me all evening. Please, look at me, Zoya."

"I don't need to. I spent seventeen years looking at my father."

He sounded hurt when he spoke after a few moments of silence. "I'm not him."

My laugh came out mixed with a soft cry. I sat up and stared at him. "Yes, you are. These bruises are an echo of my life there. Look at me!" I said, throwing his own words at him. "This is what *you* did! You *hurt* me, Idris!"

He tried to brush his fingers over the injury, but I moved away. "I was angry. And you said you were going to leave me. You said you wanted *him*."

"Because it always comes back to him! Nothing I do is enough. So just set me free." My hands rested in a prayer position as I begged him to let me be alive again. "I'm not enough. I'm disobedient. I'm a liar. I'm filthy. Used. Immoral. Shameless. Disrespectful."

Idris recognised those words. They were the same ones he and my father used to describe me at some point. "I was angry." He brushed his fingers faintly over my bruises and clenched his teeth. "Let me make them go away. I'll make it go away."

"Nothing will ever make this go away."

We both knew I wasn't talking about the bruises. They would fade with time, but the events of today left a crack that couldn't be healed.

"It won't happen again," he promised as he wiped my tears.

"My father said that the first time he slapped me. I was four. And like you he was angry; only he was angry because I broke a glass while carrying it to the kitchen to get him water."

"Zoya—"

"I forgive you, Idris. Not because I want to. But because it is my duty as a woman and wife. We are forced to forgive those who haven't issued an apology or even understand why we are owed one."

CHAPTER THIRTEEN

I IGNORED IDRIS' LOOK of confusion when I called for my mother-in-law. I stared at my reflection in awe and pride. With much help from her, I successfully made my outfit for Rizwan's wedding. It was a simple outfit, as my sewing skills were still mediocre. The embroidered top and silk skirt didn't look like hours upon hours of work. But my fingertips had been stabbed by a needle enough times to remind me how much effort went into it.

"Perfect fit!" she gasped. "Very good."

The fabric clung to my body in a very flattering way. It gave the illusion of an hourglass figure that made me feel sexy. Or perhaps it was the confidence I was feeling.

"Thank you," I grinned. "Does the colour look nice?"

Since that argument a year ago, the dynamics between us had changed slightly. Or perhaps I appreciated her more. The small things she moaned about didn't bother me as much. I actually spent my evenings sharing a cup of tea and making small talk with her.

She crinkled her nose at the dark grey. "You should have got something bright and colourful. You looked very nice in the pink you wore to your friend's wedding last week."

She was referring to Halima's wedding. She was currently on her honeymoon in Bora Bora and, from the pictures she was sending, Nazir spared no expense.

I ran my hands over the 3D work and grinned. "Your son would never wear bright colours, and Farrah said all couples had to match."

She tutted under her breath and left us alone. I couldn't decide if I should wear my hair up or down. I had gone through the effort of curling the long strands, but a bun would showcase the decorative buttons down my back I lost sleep to sew on.

"Up," Idris said without looking away from his laptop.

I stared at him. "Okay."

After our argument, Idris never broached the subject of babies for a few months. In fact, it was as if he was walking on eggshells around me. I thought maybe seeing me so distressed and desperate to leave him forced him to change his ways. I still did my part in our marriage by the way of cooking, cleaning and staring up at the ceiling while he was on top of me. But something in me broke that day, and I lost all strength to keep fighting against him.

I joined him in Pakistan for six weeks before he surprised me with a holiday to the Maldives. It was seven days of no escaping him. He tried to engage me in conversation, but even he knew I had become a shell. I saw too much of my father in him that day and was terrified of stepping out of line. So I kept my head down and did whatever he asked.

Just after the new year, we went to visit Iram after the birth of her son. The next morning Idris booked an appointment to have my IUD removed later that week. It would have needed replacing within months. I told myself that's why I didn't fight against him. I talked myself into believing motherhood wouldn't be so awful.

But the truth was, I was too scared to retaliate. One memory of the anger I saw in him silenced me. My parent-in-laws were in Pakistan and there would have been no one to save me from him. So, I went to the appointment. I let him try for a baby at every opportunity. Six months had passed, and I was yet to fall pregnant.

Idris closed his laptop and stalked towards me. "That top is a little tight, no?"

After zipping up, I could barely breathe, but it was a sacrifice I was willing to make. "That's the design."

"The shape of your breasts is on show."

I held the matching scarf up. "I'm going to drape this to cover them." I recognised the look in his eyes. I had spent too long getting ready to ruin my hair and makeup. But I didn't know how to say no without making him angry.

"If you wanted to wear a different colour, you should have said."

"You wanted to wear the outfit you bought from Pakistan."

"I could have bought a new outfit."

I didn't want to argue while he was trying to instigate it. "It doesn't matter, Idris. It's just clothes."

"I want to know why you never told me."

Choosing to be honest, I said, "Because I was scared."

"Of what?"

My silence said all I couldn't.

"You're too scared to talk to me? To ask me for something as trivial as wearing another colour?"

"Yes, because I never know which version of you I'm going to get. If I'm lucky, I'll get this version; the husband who tells me to wear my hair up. But most of the time I get the husband who might grab me by my throat so tight I have to wear my hair down to cover the bruise."

"That's only happened once in five years. And you know you provoked me."

I had given up with expecting more from him. "Okay. I apologise for that."

"Zoya," he called as I walked away. "That's not fair."

All I wanted was a day free of this torment. "Just forget I said anything. Next time I'll ask before buying my clothes."

Idris was in front of me, blocking the door. "Do you think I *wanted* to be like that? You forced my hand."

"I can't force you to do anything. It's why I never asked you to change your outfit. It's why I never ask you for anything."

"When we first married, I told you all you had to do was ask me if you wanted something. I told you I would take care of you."

"And then you put your hands on me."

"Because you *lied* to me for four years, Zoya!"

I shrugged. "Okay. I lied. It was my fault. I said sorry. Can you let me out?" When he refused to move from the door, I sighed. "Please, Idris. I don't want to argue with you."

"I'm trying to talk to you."

"No, you're trying to trip me into saying the wrong thing. You want me to give you a reason to be angry because this is what you always do."

"You said you're scared of me."

I couldn't help but laugh. "Why are you acting like you're surprised? Isn't that what you wanted? You set that tone right from our first meeting. If I'm scared, I won't dare to step out of line. You've done that. I'm scared, Idris. I'm scared to ask you for anything. I'm scared to say the wrong thing. I'm scared to cook, in case it's not good enough. I'm scared whenever you walk through that front door because I know something I have or haven't done will set you off. I'm scared to look at you. I'm scared to even *breathe* in your presence."

The look of despair on his face was hard to stomach. "That isn't what I wanted. That was never my intention."

"It doesn't matter anymore. I've accepted you and this marriage for what it is. I need nothing more from you. I expect nothing more from you. A woman like me doesn't deserve more than you've already given."

"Is that how you see yourself?"

"It's what you've repeatedly told me."

❀❀❀❀

Rizwan's wife, Emaan, was a lot more relaxed than I was on my wedding day. She laughed with us as we played the traditional games.

"Want to bolt yet?" I joked.

She fanned her melting makeup. "It's a lot to take in. There's so many names and faces to remember."

"It is a big family, but everyone is really welcoming. No matter what you fancy doing, someone is always available. One of the few perks of a big family."

"Which one is your husband?"

I searched the crowd of people and pointed at him. "That's Idris. Don't be put off by his grumpy expression."

That started a conversation about who-is-who. Rizwan, Farrah and a few other cousins joined in to explain the large family tree. Emaan did well to keep up, but lost focus when it got to second cousins.

"That's enough. If we tell her about Mizhur Mamu, she might run for the hills."

"Who's that?" she asked, wanting to understand why we were all laughing.

I shook my head. "The man can talk for days and takes pictures of absolutely everything."

"The best is when he learned what selfies were!" Rizwan added. "He took so many pictures with Bhabhi and got one framed as a gift."

"What did you do with it?" Farrah asked.

"I wanted to chuck it in the bin, but Ammi stored it away and takes it out when he comes to visit to make him happy." I gave Emaan a look of warning. "Be careful. You might end up with a picture of him on your bedside table."

She shook her head with a chuckle. "Absolutely not."

"What is all this laughter about?" Aunty Jahan asked. "I hope you're looking after my daughter-in-law," she said to me.

I took the hand she offered me and squeezed tight. "It is our job as women to take care of one another. So, if Rizwan ever steps out of line, we've got your back."

He held his hands up in surrender. "I wouldn't dare to. She works in a women's refuge home and isn't afraid to kick ass when the abusive partners turn up."

"You're much stronger than me. I don't think I could handle any of that."

"When dealing with pathetic men like that, you just have to re-member they are cowards. You'd be surprised at how fast they back down when faced with a woman's strength."

Farrah, stroking the fabric on my arms, gleamed at me. "I'm ob-sessed with your outfit. Can I borrow it sometime?"

"You can have it. When would I ever wear it again?"

"How much are you selling it for?"

My eyebrows furrowed. "Don't be silly. You don't need to pay for it. I'll dry clean it and send it to your house."

Aunty Jahan hugged me. "You've always taken such good care of my children. So, it is my job to take care of you. You've done a wonderful job as the eldest Bhabhi today, but you look tired."

Her statement prompted a yawn. "I slept late and have been awake since five."

"Your Mamu is going to drop Fatima home. Your house is on the way. Why don't you go with them?"

I knew my mother-in-law would have something to say, but I couldn't keep my eyes open any longer. I walked over to Idris, who was in conversation with a distant relative. I waited until he noticed me and stepped to the side. "I'm going to head home with Farhan Mamu."

"I can take you."

"It's fine. You enjoy yourself."

"I don't need him to drive my wife home."

"I never meant it like that. His car has an empty seat and you're not ready to leave yet."

His mind was already made up. "My keys are in your bag."

I told them to head off and did my round of farewells, which took longer than expected. The car ride was warm and silent, which had my eyelids drooping. Desperate to get some sleep, I unbuckled my heels the moment I was in my bedroom. A sigh of relief passed over my lips.

"Why didn't you tell me you wanted to leave?" Upon receiving silence, he spoke again. "Were you too scared to ask me?"

Not this again.

"You were talking to family you haven't seen in ages. I didn't want to interrupt that."

"You should have asked me."

I unzipped my top and slid my body free of it. Being able to breathe normally again felt amazing. Wanting to be done with the conversation, I sighed. "I'm sorry. Next time I'll ask." I hung my outfit so it could air out. "Are you going to work tomorrow? If you are, I need to iron your clothes and pack some food."

"Leave it for tomorrow."

"I won't have time in the morning. After making everyone breakfast, I have to clean the house and cook a few dishes to take for lunch at Rizwan's house tomorrow."

His stare was intense. "Aren't you tired?"

"Yes, Idris. I'm tired. But a good wife doesn't complain. She understands her role. She doesn't ask for more. She just does whatever she needs to do to survive another day."

He showered while I got everything ready. Only once his clothes were crease-free and his lunch stored in the fridge did I finally wash the day away. I stepped out of the shower and into the steamy room. I hoped today would be the day, but I knew I couldn't wait any longer.

I took out the pregnancy test. Idris bought it six months ago when he was certain his super-sperm would get the job done straight away. But before we could use it, my period would come.

My heart pounded in my chest. I felt sick to my stomach as the two minutes stretched into what felt like a lifetime. I choked back my sob when I saw the positive test. I took my time moisturizing my body because I knew the world would judge me for the tears that streaked down my cheeks. More importantly, I knew the sight of me crying would piss my husband off.

With dry eyes and an emptiness inside me, I entered our bedroom. Idris was reading the news on his phone. He only looked away when I silently placed the pregnancy test on his bedside table. I said nothing. There was no warm embrace or exclamations of excitement at becoming parents. His eyes stayed trained on me as I walked back across to my side of the bed and climbed under the sheets.

But no matter how hard I tried to stifle it, my cry broke out as I mourned the death of the small piece of Zoya I had left.

Chapter Fourteen

I wailed when another contraction hit, questioning why I had given in and become pregnant. But the very reason was standing at the foot of my hospital bed, staring at me in horror.

I wanted to pump myself with all the pain relief available, but Idris worried something would happen to the baby. He argued women in Pakistan gave birth with no medical attention at all. I would have reminded him we weren't in Pakistan and told him his opinion meant nothing because he didn't have a vagina that was opening ten centimeters, but I could barely breathe from the pain.

My pregnancy had dragged under his watchful eye. If Idris was overbearing before, there was no word to describe him for the past nine months. I wasn't allowed out of his sight. I was certain he thought I would try to force a miscarriage. Being pregnant didn't give me a break from the housework or sex. With no period to stop him, it became a nightly chore that only got more difficult as my bump grew.

I tried to love my body as it changed, but I couldn't tolerate the sight of it. Guilt consumed me every time I caught my reflection. I hoped to savor the pregnancy, but my mind was overwhelmed with the responsibility of caring for another person. This baby would be another chore to add to my list. It had already taken my body hostage, and soon it would steal everything else.

There were moments when I wondered who it would look like. Idris didn't want to find out the gender, so my imagination was left to run wild. Whenever someone asked which I preferred, I'd always say I didn't mind. But truthfully, I wanted a boy. A son had privileges a daughter would never get. A son had the world at his feet. A son had freedom. I knew what a daughter's life would become. Like me, she would become Idris' hostage before being sold to endure a fate similar to mine. And there would be nothing I could do to stop it.

The midwife entered the room and smiled at me. "How are you doing, mum?"

"Get this baby *out*!"

She snapped her gloves on and measured me. "I think the baby is ready to say hello," she laughed.

With a grimace, Idris said, "Let me see where mum's gone."

Another contraction came, and I let out a scream. I found myself reaching for him. "No! Don't leave me. Don't go."

He looked surprised at my request. "Ammi will be here with you."

It wasn't fair that I had to do this alone. It wasn't fair that I had given up my body to give him the baby he so badly wanted, and he gave up nothing. Perhaps having my mother-in-law with me would have been the smarter decision, but I didn't want her to see me in that state. It was mortifying.

"Idris, *please*. Stay with me," I cried. My head fell back onto the pillow. "I'm scared. Please don't leave me."

He stood in the middle of the room, looking completely out of place. "What should I do?"

The doctor grinned at him. "Hold her hand. Calm her down. Just be there for her."

Idris awkwardly stood by my bedside. He stared down at me before timidly taking my hand in his. Considering he had gotten me pregnant, it was weird holding hands with my husband. It was something we had only done once for our wedding photoshoot. The intimate action didn't belong to us.

But as the pushing started, I didn't care. I gripped his hand so tight I was surprised it didn't break. The room was filled with my scream, the medical staff's encouragement and Idris' disgusted silence.

I fell back onto the pillows. "I can't," I sobbed. "Take it out another way."

"You're almost there. I can see baby's head. Just two more pushes."

As I shook my head and refused to push, Idris scowled down at me. "Do you want something to happen to the baby?"

"No. I can't do this. I can't be a mum."

The midwife waited to see if Idris would offer any comfort and when he didn't, she stepped in. "You're already a mum. You have grown your baby and kept them safe all this time. I know you're tired, but you're almost there. Take a big breath in and then, when we say, give a hard push. You've got this, momma. Okay?"

The two pushes she promised turned out to be four. But then the most wonderful noise silenced everyone. A loud wail filled my heart with relief. *I did it.*

Idris peered over. "Boy or girl?"

Please don't be a girl.

"Congratulations! You have a beautiful baby boy!"

And I finally let out a breath and sobbed. Idris snipped the cord and then I caught a glimpse of my baby. His blotchy skin was covered in a white substance, but I instantly fell in love.

In just a single moment, my entire world shifted. The pain faded into nothing. Everything seemed more vivid. My eyes latched onto him and didn't move. My heart broke at the sound of his cry and I wanted to beg them to stop hurting him. I wanted to hold him in my arms until he knew he was safe. My heart filled with the intensity of a mother's love. It was as if all the hurt and heartbreak was worth it because it gave me him. As they laid him on my chest, I knew I would lay down my life for him.

Idris whispered the *Adhaan* in his ears.

My forehead rested against his tiny cheeks. He whimpered as I sobbed on him, and then he did the most wonderful thing. He looked at me as if he already knew who I was. The bright lights had his eyelids dropping.

I stroked his cheeks, unbelieving I thought I wouldn't love him. "It's okay. Ammi is here. You close your eyes. I'm not going anywhere."

My midwife smiled at me. "You tore a little. So, while we take his measurements, we're going to stitch you. But I promise you'll have him back in a few moments."

I didn't even feel the stinging of the needle. My mind was too focused on making sure they didn't hurt him. The weight on my chest only eased when they gave him back to me, this time dressed. I couldn't stop looking at him. I found peace in watching his chest rise and fall.

"My son," I whispered with a small laugh.

"Our son," Idris said, reminding me of his presence.

I counted his fingers to make sure all ten were still there. "*Mine. My sweet little boy*. Look at how *perfect* he is." My index finger brushed over his tiny button nose. I kissed his temple. "I love you so much."

Idris tried to take him. "You need to sleep."

"No. I want to hold him."

"Zoya, you've been in labour for almost seventeen hours. You need to rest."

I didn't care. All that worry about not being able to sleep or eat seemed ridiculous now. I couldn't imagine wasting the time I had with him by sleeping. What if something happened to him while I was dreaming of a life that couldn't compare to holding my son?

So, I refused to let him go; even when my mother-in-law entered and tried to take him from me. She took it less personally when I also refused to hand him over to Idris, Abbas, and my parents. Idris gave me a look of warning, but I didn't want this moment to end.

"Have you decided on a name?" Shazia asked.

The question wasn't for me, but for her son. Regardless, it was me who spoke. "He's going to be a good person. He won't be like the rest of them. He's going to be kind. And sweet. And generous. And noble." Knowing his name was his dad's decision, I looked at Idris. "Name him something worthy of that title. Because he's going to be good, Idris. He's not going to hurt me. He won't shout at me. He won't put his hands on me." My voice dropped to a whisper. "He won't be like you."

Maybe it was the lack of sleep that caused the hallucination, but Idris looked hurt at my words. The lights reflected in the tears that brimmed in his eyes. "Zoya..."

I kissed my baby. "I know there's not much I can give you. Your mother is shameless and dishonourable," I whispered. "But please don't hurt me. I'm tired of being hurt by the men who are supposed to love and protect me."

Both sets of parents left when the midwife entered. She eyed the uneaten toast and juice. "You need to fuel up if you're going to breast-feed."

I smiled. "I'm not hungry yet."

"You are the first mother ever to say that to me!" she laughed. "Has your milk come in? Would you like to try nursing him?"

When I nodded, she helped me untie my hospital gown until my breasts were exposed. Idris' cheeks warmed in embarrassment. He awkwardly cleared his throat and backed into a corner of the room.

"It might be a little uncomfortable. If your milk hasn't come in yet, don't worry, as it can take a few days." She taught me how to get him to latch, and her encouragement kept my spirits up every time I failed.

Finally, his tiny mouth wrapped around my nipple and he barely sucked before he stopped. I tried again, and this time he managed a few more pulls before he dropped my breast. "What's wrong, baba? You're not hungry?" I looked at the midwife in despair. "Am I doing something wrong?"

"Colostrum is very concentrated, so he doesn't need much. He'll have very small but frequent feeds over the next week or two." She turned to Idris. "Dad, you'll have to make sure mum is eating so she can produce enough healthy milk."

The words weren't registering with Idris. His stare was fixed on me as I tried to feed the baby again.

I broke out into a laugh. "Look! He's doing it! My smart boy."

Idris stood over us and watched the few pulls he managed. After a little more skin-to-skin, he helped tie my gown.

"Would you like to hold him?"

He stroked my cheek. "It's okay. You hold him."

It wasn't long before the eager grandparents joined us again. Their chatter was background noise to me. My mind was too busy trying to figure out how I created something so perfect.

Idris sat in the chair, engrossed with whatever he was reading on his phone. When his mum tried to take the baby again, he stood up. "Let him sleep on his mother." And then he left the room, with the phone pressed against his ear.

"Ayyub is a nice name," my dad said, as Idris rejoined us a few minutes later.

"I've decided his name and just confirmed its meaning." Idris stood by my bedside, tall and assured. "Karim Qadir. It means generous, kindhearted, noble and *honourable*." He looked at me. "I'm sure he will live up to his name. After all, he is his mother's son."

CHAPTER FIFTEEN

"I can't believe he's already one!" Asma cooed.

Karim buried his head into my neck when she tried to pinch his cheek. I rubbed his back. "I know. It's flown by," I said, my attention being stolen by Rani walking towards our friends. I waved at her when she caught my gaze. "Help yourself to the snacks and drinks." Before I could reach my friends, another voice stopped me.

Just as I promised on my wedding day, I had never forgiven my father. We were rarely ever alone together, and when we were, barely two words were exchanged. Even after seven years, he couldn't see how much he stole from me; nor was he sorry about it.

"Of my ten grandchildren, I see your son the least. Yet, you live the closest."

"Take it up with your son-in-law."

His eyes widened in horror. "How can I say such a thing to him? It's not my place to talk in your marriage."

I arched my brow. "Why not? You orchestrated it."

The false sorrow quickly faded to anger. "You will not speak to me like that. I am your father."

I shook my head. "No. I was borrowed property, remember? The day you sold me off to the most willing bidder, I became nothing to you." And with that, I joined my friends.

"Happy first birthday, bubba!" Rani's loud voice only had Karim clinging even tighter to me.

I rubbed his back. "He's been unwell for a few days. Getting him to eat and sleep has been a headache."

Sumayyah pouted. "Poor thing. Make sure he's drinking fluids and even if he's not eating full meals, give him little bits he can pick at."

"Is that another outfit you made?" Rani asked.

I looked down at my dress and admired the simplicity of it. Pregnancy changed my body, and I felt self-conscious in everything. While I had lost most of the baby weight, my belly still jiggled and my breasts had doubled. I enjoyed making clothes that were made for my new mother's build.

With a nod, I said, "Do you like it?"

"You're getting good at it," Sumayyah complimented.

"I like the regal look you have going on today. Totally suits this *huge* house," Halima gawked.

"When you eventually come to visit my new flat, don't expect something of this size," Rani added.

It had been months since Rani moved into her two-bed apartment. I felt bad about not going to see it, but motherhood had truly taken over my life. It was a tough year. There were moments of feeling so overwhelmed that all I could do was cry, especially in the beginning, when I was sleep deprived. I did all the night feeds and nappy changes on my own. Idris excelled only at criticising me. It was exhausting, but I wouldn't have changed it for the world.

I found peace in the moments I had alone with him. They were far and few because I wasn't allowed to have him upstairs during the day. Everyone, including both grandmothers, had their opinions on how I should take care of him. While I'd be slaving away in the kitchen, my mother-in-law would start using her home remedies on him for ridiculous things. When I started weaning him, I was glad I exclusively breastfed. Everyone had an opinion on what he should or shouldn't be eating. There were conflicting comments about whether I was overfeeding him. It was only then that I realised women can never get it right. No matter what we do.

"I'm sorry. But I'll definitely be seeing it soon."

Rani understood my cryptic words and winked at me. I wanted to ask how she was getting on with planning Sumayyah's surprise bridal shower, but was forced to keep quiet. Not that the bride-to-be was paying any attention to us.

She smiled at her phone like a teenager in love. When she looked up and caught us all smirking at her, her cheeks warmed. "What?"

"Is that Mr Yousef Hasan?" Rani teased. "What love message did he send this time?"

She playfully shoved Rani. "Be quiet and behave yourself. You're at a kids' party."

"You're the one reading dirty messages from your husband-to-be. I'd love to be in the honeymoon phase again. That fluttering excitement when you hear your phone go off. Your heart racing at the thought of them." She squeezed Sumayyah. "I'm so glad you're *finally* falling in love."

"Look at her blushing!" I laughed. "Are you ready to be married in three months?"

Like the Sumayyah we knew, a look of stress came about her. "There's still so much to do! And his mum takes forever to make a decision about anything."

Halima excused herself when Nazir called her.

"I have never met a man more obsessed with his wife than Nazir," Rani remarked as Halima walked away with the phone pressed to her ear. "It's cute. Ravi doesn't even wear trousers when he stays at mine."

"He hasn't moved in yet?" Sumayyah asked.

One of the main reasons Rani bought her flat was for Ravi and her to live together. After nine years of dating, she was tired of sleeping in different homes.

Her eye roll depicted her irritation. "Not yet. He's really pissing me off, though. He'll come and spend the entire day there and spend a few nights in the week. But he's too busy to pack his stuff and move in."

"Sounds like an excuse," I muttered.

"That's what I said." She sighed. "Look at you guys. You've got a baby. Halima has a husband. Sumayyah's about to get married. And then there's me. No ring. No husband."

"Uh oh," Halima said as she rejoined us. "Why is Rani pouting?"

"Is everything okay?" Sumayyah asked.

She shook her head with a small smile. "You know Nazir; he can't do anything without me."

My arms ached from carrying Karim. I shifted him so my left arm could get some relief. "Where is your dad?" I asked him, even though he couldn't answer.

"He's over there talking to that woman," Halima answered.

Rani's eyes narrowed into slits. "Who is that? He sure seems friendly with her."

I looked over my shoulder. "That's his cousin, Sanam."

"For a man with such traditional views, he sure seems comfortable talking to a woman." She gasped. "I bet he's screwing her."

"Why would you say that?" Sumayyah asked.

"Look at them over there, all smiley and whispering. What do you think they're talking about?"

Halima shook her head. "You've been watching too much TV. Just ignore her, Zoya."

I paid no mind to it because I knew Idris would never cheat on me. "If it gives me a break from him, she's more than welcome to satisfy him," I remarked.

Sumayyah looked appalled. "You don't actually mean that, do you? If Yousef ever..." She couldn't finish her sentence.

"I'd literally castrate Ravi and then feed it to him."

"He's coming over," Halima squeaked.

Idris greeted my friends, who offered a hello back. His eyes gave a silent command to speak privately. I excused myself before following him to the corner of the garden, away from everyone else.

"Can you take him? He's not going to anyone else and my arms are aching."

Idris ignored me. "All of my family is here. As are yours. And you are standing there talking to your friends instead of helping in the kitchen."

"I was just—"

"This is your house. Why should the guests be serving you?"

"He isn't getting down. How am I supposed to get anything done?"

"Stop using him as an excuse for why you can't do your job right."

I knew why he was frustrated, and it had nothing to do with cooking or cleaning. But I kept my mouth shut, and with Karim still in my arms, I sauntered back to the kitchen.

We were swarmed with hands desperate to cuddle him. No matter how much we tried to coax him, Karim clung to me as if I would disappear should he let go. Regardless, I helped prepare the food and carried it out to the tables in the garden.

"You have such a great daughter-in-law," an aunt praised. "When will you bring Amal over?"

Conversations about Bilal and his family migrating here had been ongoing for months. Nobody spoke to me about it, but I'd overheard Idris and his dad discussing it. Their concerns were about who would manage the businesses in Pakistan should he leave. Mine were about having additional people to cater for. With a baby to take care of, it was hard to get everything done. I told myself it might get easier having Amal to help, especially as Shazia was getting older and less able. The decades of being a hostess were finally taking a toll on her.

Knowing she wouldn't openly discuss her family matters, I carried the tray of food while balancing Karim in my other arm. When Rizwan tried to help me, I rebuffed his offer.

"Then give me Karim," he offered.

"If you can take him, you're more than welcome to babysit your nephew."

After pulling some funny faces and promising to show his car, I was finally child-free. I told Rizwan to escape quickly before Karim changed his mind and started wailing. He laughed as he scurried away. My smile faded when I felt Idris boring holes into my face with his deathly stare.

The party passed with much laughter, food, and conversation. The children, hopped on sugar, played the games I had prepared. Karim never grew fond of the attention and spent almost the entire time in my lap. Idris only took him when we posed for a family picture. He stood next to me with our son in his arms as we smiled at the lens.

Most of the guests, including my friends, had left. I was helping to tidy up when I heard Idris call for me again. "What's wrong?"

"How many times did I have to call you?" He practically threw Karim into my arms. "Put him to sleep."

I looked back towards the kitchen. "I'm still cleaning."

"He's tired and won't stop crying because he can't sleep without you." The hostility in his tone made my heart hurt for our son.

Instead of responding, I turned on my heels and walked back into the house. "Baba, can you sit while Ammi finishes tidying up?"

"Don't worry about it. We'll help mum," Sadaf said.

I stared at Idris' back as he stood laughing with his friends. "But…"

"There's enough people here to help. Go to bed."

ꝗꝗꝗꝗ

It was almost midnight when Idris bid his friends goodbye and came to bed. His nostrils flared. "Why is he still awake?"

I rubbed my eyes, feeling exhausted from the long day. "He woke up crying twenty minutes ago." Holding him closer to my chest, I stroked his cheek. "What's wrong, baba? Why don't you want to sleep?"

"You've spoiled him."

"He's a *baby*."

"A baby you didn't want," he threw in my face. "You only have him because of me." Idris was angry, which meant he was fishing for an argument.

I was too tired to give him what he wanted. "Okay. Thank you for giving me a son."

It wasn't the reaction he wanted, so he tried again. "Why did you give my son to Rizwan instead of me?"

"You refused to take him. What was I supposed to do?"

"I'm sick and tired of you disobeying my orders. Put him to sleep before I finish showering."

It didn't take a genius to know why Idris was so desperate to have Karim asleep. The sex he so badly needed me for had practically become non-existent. Between feeds, nappies and me being half-asleep, there was no room for his affection. It got better after the first few months, but with Karim's cot attached to the bed, we were often interrupted. *And it put Idris in a foul mood.* He accused me of using Karim as an excuse to not fulfil that part of our marriage.

Initially, Idris wanted another baby soon after, but he couldn't tolerate the thought of a marriage without intimacy. So I was on the pill until last month when he decided he wanted to try for a second. It wasn't a discussion. *It was his decision.*

I laid on my side and watched his chest rise and fall. I paused, reflecting on surviving a year. While it wasn't the dream I visioned, motherhood still filled me with happiness and love. A part of me still felt empty, but I accepted this was all I would be. My life wouldn't be more than I was offered.

My mind took me back to a year ago when Idris did the first selfless thing for me and named our son Karim. I just wished he looked at him with that same level of pride and joy. I suspected he carried the resentment I felt while being pregnant. I couldn't understand it. *How could he not be completely in love with perfection?* Karim was half of him. Yet, it was as if Idris was content with ticking off the box titled *have a son* on his life's to-do list. It meant nothing more to him. If anything, his son was a nuisance because he couldn't get laid.

As expected, his hands were on me as soon as he climbed into bed. His lips travelled from my neck to my shoulder. "Come here."

I shuffled closer to him. "I haven't showered yet and I've been cooking and cleaning all day."

He removed my top and palmed my breasts. "I don't care. Between your period and him, it's been two weeks. I'm having you tonight."

My clothes were gone faster than usual. My arms laid immobile by my side as he explored my body. I stared up at the ceiling and thought about how everyone spoiled Karim today. The table with his gifts was overflowing, and I wasn't sure where I was going to store all those toys and clothes.

Idris eased into me and let out a throaty groan. "Zoya," he snapped. "Look at me."

I lowered my gaze to his face. Exhaustion overwhelmed me. And if the last few nights were any indication, Karim would be crying soon.

"What are you thinking about?"

"Nothing."

His jaw clenched. "Don't lie to me."

Scared the sex was about to turn from feverish to rough, I softened my gaze. "I'm here."

"No, you're not." He slammed into me. "Even when I'm buried inside you, your head is up in the clouds!"

I winced and looked into the cot to make sure the raised voice didn't wake him. "What do you want me to do, Idris?"

"*Want* me. Do more than just fucking laying there."

Wrapping my arms around his neck, I thread my fingers through his hair and locked my legs around his waist. Now actually focusing, a few of my moans fueled his arousal. My eyes snapped open when Karim let out a cry.

Idris held me in place when I tried to move. "He's fine."

I unwrapped myself from around him. "He's crying."

"Let him cry." He gripped my hips as he thrust deep inside me. His groans were trumped by Karim's cry.

I shushed Karim, who was now sitting up. "I'm here. It's okay." But it wasn't enough to silence him. "He's going to wake everyone up. Idris, stop!" I pushed against his chest and climbed out from under him. My panic only eased once he was in my arms and soothed.

"I told you he was fine!"

"He wasn't fine! Babies don't cry for no reason." I walked around the room as I tried to get him back to sleep.

Idris eyed my naked body with nothing but anger. "I can't even have sex with my wife. Even when she's under me, she's a million miles away."

"*You* wanted a baby. This is the only sacrifice you have had to make. What else have you given up? *Nothing*. And if it is too big of a price to pay, maybe you shouldn't be forcing me to give you another."

He scoffed at me. "What difference would it make? You can't even give me proper relief after a year. If you can't do that, I might as well put you to use elsewhere."

Chapter Sixteen

Nadim's cry pushed the throbbing in my head into a pounding. Karim tugged at my trousers and I let out a frustrated groan. I dropped my eyeliner onto the dressing table and picked him up.

"What's wrong?" I tried to sound soothing, but I had been trying to get ready for Rani's engagement party for almost two hours. Between my two children and my mother-in-law constantly calling for me, I wasn't anywhere near done.

I accepted that Karim and Nadim were my responsibility, but Shazia could have asked Amal for help. However, despite her having moved in ten months ago, my mother-in-law seemed to have forgotten she had two daughter-in-laws that lived with her. Any hope I had of Amal's presence lessening my housework was quickly squashed. If anything, it seemed to have doubled since Bilal and his family moved in. Somehow, it became my responsibility to cater to whatever he wanted. I was making tea at his request. I was cleaning bathrooms they were using. I was washing their clothes. I was picking up after their kid. Despite being heavily pregnant with Nadim and having a toddler to look after, I still did everything.

"Give me a cup of tea." Idris inspected the clothes I had ironed for him before picking up Nadim. "Stop crying."

"He's four months old. He doesn't understand what you're saying."

Idris stood behind me and caught my eye in the mirror. I took the opportunity to study him. I hadn't noticed how broad his build had become. His beard was full and well-groomed. His eyes were as stern as they were on the day we met, but I felt an odd sense of normal in them. Idris had barely aged in our eight years together and the parts of him that had made him look more mature and handsome. Then there was me, two children later, who looked older than him despite being seven years younger.

He was trying to hold back one of his rare smiles. "What?"

I just realised how handsome you are.

I shook my head, also biting back a smile. "Nothing." I stood and took Nadim from him. "Would you like me to bring your tea upstairs?"

He held me against him. "I'd like you to take the kids downstairs with you and come back alone."

"We're going to be late."

And just like that, his good mood vanished. "I'll drink it downstairs."

Wanting to have an evening free of tension, I tried to make up for my rejection. "I didn't mean it like that."

"Just go."

❀❀❀❀

It seemed pregnancy had cost Halima her appetite. She mindlessly swirled her spoon around her full plate. While her makeup was flawless, she looked tired. But I knew how exhausting the first trimester was. My easy pregnancy with Karim gave me false belief my second would be the same. But with Nadim, I was sick throughout. If I wasn't vomiting, the sciatica made even the simplest of tasks a struggle.

It was shaping up to be a nice evening. Rani and Ravi made their grand entrance and were sitting at the head of the table. Yousef, Sumayyah's husband, and Nazir were talking about cars while Idris ate silently. He didn't want to be here, but as always, was worried about a past ghost turning up.

Sumayyah just celebrated her one year wedding anniversary, and from the glances she kept stealing at her husband, it was clear they were still in the honeymoon phase. Yousef treated her like a princess with holidays and date nights. When he looked at his wife, the love was abundantly clear in his eyes. He was as gentle as she was. He was as softly spoken as she was. They were perfect for one another and I was happy for my friend.

"Zoya, take him," Idris said, when Nadim starting fussing again.

Just as I took him, Sumayyah spoke. "Let me take him. You finish eating."

Already in a foul mood from my earlier rejection, Idris shot me a look of warning.

I shook my head. "It's fine."

But Sumayyah was already standing up and reaching for him. "I'm done. Here, just give him to me."

Idris gripped my thigh under the table in warning. Trying to hide my panic, I forced a chuckle. "When you're a mother, you master eating with a child clinging to you. It's no problem."

Her brow arched. "Zoya, I'd love some time to cuddle him."

Knowing Sumayyah would not take no for an answer, I ignored the sharp look Idris was directing at me. "Are you sure?"

Her answer was to sweep him out of my arms and cradle him close. It was a sweet view. My friends hardly got to enjoy Karim as a baby, and he was at the age where he didn't want anyone unless it was me or his dad.

Halima was smiling too. "You look like a natural with a baby."

Sumayyah stroked his cheek. "He's just so precious."

Our favourite pastime was making Sumayyah blush with embarrassment. When she returned home for the first time after getting married, we immediately asked her how it felt to lose her virginity. Her wide eyes and stuttering made us all burst into laughter.

I winked at her. "Soon you'll have your own."

She looked at us with alarm and shook her head. "No. Not anytime soon."

My heart dropped when Idris scoffed at her. "Why not? You're a woman. What are you waiting for?"

Looking at me in surprise, she asked, "What is that supposed to mean?"

Knowing he was in a bad mood and not wanting to ruin the evening, I tried to shut the conversation down. Especially when I saw Rani standing behind her, ready to pounce. "He meant nothing by it."

A forced smile was directed at us. "I think he did. We're adults. We can share our opinions."

"I agree. So what if she's a woman?" Rani's unimpressed stare was directly on Idris.

They were foolish to think they could win against him. Idris was never one to shy away from telling a woman what her place and role were. "You're here to carry children. You get married to carry the next generation. What could be more important than that?"

Unsurprisingly, his statement struck a nerve with Sumayyah. She put off finding love to pursue her dream of becoming a doctor. While having a family was part of her plans, she made sure she made a name for herself first. It was that determination why she was now a doctor. "Who declared that a woman cannot work *and* be a mother?"

Idris let out the first laugh I heard from him in months. "A woman has no reason to work. That's what us men are here for."

She met my pleading eyes. I subtly shook my head, wanting her to drop it. The irritation in her gaze melted into pity as she understood. It felt like she was begging me to stand up for myself, but I knew the consequences of defying Idris and I never wanted to experience that again.

However, Rani was a force to be reckoned with. She was too busy being repulsed by his mindset to see my silent begging. She stood tall and stared down at Idris with hostility. "I'm not sorry to say this, but you're wrong. The times have changed, Idris. You live in a first-world country. Women in Pakistan, India, and Bangladesh may be trained to stay home, but not here. We educate our women. We encourage our women. We *empower* our women. It's no longer a man's world."

Neither backed down from the staring match that had begun. Idris was looking at her in disgust while Rani met it with a challenging gaze.

If Yousef hadn't spoken, I was certain an argument would have broken out. "There's nothing wrong with having tradition. It's good to have a balance. If the couple can afford to have one parent at home, then what's the harm?"

Sumayyah's head snapped to her husband, and it was the first time she looked at him with something other than adoration. She mocked a laugh. "*One* parent? By that, you mean the woman, right?"

"Well, that makes sense," Nazir said, joining the conversation.

Rani scoffed. "Why?"

He looked at her in bewilderment. "She's the *mother*. The baby's food is literally in her chest."

"Baby formula exists," Sumayyah argued. "So, I assume Halima will stop working when your baby comes?"

When he agreed, Rani propped her hand on her waist. "Did you ask her if that's what she wanted?"

His soft chuckle couldn't hide the irritation in his voice. "Ask her what? She wanted a baby so she can stay home and look after it."

Halima was the only friend who wore the same panicked expression as me. It was only I that saw her cower back into her seat at his harsh words.

Sumayyah was too busy throwing a dig at her husband. "And what about the men who want a child? Should they stay home instead, Yousef?"

What was happening between them?

Whatever it was made Yousef lose his relaxed demeanour. He stared his wife down and spoke as a matter of fact. "Honestly? *No*. Women have been homemakers since the beginning of time. Women have a genetically built-in device called mother's instinct; it's there for a reason. I understand wanting to work, but it's not a requirement. The generations before us have been following these ... these..."

Rani didn't let him finish digging his own grave. "I think the word you're looking for is stereotypes, because it *is* a stereotype. It's a little box us women have been shoved and forcefully moulded into."

Dismissing her, Idris said, "The problem is you are too modern."

She gritted her teeth as anger flashed in her eyes. "And you like your women to be obedient."

My heart completely stopped.

That statement told Idris just how much I shared with my friends. He knew I had complained about him. He knew I had told them I was unhappy with him, our marriage and life.

The tension didn't waver even when Ravi joined the group. His smile morphed into a look of worry when he saw Rani fired up. "What's going on here?"

Nazir tried to lighten the mood. "Your bride-to-be is terrorising her guests."

Her head snapped in his direction. "Maybe you feel terrorised because you like *your* women to be silent. I haven't heard Halima say a word."

"Okay. Let's get some fresh air."

Rani pushed his arms off her. "*No.* Why is a woman vilified for standing up for herself?" She pointed at Idris. "He carelessly offended Sumayyah because it's okay for a man to say whatever he wants. The woman should just shut her mouth and take it. Her husband didn't defend her and instead wanted her to back down because his wife can't be anything short of perfect."

Nobody dared to respond, except Idris. "This conversation had nothing to do with you. I wasn't talking to you."

Perhaps what she did next was my fault for telling her what happened after I met with Adeel seven years ago. It was that moment that made me realise my mother-in-law was right; those who love us carry our anger for us. I was forced to let it go, but Rani had clearly let it form her judgement about Idris.

She bowed at him. "Apologies, master. I should have waited for permission to speak. Except it had something to do with me because you were talking about *women* and last I checked, I *am* a woman. If anything, this topic has nothing to do with *you* because men don't get a say in how we live."

Ravi tried to pull her away again. His warning was low, but loud enough for us to hear. "That's enough. They're your guests."

Nazir shrugged. "We're all entitled to our opinion. If that's how he wants to live, we can't judge him for it. If their arrangement makes them happy, then so be it."

She looked directly at me. "Are you happy, Zoya?"

All eyes were on me and the air felt too thick to breathe. She may as well have blatantly asked me to choose between her and Idris. But I couldn't do that, no matter how much she was willing me to stand up for myself. I cleared my throat and forced a light tone. "Guys, this is ridiculous. Let's all just enjoy ourselves."

Idris' stormy eyes were on me and I knew if we were alone, I'd be feeling the physical brunt of his rage. "Answer."

I was seventeen again. Scared and alone. No matter how badly I wanted to escape, I was forced to make a decision I didn't want to. I knew no matter what I said, I would be failing someone. But I had a duty to protect my two children and that included making sure they never witnessed their father's anger.

So, ignoring the sinking feeling in my chest, I blinked my tears away and whispered, "Yes. I'm happy."

❧ ❧ ❧ ❧

I was foolish to believe my false admission would cool his temper. I was glad to be sitting in the back between the car seats. I tried to tune out his lecture by counting their sleeping breaths. But once we were in our bedroom, there was no eluding him.

"I've let you talk to those girls, but that stops now."

I shook my head, but was too scared to fight for my friendships. It was almost as if I could feel his hands wrapped around my neck. I was alone, facing the storm of anger in his eyes.

His nostrils flared at the sight of my tears. "What have you been telling them?" He stepped closer. "Why does she know what happens in our home?"

"She doesn't. I swear I never—"

He squeezed my cheeks tight, stopping me from speaking. His voice was eerily calm. "Don't fucking lie to me."

"Please, don't," I begged. "I'm sorry. I'm sorry. I'm sorry."

"I'm getting tired of you."

I grabbed his wrist. "I'm sorry."

"Go back to your dad." He released me with a slight push. "Get out of my house."

Paralysed, I watched as he slowly undressed. A wave of panic crashed over me, stealing my breath and constricting my chest. The frantic rhythm of my racing heart pounded in my ears.

"Why are you still standing there? Get out, Zoya. Go. I release you."

"Idris—"

"Don't say my name. I don't want you. Get out of my house." He pulled the sheets back and climbed into bed.

This was all I wanted. For years, I was desperate for him to divorce me, yet I stared at him in disbelief. After everything I had given up for him, how could he discard of me like yesterday's newspaper?

It's because he knows you won't survive in the real world alone.

And that thought had my back stiffening. I didn't know where I would seek refuge, yet I plucked strength from some unknown place and stood taller. "Okay."

When I opened the wardrobe, his voice made me halt. "What are you doing? Those clothes don't belong to you. I bought those with my money. Take what you came with. Nothing else." He was trying to belittle me and was successful in doing so. "That includes my sons."

I stared at him in disbelief. "*What*?"

"*I* gave you those children. You never wanted them. Everything they have was bought with my money. They carry *my* bloodline."

"I'm their mum."

"Not anymore. My children remain with me. If you want to leave, you will do so without them."

There was the catch I knew was coming. Idris never planned to let me walk as a free woman. And after eight years, and two children, I finally understood why he was always so desperate for me to have his children. Before them, there was nothing truly tying me to him aside from fear. And if he pushed me enough, I would have lost it all to win freedom. But Karim and Nadim were lifelong chains to him that were formed with love. And a mother's love was unbreakable.

Knowing he had me trapped, his shoulders relaxed. "If you ever speak about our marriage to those girls again, I will kick you out and make sure my sons never utter your name. What kind of friends do you have? Look at their lives. Look at how little they respect their husbands. Choosing to work instead of being a wife and mother," he scoffed. "It's disgusting."

I was betraying my friends by not defending them. They weren't doing anything wrong. Idris's condescending treatment was unwarranted. But I was too scared to say anything. His actions that night reminded me I had too much to lose, which was ironic because nothing in my life was mine.

CHAPTER
SEVENTEEN

RANI'S WEDDING WAS EVERYTHING Bollywood movies built my expectations of an Indian wedding to be. A breathtaking array of flowers decorated the grand venue; their vibrant colors creating a magical atmosphere. A spacious dance floor separated the main stage and the tables. With the music booming, her family danced and sang with unbridled joy.

But nothing was as breathtaking as the bride herself. Rani designed an outfit that was the perfect blend of western and traditional. The white fabric was littered with thread work and small diamonds that were invisible to the naked eye but glimmered under the bright lights. Opting for a short top with a deep v-neck plunge, she looked like a sexy Indian Barbie doll.

"Let's go on the stage and say hello," Sumayyah suggested.

I handed Nadim to his dad. "We're just going to congratulate the couple."

Karim wanted to stay with his dad, who was engrossed in a conversation with Yousef. Jannah, Halima's eight-month-old, gave a toothless smile when her mum stood with her. She was an inquisitive baby and desperate to see more of her environment. We walked in unison to the stage and hugged our friend one at a time, before taking a seat on the stage and getting our picture snapped.

Rani flashed her hand, which was stained with the most intricate henna. "I'm a wife!"

I wanted to ask her how long she planned to wear her green choora, *bangles*, because I knew traditionally Hindu brides wore them for up to a year. I couldn't imagine getting any housework done in those.

"Welcome to marriage. It's a lot of hard work," Sumayyah laughed. When Ravi cleared his throat, she put her hands up in surrender. "But worth it."

"You look so beautiful. I absolutely *love* your outfit," Halima gushed.

"At least someone does," she remarked with an eye roll.

"Rani," her husband warned. "Not today."

"The fact that it's our wedding day hasn't stopped your mum from telling everyone how much she hates my clothes."

He awkwardly avoided our gaze. "She doesn't hate it. She only said it wasn't appropriate for the day."

She scoffed at him. "Whatever you say."

The rest of us shared a look, and an awkward silence fell upon us.

It was Sumayyah that broke it with a soft gasp. "Is that ... Zoya, don't look."

But when someone says that, it's instinct to turn that direction. And when I did, my eyes fell upon an adult Adeel. His hair was shaved to a buzz cut, and it felt like he had a growth spurt. He laughed with the friend he was walking in with, and his smile filled me with a familiar warmth. But oddly, it wasn't a warmth I missed or craved. It felt like I was peering into a memory I was fond of. He looked healthy. He looked happy. And then he was looking at me.

He stopped walking and stared at me like he couldn't believe his eyes. It was like I could hear his soft chuckle over the music as he waved at me.

"Why the hell would you invite him when you knew Idris was going to be here?"

Rani's scolding brought me back to reality. My head snapped towards Idris, who missed the whole moment, and I let out a breath of relief. "It's okay," I said.

Ravi grimaced. "I'm sorry. I never really thought about that. I just sent a message to the group and ... I'm sorry, Zoya."

I shook my head. "He's your friend, and this is your wedding. Don't worry about it."

It was like a magnet pulling my gaze back in his direction. He was already looking at me. He lifted his thumb as if asking *you good?* I smiled and gave him a small nod in response. That seemed to satisfy him because he started a conversation with his friends.

"Is he married?" Sumayyah whispered.

"Because the way he was just looking at you..." Rani added.

"He's engaged. It was arranged by his family," Ravi answered. "The wedding is next April."

"I'm happy for him," I said and meant it. "He deserves to be happy."

❀ ❀ ❀ ❀

The DJ paused the music when Rani grabbed the microphone and stood centre stage. She was breathless from the dance she and her cousins entertained us with. "For this next dance, I would like to invite someone special to the dance floor. She may be a little rusty because it's been eleven years since we've practiced this. We always dreamed of dancing to this at her wedding, but were robbed of our chance. However, I am determined to make one of her dreams come true." Her eyes were on mine.

I was already shaking my head. I refused to dance before a crowd. The Zoya she was talking about didn't exist anymore.

Having abandoned her microphone, she stalked towards me with open arms. "I'm not taking no for an answer!"

I tried to escape her hold. "I can't even remember the dance!" I argued as she dragged me with her.

"Then we'll make it up as we go along."

As we stood on the dance floor, the crowd cheered, with Halima and Sumayyah being the loudest. Halima's phone was ready to record my most mortifying moment. I awkwardly swayed as the opening vocals to *Sajan Ke Ghar Jana Hain* played. The guests clapped in sync with the beat and then I was expected to remember the moves.

I tried walking away, but Rani spun in front of me and forced me to see the song through. As we danced, I felt the room fade away. I was sixteen again in her living room; we were having the time of our lives hanging out after school. By the time the chorus rolled around, I wasn't even thinking about the next move. It was all muscle memory. I felt a confidence I hadn't experienced in a long time.

I didn't realise the song was ending until her brother Veer glided onto the dance floor and took the role of the male dancer in the song. It wasn't quite like the first time, but that was probably because I couldn't stop laughing. I followed his movements and before I was ready, the song was done and we were bowing before a standing ovation.

I hugged Rani tight, ignoring the flashes from the camera. Two more arms wrapped around us and I felt complete. When we broke apart, I held both of Rani's hands. Tears welled in my eyes. "Thank you."

"You're going to make me ruin my makeup." She blinked up and sighed. "I haven't seen you that happy in a long time. I've missed it."

"I see you've still got the moves," Ravi laughed as he and our school friends joined us. He pointed at the photographer. "Let's take a picture for old times' sake."

My gaze caught Adeel's. It wasn't a look of love or heartache. It was mutual respect. We both paved different paths in life, and that moment felt like looking through a peephole at the dream we once craved. But I truly couldn't see myself living that dream anymore.

I smiled. "I'd love to, but I need to get back to my children and husband."

🎀🎀🎀🎀

My fingers brushed over my lips as I stared at my reflection. I couldn't stop smiling, no matter how hard I tried.

Our bedroom door closed quietly. Idris stopped to watch me study myself. Then he padded over and stood behind me. His fingertips ran through the length of my hair before his nose took a dive and he inhaled deeply. He unpinned my dupatta and let it drop to the floor. With his hands on my waist, he kissed from below my ear to my shoulder blade.

"You looked beautiful tonight, Zoya," he whispered against my skin.

He'd never called me that before. While he was quick to criticise me, Idris never complimented me on anything. Unable to hold his intense stare, I bowed my head.

His fingers lifted my chin until I was forced to watch our reflections. "Look at me. Watch me undress *my* wife."

A shiver ran down my spine as he stripped me. I felt vulnerable being naked against his dressed form. Pregnancy had changed my body, but I didn't care. The skin around my belly was loose, jiggly and marked with stripes of my pregnancies. Idris never really explored my body and I don't think I could have stomached the repulsion in his eyes. So I closed mine as he rolled my nipples between his fingers.

"Look at me," he ordered. His eyes were dark with lust at the sight of watching ourselves. His hand travelled to between my legs, forcing them apart.

I felt embarrassed to watch him touch me *there*. My mouth opened and let out a silent gasp when he inserted two fingers inside me. I gripped his hand, trying to stop him. "Idris."

He pressed his crotch against my ass. "Do you feel what you do to me?" He was trying to work me into a frenzy, but I couldn't get comfortable in front of a mirror with our bedroom light on.

"Can you turn the lights off?"

He bit down on my shoulder lightly. "No. I want you to look at me."

My teeth clamped down on my lip. "It feels too awkward like this." I was used to sex in a bed, with the lights turned off. I was used to Idris being on top and doing what he needed to get himself off. But tonight,

Idris was looking at me with a heavy expression and it was making it hard to breathe, let alone relax.

"Lie on the bed."

I waited for him to undress and join me. My legs were spread, an open invitation. Idris eagerly embraced it. He hovered over me as he connected us physically. It was one of the rare occasions where I *wanted* to sleep with him. I wanted to experience the oblivion of an orgasm. Few had come from my side during our marriage. The ones I had were achieved because pregnancy heightened every sensation.

"Look at me."

My gaze moved from the ceiling to him. I didn't know where I was supposed to be looking. He was searching my face for something unknown. My eyes snapped shut when a shiver of pleasure travelled from my core to my toes.

Idris gripped my hips with force. "Zoya. Look at me."

The warning in his tone had my eyes wide and on him again. "Slower. That hurts."

"Touch me."

"Where?"

His jaw clenched, and the veins in his neck throbbed. "*Anywhere.*"

Even after almost a decade, I didn't know what to do. My hands gripped his biceps as he picked up his pace. I could feel that vaguely familiar feeling. My stomach tightened and I let out a small moan, afraid to wake everyone in the house. Desperately racing him to the finish line, I focused on chasing the euphoria.

"Look at me," he growled. His hand was on my neck. "Look at me!"

Taken back to that night, all my pleasure vanished. I tried to pull his hands off me as panic took away my ability to breathe. "Idris."

But I had lost him to his anger. "How many times do I have to tell you to look at me? *Look* at me!" His grip tightened as he repeatedly screamed the demand.

My nails dug into the back of his hand as I begged him to let go because he was hurting me. The happiness I felt only minutes ago was slipping through the guards and leaving me lonely. I tried to climb out from under him, but I couldn't move. My tears blurred his face. "Idris, please stop."

"Look at me the way you looked at him!" he screamed in my face.

And only then did I realise he'd seen my silent interaction with Adeel.

I choked on my gasp as he held me in place. "I can't breathe. You're hurting me!"

Jumping back, he climbed off me and yanked his trousers back on. "And you don't think I hurt when I see my wife looking at another man like that?"

Wrapping the blanket around my naked form, I begged him to see sense. "You're wrong."

"That wasn't him tonight?" he challenged. "Is that why you dressed up? Is that why you danced? To impress him? To seduce him?"

"Rani forced me to—"

"Is that why you haven't stopped smiling? Because you saw him?"

Knowing what would happen if the situation didn't calm down, I took my chances and stood before him. I placed my hands on his chest and sobbed through my begging. "I didn't know he was going to be there. Please, Idris. Can we just go to bed?"

He pushed my hands off him. "Put your clothes on. And stop that fucking crying."

I bit down on my cheek to silence myself. With trembling hands, I pulled my pyjamas on and stood before him, waiting for his next order.

Idris stood at his full height, so he was looking down at me with disgust. "Now get the fuck out of my house." He was being serious. This wasn't an empty threat.

"What ... no. You've misunderstood. Idris..."

"Get out."

"It's the middle of the night. Where am I supposed to go?"

He shrugged. "Your father. Your lover. I don't care. Say goodbye to your children and leave."

I shook my head. "I didn't do anything!"

"You *looked* at him. After all this time, after everything I have given you, you still haven't forgotten him. Even when I'm fucking buried inside you, you can't look at me the way you looked at him. Were you thinking about him when it was *me* touching you?"

"No! Please, Idris. Can we stop this? Can we just go to bed? I didn't do anything. I'm sorry for dancing with Rani. I'm sorry for looking at him. I won't do it again. Please..."

Nine years ago, I never would have belittled myself by begging him, especially when I did nothing wrong. But without Idris, I had nothing. Without Idris, I would be a childless mother.

He grabbed my hand and dragged me out of the room. I almost tripped down the stairs as he led us to the front door. No matter how much I pleaded, it fell on deaf ears.

"Bhaiya?" Bilal called from the top of the stairs.

"This has nothing to do with you! Go away!"

Another door opened, and his mum descended the stairs. "What's happened?"

"Tomorrow I'm going to the mosque to rid myself of this woman."

"What has she done now?"

I shook my head. "I didn't do anything."

Idris opened the door. "She belongs to the streets."

His mum stood at the bottom of the stairs, too scared to get any closer to him. "It's the middle of the night," she tried to reason.

He didn't care. He pushed me out of the house and slammed the door shut.

The cold air nipped at my skin. I stared out onto the empty street where the wind howling competed against my own. As a flock of birds flew away, I desperately wished they could take me with them. But I knew there was nothing out there for a woman in my state. I would be shunned by the community. I had no means to make it out there in the real world. I had no real qualifications. No income. *Nothing*.

But most importantly, my children were still in there.

I slammed my palms on the door. "Idris! Please. Open the door."

Their raised voices allowed me to hear what was still being said. His mum was begging him to open the door.

Idris' threat was clear. "If you open this door and let her in, you will be responsible for cleaning her blood off the floor."

"Yeh kaffe heh!" *That's enough*. His dad's voice boomed above their argument. There was a slight pause. "Darwazah kholen." *Open the door*.

"Naheen." *No*.

I'd never heard Abbas so angry. "I have given you much freedom, Idris. I have never spoken in your private matters. But if you don't open that door, I will break every relationship between us. Let her back inside the house."

The door swung open, and I tumbled into the foyer. Unable to stomach the shame I felt, my head stayed bowed to the ground.

Abbas commanded his second son to return to his room before he addressed us again. "What happened?"

When he spoke, it was with a coldness that even the weather couldn't achieve. "I have tolerated enough of her. She doesn't listen to a word I say. She doesn't cook. She doesn't clean. She can't even iron my clothes properly."

"Is that a reason to create such drama at this time of night?"

"She danced with another man today."

"Is this true, Zoya?"

I looked at my father-in-law and shook my head. How was I supposed to explain that Veer joining in wasn't something I could control? Would he understand it was a harmless act? More than that, how could I explain the true reason behind Idris' anger?

"If he wants a divorce, give me my children and I will leave."

"Nobody is getting divorced," he declared.

"I can't do this anymore," I sobbed. "No matter what I do, he is never happy. I have given him everything he wants. I have done everything you have asked me to do. When Amal went into labour, I dropped everything and left my children for hours to be with her. I'm pulled in a million directions and I have killed myself to be there for everyone. But he's never happy."

Abbas took pity on my grieving self. His hard eyes softened. "There is hardship in every marriage. These pass with time. Seek forgiveness and go to bed."

I wanted to ask why *I* was the one apologising when he had assaulted me. But all I wanted was for this night to end. I wanted to tuck this moment away with all the other memories I was forced to forgive and forget. My knees wobbled as I walked towards Idris. My heavy chest felt like it was going to explode. "I'm sorry. Forgive me."

Idris said nothing as he stared down at me. And then he clambered up the stairs into our bedroom. When I joined him, he was staring out of the window with a stiff back.

Part of me selfishly wished Nadim still slept in our room because I craved affection from my children. I wanted something pure and innocent in my arms. Instead, I picked up the clothes we had discarded earlier and neatly folded them. I couldn't hold back my whimper when I saw the mark his hand left on my neck.

Idris turned and locked eyes with my reflection. He too was looking at the bruise. "You need to ice that."

I pulled my lips together to stop myself from crying. "Before I go to bed, do you need anything?"

Gone was his raised voice, fuelled by rage. When he spoke, it was low and gentle. "The ice will reduce the bruising."

"I'll wear something to hide it." When he took a step closer, I turned on my heels and climbed into bed. I couldn't handle him touching me tonight.

But always determined to get what he wanted, he walked around the bed and kneeled on the floor. His thumb brushed the tops of my cheek. "You are *mine*, Zoya. I will not share any part of you. Is that understood?"

"Yes."

I couldn't sleep, even when Idris was letting out soft snores. My heart cried for a younger Zoya who dreamed of a life much larger than this; one where the world belonged to her. *If she could see me, what would she say?* She would have scowled in disgust and berated me the way Idris had done. She would have concocted a plan to get me out of this.

And as I laid next to my husband, I did exactly that. I told myself that next time he threw me out, I would be prepared. I would do anything to make sure I never had to walk back into this prison.

CHAPTER EIGHTEEN

I scanned through my essay one last time before hitting save and letting out a breath of relief. "Okay. I can actually help you now."

Rani was moving the taped boxes to one side with much struggle. "Where am I going to fit all this stuff in that one room?"

After a year of marriage, and no sight of her and Ravi moving into her flat, she decided to pack it up and take the rest of her belongings to her in-laws. She asked all three of us for help, but Sumayyah was working and Halima was stuck with a poorly Jannah. I was surprised when Idris agreed to let me go and I was making the most of my time away from him by getting this assignment done.

I eyed all the items still strewn around the room. "It won't fit. You need to get rid of some stuff."

She pouted and hugged her knee-high boots. "But these are so pretty."

Shaking my head with a laugh, I stood. "Can you check over my work before I submit?"

"You could just send it to Sumayyah to check over. You'll be guaranteed top marks that way."

"She's too busy and you know I don't want anyone else to know about me doing this course."

"I'll never understand why, but fine. How many more modules do you have left?"

"Four. It was only meant to take me nine months, but I'm on month thirteen and have so much left to do. It's hard finding the time between everything else I need to do. And then there's the fact I can't study at all when he's off from work."

"That's the reason you went for this user-led online course. The nine months were only a guide. Don't sweat it. You don't even need this qualification to start a business. Just open a social media page and the customers will come to you."

Remembering what my sister said to me all those years ago, I repeat her words. "Uneducated people don't get to own businesses. And anyway, I don't even have a business idea yet. I need something that Idris won't start asking questions about."

"Then you'd need to charge people a subscription to watch you cook, clean, be a mother and have sex with him."

I bit down on my lip to stifle my laugh. "Touché."

She sighed. "Why don't you just tell him? He can't possibly get mad at you for earning money while sitting at home."

"Really?" I asked sarcastically. As I made a fresh box, a thought occurred to me. "If most of your clothes are still here, what have you been wearing?"

"According to my in-laws, my clothes aren't appropriate for a daughter-in-law. They practically want me dressed as a nun." She rolled her eyes. "What's wrong with showing a little skin?"

I shrugged, not knowing how to comfort her. "Idris throws a hissy fit if my hair isn't covered properly at home. If Ravi doesn't care, then wear whatever you want."

"If his mum cares, so does he. Before we got married, he loved me wearing sexy outfits. Now it's all about saving face with his precious family." She ended the conversation when she gasped. "I can't believe I forgot about this."

I helped her push the large cardboard box to the centre of the room. "Why is it so heavy?"

Her green eyes gleamed with excitement. "It's your birthday present from ten months ago! While I was in India for my wedding shopping, I came across all these beautiful fabrics and it was dirt *cheap*. I bought a couple back for you since you're totally into all that. Between the wedding and everything, I forgot to give it to you."

My heart warmed at her thoughtful gift and I hugged my friend before playfully slapping her back. "I think that is more than a *couple*."

Rani was excited now, and instead of packing, she was cutting through the layers of tape to show me the contents. She was right; they were beautiful. They were also of much better quality than anything I could find in London. My mind was going into overdrive as I started imagining the different style and forms the fabrics could take. My ideas were coming out as word vomit. I paired the different patterns and colours, asking Rani what she thought, while not giving her the chance to share her opinions.

She sat on the floor, cross-legged, and smiled at me. "I've missed seeing you like this. There's this fire of youthfulness in your eyes that hasn't been lit in a decade."

My cheeks warmed. "I never understood how versatile textiles was. Each fabric is made for a different purpose. And it sounds weird, but I find an odd sense of freedom in it. I can do whatever I want with my designs. I can match anything and everything together." I shrugged. "It's dumb, I know."

"I don't think it's dumb. I think you're pretty phenomenal at it. I would literally buy everything you've made."

Rani and I had been friends for seventeen years; and during that time we had gotten up to enough mischief. Of my friends, she was always the one who helped me plan and execute my forbidden ideas. It's why I recognised the wild look in her eyes as an idea came to her.

She jumped up. "Oh, my god! That's it!"

I arched my brow. "What's it?"

"Your business idea! Why don't you sell your dresses?" Her words were too fast for me as she paced her living room. "You could literally do it from home. You open a social media page, advertise them, and customers come to you. It won't interfere with your wife duties and Idris would never know."

Standing up, I ignored the stabbing I felt at bursting the bubble that encased me for just a moment. "That won't work. I can't even leave my house for bread. Where would I buy the fabrics?"

She spread her arms towards the materials littered across the floor. "Buy them from India."

"And how would I get to India?" I asked dryly.

"You don't. *I* get them from India. My parents literally go twice a year. I have *so* much family that travel out there. We ask them to buy fabrics in bulk and ship them to us."

"Yeah, and when a huge box turns up to Idris' house every few months, what am I supposed to say to him? *Oh, just ignore that. It's for my secret business,*" I said sarcastically.

Rani was stumped for a moment. "Ship it *here*. It can be your little warehouse."

"You're meant to be putting it up for rent."

"When you make enough money, you can pay rent. *Or* we become business partners and this is part of my investment." She clicked her fingers. "We become business partners! I supply the materials and you can make the dresses. Obviously, that isn't fair to you, so I can run the social media accounts and bring in customers."

"I love the idea, but it won't work. I'd need to meet customers to take their measurements. I'd need to be available for the fittings."

"*I* can learn all that stuff. If it needs alterations, I'll take the revised measurements and give it to you."

"And how am I supposed to get the outfits to you?"

"The boys are in nursery. I can meet you there at drop off and pick up time." She grabbed my hands. "We can do this, Zoya!"

As much as I wanted to feed into the plan, I wasn't a delusional teenager anymore. It wasn't only the practicality of it all, but I feared what would happen if Idris found out I was lying to him. What if this all fell through? Where would that leave me? Idris already proved how easily he could throw me out and take my children away from me. And nothing was worth the risk.

Shaking my head, I said, "I can't. I won't be able to hide making the dresses. When he asks why I'm suddenly making all these outfits, what excuse do I give? When he sees outfits that clearly aren't my size, how do I explain that? And when he realises I haven't ever worn them and notices they aren't hanging in my wardrobe, what do I say?"

"I don't know!" She took a deep breath and rubbed her face. "But you have to try. You are too good to be stuck standing over a stove with a child in one hand and spoon in the other. Where is the girl who would have *made* a way for this to happen? Where is the girl who would have spun whatever lie she needed to see this through? Where is the girl who dreamed of having the world in her hands?"

"She grew up!" I snapped. "I grew up. I got married. I became a mother."

"No! You stopped believing! You let him steal your dream!" Guilt cast a shadow on her face. She walked until we were face-to-face before wiping my stray tear. "You deserve so much more, Zoya. You can't let him stifle you like this. I remember the day we met and how enthralled I was by your determination to be something *more*. You had dreams beyond our wildest imagination. You were so tenacious."

I couldn't stomach the pain in her expression. "I don't even know what that means," I tried to joke.

She let out a soft laugh. "It means you are someone who is unwilling to accept defeat. It means you are persistent in meeting your dreams. You cannot give him so much control over you. You are magnificent, and he doesn't deserve to steal that for himself. The world deserves a piece of you. He doesn't deserve you. He's just an insecure—"

I stepped away from her. "He's my husband."

Rani never liked Idris, especially after her engagement party. But how could I, as his wife, let someone degrade him like that?

"He's controlling."

"That's not fair. You don't know him."

"Do you?" she fired back. "What's his favourite colour? What is his earliest childhood memory? Do you even know how much money he makes? Where did he meet his best friends? What's his comfort movie?"

She was right. I couldn't answer any of those questions because Idris and I didn't talk. With seven years between us, there was no common ground. In the beginning, I didn't want to talk to him; I wanted to pretend he never existed. Somehow, that had become the norm for us. We were in a silent marriage and I needed that; because every day was chaos in that house. There was always somebody who needed something from me. And truthfully, a silent Idris was better than an angry one.

"He's the father of my children. Maybe he doesn't take me out to dinner, or on holidays, or buy me lavish gifts like Ravi does for you. But he has taken care of me and our sons."

"The Zoya I met would have rather died than let a man *take care of her*. She housed a strength he has spent over ten years stealing. If the Zoya I met was standing here, she would remind you that you've already lost if you haven't tried. And then she would have shown you how to win."

🎀🎀🎀🎀

We were welcoming 2021 with Idris' extended family at his grand-mother's house. The weight because of my conversation with Rani last week only faded with the chatter of Idris' family.

"Can you believe the first year of this decade has passed?" Rizwan asked to the room. "I've been married for *five* years. Idris bhaiya has been married for a whole decade and he's got two sons. How crazy is that?"

We spent our ten-year wedding anniversary apart, with Idris being in Pakistan. It wasn't long after Rani's wedding when he left, and I wondered whether he went to search for another wife. He came back empty-handed. So that was that. Neither of us wished each other a happy anniversary. It would have been hard since neither of us were genuinely happy. Life with Idris had finally found normalcy. We had become somewhat of a harmonious system. But the harmony only remained if I catered to his every need.

Wanting the attention off me, I pointed at Amal. "They've been married for eleven years and are welcoming their third baby in two months."

Our home was too full. Now that Hamza and his wife had migrated here, there was thirteen, soon to be fourteen, people living in the five-bed house. As Idris refused to have his children disrupting his sex life, our boys shared a room. Amal and Bilal were co-sleeping with their two children. She mentioned she wasn't sure where they were going to fit the baby's crib once he arrived. Hamza's wife, Anisa, gave birth to their daughter three months ago and somehow fit a cot in the smallest room in the house. All those people meant cooking larger volumes of food more frequently and constantly cleaning up after everyone. No peace or solitude existed.

I asked Idris if his brothers ever planned to move out. He said there was no need as there was room in the family home. I never brought it up again.

"Impart your wisdom and advice on marriage," Farrah said.

My elbow nudged Amal to take the reins. She smiled. "Understand one another. Be there for one another. Marriage is a partnership. You are a unit that has to work with one another."

The boys cooed at a red-faced Bilal who swatted them away. Then they were looking at me expectantly.

I cleared my throat. "I think that sums it up."

"You don't believe you need to love your spouse?" Idris' question to me silenced the noise.

In ten years, neither of us said we loved one another. Saying it would have been a lie. A younger Zoya yearned for an all-consuming love story the movies would have envied. I never received that because Idris and I didn't love each other. We tolerated one another.

Farrah grabbed my hand with a giggle. "Who knew he was such a romantic? You're so lucky."

My heart squeezed tight. "In this culture where there are so many expectations placed on us women, there is no room for romance or love. We are bound by our duty to serve our husbands. How can we be expected to love another when we are taught, we as women, are not good enough to love ourselves? We are not good enough. We are not worthy enough; not even of our father's love. Why should he waste his time loving something that is only his temporarily? How could a mother love something that is only a burden? How does a husband love something that is so easily replaceable? We are viewed as something to own, not to love. We are puppets bound by the strings tied around our wrists. They are careless with us. They break us as a child breaks his toy. Why? Because we hold a numerical value to them. We are not people. We are not human. We are women and to this culture, that makes us worthless."

The room's gaze was split between my solemn expression and Idris' stunned one. Farrah's eyes never wavered from the tears brimming in mine. She held onto me tighter.

I forced a smile and tucked her hair behind her ear. "It is *you* that is lucky. You have parents that wish to see your dream come to fruition.

I once had a dream too. Over the last ten years, life has taught me it is not a woman's place to dream. And I accepted that. I didn't fight. I didn't stand up for my dream. I simply bowed because I was taught a woman is to be obedient. We are taught that duty and toleration is love." I shook my head. "But it's not. It's a system created by men to make sure we never have the courage to say no."

"I forgot how skinny I was when I made this!" I laughed, handing the bag to Farrah. "I've taken the sides out a bit, so it should be a perfect fit now. You can keep it."

"Are you sure? You loved it."

I waved her off. "There is no way, after two children, I can squeeze into that."

She rummaged through her bag and took her purse out. Grabbing my hand, she forced something into my palm. "It's not much, but it's the only cash I've got on me."

I frantically shook my head. "Don't be stupid. You don't need to pay me for it. It's handmade *and* secondhand."

She shoved my hand away. "You spent your money to buy the materials and put a lot of effort into it. If I was to buy this from the shops, it would cost me double, if not triple."

"It was Idris' money."

She winked at me. "Keep it for yourself. I won't tell him if you don't." Her gaze softened, and I knew my vulnerability from earlier was on her mind. Her shoulders braced back. "We need to be the change. Women are worth more than this culture can ever give us.

We cannot sit back and let them treat us like this. We are not their puppets. We are *women*. Do you know how powerful that makes us? How *strong* that makes us? Men walk this Earth thinking they have won. That is only because women have been too afraid to start a war. If we found that strength and courage, victory would easily be ours."

With those powerful words, she hugged me goodbye and left me to absorb her determination. My legs didn't move, even when Idris called for me. I stared at the small bundle of cash in my hand. It was sixty-five pounds. And it was *mine*.

There was a fluttering in my chest. It was the first time I ever held money that belonged to me. And it was liberating. I clenched my fist close to my chest and broke out into a laugh.

And somewhere in the distance, I heard the first chain on my handcuffs break free.

Chapter Nineteen

I pressed the phone against my ear as I left the room, shutting the door behind me. "Is everything okay?"

"How much longer are you going to be?"

I was cutting it close to my imposed curfew, but my customers were running late and I had to be here to hem their skirts. "We're going to make our way home soon."

"I told you to be back by five."

Knowing it was a lie, I said, "We should be back by then. I need to go. Farrah's calling me."

"You've been out since eleven. You're still in the risky stage of the pregnancy. What if something happens to the baby?"

Compared to my normal routine, shopping with Farrah was a breeze. Her wedding was six months away, which left me with little time to make everyone's outfits. Farrah wanted all the women to match, but with a family of that size, it was impossible to agree on a design. It was the bride herself who suggested buying material and making outfits would be easier. *Well, easier for everyone except me.* Farrah was the only other person aside from Rani who knew about my small business, and she believed it would be good practice for me. Neither of us could have known I would be pregnant during this time.

Only a few days after New Year's with his family, I was searching for my pill, only to discover Idris had thrown it away. I didn't ask him about it, but he knew it was another thing he forced on me. His wish came true because only two months later, I produced a positive pregnancy test.

Nobody knew I was pregnant because my mother-in-law told me to wait until I was past the twelve-week mark. I wasn't sure if I could hide it from Farrah for another four weeks because the smell of everything was making me gag.

"Nothing is going to happen to the baby. I'll see you later." I hung up and rejoined them.

The girls were twirling in their dresses. "It's perfect!" one of them gleamed. "It's exactly what we wanted."

I quickly made the minor adjustments they needed while Rani collected the money. It was already twenty past five when they left the flat.

"You are smashing this!" Rani shrieked. "We've already made over two thousand pounds this month."

Normally I would have celebrated the milestone, but panic was filling me by every minute I was past my curfew. "Idris has already called me. I need to go."

"Okay. When is the pink outfit going to be ready?"

My bag was slung over my shoulder, and I was practically out of the front door. "I'll text you!" I turned my pleading eyes to Farrah, who understood and sped the way home.

My fingers were turning purple from the weight of the bags. I rang the doorbell again, wishing someone would hurry and open the damn door. When Hamza eventually did, I rushed past him and dumped the bags on the living room floor before going back to the car for a second round.

"Bilal, get the rest!" my mother-in-law screeched. She tried taking the ones in my hand. "You shouldn't carry such heavy bags in your condition," she hissed, so Farrah couldn't hear.

Despite the outside world being unaware of my pregnancy, everyone in the house knew as nothing remained a secret in this place. Everywhere you turned, someone was always there. My morning sickness basically announced the news for me. It didn't make anyone help me with the chores, though. Unlike Amal and Anisa, I didn't get a free pass because I was pregnant.

"It's okay. It's not that heavy." I walked straight into a body.

Idris stared down at me. "Put those down right now."

It was an automatic response. The bags dropped to my feet, and I swallowed hard.

He was still in a foul mood. "Go upstairs," he ordered.

I hid my nerves and kissed my sons hello. I smiled at Farrah, telling her I would be back in a few minutes. I climbed the stairs and braced myself for the anger about to be hurled at me.

"What time do you call this?" he asked as he entered. He shut the door behind him. "I said five o'clock. What time is it?"

"Six-fifteen. I messaged you to say we were stuck in traffic." There was no excuse good enough for my tardiness. So, I gave him what he wanted. "I'm sorry I'm late."

"And then you come parading in carrying those bags like you're not carrying *my* baby."

"It wasn't that heavy."

"I don't care!"

"The baby won't die if I carry a few bags."

"As if you would care, even if it did."

I stepped back from his harsh words. It took me a few seconds to realise he did actually say that, and it wasn't something I imagined. "How could you say that?"

"That's what you want, no? You've always made it clear you've never wanted my children. The thought of carrying a piece of me horrifies you. The notion of having to love half of me makes you sick."

It was no secret that my pregnancies were forced on me. And while my life was far from what I wanted, I loved my children. Even when I wasn't emotionally attached to Karim while he was in my womb, I did everything to make sure he arrived safely. I sacrificed everything for my children. It was the only reason I was still trapped in this marriage.

He scoffed at me. "You can't even deny it."

"No. I just won't dignify you with a response." I stripped my jeans and top and dumped them in my laundry hamper.

"I'm not done talking to you."

"You don't want to talk. You want to argue because you're pissed about something else. But I won't be your punching bag today." Knowing I'd eventually be alone to face his anger, I changed into a dress and took my escape.

The rest of the evening passed with a never-ending discussion about design ideas. With the fabric now in front of me, my creative juices were flowing, and I was eager to begin this project. With the little time between now and the wedding, it was going to be a struggle to make this many outfits. Plus the upcoming pregnancy fatigue wouldn't help. But I was determined to get every outfit perfect. A group chat was created, and it seemed everyone had a unique style they wanted to wear.

After bidding everyone goodbye, Farrah told me to wait at the front door as she ran to her car. When she returned, she handed me a wrapped gift. "This is a little present from me to say thank you for doing this. I know you're already busy, so I really appreciate it."

Taking it from her, I unwrapped it to reveal a large sketchbook and pencils. "Thank you. You didn't have to get me anything."

"I thought it would be helpful to jot down everyone's measurements next to a sketch of their outfit. You know, just to keep on top of it."

I flicked through the empty pages, unable to stop smiling. "This was so thoughtful."

"When you eventually think of a company name, we'll emboss it onto the front."

My mouth hung open in mock surprise. "You don't think *Bespoke Pakistani Designs* is a good company name?"

She chuckled. "I don't know how you got Rani to agree to that. Your name should be on the labels of your work."

I hugged her tight. "This is enough for me," I said honestly.

❦❦❦❦

"Where are you going?" Idris asked, in his sleepy state.

"Toilet. I don't think the baby liked the food Farrah and I ate." My stomach cramped again and I practically ran. A bead of sweat ran down my temple from the strain of holding it in. I just about made it to the seat when I released.

172

But nothing came.

I tried again, but faced the same outcome. The cramping was only getting worse. Feeling confused, I stared into the toilet bowl and saw nothing. *What the hell?*

Putting it down to indigestion, I washed my hands. I was about to turn the light off when I noticed the droplets of water on the toilet seat. Because I knew Idris would tell me off for the mess, I quickly grabbed some wipes to clean it. But my eyebrows furrowed.

Water isn't red.

Another surge of panic came over me. Yanking my trousers down, I checked my underwear. There was nothing there. My heart was racing as my fingers slipped between my legs, and it took everything to not scream the house down at the sight of blood covering them. Quickly washing my hands, I raced back to my bed and shook Idris.

"We need to go to the hospital." I grabbed his shoulders, almost on the verge of tears. "Idris! I'm bleeding! Take me to the hospital."

He was wide awake. "Where?"

"Down there. Come on. We need to go."

It was a flurry of chaos. I woke his mum up to let her know and to keep an eye on the boys. She gave me a list of prayers to read, but I only had one on my tongue.

Please God. Save my baby.

The car ride was silent except for my heavy breathing. I was re-searching online, and some mothers said they experienced bleeding and had a healthy pregnancy. I held hope that was the case for me. But every sharp pain in my lower stomach ebbed at that. I wanted to beg Idris to drive faster, even if it broke the speed limit. But his hard expression stopped me. His knuckles were white from his tight grip on the steering wheel.

It was one of the few times I craved his affection. I wanted him to tell me not to worry; our baby was safe and even if he wasn't, we'd make it through this together. But his silence only reinforced how alone I was in this marriage.

We were rushed through triage and before I knew it; I was wincing from the coldness of the gel. My eyes never wavered from the screen. Idris stood stiffly next to me, staring in the same direction. I waited with bated breath to see my baby for the first time.

And then he appeared. A small blob that already housed a third of my heart. A small cry escaped me; something crucial was absent.

"Why can't I hear his heart?" I asked the midwife. "Where is my baby's heartbeat?"

She ignored me and continued to move the transducer around my belly. The coldness from the gel didn't even register anymore. "I'm just going to get a doctor."

"No! Come back and find his heartbeat! Why isn't my baby breathing?" My head fell against the bed. "Why isn't he breathing?"

Idris said nothing. He didn't move as I stared up at the ceiling and sobbed.

She's just rubbish at her job, I reasoned. *A doctor will locate his heartbeat. The doctor is going to tell me my baby is fine. He is alive, breathing, and safe inside me.*

When the doctor entered, she smiled at me and moved the wand around for minutes. Only my cries broke the tension in the room. No matter how hard she tried, she couldn't locate his heartbeat.

"I'm sorry, Mrs Iqbal."

I heard nothing else over the shattering of my heart. My mouth opened as I let out a scream that shook the walls of the hospital. Words were coming out of me, but even I couldn't understand them.

When she put the transducer down, anger filled me. "What are you doing? Keep trying! He can't be gone. He's in there. You can't just stop trying to save him."

"I'm really sorry, Mrs Iqbal. This early into the pregnancy, there's nothing we can do."

I held my stomach and silently begged God to breathe life back into my baby.

I'm sorry. I'm sorry. I'm sorry.

Idris never spoke until we were moved to a private room to process the news and wait for the next steps. The part of me that hoped he would comfort me cowered from his hostile tone. "Stop that crying."

I couldn't control it. I covered my mouth, hoping it would silence me. But a mother's grief was unstoppable. It filled every pore of my body until it was the only thing I was made of.

"Didn't I tell you to be more careful? I told you not to go out. I told you carrying heavy bags isn't good for a pregnant woman."

I shook my head. "I didn't do anything. I didn't kill my baby."

"Stop crying, Zoya!" he snapped. "You're always fucking crying! This is what you wanted. God answered your prayers, so what right do you have to cry?"

"I never wanted my baby to die!"

"Yes, you did! You never wanted this baby! You didn't have it in you to love another piece of me."

I shook my head, refusing to believe him. "That's not true. I would have loved him."

Idris stared at me. "In order to do that, you would have to love me first. But you have made it your mission to hate me. Everyone is worthy of your love. Except me, who is half of the unborn child you are crying for."

Words failed me. I had lived this dynamic enough times to know there was nothing I could have said to ease his rage or my pain. It felt like I had been stuck in the same moment my whole life, and I was tired of always being the one in pain. I wished I could have felt angry at him for leaving me to die on a sinking ship.

But all I wanted was to rewind a few hours to when I was still a mother of three.

CHAPTER TWENTY

IF I DIDN'T PULL all my focus on kneading the dough, I would have collapsed from the pain. Every few minutes a sharp cramp would hit me and having me clenching my thighs as if that could stop nature from doing her job. It had been a week since my miscarriage; and it was *my* miscarriage because Idris pretended it had never happened. In fact, he acted as though I didn't get pregnant. We returned home, and it was business as usual. I made him breakfast and got his clothes ready for work. All the while, it felt like my world was crumbling.

"Ammi, Nadim took my car again," Karim whined.

I sniffled back the tears I didn't realise were falling. "Let him play with it, baba. You're the big brother." *And you would have been the best big brother to another sibling if you weren't robbed of the chance.*

"It's not fair!" He stomped away.

"Idris and Bilal were the same when they were that age," my mother-in-law said while rolling out the roti. "Always fighting over toys."

The most I could offer was a timid smile. For the past seven days, I wondered *why* this happened to me. *Was Idris right?* Did this happen because I didn't truly want another baby? Was it a result of overexerting myself? I read enough articles to know that it was common in the first trimester and was usually because of a chromosomal defect. It still didn't stop me from blaming myself.

"Take some paracetamol before the guests come. It will help with the pain."

I wiped my tears. "Okay."

"There's no need to cry. These things happen. At least it happened before it was a proper baby." She was too busy making sure her roti was circular to notice I had frozen. "It didn't even have a soul yet. If it did, we would have had to have a proper janazah." *Funeral*. "You won't even feel it coming out. It will be like a normal period."

I wanted to tell her to stop calling the baby *it*. I didn't care that he was the size of an olive. I didn't care that he had no soul. He was my baby, and he didn't deserve my body to fail him. He should have been safest inside me; yet I couldn't save him.

"Once the bleeding stops, you can try again."

I didn't want to try again. The thought of ever going through this again terrified me. I no longer trusted my body to protect my unborn child.

"It's a good thing we didn't tell anyone. Can you imagine what people would say? Even though you were blessed with two healthy sons, they might think you've aged and now there is something wrong with you. It's good to keep these things within the family." That was her way of telling me to keep my mouth shut about it.

Thankfully, I didn't have to respond because Idris was walking towards me. His jaw clenched when he realised I had, once again, been crying. "Hashim and his wife are coming tomorrow. Do you need any groceries to cook dinner for them?"

"Get some chicken and flour," she answered for me.

I lowered my gaze and went back to prepping the dough.

His stare bore into the side of my face. "Anything else?"

"Ghee," she added. "And cloves."

"I haven't had *Kheer* in a long time."

Kheer was a Pakistani take on rice pudding that required standing over the stove for hours. He was the only one who would request that of me while I was in such pain.

"Then get two bottles of milk as well."

His eyes darted to his mother when she responded on my behalf again. He was clearly getting agitated that I wasn't answering, but it wasn't intentional. After a week of skimming around each other, I thought it's what he wanted.

Giving me no opportunity to ignore him, he said, "Zoya, do you need anything?"

I need you to stop blaming me for our baby dying.

❀❀❀❀

"Kya yahan koei party hai?" *Is there a party in here?*

Farrah batted her dad away with a laugh. "Bhabhi is taking everyone's measurements."

I couldn't blame her dad for thinking otherwise. The room was packed with all the women of the family. One-by-one I was working my way through the crowd, taking their measurements and making a rough sketch of their desired outfit. Thankfully, most of them were simple enough.

"Your wife is quite the businesswoman," he joked to Idris.

"With that title, I'll have to charge you," I said, making him laugh. "Emaan, come on. Your turn."

She came close and whispered, "Can you leave some extra material inside mine in case I need to take it out?"

I furrowed my eyebrows, eyeing her thin frame. "Why would you..." It was selfish that my heart dropped in envy. "You're expecting?"

A shy smile spread across her face. "Just had my first ultrasound."

Blinking back my tears, I hugged her. "Congratulations," I whispered. "I wish you a healthy pregnancy."

A squeak came from Farrah. "Are we telling people?"

Emaan gave everyone a sheepish smile. "Let's just say I'm bringing a plus one to the wedding."

Happiness erupted within the room. Iram and Sadaf, who knew about my loss, caught my stare and silently asked if I was okay. *But how could I be?* If everything had gone as planned, I would have announced the new addition to my family as well. Instead, I had to swallow the lump in my throat and pretend that I was fine. I had to act as if someone wasn't clutching my heart so tight I felt like I couldn't breathe. I could feel Idris' stare from across the room and I knew any sight of me crying would have him flying off the handle.

So, I joined in with the celebration. "I think it would be best if I saved your outfit till last. I'll make everyone else's and then take your measurements. That way we won't have to alter as much. Pregnancy makes you swell in places you don't think possible."

She nodded. "Okay. Whatever makes it easier for you."

"It's been three years for you, Zoya. When are you going to give Idris another one?" an aunt asked.

All eyes were on me and I felt like a deer in headlights. My heart pounded in my chest as I struggled to come up with an answer that wasn't *my baby just died.*

"When Allah wills it, it will happen," my mother-in-law answered.

"Her two are a handful," Iram said with a huff. "She can't catch a break. How is she supposed to add another baby to that?"

I was grateful they answered for me because I was immobile. Every crevice of my body ached with grief. I needed to get out of there, but didn't want to create a scene.

It was like Sadaf could read my mind. "Zoya, remember that outfit we bought last summer? I want something like that for Farrah's wedding. If you show me yours, I'll tell you which parts I want to change."

I nodded and excused myself from the room. Practically running up the stairs, I let out the first sob as soon as I entered my bedroom.

Sadaf wrapped her arms around me and rubbed my back. "I'm so sorry. I can't imagine what you're feeling."

"It's not fair. I know I have two children, and some people can't even have one. I know he was barely formed, so it's stupid crying over something that wasn't real; but my heart refuses to understand that. It's in so much pain and I don't know how to make it stop."

"You have a right to grieve. It doesn't matter how early in the pregnancy you were; for a mother it's always different. Our lives change and our heart expands the moment we see a positive pregnancy test. It's okay to mourn."

"Who am I supposed to mourn with? I'm not even allowed to talk about him. Nobody understands my heartbreak; and the one person who should, is so angry at me for killing his baby."

"Sadaf, get out."

I wasn't sure when he walked in or how much he heard. I wiped my tears on my sleeves and stared down at my fingers.

She held onto me tighter. "She's upset and needs someone to talk to."

"She's *my* wife. I'll deal with her as I see fit." He opened the door. "Get out."

With an apologetic smile, she kissed my temple and took her leave.

Not wanting to argue, especially with guests downstairs, I forced my tears to stop. I erased the evidence from my cheeks and cleared my throat. "I'm sorry. I won't cry again." I swallowed hard when he locked the door and blocked the exit. I backed away. "Please, Idris. I said I won't cry anymore. I was just caught in the moment."

He walked towards me. "Look at me."

Our eyes met, and I was surprised by the anguish reflected in him. I flinched when he lifted his hand.

"I'm not going to hurt you," he said.

He cupped my face and forced me to hold his gaze. My chest rose and fell so deeply it was the only sound in the room. His thumb brushed the top of my cheek with a tenderness I never received from him. He wiped away the single tear that escaped. My lip quivered as the echoes of laughter from downstairs reached our ears.

"Let it out." His gentle whisper pushed me over the edge and into his arms.

I gripped his t-shirt as the dam to the wave broke free and my heartbreak poured out of me. My cries muffled against his chest. Every knot in my body came loose, and I fell to the floor, unable to carry the pain anymore.

Idris didn't let go and wrapped his arms around my curled body. He held me tight in his embrace, as if he knew by letting me go I would shatter into a million pieces.

"*Why*?" I asked to no one. "What sin have I committed to be punished so severely?"

And finally, Idris took away the burden of blame from me. "You did nothing. This wasn't you."

"I want my baby back. My body feels empty without him."

"We can have another baby," he promised. "If that's what you want, I'll give you that. I'll give you anything you ask for."

I shook my head. My fingers found his hands before I squeezed them tight. "I *can't*, Idris. I can't put myself through this again. I can't tolerate this heartache again. Please don't make me do this."

He held my face. "We can wait until you're feeling better."

"What if it happens again?" I tilted my head back and closed my eyes. "I loved him. I know you don't believe that, but I did. I never wanted him to die. He was going to be kind and handsome. He was going to steal my chance to sleep and drive me crazy with the constant crying. He was going to make my nipples sore from breastfeeding and wee on me. But I would have loved him despite all that."

"I know you would have loved him."

"Another baby won't make me forget. It won't erase this pain nor fill this void."

"Let's see what happens." With a sigh, Idris wiped my tears. "In my moment of shock and grief, I said some hurtful things."

It was the closest thing to an apology I had ever got. "That doesn't make it okay. I was hurting too, Idris. I needed you the most in that moment, and instead of easing my pain, you amplified it."

"Part of me truly believed you wanted this because you hate me."

"How could you think that? Before anything else, I am a mother."

"Not to me, Zoya. Before anything else, you are my wife. *My. Wife. Mine.* I can't tolerate the idea of sharing you. When I see you talking and laughing with anyone else, I *burn* because I know I will never get that. I will ask you a simple question and you can't even look at me, let alone speak to me. When I see someone sitting next to you, I want to flip the room upside down. I want you to myself. And just the *thought* of anyone else getting your time, voice, and laugh blinds me with rage. But most of all, I hate that you love our sons more than you could ever love me. You gave them a part of you I was always denied."

The deranged look in his eyes equally terrified and confused me. His jealousy over small things was unhealthy and bordering on insanity; especially with our children.

"They're *our* children. It's our job to love them because that is what protects them. How could you hate them?"

He shook his head. "I don't. I *can't* hate them because they're the only parts of you that accept my love. It's why this loss hurt so much because I knew with it died my chance of loving more of you."

CHAPTER
TWENTY-ONE

My pointed expression went ignored as Rani parked the car. "We can't take on anymore orders. I barely have the time to make the ones we've agreed to."

"If we keep rejecting people, we won't have any customers left. You're on a roll, Zoya. Let's keep the momentum going."

"The momentum only exists because Idris and his parents have been in Pakistan for two months. They're back today, which means my working hours will significantly drop as of tomorrow. He can't see me making these outfits because he's already asked why I'm always drawing or sewing."

"What did you say?"

My mouth snapped shut before the truth slipped out. My friends didn't know about my miscarriage. Nobody knew about it because it was easier to take Idris' approach and pretend it never happened. Longing came over me around the time he would have been born, but it was too overwhelming, so I pushed it to the back of my mind and focused on Karim, Nadim, and designing. That was the explanation I gave to Idris when he asked about the number of hours I spent making outfits he'd never seen me wear.

Ignoring her question, I said, "We've got to slow production down. I can't keep up." I waved at Sumayyah, who was already at the table. "Please don't mention it to them."

"Why? We've kept this secret from them for two years. I don't like it."

"Neither do I; but the more people that know, the higher the chances of him finding out."

Rani wanted to shout our achievements proudly to the world. However, she reluctantly agreed. "Don't tell me Halima's flaking on us again?" she asked once we were seated.

"She hasn't sent a message, so I assume she's coming. How are you guys?" Sumayyah asked.

"Bloody tired. My parent-in-laws have gone to Pakistan and Amal and Anisa are useless. They haven't helped me cook or clean *once* since. Not that they're asked to do much when my mother-in-law is here," I muttered with an eye roll.

She frowned. "I thought you liked your sister-in-laws?"

"They're fine as people, but it wouldn't kill them to clean up after themselves. How is life at yours?"

Sumayyah nodded her head. "Good. Thankfully, Amina is very helpful around the house. She's the perfect bou." *wife / daughter-in-law.* "Compared to her, I'm a useless monkey." She almost choked on her water when she jumped from excitement. "Nafisa's pregnant!"

"Little Nafisa is going to be a mum?" Rani shrieked.

I laughed, also finding it hard to believe. "I remember when her first tooth fell out. Can't believe she's going to have a baby!"

"Are you excited to be an auntie?"

There was a look on Sumayyah's face I couldn't decipher. "Of course. My parents are ecstatic that they're finally going to be grand-parents."

Only a month ago, Sumayyah mentioned she and Yousef had start-ed trying for a baby. From her expression, I sensed she was envious that it had happened for her sister before it happened for her. Culture dictated that elder siblings have children first. But it wasn't a big deal. Bilal had a child before Idris and me.

Trying to reassure her, I smiled. "Trust me, your kid is still going to be the favourite. My in-laws fawn over Karim because he's Idris' child."

Rani answered her phone and pressed it against her ear. Completely unlike herself, she was softly spoken and overly sweet. "I'm just out with my friends for lunch. It's fine. You guys eat." *Pause.* "I'm not sure yet. I'll let you know once I'm on my way back. All righty then. See you later," she ended in a singsong voice. She cut the call, rolled her eyes, and dropped her phone. "Fucking fake bitch," she hissed.

The complete change in her demeanour had me biting down on my lip to stop my laughter from bubbling out. "And *who* was that?"

"Devi."

"I thought you got on with Ravi's sister?" Sumayyah asked.

Her pointed expression was the true Rani we all knew. "That bitch is the fakest person I have ever met. She didn't call because she was waiting for me to eat. She's calling because her fucking cow of a mother wanted to know where I am, who I'm with, and what time I'm going back."

"Why didn't she just call you?"

"We're kind of not speaking right now." She clearly didn't want to delve into whatever had happened. She found her escape from our questioning looks when Halima took the empty seat at the table. "Why are you late? I'm starving."

"Nice to see you too," she remarked sarcastically.

Despite her asking, Rani was adamant we ordered food. Then she turned to Halima with a wide grin. "You may proceed."

Halima couldn't hide her smile. "Thank you, your highness. But it's not that exciting. Naz and I went to speak to a mortgage broker because we're looking to buy our own place."

"That's exciting," Sumayyah said. "Do you plan to stay local to here?"

She nodded. "Definitely. Jannah is settled in nursery and has a little group of friends. I don't want to disrupt that."

"Well, despite how jealous I am, I'm thrilled for you." Being the only one of us to have gone through the process, Rani offered Halima any advice she could.

Eager to absorb it, Halima couldn't see just how envious we all were. I would have given anything to be free of living with my in-laws. It was exhausting being the eldest daughter-in-law of the house. I wasn't allowed to make a cup of tea for just myself or a snack for just my children. It was for everyone or for no one. I was tired of having to cook five different dishes because I had to cater to everyone. I wanted a space where I could have a moment to myself.

When my gaze fell on Sumayyah's longing expression, I wondered why she was jealous. Her in-laws were tiny compared to mine. I knew she cooked on her days off, but her mother-in-law preferred cooking on her own. Sumayyah told us, most days, the cooking was done before she was even awake. Despite her age, Yousef's mum was a whizz at maintaining her house and didn't expect Sumayyah to slave away for them.

It was a known fact that Rani never wanted to live with Ravi's family, but she changed her mind just before the wedding. She knew it was going to be temporary, so she didn't mind. Her in-laws were even smaller than Sumayyah's; with only Ravi's parents and sister living there. She had a difficult relationship with her mother-in-law, but that didn't seem to stop her from living her life.

But as I looked at my friends, I questioned whether their lives were any easier than mine. Perhaps, like me, they were hiding behind a mask. I hadn't told them about my miscarriage. Rani avoided telling us what happened with her mother-in-law. Sumayyah didn't openly say she was struggling to get pregnant.

"How come you're moving out?" I asked. For as long as I could remember, Halima was happy to live with Nazir's family.

She looked at us and shrugged. "Mainly for space."

It was a lie. Whatever the truth was, she couldn't bring herself to admit it to us. And it made me wonder how many false smiles had we paraded while bragging about our marriages? I would never know the answer. But I was certain of one thing.

Around the table were four women who hoped concealing their heartbreaks would erase them. We hid behind our forced smiles and the armour we thought our wedding rings would provide. We hoped that if we spoke of love and happiness, it would be the same as having it. But words that aren't heard are the same as silence.

And the silence that enveloped the table spoke louder than any words we could muster.

❦ ❦ ❦ ❦ ❦

"I know you dry cleaned these over there, but I'm still going to give them a wash," I said as Idris pulled his pyjama bottoms on.

Once they arrived, I served them dinner and listened to Shazia prattle on. Idris ate silently, only speaking once or twice when Karim or Nadim asked a question. I cleared the table and dishes while they showered and the other siblings went to bed. Thankfully, the boys were asleep when I came up. Knowing Idris preferred his luggage to be unpacked straight away, I sat on the floor and started tidying it all away.

"I'm going to the restaurant tomorrow morning to speak to the contractor about the extension."

It was the first I had heard he was even extending it. "Okay. I'll iron your clothes. Will you be home for lunch?"

"Yes. Prepare something for tea time. Yousef is coming to discuss building plans."

My eyebrows furrowed. "Sumayyah's Yousef?"

"He's an engineer," was the only explanation I got.

I hadn't realised the two kept in touch, but I shrugged it off. "Okay. What did you want me to do with that?"

Idris looked up from his phone at the large cardboard box. "Whatever you want. It's for you."

"What is it?"

"Open it."

I felt nervous as he watched me. The nerves turned to confusion as I eyed the folded material. "I didn't ask Ammi for fabric."

"I bought it for you." He paused before awkwardly adding, "As a gift."

"*Oh.*"

"I thought you'd be a bit more enthusiastic considering how much you enjoy the hobby."

It's not a hobby, I wanted to argue but couldn't.

"You were jumping for joy when your friend gave you some from India."

The hostility in his tone forced me to face his jealousy. "No, I love it. I just wasn't expecting it, that's all."

"Do you not like the colours and patterns?"

"They're beautiful."

"Is the quality not good enough?"

"They're perfect."

"So, it's simply the fact that *I* bought them that's the issue then."

I shook my head. "No, of course not. I was just surprised. I really like them and appreciate the effort. Thank you."

Idris said nothing else as I finished sorting his clothes for the next day. By the time we climbed under the covers, it was nearly one in the morning. I was expecting him to be all over me, but he remained on his side of the bed. He laid on his back, staring up at the ceiling.

For a second, I wondered whether he had found someone to satisfy him in Pakistan. Had he gone and found himself a wife that fit his ideal? Did he lay in bed with another woman and reluctantly return to me because he had to? If his businesses weren't here, would he have come back to me?

"Did you enjoy yourself?" I found myself asking in the darkness.

"Did you?" he fired back.

"I enjoyed being able to sleep without your snoring," I teased.

He let out a soft chuckle. "I enjoyed being able to sleep without someone hogging the blanket."

"It was Pakistan. Did you really need a blanket?"

"I needed something to fill the warmth I was missing."

We fell into a silence again.

"What's your favourite colour?" I thought he had fallen asleep because he didn't speak for a few minutes.

"Brown."

I scrunched my nose. "That's one of the worst colours."

"It's beautiful; especially when the sun hits it at the right angle. I could lose track of time falling into it."

A silly smile took over my lips because I knew what he was talking about.

"What's yours?"

The first thing I noticed about Idris were his eyes. They were this perfect blend of varying shades of green. Nobody could deny how beautiful they were, and it was one of the few things he passed down to our sons.

"Green," I whispered. I turned my back to him, pulled the blanket to my chest, and sighed. "Goodnight."

The bed creaked as Idris closed the distance between us and wrapped his arm around my waist. When he spoke, his voice was so gentle it could have lulled me to sleep. "I enjoyed myself. I got to admire how well my companies were doing. I ate fresh fish, poultry, fruit, and vegetables. I walked the streets of my home country and when it was too hot, I sat under the air-con in a home I built on the land my father and forefathers bought. But I missed London. I missed my children. I missed the smooth roads and the ease of driving. I missed the grey skies and drizzly rain. But shall I tell you what I missed the most?"

"What did you miss the most?"

"You."

"I've been taking the pill. We can have sex if you want."

"I'm not talking about sex." He kissed my temple. "I'm talking about *you*. I missed you, Zoya."

CHAPTER TWENTY-TWO

OUR BEDROOM DOOR FLUNG open as the boys ran across the room and jumped onto the bed. "Happy birthday, Ammi!"

"Thank you, baba. What do you have there?" I asked, pointing at the paper in his hands.

"We made you a card," Nadim stated proudly.

My eyes widened and I let out a gasp. "This is my favourite card ever! I *love* it. Thank you."

"How old are you?"

"Mums don't have an age."

"Everyone has an age!" Karim laughed. He turned to his dad. "How old is Ammi?"

Idris smiled when I shook my head. "She's very young. I think she's only twenty."

"That's a big number," Nadim gasped.

I pinched his cheeks. "That's because you're only five."

"How old are you, Baba?"

I crinkled my nose. "Your baba is thirty-eight!"

Their faces contorted in horror before they yelled, "That's so old!"

I burst into laughter. "You're right, he is an old man." I looked at Idris. "I'm going to have to put you in a care home soon."

His shoulders shook as he chuckled. "This old man is hungry. Let's have some breakfast."

Knowing Idris was naked under the sheets, I told the boys to brush their teeth. The second the door slammed shut behind them, Idris' arms circled around my waist and pulled me into them.

"You've got approximately four minutes before they scream in hunger."

His lips travelled from my collar bone up my neck. He kissed just below my ear. "Happy birthday," he whispered. "*Thirty-first* birthday, should I remind you?"

I groaned as I climbed out of the bed and stretched. "Believe me, my body reminds me of my age every day. I can't do anything without my bones clicking."

Sitting up, he stared at me for a few minutes. "Then maybe we should start trying for another baby before your body completely gives up."

Despite his light tone, I froze. Echoes of my cries and pain filled me. Since the miscarriage two years ago, he hadn't brought up having babies. He respected my request and silently placed the contraceptive pill in my bedside draw a few days later. And every month a new packet replaced the empty one.

I sighed. "I can't put myself through that again."

"Your body has healed. Enough time has passed. And despite how much we can joke about it, you are getting older. We don't have much time before the window of opportunity closes."

"But life is finally normal."

My boys were both in full-time school. While Idris and I weren't always on the same page, we had at least spent the last five months in the same story. But most importantly, those two elements meant I could fulfil orders and make a decent salary from my small business. I had established a routine that meant I could get everything done without arousing suspicion. A baby would disrupt all that and before I knew it, I would be back to square one.

My only option was to change his mind. "Where are you going to put another body in this house? Your brothers have five children between them and it doesn't seem they ever plan on moving out. Are you really going to spend the rest of our marriage with a child between us?"

"They can share a room with Karim and Nadim."

"There's hardly enough room for the two of them. And what happens if we have a daughter? She can't share a room with them."

"I'll build an extension. I'll buy a bigger house. I want another baby, Zoya."

"Why? We have two healthy, happy sons. You have an heir to continue the legacy you've built."

"I don't understand why you always have to fight me on this," he snapped.

"Because I don't want to be pregnant! I don't want to put my body through that again. You are a man, so you couldn't possibly understand how *hard* it is. It's not just being pregnant, but everything that comes afterwards. I finally have some time for myself."

He got out of bed and started pulling clothes on. "What do you need time for? To waste it aimlessly drawing?"

I didn't want to argue with him. This was the longest we had got on. Our marriage wasn't anything to inspire a love story, but it worked for us. Maybe we didn't know every small detail about each other, nor did we have heart-to-heart conversations; but we both finally understood our roles, and we did them well.

"*Please*, Idris. For the first time in my life, I feel somewhat happy. I feel like I can breathe again. You said I can ask you for anything, and I am asking you to not take that from me."

ᎧᎧᎧᎧ

It was the first time I had been inside Idris' restaurant. *Balti* was arguably the most successful of his restaurants, serving traditional Pakistani cuisine. I had only seen the exterior once while sat in the car when Idris stopped on the way home to speak to his head chef. Since then, he had remodeled the whole interior. The combination of dark walls, crystal chandeliers, and pops of greenery produced a luxurious atmosphere.

Idris kept his hand on my lower back as we were ushered to the private room. I couldn't help but giggle at the hard expression he wore.

He peered down at me. "What?"

The rest of our party walked ahead when we stopped. My heels made it easier to cup his jaw. "Would it hurt you to smile?"

"I've counted four tables who haven't received their complimentary cold starters."

"I've also counted only two tables that are empty. It's busy and they are trying their hardest. I'm sure it doesn't help they have to serve *you* tonight, either."

Trying to fight his smile, he asked. "What's wrong with serving me?"

"It's an absolute nightmare. Believe me, after thirteen years, I can say that with certainty."

He tucked a loose lock of my hair behind my ear. When he leaned forward, I thought he was going to kiss me. Instead, his lips pressed against my ear. "You did a wonderful job serving me last night."

I playfully slapped his chest. "Behave yourself."

His boyish smile made my heart waver. "Only if you promise to reward me later." He surprised me by taking my hand and walking alongside me to rejoin our party.

I couldn't recall the last birthday I enjoyed celebrating like this. My cheeks ached from the laughter I shared with Farrah, Emaan, and Rizwan. I was glad Idris thought to invite their families and our household. The room was abuzz with chitchat, except from Idris, who sat next to me in silence. It wasn't his usual broody silence. It was a content one. His hand hadn't moved from my thigh since we sat down. Every once in a while, he'd squeeze tight, almost as if he was checking I was real.

"Sir, are you ready for the dessert menu?"

"Baba, I want a *big* ice cream!" Nadim yelled.

"I know what I want for dessert," Idris muttered to me. He stared at me in panic when I removed his hand. "Where are you going?"

"Bathroom." Excusing myself, I closed the door behind me and followed the signs to the ladies' room. I made a note to compliment Idris on the interior design of this place because even the toilets were stunning.

"I thought it was you," a voice said as I was making my way back. Adeel smiled at me. "I saw you walking in."

My heart hammered in my chest. Had Idris left the private room, we would have been the first thing he saw. He was in a good mood and our marriage was in a great place. I wasn't willing to sacrifice that for Adeel. Even if he didn't catch us tonight, I was certain there were cameras everywhere. Knowing that, my plan was to tell Idris on our way home before he found out himself and thought I was lying to him.

I forced a smile. "I didn't see you. I was with my family, who are waiting for me. Please excuse me." I barely made it two steps away from him when I halted.

"Happy birthday, Zoya." He arched his brow when I faced him. "Did you think I forgot?"

"You need to forget."

"How can I forget the plans we made? I hadn't heard from you in two months, yet I waited for you to come back to me. I was going to propose to you! I put together all the money I had to buy you a ring."

Looking back to make sure his raised voice didn't garner any attention, I walked towards him and kept my voice low. "It's been thirteen years. I'm married. *You're* married. We are not doing this. So pretend you never saw me and go back to your table."

"I love you."

My lip quivered. "No, you don't. You love your wife. So I am begging you, don't do this to her. Don't make me become that woman."

His fingers rested under my chin. "I never stopped loving you. It's why my parents had to find me a wife."

I pushed his hands off me. "We were kids! We didn't know what love was."

"So you didn't love me?"

I struggled to give an honest answer, but settled on, "Yes, but that was a different time."

He looked at me in disgust. "I saw the two of you when you came in. All smiles and touchy. Do you love him?"

My eyes latched onto his as my silence hung between us. I didn't know if I loved Idris. All I knew was I didn't hate him anymore. "He's only on the other side of this wall. Please, just walk away and forget about me."

"We're older now. I have a good job. We can go anywhere we want and start again."

"I have children! I have a husband! I can't abandon them. I have given too much to my marriage to do what you're suggesting."

"He will never love you the way I do. I loved you when you were wild, crazy and completely yourself. How much did you have to sacrifice to earn his love? How much of yourself did you have to give up in order to find happiness? I remember how he got you, even if you don't. You *hated* him. You wanted him to leave you so we could be together. That wasn't fake."

I stared at his desperation and felt sick to my stomach. My heart broke for his wife, who was probably at home looking after their children. Did she know her husband was yearning for a past ghost?

Not wanting to waste anymore time on him, I turned around.

My heart completely stopped.

Idris stood tall and glared at us. His lips settled into a thin line and his fingers curled into fists. "What's going on here?"

I knew his calm voice was a facade. "Nothing. Let's go."

"I was coming to see what was taking you so long. I have my answer."

"He bumped into me."

"Is that right?"

I held his arm. "Idris, please. Let's just go."

But he wasn't looking at me. His icy stare was directed at Adeel. "Get out of my restaurant." He stepped closer. "And if I ever see you looking at *my* wife again, I'll break every bone in your body."

Adeel saw Idris' threat as empty. He laughed and stepped up to him. "And what if your wife *wants* me to look at her?"

"She doesn't."

"How do you know what she wants? You never took the time to ask her. But me? I know *exactly* what she likes." The suggestive tone made him grin.

Idris laughed, but there was no humour in it. "Is that right? What do you know?"

"Every damn thing about her. She wasn't afraid to tell me what she wants and how she likes it."

I pressed my hand against Idris' chest, trying to break through the testosterone they were exuding. "He's lying. Please, just walk away. Let's go home."

"You never forget your first," Adeel goaded.

"You never had her," he spat out.

But Adeel was pressing all the right buttons. Idris' jaw tightened. With narrowed eyes filled with ice, his fingers curled into fists.

"Yes, I did. She was mine first."

My head snapped to him. "Stop lying!"

"What lies, Zoya? I wasn't your first? I still remember the way your lips felt against mine. I remember where we were when you first said you loved me. I remember the first time I got a boner because you—"

The sharp crack and blood were the telltale that Idris had broken Adeel's nose. And he wasn't done. He threw him against the wall and pinned him there. "I'm going to kill you," he snarled.

Scared he would lash out at me if I touched him, I hoped I could beg him to see sense. "Let him go before someone calls the police."

"Is this what he does to you?" Adeel asked, looking at me.

Idris slammed his head against the wall. "Don't look at her!"

"You're going to hurt him, Idris! Please, just let him go."

Without looking away from him, he asked, "Is his pain hurting you? Do you want to save him?"

I shook my head. "No! But our children are just steps away and I don't want them to see you like this. Please, let's just go home."

Nothing was making Idris waver. He held Adeel in place as he barely controlled his breathing. I knew what he was capable of when pushed past his limit.

"Please come back to me. Where is the husband I had all evening? I need him because this one is scaring me," I cried. "Let him go. He's not going to call the police and we can pretend he doesn't exist. It will just be you, me and our children. Idris, please look at me."

Slowly, his head turned towards me. "Say it," he ordered.

My fingers twisted together, and I gave him the reassurance he needed. "I'm yours. I belong to you and only you."

I didn't have the stomach for dessert and shortly after, we gathered our belongings and made our way home. As I got the boys ready for bed, all I kept thinking was I couldn't revert to the early days of our marriage. I needed to make Idris understand none of it was true.

I knelt on the ground and put my supplies next to me. With shaky fingers, I took Idris' injured hand and began wiping away the dried blood. "He was lying. I never did that with him. You know that, right?"

"It wasn't all a lie, though." He stared down at me. "You did kiss him. You did love him."

"That was a long time ago."

He hummed under his breath. He said nothing else while I finished cleaning his hand and put the items away. "Where do you go after you drop the boys to school?"

Trying to act neutral, I brushed my hair. "What do you mean?"

Idris stood behind me. "It doesn't take more than twenty minutes to drop them off. Yet, you return after forty minutes. The school is only five minutes away, so why do you leave half an hour before the bell rings?" He met my gaze in the reflection. "Did you think I never noticed?"

Denying it wouldn't achieve anything. So, I tried a lie. "I walk the long way home for some fresh air and a break from the house."

"Who do you walk with?"

"Nobody."

"If that's true, how did he know where you were tonight?"

Oh god. Idris was putting together a completely wrong picture.

"It was coincidence. I tried to walk away from him tonight. If you've got cameras, you can check for yourself."

"I will." It was a threat. "Do you love him?"

"No."

His knuckles ran down my spine before he gripped my hips. "Good. Now take your clothes off." He took a seat on the bed and watched as I followed his order. "What did you do to give him a boner?"

"Nothing. I only ever kissed him."

"You're going to show me how you kissed him."

I knew what was coming. Tears filled my eyes again. "Please don't do this."

"Stop fucking crying. Did you cry when you kissed him? Or did you throw yourself at him?"

"It wasn't like that."

"Then show me!" he roared. "Show your husband how you pleasured your boyfriend. You must have done a mighty job if, after all these years, he can't forget about it. What did you do after you kissed him? Did you pleasure him with your mouth? Did you lay on your back, spread open for him?"

I rubbed my face. "This is what he wanted! He was trying to get under your skin!"

"Well, he's there! The image of the two of you is burning in my mind! All I can see is your hands touching him in ways you've never touched me. All I can hear is you telling that animal you love him! And I don't know how to get rid of it! Every time I think I am over it, you remind me of him. You remind me that your love belongs to someone else."

"It doesn't. Tell me what I need to do to make it stop," I begged. I gripped his shirt. "What do you want from me? What else can I give you?"

"I want *you*."

"I have given you all of me. There's nothing left."

He stood tall. "Yes, there is." Idris stripped his clothes and took the only part of me that truly mattered to him. "I had you first," he moaned. His hands touched every inch of my skin, grabbing and clawing at it. He pressed his body as close as he could to mine. His lips trailed over my face and down my neck. But it wasn't enough to leave a mark on me.

My legs tightened when he bit down on my neck. I held back a sob when his teeth plunged into my shoulder. Unable to take the pain, my fingers gripped the bedsheets.

"You have always been *mine*." He buried his head in my neck.

And I was glad because it meant he couldn't see my tears. "Yes."

"Nobody else has had you."

"Nobody."

"I'm the only man who knows what you feel like."

"Yes."

"I'm the only man who has filled your womb with life."

"Yes."

"And I'm going to do it again."

"Okay," I whispered.

The next morning, my contraceptive pill was no longer in my bedside draw.

Chapter Twenty-Three

"Have you checked in with Sumayyah?" Halima asked.

Two weeks ago, while at Halima's mini housewarming gathering she had just for us friends, Sumayyah opened up about her struggles with infertility and the impact it was having on her marriage. My heart broke when she started crying. If I had just one wish, I would have used it to make her dream come true.

Her reality amplified the guilt I felt when my pregnancy test came back positive. Since my birthday five months ago, neither Idris nor I discussed what happened. The progress we'd made had regressed, but not all the way to the starting line as I worried about. But pregnancy meant life was about to turn into a nightmare again.

Because of that, I wanted to spend the day moping, but Halima and I planned this playdate weeks ago. So, I pushed aside my foul mood, got my boys dressed, and was sitting under the July sun in a park.

"She said things are better with her mother-in-law and Yousef and her are doing well."

She frowned. "I can't imagine how hard that must be for them. It makes you feel really grateful, huh?"

"Sure."

"Are you okay? You're very quiet. Or am I just boring you?"

I smiled at my friend. "Ironic coming from you. You've always said so little. We practically have to force conversation out of you."

Her gaze dropped to the ground. "Sometimes I think what's the point in speaking when nobody really listens?"

Taking her hand in mine, I gave it a squeeze. "You know you've always got us, right? We're always here to listen to whatever you want to talk about. Even if it is just to brag about how perfect your husband is."

Her smile wavered, but she squeezed back. "Do you think Jannah will always be friends with your boys like this?" She jutted her chin towards where they were running around with the ball.

"I hope so. As great as family can be, nothing beats having friendships that become family. To have a great friendship is rewarding because it's a choice, you know? Those people aren't with you because of obligation. They love you for you."

"I don't know where I'd be without you girls. When life gets hard, you guys inspire me."

"Nothing about me is inspiring."

She shot me an unimpressed glare. "Every so often, I think about prom. We were so young and terrified about the future. But not you. You always knew what you wanted from life."

"And then I let it slip through my fingers. I became the very thing I hated."

"No," she whispered. "You chose to survive and there's no guilt or shame in that."

The night my father learned about Adeel was a memory I never allowed myself to think about. Over a decade later, I still felt choked by the trauma from that night. I could still feel the stinging of my wounds and the metallic smell of blood.

But in the safe comfort I found in Halima, I let it rise to the surface. "I'll never be able to explain it. Even as a grown woman in her thirties; even as a mother of two, he still scares me. I haven't lived in that house for years, but whenever I step over the threshold, I can hear my cries. How could he do that to his own daughter? How do you hurt someone you're supposed to love?"

She wiped my tears even though her own were falling. "Because this culture teaches men that they have a right to our bodies."

"Sometimes I ask myself why I didn't just run as fast as my legs could take me. Why didn't I stand up for myself? But then that same panic sets in and I understand how helpless I felt. I believed him when he said I was the one in the wrong and deserved the way he treated me. His sharp tongue marked my skin until I accepted his version of the truth." I shook my head and took a deep breath. "It's stupid I know. It's something you can't understand unless it happens to you."

Her eyes glazed over. She was looking at me, but she couldn't see me. "When the first slap comes, you're too stunned to do anything because you're still trying to register what just happened. And when you realise, you're crying and asking why he did that. Then before you know it, you're apologising because you *must* have deserved that. So, it happens again and again and again. And by the fourth or fifth time, you don't even cry anymore. You don't ask why, because it was drilled into you it is always your fault."

Goosebumps rose on my arms. "Halima ... how... why..." I couldn't finish the question because the idea of Nazir being violent was laughable.

She arched her brow. "I've read so many of these stories, and they're all the same." Her light tone did little to ease my worry.

"If he's done something, you would tell us? You know we would stand with you the whole way. We would protect you."

"I know," she whispered. "Sometimes I wish we could go back to being sixteen at prom, wearing our pretty dresses, with those bows tied around our wrists."

"Why?"

"Because as scared as those girls were, they were also determined to step into the real world and take it head on. They weren't afraid to dream. They wanted to change the world. Between them, they housed so much hope, strength, courage, and resilience."

"Young Zoya truly believed she was going to revolutionise the world."

Halima laughed. "If you could meet a younger you, what would you tell her?"

"Nobody is coming to save her. If she wants to survive, she needs to be smarter than them. How about you? What advice would you give to a young Halima?"

"A flower, no matter how damaged, is delicate and deserves the best care. Sometimes we accept the wrong treatment. And if that happens, it's okay to admit we made a mistake. But we must stop letting that treatment continue, even if some damage is already done. Because it's always better to lose one petal than it is to let the whole flower wilt."

I felt heavy-chested for the rest of the day. Halima's haunted look tormented me. My gut told me something was wrong, but she promised me she was okay before she dropped me off.

"What's on your mind?"

I snapped out of my daze and smiled at my father-in-law. "Nothing."

"Did they have fun today?"

Their playdate exhausted all their energy. They could barely keep their eyes open during their dinner and shower. It made it an easy battle to get them asleep, which is always a mother's dream.

"Yeah. Nadim scraped his knee though."

He waved me off. "Children hurt themselves all the time. Don't worry."

"Their dad doesn't seem to understand that."

"Their dad doesn't understand many things, though he walks around as if he does."

His dry tone made me smile. I didn't make any comment because a good wife doesn't slander her husband.

"I know he is difficult because I made him that way. I broke his back until he had the strength to stand as a real man."

"He is a good son," I said honestly.

"Being a good son does not make him a good man. In order to achieve that, he must also be a good husband and father."

"Is that something you believe you have taught him to be?"

"You would have to ask your mother-in-law that. But I see much of myself in Idris and, as a result, I wonder if my wife endured the same hardship I see in you."

His ghostly tone made my throat close up. Abbas was a traditional man with strong beliefs set from generations ago. He could have blindly agreed with Idris' treatment of me. Yet, he was reflecting on his own actions as a husband; and I hoped it made him appreciate his wife, and all she did and continued to do for him.

"He's better than before."

With a nod of his head, the conversation ended. "Get to bed. It's late."

"Did you want anything special for breakfast tomorrow? I can make *halwa puri*," I offered, knowing it was his favourite.

"I cannot say if you are a good wife or mother. That is not my place. But know you are a good daughter-in-law," he said sincerely.

A warmth spread through me as I left him to his own company. "Ammi, do we have semolina?" I asked, as I entered the kitchen with a smile gracing my lips.

"What are you making at this hour?"

"I told Baba I would make him halwa puri tomorrow for breakfast."

Pride shone in Shazia's face. She turned to her son. "Your wife clearly has a favourite," she joked.

"Don't worry. I'll make some for everyone."

Idris said nothing as his phone rang, and he left the room. I prepared ingredients, ready for the morning. Once the kitchen was spotless, I turned the lights off and headed upstairs.

Idris looked over his shoulder at me as I joined him in our bedroom. "I have to go. I'll call you tomorrow."

"Who was that?" I asked once he hung up.

"Sanam."

I checked the time and wondered why she was calling him so late into the night. Suspicion rose in me but I realised if it was anything untoward, he wouldn't have told me it was her on the phone. A small part of me wanted to create a scene because if the roles were reversed, and it was *me* talking to a man this late, Idris would have flipped his shit. He would have interrogated me before forbidding me to do it again. But I let it go because I wasn't in the mood to argue with him.

"Will you be having breakfast with us or going to work early tomorrow?"

"I'll be home." He raised his eyebrow. "What's wrong, Zoya?"

"Nothing." *Except why were you talking to her? And why did you hang up as soon as I walked in?*

"She called to ask for a ride."

Of what? Your penis?

"I didn't say anything. You can talk to your cousin about whatever you want whenever you want. You didn't need to hang up because I walked in."

"That isn't why I hung up."

"Okay. I'm just saying, I don't really care what you two secretly talk about."

"You don't seem to care about anything when it comes to me," he muttered.

Ignoring his self-pity, I changed the subject. "Can you make sure you're home Thursday morning? I have a doctor's appointment."

"What's wrong with you?"

I rummaged through my draw and held up the pregnancy test. "Congratulations. You're going to be a father again," I said blandly.

His eyes followed me as I moved across the room and got ready for bed. "When did you find out?"

"This morning."

He sighed. "Is this how the next nine months are going to be?"

"What were you expecting? Did you want me to throw my arms around you and thank you for putting me through this again?"

"I thought you would have been a little more grateful, considering what happened last time. This is a second chance."

That was a low blow, and he knew it.

"A new baby won't make up for the one I lost."

"*We* lost," he corrected.

I stood tall and braced my shoulders back. "In the last thirteen years, what have you exactly lost? What have you had to sacrifice? From where I'm standing, I'm the only loser in this relationship. I lost the ability to make my own decisions, my body, my voice, my freedom, and *myself*. I don't know who the hell I am anymore. I'm just a collection of broken pieces."

"What do you want me to do, Zoya?"

"Nothing, because I would be a fool to think the hands that broke me are capable of fixing me. I'll do that on my own."

CHAPTER TWENTY-FOUR

I STARED AT MY mother in disbelief while she smiled with pride at her news. It seemed my sisters shared her excitement because they rushed over to get a good look at Zain's wife-to-be.

"She's a little plump, but that's okay," my mum said. "In real life her skin isn't *that* dark. The lighting in this picture is quite bad."

"She's pretty," Maliha said. "When's the wedding?"

"October."

Asma's mouth hung open. "How are we going to plan a wedding in two months?"

"Now that everyone knows, neither side wants to delay it. There's no point dragging out an engagement."

I scoffed. "What difference does a few more months make? They've been dating for *years*."

"Zoya," Asma pleaded.

"How come your father never beat Zain when he found out he was in a haram relationship? Is it permissible because he's a man?"

"*Our* father—"

I held my hand up. "That man is not my father. He stopped being that when he beat me because I had a boyfriend. So, I want to know why Zain never suffered the same punishment."

"You know how it is now. The times have changed."

"For men," I finished for her. "The times have changed for men. This culture has continued to hold us women back. Because I guarantee that girl's family is talking about her behind her back. Her family is rushing this wedding because they feel ashamed she found love on her own. Do you think they've told anyone she had a boyfriend? They're probably telling people it was all arranged. They want to contain all the whispers by getting rid of her as fast as they can."

My mum's eyes narrowed. "We tried to get him married years ago. He said no."

"So did I," I spat. "I *begged* you to put an end to my suffering. Instead, you dressed me up for my husband and shipped me off to his bed."

She looked horrified at my suggestive words. "We married you to a good family, to a good man. We didn't just accept any girl for Zain. Ilham comes from a respected family. Her values align with ours."

A humourless laugh slipped out of me. "Isn't that ironic? A stranger who committed the very sin I did is good enough to be loved as your daughter, but you guys were so quick to disown me. I'm happy for you guys. I hope she can be the daughter I failed to be."

"That's not what she meant," Asma tried to argue.

"I know what she meant. I was never good enough for this *respectful* family. I was labelled as dishonourable and shameless when I fell in love. Yet, Zain's love is celebrated. I'm not surprised because the only way to remain unscathed in this family you have to be one of two things: obedient or a man."

∾∾∾∾∾

"God, your boys get more energetic the older they get," Zain sighed as he joined me in my childhood bedroom.

I didn't respond, choosing to focus on weaving my needle in and out of the fabric.

"What are you making?"

Most of the outfit was done. I just needed to take in the waist a little before Rani delivered it to the customer tomorrow. As it was the school holidays, I had no way of dropping it to her, so she'd have to pick it up from here.

"Did you want something?"

My brother and I never really spoke except for pleasantries. It wasn't personal. That's how we were raised. Despite living under one roof, we had upbringings that were worlds apart. The only thing we had in common were our parents, but I'd argue he was raised by two people I never recognised.

He took a seat at the foot of the bed. "Bhaji," *sister,* "told me what happened earlier. Ilham is a nice person. You'll see when you meet her."

"I never said she's not a nice person. And even if she's not, what do I care?"

"Do you actually mean that?" His hurt tone made me regret my harshness.

"I've got to get this done before your brother-in-law comes to pick me up. So, what do you want?"

He went mute, but I could feel his heavy stare on me. "Nothing. I..." He sighed. "Do you hate me?"

That caught my attention. My fingers stopped working, and I looked up at my brother. He was no longer the baby-faced kid I always thought of. Zain had grown into his long nose and round eyes. His chubby cheeks had melted and set into a sharp jaw. Once upon a time, he could only grow a sparse moustache, but he now had a full beard that was well-groomed.

"I don't hate you," I answered. "I resent you."

"Because you blame me for what happened? If I never showed him those pictures..."

"He still would have done what he did. He already knew the truth before he saw the proof. That isn't why I resent you."

Zain looked like a little boy when he asked, "Then why?"

"Because you got everything I dreamed of without even having to ask. You went out with your friends whenever you wanted, with no limitations. I would have to wait until they were in a good mood before I begged them to let me see my friends. If they agreed, I had such strict constraints and had to deal with the guilt when I came back. She would call me way before my curfew to ask where I was and what time I would be back. If I was ever a few minutes late, panic would consume me until I felt sick with worry about his violence and her silent treatment."

"I never knew it was that bad."

"Why would you? You were given all the freedom in the world because you are a man. It didn't matter what you did out there, because everything was justified for you. But a woman's actions out of the home determined her worth inside of it."

"That's a culture thing. It was what they were taught, so it's all they know. I'm not saying they were right, but they wanted to protect you." He shuffled closer. "I've seen it with my own eyes how cruel men can be."

"And I experienced how cruel they can be when my own father strangled me and promised to kill me. You were there, Zain. It was you who pulled him off me. Am I supposed to thank him for that?"

He shook his head. "I'm not saying that, but he was angry and didn't want you to make a mistake you couldn't take back."

"The only mistake I made was falling in love with someone *I* chose. I dreamed of a life better than the one they planned for me, and that was unacceptable. I didn't bow to their commands, so they held a gun to my head until I did. And then they framed me for their crime and handed me a life sentence."

Sadness clouded his features. "I really want you to be happy for me, but I get why you can't."

"I am happy for you, Zain. *I'm* just not happy." I blinked my tears away. "Do you love her?"

His cheeks burned bright, and he looked away, feeling flustered. "I suppose," he muttered.

"Then complete my dream all the way. Lead your marriage with love and protect her. Don't make her conform to what *they* want. Love her for who she is."

He swallowed hard. "Did you fall in love again?"

Before I could answer, the door opened, revealing Idris. His eyebrows furrowed in confusion as he stared at us. "Let's go."

I picked my needle up and quickly finished the stitch before folding the dress, ready for Rani tomorrow. "Can you tell the boys to put their shoes on?"

Idris still hadn't budged. "They're ready to go."

I nodded and turned to my brother. "You have the choice to copy what you have learnt, or learn from their mistakes. Anger does not make love grow. Only love can make love grow."

"I understand."

"And to answer your earlier question, I don't know. But I'm working on it."

Zain smiled at me. "You deserve a lifetime of dreams. So, I hope they are worthy of it."

Catching my reflection in the mirror, I smiled too. "Yes. She is worthy of it."

CHAPTER TWENTY-FIVE

"I THOUGHT YOU WANTED to keep that one for yourself?" I asked Rani as she folded the teal dress away.

Her eyes darted to Ravi, who was tapping away at his keyboard. "The colour is a bit too bright for me."

"Since when has a colour been too bright for you? You've literally worn neon yellow before," I laughed.

"I've been told to tone my wardrobe down to match my skin colour."

My mouth hung open in shock and disgust. *Who said that to her?* I didn't have to ask because the defensive look that overcame Ravi made it clear it was someone in his family.

"Don't twist what she said," he warned.

Her brow arched. "I put it politely, but I'm more than happy to repeat her exact words."

I'd heard enough to grasp what was actually said and my heart hurt for my friend. Rani had always been unapologetically herself. I'd never seen her second-guess who she was and what she liked.

"You take everything out of context and twist it to your viewpoint," he retaliated. "You have a problem with everything she says."

"You'd have a problem with it too if you were ever there to hear how much of a *bitch* your mum is."

Throwing his laptop onto the sofa, he stood up and glowered at her. "What the fuck did you just call my mum?"

The word filled her mouth, but she didn't repeat it. She stared her husband down with a look of rage and hurt.

"You constantly push her limits. You live under her roof, so you are to follow the same rules as the rest of us."

"Well, right now you're under *my* roof, so get the fuck out." She turned her back to him and resumed organising the mess.

My gulp was loud in the awkward silence. Picking up my fabric pen, I began making markings on the material just so I had something to do.

"Why would you respect my family when you have none for me?" he asked a few minutes later.

"And how can I expect your family to respect me when you have none for me?" she fired back. "All you care about is them and what they want."

"That's not true."

She tried wiping her tears away inconspicuously, but I saw it. "Just go, Ravi. I don't want to talk to you right now."

"Whenever I've tried to mediate between you two, you—"

Her head snapped towards him, and if looks could kill, Ravi would have dropped dead. "*Mediate*? Is that what you call blaming me and excusing *everything* your family does and says?"

"Well, if you gave me an ounce of respect as a man and husband, you would shut your mouth and let me handle it. But you just have to have the last word."

I stood up, ready to break up a fight, when Rani stepped towards him.

"The day you act like a real man and husband, I'll give you a speck of respect. Until then, I'll continue to play *both* parts in this marriage."

Glancing at me, he shook his head in disbelief. "This is the problem with you."

"Oh, just *fuck* off, Ravi. Get the hell out of my flat." When he stepped closer, she stepped back and pointed at the door. "Go! I don't want to fucking look at or talk to you."

His guilty stare turned to me, and he silently pleaded with me to fight his case for him. When he realised I wasn't getting involved, he resigned and packed his stuff away before taking his leave.

"I'm sorry you had to see that," she said once the door closed behind him. "He gets so precious over his mum."

I wanted to hug my friend, but I knew she didn't want to make a big deal out of it. "You should see me and Idris when we argue; the whole house gets turned upside down," I said, hoping to lighten the mood. "For what it's worth, I think you should keep the teal one. You'd look beautiful in it."

She said nothing, and we continued to work in silence until the doorbell rang. Rani let the customers in and masked her sadness with a chirpy voice as she led them to the living room.

I secured my needle and stood to shake their hands. "Hi. It's nice to meet you."

The husband looked around the room. It would have been professional to tidy up before they arrived, but I had multiple orders that required alterations, as well as finishing a few designs to be sold readymade. And it all needed to be done today while Idris thought I was at my sister's house helping her cook.

"Do you live here?" There was a playfulness to his tone that eased my worries.

I chuckled. "No. This is just our workshop. What are you looking for today?"

His wife's grin was so wide I was worried her cheeks would split open. "I am *obsessed* with your dresses! Everything I see on your page is absolutely stunning!"

Pride filled me at that. "Thank you. Did you bring your fabric with you?"

"I wanted to buy something off the shelf."

"Okay. If you show me which piece you want, I'll see if we have it in stock."

She shrugged. "Anything."

Rani shared the same look of bewilderment as me. "You didn't have one in mind?"

"All I know is I want something you made. I'm open to any colour or cut."

It felt like I was dreaming. There she was, a complete stranger, who was desperate to wear something *I* designed. I let out a laugh. "Okay. What event is it for?"

"My sister is getting married," her husband answered.

Rani's real estate experience kicked in and she started bringing out a range of options. She advised the woman on the most flattering colors and fit.

All the while, I stood there dumbfounded. It was like watching a movie. Every new outfit made her eyes widen and mouth gape open in awe. Her fingers ran over the fabrics as she tried to make her mind up.

Then she was looking at me. "What do you think?"

"The *sharara suit* is my favourite. The flowy trousers give you the best of both words. They're practical but also give the illusion of a skirt when stood still."

Her husband was looking past my head. "What's that?"

I eyed the incomplete beige outfit. "That's a palazzo suit."

She was already walking towards it. "What's that?"

"It's like a *sharara,* but it's not fitted at the knee. It's essentially got wide leg trousers. This design has a long peplum top instead of a traditional *kameez.*"

Rani held up the heavily embroidered fabric for her to admire. "This is a brand new piece and definitely a showstopper."

"I *love* it." She turned to her husband. "What do you think?"

He nodded. "It's definitely my favourite."

"It's also not made," I said, bursting their bubble.

"Would you be able to get it done within a month?"

My eyes scanned all my outstanding orders, and I hesitated. "I don't want to make a promise I can't keep."

"I will pay you *anything* if you can get it done for me. I've literally been waiting for a family wedding just so I can buy something from you."

It wasn't only my orders I had to fulfil. I was coerced into making mine and my sisters' outfits for Zain's wedding. But I didn't want to disappoint her. "Six weeks," I countered.

She let out a shriek and *hugged* me. "Thank you so much!"

I awkwardly returned her embrace. "You're welcome. Let me take your measurements."

"We have more of this fabric. Do you want to match with your wife?" Rani asked.

"It's a bit flashy for a man," he chuckled.

She shook her head. "Absolutely not! We could make you a *sherwani* out of plain fabric to match her beige trousers and use the embroidered fabric to make a waistcoat."

He scratched his head. "I don't know. Naima, what do you think?"

"You *are* the only brother. And the colours are neutral enough for you to pull off."

"Perfect!" Rani declared. "Zoya will take your measurements."

Nobody thought to ask me, the person who had to make the damn thing, what I thought. Had they asked me, I would have told them I had no idea where to begin with a man's outfit. I had zero experience with it. But it was too late to say anything because Rani was writing up a receipt and I was taking his measurements. Reality only hit me once they walked out, and Rani slammed the door shut behind them.

"Why would you agree to that? I don't know how to make a waist-coat!"

She waved her phone at me. "That's what the internet is for."

"It's not that simple! What if I get it wrong and there's not enough material left for me to start again? This is his sister's wedding! If I fuck it up, our reputation is down the drain."

She gripped my shoulders. "Zoya, baby. *Breathe*. You'll be fine."

My eyes narrowed. "I also don't have the *time* to make another outfit. I don't know if I can even make hers! Why would you suggest that without talking to me first?"

"I saw an opportunity to make extra money, so I took it. And we'd eventually have to branch out. Just close your eyes and imagine this: a family collection; matching outfits for the *whole* family."

I could see the vision. I had drawn enough sketches of a '*mummy and me*' collection for both daughters and sons. The problem was I didn't have the luxury of time to do it because I was limited to the few hours I had away from Idris.

Taking a deep breath, I calmed myself down. "No more orders until we've got through all of these."

She held her hands up in surrender. "Yes, boss. We've made enough cash to see us through the next few months. Speaking of which, when are you going to spend your share?"

"When I think of something I want."

"You've got about forty-five *thousand* pounds, Zoya. You can't think of *anything* to buy with that type of money?"

"What did you buy?"

"A *Chanel* bag. *Dior* sandals. *Gucci* earrings. Anything I freaking wanted."

"Well, I can't exactly walk home with those, can I? I would be in Idris' firing range before I could even blink."

"So, leave it here and wear it when you're not with him."

"What's the point of that? And anyway, I don't really care for that stuff."

She flicked through my sketchbook and sighed. "What's the point of having money if you don't spend it?"

"I like knowing that it's there." *And if Idris ever kicked me out again, I could take care of myself and my children.*

"These are so beautiful."

Standing behind her, I eyed my sketches. "I know. If only I had a magic wand to turn them into real fabric."

"Maybe we could." She turned to face me. "I mean, there must be a factory somewhere in the world that can turn your designs into tangible fabrics."

I shook my head with a smile. "You're a nutcase. Come on. I don't have long before I have to get home."

But Rani didn't move. "I'm being serious. Prints and embroidery don't just appear. Someone must send off their designs to get made. We just need to find where to send your drawings."

"Of course there are people that design the materials we buy. But that isn't an easy job. You have to meet with suppliers and build relationships with these factories."

"Let's do that, then."

"These factories are in places like India, Bangladesh, Pakistan, Dubai, and Turkey."

She shrugged. "I have a passport."

I stared at her. "You can't be serious."

A smirk took control of her lips and determination shone in her eyes. "The dream, Zoya. It's all about making the dream a reality."

⟡⟡⟡⟡

I quickly changed my clothes before Idris could ask why I didn't smell of curry. I stared at my reflection and wondered how amazing it would be if Rani could find a factory that could make any fabric I wanted. *What would that mean for the business?* And at that point, would I be able to keep lying to Idris?

227

I wanted to tell him the truth and tell him to deal with it. The past two and a half years were proof I could run a business *and* be a good wife, mother, and daughter-in-law. It was exhausting running on my current cycle. It was difficult to keep up with lying to him. More than that, I didn't want to lie to him. I wanted to share my success stories. I wished I could tell him about today and how amazing it felt.

Our bedroom door opened, and an exhausted Idris walked in.

"You finished extra late today."

"Hashim messed up the food order."

"Is it all sorted now?"

His arms wrapped around my waist. Instead of answering me, his lips met mine and kissed them gently. He tucked my hair behind my ear. "I'd like you to pack a bag."

"Where am I going?"

"*We* are taking a short holiday to Bali."

"And where are we leaving our children?"

"There's enough people here to take care of them. But this one," he rubbed my belly, "Will have to come with us."

Worry filled me because I had never left the boys longer than a few hours. "I don't want to leave the boys."

"It's only five nights."

"Without either their mum or dad."

"They're seven and five. Ammi is here. Plus, Bilal said he'll keep them entertained."

"It's too risky to fly this early into pregnancy."

"I checked with a doctor before I booked the tickets." He kissed my neck and sighed. "Come on, Zoya. I'm really trying here."

I couldn't afford to lose the little time I had to deliver on my orders. But his desperation pulled at my heartstrings. He held onto me tightly as he begged me to give him a chance.

So I nodded and told myself I would come clean and tell him about my business before we returned from our holiday.

CHAPTER TWENTY-SIX

SOMETHING WAS DRIPPING ON my cheeks and stealing my slumber. I grumbled and hid under the blanket. "Leave me alone," I moaned.

Idris laughed and stripped the blanket off me. "You've wasted our first afternoon here sleeping. Get up. Let's grab a late lunch and walk down the beach."

I eyed him with suspicion. "Who are you? And where is my husband?"

His eyes softened. "Your husband has explored this resort on his own and had a swim while you've been napping our holiday away."

I sat up and rubbed my eyes. "This morning sickness is killing me. While you were in the sun, I was hung over the toilet bowl."

He grimaced. "Take a shower. You'll feel better."

With a groan, I lugged myself out of the bed and walked over to the wide windows. Below us, the resort was bustling with people enjoying the sun we would never find in London.

"Did you check in with the boys?" I asked as I unzipped my suitcase.

"They're fine. Stop worrying."

"I'm a mother. It's my job to worry."

"Well, I need my wife here," he retaliated. His features softened as he took in my alarmed expression. He let out a deep breath. "Can you stop being everything else and just be my wife? For the next few days, I don't want to share you with the world."

My lips barely curled into a smile as I nodded. "It felt good to lie in. I can't remember the last time I slept past seven or wasn't woken up by someone yelling for me."

He wasn't listening to me. He held up the underwear I tossed onto the bed. His irises darkened to a forest green at the lacy material. "What is this?"

Trying to hide my laugh, I bit down on my lower lip. "Are you really asking me that?"

"You've never worn anything so..." He swallowed hard. "Where did you get it?"

"Rani bought me a gift card once as a joke and it was going to expire." My cheeks burned bright in embarrassment. It was ridiculous that I felt so shy considering how many years we'd been married. But I'd never needed to wear fancy underwear to seduce him.

"And you're going to wear this..." He looked at it again. "All day?"

I couldn't stop the giggle. "I plan to wear clothes on top of it. But, yes." With my toiletries in tow, I sauntered to the bathroom with Idris on my heels. The warm water unraveled the knots in my body. "Where did you want to eat? Hotel or somewhere else?" I looked at him when he never answered.

Idris was too busy eyeing my body. His eyes raked up and down my naked form. Only when I cleared my throat did he snap out of his daze. "Whatever you want."

Wanting to get him into a good mood before I broke the news about my business, I smirked. "Want to join me?"

His eyebrows shot up. "Really?"

"I could do with some help to scrub my back."

$$\mathcal{R}\mathcal{R}\mathcal{R}\mathcal{R}$$

After spending the morning emptying my stomach's contents, I gorged on everything the buffet offered. Idris barely touched his food but was amused by how much I consumed. My stomach was bloated and made me look at least five months pregnant.

I covered my mouth. "I think I'm going to barf."

"You ate four slices of chocolate cake," he remarked as he led us back to our room.

"That's your baby's fault. We're going the wrong way, by the way."

Idris carried on walking ahead. "I upgraded our room."

"When? Why?"

He swiped the key card and held the door open for me. "I wanted a private pool."

This room was more of an apartment. The small living room housed a corner sofa and a large flat-screen TV. The smaller balcony looked over the resort. But the one attached to our bedroom was secluded. Our bags had been brought up and placed in the bedroom. Ready to drop into a food coma, the extra large bed looked too enticing.

I jumped into the middle of it. "I'm about to sleep like a queen."

"You can sleep after we check out the pool."

"No pool use for the pregnant lady. Why don't you relax while I nap?"

"You can sit on the edge and keep me company."

With a pout, I moaned. "I would rather sleep."

"And I want to appreciate the view."

"What view? You're going to be staring at nothing."

He stood in front of me and stared down at me. His jaw clenched tight. "Take your clothes off, Zoya." The huskiness in his soft yet firm command made my core tighten. "I couldn't fucking eat knowing what you had on underneath."

"We *just* had sex like an hour ago," I laughed.

"I said nothing about sex. I want to look at you."

I had lost count of how many times I undressed for Idris. But that moment felt different. His attention made me feel desired, like never before. His eyes darted around my body, as if unsure where to look.

I ditched my dress on the floor and leaned back on my elbows. "Happy?"

Taking a few steps back, he crossed his arms over his chest. He hummed in approval. "Legs a little wider," he instructed. He tutted. "Don't look away from me." With my gaze on him, he clamped down on his bottom lip. "Now that's an exquisite view."

Could he see how fast my heart was beating? My throat ran dry and I couldn't look away from his face. Idris had always been handsome, but he had aged with grace. His sharp features were perfectly balanced and came together to make something divine to look at.

"What is your obsession with me looking at you? Whenever we're intimate—"

He was fighting his smile. "Intimate?"

"You know what I mean."

His soft laugh filled the room. "Are you too shy to say the word sex to your husband?"

My hands covered my face in embarrassment. "Forget it."

"Look at me, Zoya," he ordered quietly. Once my gaze was back on him, he said. "When we are sharing those private moments, I want to know it is me you're thinking about. I don't want there to be any chance of you imagining anyone else."

Guilt ate at me because I knew where that insecurity came from. "I wouldn't ever think about anyone else. Not during sex or any other time."

He hummed under his breath. The thick emotion in his voice filled the room and made it impossible to breathe. "I don't exist in your life; I know that. But there are moments when your eyes look at me and it's like you can see me. And when that happens..." His jaw clenched. "I want you so bad."

"What do you want, Idris?"

He stalked towards me with a look of hunger in him. Unlike himself, his fingers felt like feathers as they skimmed over my skin. "The things you do to me without even trying." He sounded angry at himself. "You live in my brain all the time."

I hooked my fingers into the waistband of his shorts. "I think I live somewhere else," I teased.

Idris grabbed my hands and pinned them above my head. "I'm trying really hard to not have my way with you right now. So, I wouldn't touch me there."

My head fell back as a laugh ripped out of me. "Good to know I have some control over you."

He released my hands to push my hair away from my face. "I love it when you laugh. Especially when it's with me." He kissed my shoulder. "Come. Let's make use of the pool."

I followed behind him and took a seat on the edge. The water rippled around my legs as I dipped them in. Tilting my head up, I enjoyed the feeling of the sun glowing on my skin. "I could get used to this."

"If that's what you want, I'll buy a villa here tomorrow."

My brow arched. "How much money do you have?"

His laugh was one of arrogance. "A lot."

"How did you end up so rich?"

"I took my ancestral wealth and started building a fortune. I invested in a business and kept doing that until I had enough to build another. Then I did the same until I started another. And another. And another."

"And here's me thinking you were a self-made man," I joked.

He waded through the water until he was standing between my legs. "I was only fifteen when I begged my father for money. He said I was too young to understand the dynamics of business. I promised to triple his investment within a year if he gave it to me."

"What did you do?"

"I went to Pakistan during the summer holidays and opened a launderette smack bang in the middle of Islamabad. I knew the rich would believe using such an establishment gave them a higher status. And it worked. I returned my father's investment after only four months."

My fingers threaded through his damp hair. "Can I tell you why I hate that story?"

"Why?"

"Because if it was your sisters who had asked for the money, they never would have got it. Not even if they had a one hundred percent guarantee of a return on investment. They would have failed at the first hurdle simply because they were women."

"Women don't work. That has been the tradition since mankind has existed."

"Traditions can change, Idris. What's the worst that would happen if a woman was to earn a living?"

His hands rested on my thighs. "Who would maintain the house? Who would raise the next generation?"

"Who said she can't do both?" *What if I was already doing both? Come on. Tell him, Zoya.* "I'm not asking to go out there and work a corporate job. But what if I worked while not having to give up my duties as a wife and mother?"

The sweet Idris I had the pleasure of having all day vanished in an instant. "Do I not earn enough for you?"

"That's not what I meant."

"What did you mean, then?" he snapped. "I don't need my wife to help me pay the bills. It is my duty to take care of you. It is my duty to provide for my children. I have done that, no? I don't need my wife to help me be a man."

Scared this was about to explode into something uncontrollable, I held his face. "Of course you have. That is something I have never worried about."

"Then what is it? Why are you so desperate to go out into the real world and leave me?"

236

"Leave you?" My arms dropped as eyebrows furrowed. "Why is it so hard for you to accept that a woman can be more than a wife and mother?"

"What do you want to be? A man? Because that is what you are asking for."

"I'm asking you to give me some freedom to find my feet in this world. I want to experience a life outside of the home."

"What will that give you that I can't? I have told you time and time again that I will give you anything you ask for."

"Except this," I pointed out. *The one thing that I really want.*

"Look at the life I have built. I didn't do this for myself. I did this knowing one day I would have a family to take care of. With my wealth, our sons would never have to work, but I will force them to graft. Because *that* is what a real man does. He takes care of his family. He doesn't send his wife out into the world to do that job for him. He protects her modesty and status as a woman by keeping her within the home where he knows nobody can touch her."

That moment solidified my decision: I'd never tell him. As I looked down at the fire in his eyes, I understood Idris could never celebrate my wins with me. Because he would never accept them. He would view my success as a betrayal to him and our marriage. It would be the same as castrating him and laughing about it with the world.

The hope and courage I held in my chest deflated like a balloon. I knew there would come a day when I would have to choose between him and the business. And that realisation made my heart clench tight because I could no longer imagine a life without Idris.

My head bowed and my voice was barely above a whisper. "I'm sorry. I won't bring it up again."

"You have spent so much time building a dream, you haven't understood the reality and force of love. But if you woke up, you'd see how long it's been waiting for you."

"It is you that has misunderstood, Idris," I argued. "There is no force in love. If you love something, you don't stifle it. You let it free into the world, trusting it will come back home to you. But most importantly, you don't hurt the ones you love."

CHAPTER TWENTY-SEVEN

"Shit. Shit. Shit."

There weren't enough people in the small venue for me to hide from the familiar faces. No matter what excuse I tried to ply my mother with, I was forced to attend Zain's engagement party. I didn't understand why money was being wasted on this, considering his wedding was only one month away.

"What's wrong with you?" Maliha asked.

I wiped the nervous look off my face as Idris made his way over to me. Looking back in their direction, I judged the distance and hoped I could lead him away before they spotted me. But I was too late.

"Hey!" Amir waved at me from across the hall. Next to him, Naima was grinning at me.

"Who is that?" Idris asked in a low tone.

Naima hugged me before I could reply. "What are you doing here?"

"It's my brother's engagement party. How about you guys?" But I already knew the answer; and I wished I let my mum show me the pictures from the day they went to visit Ilham and her family. Had I done, I could have easily explained away how I knew them to Idris.

"What a coincidence! My sister is the bride!"

"This is my husband," I blurted out.

He shook Amir's hand. Then he was staring down at me with a deadly expression. "Do you want to introduce them?"

"This is Ilham's brother and sister-in-law."

"And how do you know them?"

Naima opened her mouth, but I jumped in. "I met Naima at the park." It was the first lie I could think of and realised how quickly it could fall apart.

She looked at me with confusion, but the panic written all over me made her play along. "I tripped, and she was kind enough to check on me."

Amir forced a chuckle out. "She's very clumsy."

I struggled to swallow the lump in my throat because I knew Idris didn't believe us. It's why he didn't interrogate us any further. He barely concealed his anger and stormed off.

"I'm sorry," I whispered to them and walked away.

The bubble we found ourselves in the past ten days had truly burst. The rest of our holiday passed in a blur. We explored the country, bought gifts for the family and ate until we couldn't. It was an enjoyable break, but I missed my boys and the best part was getting home and squeezing them until they started moaning to let them go.

Ilham was beautiful and a perfect fit for Zain. They kept stealing glances at one another, and when they locked gazes, they both wore timid smiles. My father was parading the venue like he was the most important person to exist. He exaggerated and boasted about himself to anyone who offered an ear.

"Who deserved that eye roll?" Amir asked, as he came to stand beside me.

"You weren't meant to see that."

"Why are you standing in the back, all on your own?"

I leaned against the wall and sighed. "I'm tired of making small talk with people I don't know. No offence."

"None taken. I've had to stand there and listen to Pakistan politics with all the men from both sides. The amount of times I've heard your dad say that the youth have ruined the country." He made a face that looked like he'd been through war and back.

Laughter burst out of me. "I've been hearing that since I came out of the womb. Did he tell you how he could guarantee a win in cricket?"

"Of course! That came right after my dad said he could win the world tournament with his eyes closed."

The laughter subsided, and I sighed. "I'm sorry for making you and Naima lie before. My husband is ... difficult."

"Can I ask why your work is a secret from him?"

I didn't want to delve into my problems with a stranger who was about to become Zain's brother-in-law. "As a man, I don't expect you to understand."

"Try me."

I shifted slightly, so I was looking at him. "My husband believes that a woman's place is the home where she cooks, cleans and takes care of her children. She cannot possibly be more than that. And if she tries to be, there is something fundamentally wrong with her."

Amir covered his mouth to contain the humour that wanted to slip out. "That's the biggest bag of bullshit, if I've ever heard it."

I smiled. "That makes you a rare jewel in this culture, and your wife a lucky woman."

"I don't know if she would agree with you. She's the one out there working to keep a roof over our heads."

My jaw dropped. "What?"

"We both worked. I was manager level in a corporate job, but my wife has a PhD in clinical psychology. She was making *way* more money than me. So, when we had children and decided we wanted one parent at home, it made sense for her to go back to work. Now that all three are in school, I work part-time hours, but she's the one taking care of us."

I couldn't believe it. I knew traditional roles were breaking outside of our culture, but this was the first I had heard of a South Asian couple breaking the norms. "And you're okay with that? It doesn't make you feel..."

"Emasculated?" he finished when I struggled to find the right word. "It took some adjusting to, but I had to put my pride aside and do what was best for my family. Naima struggled during her maternity leave. She was itching to get back to work. My pride and ego were the sacrifice I made for her happiness. And if she ever decides she wants to switch roles, we'll do that."

Something warm spread through me at the love and devotion in his tone and eyes. Standing before me was a man who truly loved his wife and family. "She is incredibly lucky to have you. Most people only dream of experiencing a love like that."

"I never would have known how great my wife is at her job if she didn't tell me all the good she achieved in a day. How can you expect him to believe in your dream if he doesn't know it exists?"

The bedroom door slammed shut and Idris pinned me against it before I could blink. "Are you fucking him?"

"What are you talking about?"

"How stupid do you think I am? I saw that fucking grin on his face when he walked in and saw you. And *you*," he spat, "You were *friendly* with him."

"And his *wife*. If I was having an affair with him, do you really think I would be friends with her, too?"

He released me and stepped back. "Well, it wasn't his wife you were talking to for ages, was it?"

"We were talking about his marriage!"

"I don't care! Why should I have to stand there and watch my wife laughing with another man?"

"It's not my fault you never bring me any happiness!" I regretted my words of anger as soon as they were out there. I shook my head. "I never meant that."

He let out a dry chuckle. "What did you mean, Zoya?"

Walking past him, I yanked all the black clips securing my bun out. I tugged at my roots, hoping it would release the tension in my scalp. "Can we please not do this?"

"If I see you crying, I am going to set this house on fucking fire."

I turned on my heels and stared him down. "I did nothing wrong, Idris! I was not flirting with him. I was not touching him. It was a conversation! I'm allowed to have those with other people."

"Not with another man!" he screamed. "Not when your husband is standing there watching you give your attention to him."

"You are being ridiculous! You can't expect me to never speak to anyone of the opposite sex."

"You weren't just talking. It was flirting."

"No, it wasn't!"

"He saw you standing there all alone and walked over to you. And you let him think it was okay for him to speak to *my* wife. Why should I tolerate such behaviour? I do not care for a man to leer at my wife. There is no shame in a man wanting to protect his wife's honour."

"What honour of mine have you maintained? How many times have you accused me of adultery? You didn't even let me explain anything before you pinned me against a wall and accused me of it again! How can anyone hold me in such regard when the man I share my bed with views me with such little respect?"

"What respect can I give to a woman who parades herself in front of any man that pays her attention? If you had any respect for me, you never would have stood alone with him and shared an intimate moment."

"It was a fucking conversation!" I screamed. "Just because you don't know how to have one of those, that isn't my problem! Not every man is desperate to stick it somewhere warm."

His eyes narrowed to slits as he stared at me in repulsion. And then he hit me where he knew it would hurt. "If you had more to offer, perhaps that isn't all I would need you for."

With just one line, he stole the little self-esteem I had. Idris stripped me down to my bones and ground them to dust with his cruel tongue. My mind was forming words just as wicked, but my heart had stopped.

I stared at him, unable to say anything back. And then I turned around and resumed removing my makeup.

Idris stood behind me like a statue. "How do you know him, Zoya?"

There was nothing I could say that would satiate him. With his temper levels already high, I was scared what the truth would do to me. Grabbing my clothes, I took the coward's option out. "If, after all these years and everything I have given up, you can't trust me, then there is nothing I can do."

"Where are you going?" he asked when I reached for the door handle.

"I think it's best for everyone if I slept with the boys tonight."

His heavy footsteps aligned with my beating heart. "You're not going anywhere." His arms trapped me on either side as he pushed the door closed.

"I'm pregnant," I reminded him. "The baby won't survive what we both know is coming."

"Tell me how you know him."

"Let me out."

"My wife doesn't sleep in another bed. A husband doesn't sleep without his wife."

"Yet the same husband just accused me of sleeping with another man. I can't keep forgiving you for the same thing. I would understand if I had taken something from you, but I haven't. Yet somehow I keep giving you a piece of me every time I'm forced to forgive you for something you're not even sorry for. It's killing me."

"And it kills me every time you give a part of yourself to someone else. Why can't I have the Zoya that he got? Why do I get the angry one who hates the world?"

If my heart wasn't breaking, I would have laughed at the irony of him asking that. After the way he treated me, what did he expect?

"Perhaps if you let me step out of *your* world, you would see the Zoya that lives freely."

"You're not sleeping in another room."

His voice's finality made me sag against the door; I sighed. "Fine." I slipped out from under his arms and changed my clothes. Feeling exhausted, I curled up on the armchair and stared out of the window. The moon and stars were fighting to be seen through the clouds that concealed their beauty.

"What are you doing?" He stood in front of me. "When I ask you a question, I expect an answer."

Without looking at him, I said, "I'm sleeping in this room."

"I meant the bed."

"I can't. Not tonight."

"Get into the bed, Zoya."

I hugged my legs to my chest. My cheek rested on the tops of my knees as I tuned out of reality. That night hurt the most because it proved the new Idris was only a facade for the one I met. It didn't matter how much I gave, it wouldn't be enough to earn my freedom. My tears slowly soaked through my trousers.

"A tantrum won't permit what you did tonight." He pulled the covers down, climbed into bed and turned the light off.

The only thing breaking the silence was the sniffles I couldn't hold back. Even in the darkness, I felt his gaze on me from across the room. I don't know how much time passed before he spoke again.

"You can't spend the entire night like that."

The part that believed in the new Idris fell for his concerned tone. But the smarter Zoya knew what would happen if I got into that bed, and she had a baby to protect. Needing something to mute my mind,

I closed my eyes and counted to one hundred. I did that nearly five times before he made me lose my place.

"Don't make me pick you up and carry you to our bed."

I started counting again. This time I made it to three hundred and seventy-six.

"What will you get by behaving like this? You can't avoid me forever. We live together."

I wasn't living. I was never given the chance to live.

I counted to two hundred and thirty-nine.

"You're going to hurt yourself."

I've only ever been hurt. I've never been worthy of love.

I counted to one hundred and forty-four.

"I won't touch you. Just come to bed."

I can't do this anymore.

"Do you want a divorce?"

He switched on the lamp and sat up. "What did you say?"

"You could be happy and free of me."

"Don't *ever* suggest that to me again."

"All I have done is disappoint you. Even when I've tried to get it right, I've failed you. I couldn't even carry your baby to term. He died before I gave him a chance. Maybe he was better off because I can't even be a decent mother to your children."

"Stop talking like that."

I could hear my father's angry yells from that night as I echoed his words. "I'm a failure."

"I don't want a divorce," he grit out.

"How about a second wife?"

"*Stop it.*"

"Maybe she can make you happy. She won't be shameless and dishonourable. She won't be used or filthy. Your mum won't have to complain about her being lazy. She won't kill your baby. She'll be everything you want."

"Why are you talking like this?"

My eyes closed as a cry broke out. "Because I don't know what else I can do. We're just so *unhappy* and I can't fix it. Every time I think we're better, you remind me how stupid and useless I am."

"I never said that."

"I'll release you from your duties towards me."

"Stop it," he snapped.

"You can live a happy life with her."

"Shut your mouth, Zoya! Stop talking like that and get back into our bed."

"It will be like I don't exist." My broken voice hung in the air.

Idris stared at me until his plea broke the silence. "I don't want a second wife."

"Then kill me. To be a woman in this culture is like serving a life sentence on death row. I've been punished enough and I can't take it anymore, so just kill me."

CHAPTER TWENTY-EIGHT

FARRAH'S WEDDING RING BLINDED me when it caught the light. She grinned at me. "Do you have any of your old maternity clothes? I've tried to shop around and everything is so frumpy, but I remember you wore nice outfits later into your pregnancies."

It took a second for my brain to catch up and when it did; I was out of my seat with a loud squeal. I squeezed her tight as happiness overwhelmed me. "Congratulations! How far along are you?"

"Only ten weeks, and I know they say to keep it a secret until the first scan and whatever, but it's *you* and I couldn't keep it in for a second longer."

"This is so exciting! How are you feeling?"

"I've had it pretty easy; a little nauseous, but otherwise I feel completely normal. Although my boobs are already hurting. Is that normal?"

"Wait until you have a tiny human sucking your nipples raw."

"It's like the skin around my belly is already stretching. I think it's psychosomatic, but I feel ugly in my normal clothes."

I pursed my lips, unsure if I should share the news of my pregnancy. Like Farrah, I was under the twelve-week mark, but I hadn't told anyone last time and something still went wrong. And there was the fact that she might already know as aunty Jahan found out two weeks ago and may have slipped the news to her daughter.

"I would give you my maternity clothes, but I'm afraid I'm going to need them at the same time as you."

The joyous shock on her face immediately ruled out my earlier suspicions. She engulfed me tight. "This is so crazy! How far along are you?"

"Eight weeks, so let's keep it very quiet for now."

"I can't believe we're pregnant at the same time! Did you ever think that would happen?"

"Absolutely not! I'm going to be thirty-two when I give birth." I looked up when Idris entered the dining room. "Your tea is ready. Let me get it for you."

Idris took a seat at the table and was forced into conversation with Farrah. His side of the conversation was half-hearted, and he didn't hide how uninterested he was. I was expecting him to take his tea and disappear into another corner of the house, but he remained in the seat next to mine.

"I hope our babies are best friends," she said in a dreamy state. "What do you think you're having?"

My hands found themselves on my stomach. "A boy. What about you?"

"I've been reading all these wives' tales, but I keep getting mixed answered. Do you have the same symptoms as when you were expecting with the boys?"

"Everyone thought Nadim was going to be a girl because of how different that pregnancy was compared to my first. I don't think you ever really know unless you find out."

"What are you hoping for? Probably a girl after two boys."

Idris' heavy stare burned through me. He probably wanted another son because what use was a daughter to him? A daughter couldn't possibly mount up to a son regardless if she was smarter and more adept than her brothers. To Idris, like my father, a daughter was only borrowed property. She was a burden he would have to go through the trouble of finding someone to unload her onto.

"A boy," I answered. "This culture is unkind to women. I couldn't bear the guilt of bringing a life into this world only for it to be trapped within a dreamless cage built upon unrealistic expectations and un-changing tradition."

He knew I was referring to our argument from three weeks ago. I never moved from the chair that night. Sleep never came to meet me. I don't think Idris slept either, but he didn't speak to me after that. He turned the light off and stared up at the ceiling.

The next morning, I made breakfast for everyone before they could wake up. They all ate together while I cleaned the mess I made. It was only Amal who called me to join them. I told her I wasn't hungry. Nobody thanked me.

My mother-in-law asked why I hadn't prepared the vegetables to cook for lunch. Idris never went to work that day, which meant the cooking had to be perfect and excessive. I cooked alone. Amal helped me clean up afterwards. Anisa was nowhere to be seen. My moth-er-in-law scolded me for not scrubbing the cooker clean properly. They all ate together while I cleaned the house. It was only my father-in-law who called me to join them. I told him I wasn't hungry. Nobody thanked me.

Hamza was working a night shift and wanted tea, but Anisa was giving her children a bath. Bilal was craving *pakoras,* so I made a fresh batch while the tea brewed. I neatly laid the table and left them to enjoy it. It was only Karim who reminded me I loved pakoras and asked me to join them. I told him I wasn't hungry. Nobody thanked me.

There wasn't enough roti for dinner time. My mother-in-law had shoulder pain. Amal had popped out with her husband. Anisa didn't know how to make them. I watched in a daze as the perfect circles puffed up as I cooked them. They spoke about their day as they ate around the table like a family while I cleaned the kitchen one last time for the day. No one remembered to call me to join them. But that's okay, because I wasn't hungry. Nobody thanked me.

I cleared the table. I washed the dishes and put them away. I kissed my children goodnight. I showered. Idris was relieved when he saw me in our bed. I undressed and had sex with my husband. And then I did it all again, on repeat.

"Why were you dry heaving all morning?" my mother-in-law asked on day seven.

"You haven't been eating proper meals the past few days," Amal said.

Idris looked at me.

I didn't look at him.

"I did eat." It wasn't a lie. I snacked on enough nuts and fruit to keep me going.

"What have you eaten?" she asked. *"I can't remember the last time you sat with us to eat."*

"You look ill," my mother-in-law added.

"I'm fine."

Idris hadn't been to work all week. He'd been present at every mealtime. Yet that day was the first time he remembered to call me to join them. I told him I wasn't hungry.

"You didn't eat breakfast."

"I did."

"Two bites of an apple don't count. Get yourself a plate before I lose my temper."

"Those curries trigger my sickness," I lied when he refused to move.

"I don't care. Force it down."

"I'll eat later." I don't know if he believed me, but he let me go.

I thought he went to work when he disappeared after lunch. He returned an hour later with groceries because he wanted specific dishes for dinner. I cooked on my own as Shazia was looking after one-year-old Uwais while Hamza and Anisa ran errands. I cleaned everything away, set the table, and called everyone for dinner.

"Where are you going?" Idris asked before I could escape upstairs.

"I need to fold the laundry."

"Come and eat first."

"I'm not hungry."

"Zoya," he warned.

"Idris, where are you?" Shazia called.

"Your food is getting cold. Go and eat," I said, before walking away.

I folded the laundry while they ate. Once they were finished, I washed their plates and put everything in its place. I kissed my kids goodnight. I showered and waited to fulfil my nightly wife duties. I began to undress when he entered the room.

"Keep your clothes on," he said. He sat on my side of the bed and tried to hand me a plate of food. *"I know these are your favourite dishes. Eat it."*

"I'm not hungry."

"It's been a week, Zoya. You need to eat."

"A corpse doesn't need food." I removed my top. *"Can you be quick tonight? I need to be up early tomorrow. Aunty Jahan is coming for lunch."*

Putting the plate down, he grabbed my hands. *"I'm not having sex with you tonight."*

"Did I do something wrong?"

"Are you trying to punish me? Is that why you're starving yourself?"

"I did eat."

"That's not proper food." He held the plate up. *"Please, just eat something."*

"I'm not hungry."

I wasn't anything anymore. I was a broken, empty vessel.

"You're pregnant," he whispered.

I climbed under the sheets and turned my back to him. *"I want to die."*

The next day Aunty Jahan gasped at my ghostly state. She refused to take a bite of her food unless I ate too. But I couldn't stomach anything. Everyone in the house knew why I had become a zombie. My mother-in-law explained it away to her sister by telling her I was pregnant. That only led to a gentle lecture from our guest and her feeding me as a mother does to her child. Before she left, she scolded Idris and reminded him to look after me.

But nothing really changed except Idris watched over me during mealtimes and asked his mother to do the same when he was at work. I only snapped out of my trance when Rani asked for updates on orders and my sisters dropped off the fabrics for Zain's wedding.

Idris stood. "Zoya, come with me."

Farrah gave me an apprehensive smile before I followed him up the stairs. I closed the door behind me.

"That's not fair."

I didn't want to fight with him. "Okay. I'm sorry."

"You're killing me."

I bowed my head. "Okay. I'm sorry."

"Look at me, Zoya." His gaze held me hostage. "When is this going to stop? I can't take it anymore."

"Okay. I'm sorry."

"Stop it! Stop saying you're sorry!"

"What would you like me to say?"

He stepped back. "What?"

"What would you like me to do?"

"I want you to wake up! I want my Zoya back." He sounded on the verge of tears.

"This is your Zoya. This is the wife you wanted. Sit. Stand. Serve. Speak. Silence. That's what you said, right? I'm finally awake, Idris. I'm not dreaming anymore."

He held my face. "How could you think I wouldn't give my daughter the world? How could you not want a little version of you?"

I was completely drained of tears. When I spoke, it was a matter of fact. "Why would I want that? I know how undeserving of love I am and I could never want that for anyone, let alone my own child."

"*I* would love her."

"That's my biggest nightmare, because I've seen what a father's love is. I've experienced a father's protection in this culture. She would just be a toy for this culture to use, blame and break."

"I would *never* put my hands on her."

"You once made that promise to me, too."

"You know I haven't..." He struggled to find the words and eventually settled on, "I haven't done that to you in years. Even when I've been angry, I haven't done *that*."

"It's funny how men always assume the only way to break something is to physically smash it to pieces. Men have been taught they can buy a toy and toss it aside when it's not exactly what they want. Men have never been taught to look after something with gentle care. Men have been told once money has exchanged hands, they can do as they please. Men have been taught it's okay to break their toys because there is always a shiny new one out there. It's why you're all so damn good at it."

CHAPTER TWENTY-NINE

THE MIDWIFE WAS TOO chirpy for my sombre mood as she spoke with too much energy. "What are you hoping for?"

"Boy."

"Girl," Idris said simultaneously. It was pure bullshit. He was just trying to prove a point.

"After two boys, I'm sure you want a daddy's girl," she said to Idris. "Well, we can't find out the sex today, but we can make sure the little one is healthy and safe inside mummy." Her childish tone was irritating me. Thankfully, she squirted the gel and brought up the scan of our baby.

I breathed a sigh of relief when a heartbeat came out of the speakers. "Is he okay?"

"Baby is a little smaller than expected, but nothing to worry about. Have you been experiencing morning sickness?"

"It's been terrible."

"As you come into your second trimester, your appetite should return. Try to eat a balanced diet. I know how difficult the cravings can get." Her shrill laugh pounded in my head. Luckily, I only had to endure a few more minutes of her. "If you wait outside, we'll get you a copy of the scan."

We thanked her and took our leave. Bursting for a wee, I left Idris and went to empty my bladder. I took my time getting back to him because I didn't want to hear a lecture about my lack of eating. But I forgot we had the drive back to his home.

"I have had enough," he started before we were out of the car park. "This nonsense you've started with food is going to stop today."

I leaned my head against the window and stared at the blurring streets. "Okay," I whispered.

"I'm being serious! You are going to eat three proper meals every single day. You heard what she said. Do you want something to happen again? Is that why you're doing this?"

"I have been eating."

"Only when I'm sitting in front of you. Mum has told me you barely eat while I'm at work." He huffed. "Is that what you need? Do I need to be home for every meal to watch over you?"

Why not? You control every other element of my life.

When he stopped at a red light, his gaze was on me. His words were coated in desperation. "Zoya, when is this going to stop? I know it was a bad argument, but it was just that; *an argument.*"

Idris couldn't possibly understand how detached I felt from the world. I felt disembodied and adrift. Nothing felt real or tangible anymore. It wasn't just an argument that night. Idris broke the last string of strength I had left and there was nothing for me to hold on to anymore.

"Can you call my mum and tell her something came up and I can't go today? She won't argue with you, but if I call, she'll make me go."

"It's the day before your brother's wedding."

I closed my eyes. "I have a headache."

"Get some rest and I'll drop you off later."

"I don't want to go."

"Why not?"

"Why do you care?"

"Because you're my wife and since that night, it's like you're not even here. You don't eat. You don't sleep. You don't even speak to your friends anymore."

I sighed as he pulled into the driveway. "Fine. I'll go."

He groaned in frustration. "Will you just talk to me?"

"I have nothing to say." Before he could say anything else, I clambered out of the car.

Bilal opened the door before I could ring the bell. I barely acknowledged him and walked into the living room. Karim and Nadim ran up to me as if I'd been gone for two weeks as opposed to two hours.

"Where did you go?" Karim asked.

"Did you buy me sweets?"

I ruffled Nadim's hair. "Sorry, baba. There weren't any sweets at the hospital."

Worry filled Karim's green eyes. "Why did you go to the hospital? Are you sick?"

"I'm not sick. Ammi just had to make sure your little brother was growing nice and safe."

Nadim jumped up in excitement. "We're getting a baby brother?"

Idris leaned against the doorframe. "It might be a baby sister."

"Is the baby inside your tummy?" Karim asked. "Adam from school said his mum had a baby in her tummy. She was really fat," he giggled.

"Yes. The baby is in my tummy and once he's big enough, we'll get to meet him."

This was all news to Nadim. His excitement had morphed into confusion and curiosity. "How are they going to get him out?"

I didn't know how to answer that without scaring him. "Er ... the doctors at the hospital will help take him out."

But that wasn't the end of his line of questions. "How did he get inside your tummy?"

I sat on the floor with Nadim on my lap facing me and Karim next to me. I wanted to avoid this conversation for as long as I could, but I knew my changing body was going to inspire more questions. "I got a special seed that grows babies."

"Where did you get it from?"

"Your Baba bought it from a special shop."

At that, Idris reminded me of his presence and laughed.

"Miss Brown said babies come when a mum and dad love each other," Karim said with a proud look. "But how come the mum always grows the baby?"

Ignoring the first part, I explained, "Because boys can't grow babies. Only girls can do that."

"Did I grow in your tummy too?"

I pinched Nadim's cheeks. "You both grew in my tummy."

They shared a look of pride and then Nadim lifted my top and yelled, "Hello! I'm your big brother!"

I squeezed him tight with a laugh. "You're going to be the best big brother!"

"And me!" Karim pouted.

I pulled him into the hug. "You're already the best big brother to Nadim."

"You're the *bestest* mum in the whole world," Nadim muffled against my chest.

My cheek rested on the top of his head, and I held my tears back. "Is that right?"

"We love you!" Karim shouted.

I held both of their faces and an ounce of life came back into me. "I love you two more than anything in the world."

Nadim's small hands wiped my tears. "Why are you sad, Ammi?"

"Don't cry," Karim added. "We were really good when you went to the hospital. We didn't do no jumping or fighting."

His brother eagerly nodded his head. "Can we have chocolate for being good?"

I laughed despite my tears. "Only *one*."

"I'll get it for them. Why don't you lie down?" Idris suggested.

But my mother-in-law called for me in the kitchen. "Coming!"

He grabbed my arm and gently pulled me towards him so there was no space between us. "I've missed your smile," he whispered.

"Please let go."

His thumb brushed over my bottom lip. "You're hurt by what I said."

"Mum's waiting."

"I was angry."

"Our children are right there."

He held onto me tighter. "You have to understand why I was angry, and then you said things to make it worse."

"Don't do this in front of them."

"I saw you talking to him and I couldn't take it, Zoya. Everything turned red, and I was blinded by rage. You wouldn't tell me how you knew him and my mind went to the worst place. It's an image I can't get out of my head, no matter how many times you give yourself to me. Every time I touch you, my mind tells me you wish it was him. You don't look at me the way you looked at him."

My watery smile didn't seem to reassure the boys. "You need to stop. You're scaring them."

"*Mine*," he pleaded. "You're *my* wife. Tell me he is nothing to you. Just promise you won't talk to him again. That's all I need to make it stop."

It was completely irrational, bordering on insanity. The look of frenzied desperation terrified me because I did nothing wrong. Ignoring Amir would be impossible; he'd essentially become family in a day. I couldn't fathom how he could obsess over something so trivial as a platonic conversation with another man.

But I shrugged. "Okay. I won't talk to him."

҉ ҉ ҉ ҉

The wedding celebrations were ongoing downstairs. Music was blaring over the never-ending chatter of my extended family. The groom himself was nowhere to be seen, but everyone else made the final preparations to bring my parent's only daughter-in-law home. Her bedroom had been decorated with silk and pretty twinkly lights. The banisters were adorned in flower garlands, and every corner of the house was bursting with colour.

I sat in my childhood bedroom, hemming the sleeves of Asma's outfit. I wasn't in the mood to join the festivities. All I wanted was to fall into a dreamless sleep. My solitude was broken when the door opened.

"Karim said he's getting a baby brother."

My dad was the last person I wanted to speak to. I suddenly wished I was downstairs so I could have avoided being alone with him. My mum was overjoyed when I told her I was expecting again and seconds later, she announced it to the house full of people.

He perched on the bed's edge. When he spoke, it was to the wall instead of me. "Why don't you stay tonight? Asma and Maliha are staying. Nadim and Karim will have fun with their cousins."

Spending a night in this house with them and the nine children my sisters shared between them sounded like hell. Then there was the fact that Idris would rather die than let us spend a night without him.

"Their dad won't allow it." Wanting this conversation to be over, I tied a knot in my thread and stood up.

"You haven't even asked him."

"And I'm not going to because I don't want to argue with him over something I don't even want."

"It's been many years. How long will you continue to be angry? Look at the life you have. Look at the beautiful children you were given. That boy wouldn't have been able to give you what you have today."

"And what do I have?"

"I did not teach you to be ungrateful."

Whenever I stood before my father, I felt like a little girl again. With just one look, he could bring back the young Zoya who felt scared and trapped.

My lip quivered as anger consumed me "No. You just taught me how to be obedient. You broke my will with every slap and kick. You marred my skin with every foul, derogatory word until I was unrecognisable."

"What you were doing..." He shook his head. "It was a sin!"

"And what you did to me wasn't? Where in the religion does it say to beat your child until she can't see straight? Which God would accept a father's desperation to kill his child?"

"I was angry."

And just like that, Idris stood before me.

Their faces morphed until I couldn't tell them apart. They were his words, but Idris' voice. My eyes squeezed shut, an icy dread tightening my chest as the storm in my mind threatened to consume me. A scream was desperate to escape, hoping it would silence everything.

I was tired of being their punching bag because they were angry. I was tired of accepting that excuse because nothing could ever justify what they had done to me.

"I was standing right here when you slapped me so hard my ears starting ringing." I took a step back and grabbed my throat. "I was standing right here when you strangled me and promised to kill me." My false bravado wavered as the first cry came out of me. "I *begged* you to let go because I couldn't breathe."

Unable to face the truth, he turned the other way.

I took three steps forward. "This is where I fell when you pushed me to the ground. Do you remember how many times you kicked me?"

"It was a long time ago."

"*Nine*. Three to my leg. One to my crotch. Three to my stomach. One on my shoulder and one on my head. I tried to get away, but you were too strong and I was too broken."

His thunderous glare landed on me as he stood up. "That's enough! What father wouldn't be angry at what you were doing?"

Disappointment filled me. Even when faced with the evidence of his guilt, he couldn't put his pride aside and apologise. I didn't even want an apology he would never mean. I wanted him to acknowledge his actions and take accountability for ending my life before it could really start.

"When you think of that night, all you remember is how angry you were; an anger that faded before my wounds could heal. As time passed, you moved on and your life continued."

"So did yours."

I shook my head. "You killed me that night, just like you promised. My ghost is still trapped in this room, begging for freedom. Every time I step inside, she pleads with me to let her out. But she can't see that Zoya never crawled off the floor when you walked away. She lays motionless watching me serve out a life sentence all because you were angry. Perhaps I did sin by falling in love before marriage. But I must be punished for your sin too, because it's always a woman's duty to pay for a man's anger."

CHAPTER THIRTY

YOUSEF THANKED ME WHEN I finished laying out the fried snacks and tea at the table. "This is too much."

Sumayyah smiled at me. "Everything looks delicious. Sit down and eat with us."

Idris' heavy stare forced me onto the seat next to him. Just as he threatened, he made sure he was home for every meal. After watching me eat breakfast, he'd leave for work only to return at lunchtime to do the same. For the first time in our marriage, he was home every single day for dinner, no matter how busy the restaurant was. Our roles had reversed to *him* plating my food. Then I was bound to the table until he was satisfied I had eaten enough.

The table was painfully awkward. Sumayyah didn't know what to say in front of Idris, and I was too scared to speak to Yousef in case it triggered my husband. Had I known Yousef would tag along, I wouldn't have invited Sumayyah. But I wanted to apologise properly for what I said two weeks ago.

I announced my pregnancy to my friends and amid venting about it; I realised how insensitive I was being. Sumayyah said she didn't mind, but I saw the look on her face. There I was complaining about something that she had spent years yearning for. I felt awful and wanted to make up for it. Neither of us were expecting Idris to extend the invite to Yousef.

"I loved your outfit for Zain's wedding," Sumayyah eventually said. "Did you make it?"

"My sisters chose the material."

"You might have to make my outfit for Haniya's wedding."

"I didn't know she was getting married."

Yousef nodded his head. "A family came to see her two months ago. I think our families have agreed to move forward."

"I think she's more excited to shop for her wedding ring than anything else," Sumayyah laughed.

"You were the same," her husband reminded her with a smile.

She stretched her hand out in front of her and admired her rings. They sat snug around her finger like they were part of her. "I think women understand the weight of a wedding ring more than men do. It's not just jewelry. It's a reminder of the promise we made. It's protection from impermissible attention. It's the beacon that calls you home." She snapped out of her daze and looked at me. "Wouldn't you agree?"

I wouldn't know because I never wore my wedding ring. It was gold, tacky, and I hated it. Regardless, I didn't need a reminder of that because Idris' unescapable presence was enough.

Flashing my hand at them, I shrugged. "My wedding ring is somewhere in my mother-in-law's safe."

Sumayyah's eyes darted to Idris' hand. She was checking to see if he wore his band, which he did. "Why don't you wear yours?"

"It's ugly," I deadpanned.

Her mouth dropped at my bluntness. "It can't be that bad."

"Well, it's certainly not the radiant cut diamond I wanted." Taking a risk, I turned to Yousef. "How are you feeling? Your one and only baby sister is getting married."

"The house will definitely be quieter. It's hard to imagine her doing all this." He gestured to the spread on the table.

"She'll get the hang of it. And she's had Sumayyah to learn from."

My friend shook her head. "I'm going to send her to you for advice. Six years later and I still don't know how to do the daughter-in-law thing."

"Thirteen years later and I'm still getting it wrong. Maybe that's the unwritten rule. No matter how hard we try, it's never good enough." Despite my attempt at a light tone, tension settled between us. I smiled at Sumayyah. "Let me make a plate for you and we can leave the men to talk about men's stuff."

Idris gripped my thigh under the table. "Take food for yourself, too."

Sumayyah grabbed her cup while I carried the plates. Like me, she let out a breath once I shut the door behind us. "Since when were they such good friends?"

The first genuine laugh slipped out of me. "I have no idea. But did you know they text?"

"My husband's second wife is his phone, so I'm not surprised. When I imagined us all married and having double dates, I wasn't banking on the awkward silences."

"I don't think any of us imagined marriage to look like this." I sighed. "I'm really sorry for what I said the other day. I've just been feeling so crap with these hormones and everything."

Sumayyah locked her eyes on mine. "It's okay to feel the way you do. I never want you to feel you can't come to me when you need a shoulder to lean on. While we're on either end of the spectrum, my struggle isn't any bigger than yours."

"One of these days someone is going to take advantage of how understanding you are," I attempted to joke. "But thank you."

Her brown orbs didn't waver from my face. Her eyebrows furrowed as she studied me. "What's wrong, Zoya?"

"What do you mean?"

"I can't explain it, but it's like you're not you. You barely call or text anymore. Whatever it is, you know you can trust me. It won't leave this room."

I slumped against the sofa's backrest and exhaled. "I know there are so many women that would give anything to be in my position. To be pregnant is one of life's greatest wonderments. And I love my children. I really love them and I know I will eventually love this one too. But right now I just can't. And I feel so guilty for feeling like that. Especially after..." My voice caught in my throat.

Sumayyah's soft gaze matched her tone. "Especially after what?"

I hadn't spoken about my loss to anyone, but my heart was bursting with pain. "My miscarriage."

In an instant, her arms were around me. "I'm so sorry."

"I was heartbroken. I begged God to give my baby back. He never heard me."

"Nothing can stop a miscarriage when it happens."

"Am I broken?"

Her heartbreak was written on her face. "You are not broken," she promised.

"There must be something wrong with me because even after that, why don't I love this baby? Why am I not grateful that I was given another chance?"

She kneeled on the floor before me. She took my hands and squeezed tight. "Because this baby isn't the one you lost."

"They told me I shouldn't cry for something that wasn't even human yet. So, I silenced my sobs. They told me I should be grateful because at least I had two children. So, I stopped mourning. They told me to never mention it to anyone. So, I told people I was a mother of two."

"Every day I mourn for something I haven't ever had. So, I can't imagine how hard that must have been. Especially because you have experienced the warmth of holding a baby in your arms and understand the force of a mother's love."

Not wanting Idris to hear my cries, I tried to swallow them down; but my desperation broke free. "How do I make this thing go away? Is there some medication you can give me to put an end to it? There has to be some medical explanation to why I feel like this."

"How do you feel?"

"Why can't I love this baby? I feel so empty. I..." I closed my eyes and let my sob free. "I can't stop it. I know I should be grateful and my children need me. But I feel helpless and so stuck and nothing makes it stop. I just want to die."

"Don't say that," she tried to scold, but she broke into a silent cry. "You are too loved to die."

"You're a doctor. Give me a word, a diagnosis, a label, ... *something* to make me understand why I'm feeling like this. Tell me this is something that will go away because I can't do it anymore. I can't keep fighting something that doesn't let up."

Wiping her tears, she took a seat next to me. "Have you been eating and sleeping?"

I shook my head. "I have no appetite and I'm always tired, but I can't sleep."

"This isn't a formal diagnosis, but with everything you've told me and how you've been recently, it ticks the symptoms of antenatal depression. This isn't something you brought upon yourself and is more common than you think. So, please don't blame yourself."

"How do I make it stop?"

"There are antidepressants available, but there are risks associated with those. Talking therapy can be very helpful. But most people find lifestyle changes help. Something even as small as talking to family and friends. I can't tell you which is best for you, but I promise it will go away and I will be with you the whole time."

The devotion in her tone made me smile. "Do you ever feel you're running with no end destination? It's like I'm constantly chasing something that isn't even there. And I'm *exhausted*. I don't know how to win."

"I wish I had the answer to that," she smiled. "A woman is confined by the boxes this culture has bestowed upon her. We must be a respectful daughter, a nurturing sister, an attentive daughter-in-law, a dutiful wife, and a loving mother. We cannot be too tall or too short. Nor too skinny or too fat. We cannot be too fair or too dark. A woman must be tolerant. A woman must be subservient. A woman must be *perfect* in order to survive this culture."

Chapter Thirty-One

The small square dining table was covered in fabric samples of different textures and colours. I held each one and tested its flexibility while mentally ruling out the ones of poor quality.

"Obviously, these wouldn't be the final designs. He wanted us to get a feel of the quality for each price point."

"The cheap ones are too stiff. It would be really hard to mould them for a good fit. Plus, it would be uncomfortable to wear. No mother with a newborn would wear something that could irritate their baby's skin."

Rani hummed in agreement. "What about the mid-range?"

I picked up a sample and tried to convince myself it was good enough, but my heart was set on the pricier fabric. We had agreed to start with a small budget for this project to test the market and the high end material was definitely outside of that; even if it was the luxury I envision for the brand.

"It's got more fluidity," I eventually said lamely.

She groaned at my hesitation. "Our taste is too damn expensive. If we were to go with the more expensive one, how would that affect pricing? The larger sizes would require more investment."

I vehemently shook my head. "No. We're not going to make people pay more because they don't fit society's beauty standards. I want to be properly inclusive. No matter the shape of your body or your skin tone, you should be able to wear any design and colour."

Her eyes twinkled in the light. "I love that. A space for everyone to shine." Her hands came down on the table. "Okay. Let me enquire with a few more factories and see what they come up with."

My hands rested at the bottom of my small bump when I felt a cramp. "Orders are good to go. Did you update our bio to say we're not taking any new orders?"

"All done. Will you get all current orders completed by February?"

"I should be okay." I winced as a sharp pain struck through my stomach.

"Are you okay?"

"Cramps."

Her face drained of colour. "Let's get you to the hospital!"

I couldn't get myself to move. I wasn't sure I could survive it happening again. I wanted to stay put because then I could tell myself it's indigestion and my baby would be safe. He wouldn't be trying to leave me again.

Rani wasn't giving me the option of being ignorant. She draped my jacket over my shoulders and practically dragged me to the lift. She jabbed the button to call the lift at least ten times before it appeared. Her foot was all the way down on the pedal as she drove us to the hospital.

I couldn't get myself to do anything. My mind had shut off, trying to protect itself from the impending heartbreak. Even when I sat in the waiting area, surrounded by other expectant mothers, I hadn't caught up with what was happening. Then I was lying on the bed, legs spread, and the panic set in. I could barely answer the questions. Rani paced the room while the equipment was being prepared.

And then I released the breath I didn't realise I was holding.

Rani's laugh shook as she shed a few tears. Her hands set into a prayer pose. "Thank you. Thank you. Thank you," she muttered.

The midwife smiled. "Baby is okay."

"What was that pain? I've never had that before."

"It could be gas or constipation." She wiped the gel off my belly. "Or even ligament pain as your body grows. But I've read through your medical history; so, just to be on the safe side, we're going to monitor the baby's heartbeat for a few hours. Is that okay?"

Relief overwhelmed me and I had to force down the lodge in my throat before I could say, "Yes, please."

She directed me to a ward, instructing me to lie down. Two small transducers were placed on my abdomen, and then the sound of his heartbeat came through, steady and present.

"We'll keep you under observation for two or three hours. Press the button just behind you if you need anything." She drew the curtains closed as she left.

Rani let out a sigh. "That was the scariest forty minutes of my life. I'm so glad you're both okay."

I held my bump, making sure to not tangle the wires. My eyes closed, and I thanked God for keeping my baby safe. "You're okay," I whispered. "Please don't leave me."

She wiped my tears. "Why are you crying? Everything is okay."

Maternal guilt hit me full force. "Just the other day I was telling Sumayyah how I don't love this baby. I have hated every moment of this pregnancy. When Idris said he wanted another one, I begged him to change his mind because I didn't want to give up the business. What kind of woman does that make me? How does a mother choose money over a child?"

Rani climbed onto the bed and helped me shuffle over. She intertwined her fingers with mine and stared up at the ceiling. "You weren't choosing money. You were choosing sanity for the sake of the children you already have." She sighed. "I don't know how you do it. You are so selfless for the sake of your children. I don't ever want to feel the panic and pain I just felt. I'm too selfish to be a mother."

"It's a huge commitment and one that never lessens. It doesn't matter how old they get, they will always be your responsibility."

"That's exactly why I don't want to have children. Why is it so wrong for a woman to say she doesn't yearn for a child? People look at me like I've murdered someone. If I gave in to the pressure from Ravi and his family, who would win? They don't have to raise it. Ravi wouldn't give up his life. I would be miserable. What kind of life is that for the kid?"

I turned to face her. "You don't need to justify your choice to anyone. Ravi knew your unwavering stance on children when you met all those years ago. You never gave him false hope. He had the choice to walk away if his mind changed."

She rolled her eyes. "I don't think he even really wants a baby, but his family wants a grandchild from him, which means he now wants one. Suddenly, I'm made to feel like I tricked him or that I'm denying him something he's craved his whole life. We had a plan and a vision of what life was going to be. We *both* wanted the same thing until they steered him away. So why does it feel like *I'm* doing it all wrong now?"

"My whole life I've been told I'm doing it wrong. Nothing I do seems to be enough. And even though I know that; I still want their approval. I'm still killing myself trying to please them. I wish I was more like you."

"You are more than I could ever be. After over a decade, you're still standing. I've barely made it through half of that and I can't do it." Her broken laugh only hurt me more. "I was a fool when I would scold you for not standing up to Idris and his family when you first got married. I couldn't fathom how you could tolerate anyone treating you like that. But over the years, I've conformed to what Ravi's family wants me to be. And sometimes I catch my reflection and I don't recognise her anymore. When you get married, everyone talks about how hard it is to leave your family. But nobody warns you about the heartbreak of leaving yourself behind. They break you until you fit into their ideal of a *bou*."

Ravi's mum wasn't the chilled out mother-in-law he claimed she would be. She was the most traditional out of them all, including my own. We all knew Rani clashed with her more than they got on. But the harrowed expression on her face made me wonder how bad it was for her.

"Have you told your parents? You know they would save you in a heartbeat."

She wiped her tears. "I can't do that to them. Seeing me married was their greatest joy. If they knew how miserable I was, it would kill them."

"What about Ravi? Can't he see what it's doing to you?"

"I've come to realise it wasn't *him* I married. It was his family, and he can only be happy when they are."

"So, you sacrifice *your* happiness to make it happen."

"I sacrificed *myself* to make it happen."

❀❀❀❀

Through the panic followed by the heavy conversation, I had forgotten an important thing: *Idris*. I didn't think to message or call him until I was on my way home and by that point, my battery was dead.

"Go upstairs," he snarled as soon as he opened the door.

"Can I say hello to the boys first?"

"Upstairs. *Now*."

But the boys were bounding towards me with joy. Their arms wrapped around my legs and waist. I couldn't understand anything as they spoke over one another.

"Go and sit down," Idris commanded them.

My heart broke at their disheartened expressions as they walked away. "Did you need to shout at them?" I asked as we climbed the stairs.

"You really don't want to push my buttons today," he warned. "If you are so concerned about my children, perhaps you should have made sure you were home."

Only because he couldn't see me, I rolled my eyes. His use of *my children* told me how this conversation was going to go and warned me to prepare myself for his cruelness.

He locked the door, then faced me. "It's nearly eight o'clock. Do you know how worried I've been? Why was your phone going to voicemail? Why are you home late?"

"I'm sorry for being late. I lost track of time and when I realised how late it was getting, my phone had died."

His fingers clenched. "Where were you?"

"At the hospital. I had some cramping and went to get checked out. Everything was fine, but they wanted to monitor his heartbeat for a few hours just to tick all the boxes."

Relief only flashed in his eyes for a moment. "You went to the hospital and didn't think to call me?"

"Rani was with me."

The mention of her name made him lose control of his temper. "*She* is not the father!" he roared. "That is *my* baby! *I* had a right to know if something was wrong."

"It all happened so fast. And you were at work."

"So what? Don't you think I would have dropped everything to be there?"

I held my hands up. "You're right. I wasn't thinking straight, and I forgot. That doesn't make it okay, but all I can do right now is apologise and make sure it doesn't happen again." I waited for him to argue back, but Idris went silent.

He stared at the ground, completely immobile. "I thought you left me." It was barely above a whisper, but his statement weighed a tonne.

"How could you think I would leave Karim and Nadim behind?"

"Are they the only reason you came back?" He took my silence as an answer. "I would have torn this city apart until I found you. *That* is how much I can't live without you. Do you know ... I..." He struggled to catch his breath. "I was so scared. You can't do that to me again."

His vulnerability choked me. This wasn't an angry man. Standing before me was a man tortured by his biggest fear.

I walked until we were standing toe-to-toe. I placed my hand over his chest and could feel his racing heart. "I'm here. I came back. We're okay."

When he lifted his hand, I flinched. "I'm not going to hurt you. I just need to feel you." His fingers tucked my hair behind my ear. His thumb brushed over my parted lips. As he stared into my eyes, I felt his body relax. "You can't leave this house anymore."

It felt good to laugh with him again. "Very funny."

But Idris wasn't smiling. He held my face in desperation. "When I couldn't get hold of you, I thought death had come for me. I felt sick to my stomach. I was ready to make a deal with the devil to get you back."

He was serious, and the heaviness in his voice wrapped itself around me. The walls were closing in on me and I couldn't breathe. I was suffocating on his despair.

I stepped back. "You expect me to sit at home every single day? What if I want to go shopping or for a walk?"

"If you want to go out, I'll take you. But from now on, I'll drop the boys to school and pick them up. If your family or friends want to see you, they can come here."

"Idris, that not fair!"

"You didn't come back for me. And for that very reason, I cannot let you free."

"This is insane!"

"Then call me crazy! I don't care because I refuse to feel what I felt today." The haunted look in his eyes made it clear he wasn't going to budge unless I forced him.

"That's fine, Idris. I'll stay home and raise my children. I'll cook, clean and keep this baby safe." I stood taller. "You want to take away the little freedom I have? Okay. Then I'll take the only thing you really need me for."

"What's that?"

"My body is off limits to you in every single way. You can't kiss me. You can't touch me. You can't have sex with me. And *only* when you give me my freedom back will you get back the wife you want."

CHAPTER THIRTY-TWO

"YOU'RE CUTTING OUT," I groaned for the second time in less than a minute.

There was some loud shuffling on her side before Rani's voice came through clearly again. "Sorry. I'm near Halima's flat and the connection keeps dropping."

I tried to keep my tone neutral, but the envy came through. "Are you all meeting up?"

"Halima asked me to drop something off." She was trying to protect my feelings, but I knew it was a lie. "I was asking how you're going to get the orders to me if you can't leave the house. I would come and get them but..."

Idris hates you.

I sighed, feeling upset that they were all gathering without me. "It's not like it's my choice."

"*Honey*, play the game. Get him to give in first."

"How?"

"Seduce him!" she said, like it was obvious. "Make him so horny he won't have any choice but to break this ridiculous wager you've got going on."

I could hear Idris' heavy footsteps coming my way. "I'm not doing that. I finally have a break from him. I'll think of something else. I need to go. Talk later."

"Keep your head up. I just blew kisses through the phone, so make sure you catch them. I love you!"

"Have fun. And I love you too." I hung up and tossed my phone onto the bed.

As I watched him work on his laptop, I considered taking Rani's advice. Idris had done well to keep his hands off me. He kept to his side of the bed and only one night did I have to remind him of our new arrangement. In his defense, he wasn't trying to have sex, but even hugging me was off limits. He huffed in annoyance and shuffled away.

But I *needed* to get the orders to Rani and school drop was my only window of opportunity. So I swallowed my embarrassment and climbed off the bed.

"You didn't eat everything on your plate," he muttered without looking at me. "Go downstairs and finish your meal."

"My stomach feels like it's going to burst." I winced. *Nothing about that was sexy.*

How was I supposed to seduce him when he wasn't even looking at me? He was too invested in whatever was on his screen. Unknowing what to do, I pulled my top over my head and that finally caught his attention.

"What are you doing?"

"I need to shower." I stood in front of the mirror and eyed my stomach. As my bump grew, the skin was becoming tight again. "Is it just me or am I so much bigger this time round?"

"That's a trick question," he mused. "I'm not falling for it."

Turning around, I stopped in front of him. "I'm being serious. This doesn't look like a four-month bump."

He looked up at me through his lashes. "It looks fine."

"And then there are my boobs."

"What about them?" Idris tried to look anywhere else. But like a moth to a flame, he was eyeing them like a man starved.

"I need new bras. These are too tight." I cringed at myself. *I can't do this. Nothing was worth pimping myself out for.* Giving up on the plan, I sighed. "Do you need anything before I go?"

He smirked at me as he closed his laptop. "How about you take those trousers off for me?"

With a tut I said, "Have you forgotten about our deal?"

"You said nothing about looking, only touching. I don't need to touch *you*."

I equally loved and hated a playful Idris. That part of him made it simple to overlook his true nature. He was witty and charming. He smiled so widely his perfect teeth were on display. His laugh was a deep rumble. And his eyes were the perfect shade of green.

"You're just going to have to use your imagination," I teased back. "I'm jumping in the shower before Farrah gets here."

"Your body looks perfect, by the way," he said nonchalantly. "It always has. It's the one thing I've never needed to complain about."

"Now you're just trying to sweet talk me into giving you a strip show."

His laptop was placed next to him, and he clasped his hands in his lap. "The day our families met, I was adamant about meeting you. Shall I tell you why?"

I assumed it was because he was a control freak, but something in his expression told me I was wrong. "I'm listening."

"When word spread that I was searching for a wife, I was inundated with proposals."

"So humble," I said sarcastically, earning a chuckle from him.

"My parents were shoving marriage CVs and pictures in my face the second I returned from work. I analysed all of them, but none of them were quite to my taste."

"Such a gentleman."

He couldn't hide his playful smile. "I had just finished eating when I caught a glimpse of your picture. I couldn't look away. I didn't ask to see your CV. I didn't even ask for your name. I stood from the table and told my father to arrange a visit with you before walking away. I knew I had to meet you because I needed to see if it was possible for someone so beautiful to exist."

"And then you saw me in that oversized outfit with my hollow face and realised it isn't," I laughed.

Idris' eyes were alive as he relived the past. He shook his head as he smiled to himself. His voice was soft and dreamlike. "You couldn't imagine my surprise when I realised you were even more beautiful in real life. I'd never been swept away by a woman before. I'd never even paid attention to a single one. *Until you*. And I just knew I had to have you."

Everything about Idris in that light was genuine and gentle. I felt the waver in my heart for him. His moments of vulnerability were rare, but every one made a home in my heart.

"After all these years and two children, I'm sure your mind has changed."

"I have loved watching you grow and age into the woman you are. I am grateful and in awe of the body that gave me two children. I find peace in waking up to you. Sometimes I lay in bed and wait for you to wake up because your eyes are the perfect shade of brown in the morning. And your smile..." He shook his head. "That is a work of art I could spend a lifetime admiring. You are a timeless beauty."

Despite being half-dressed, it was the way he looked at me that made me feel naked and vulnerable in the best way. For the first time in our marriage, I stood in front of my husband, held his face, and gently kissed him. He didn't dominate the kiss or turn it into something more.

He tucked my hair behind my ear. "I thought I could survive the two weeks until our wedding, but I couldn't; so I forced our parents to agree to joint events. Those days in between were excruciatingly long because I just wanted to see your face. And even after all these years, yours is still the first I look for in a room full of people."

☙❧☙❧

"Bhaiya!" Farrah called as Idris walked past the living room. "Can you come here, please?"

"He's not going to agree," I muttered.

"Agree to what?"

She grinned. "A joint gender reveal!"

He looked less than impressed. "What's that?"

"To find out the gender of our babies." She went into a detailed explanation of how the party would be put together.

"What's the point?"

"It's a fun way to find out what you're having. Come on! We'll invite everyone and play some games and eat some food."

I laughed at his blank expression. "I told you there's no point asking him. Why don't we host one for you here? I'll think of some games."

She pouted. "We are literally twelve days apart in our pregnancies! What are the chances of this ever happening again?"

"*None,* because I'm getting myself sterilised after this baby." I ignored Idris' look of surprise at my statement. "We should get some *team boy* and *team girl* stickers for people to pick from when they come in."

"Fine," Idris said. "You can do a joint party."

Her eyes widened. "Really?" She playfully pushed me. "I told you I could convince him!"

Never one to shy away from bursting someone's bubble, he said, "It had nothing to do with you." He looked at me and then walked away when the doorbell rang. "Zoya!"

With a groan, I pulled myself off the sofa. When I recognised the familiar faces, I broke into a run and threw my arms around my friends. I let out a childish squeal. "Come in!"

"We just came to drop something off," Halima said.

I opened the door wider. "Please come in! It's only Farrah here!" Joy was making me jitter and I couldn't stop smiling. I summoned the boys when Jannah asked for them.

My mother-in-law followed suit and greeted my guests. Despite a language barrier limiting conversation, positive spirits reigned. I warned Karim to play gently with Jannah before they could scurry away.

"Let me get you guys something to drink."

Sumayyah grabbed my hand. "Please, no. We didn't come to trouble you."

Unable to stop myself, I hugged her tight. "It's no trouble at all! Please sit. I'll be back. Tea or coffee?"

Farrah laughed. "I'll come and help before you topple over with excitement."

As she helped me put together a quick spread, we compiled a list of things we would need for the party.

"I'll buy the bits and pieces we need and drop them here. My flat is already a mess with the baby furniture being delivered."

And the idea hit me. Making sure the coast was clear, I edged closer. "Idris has a new thing about me going out and I can't do school run anymore." I waited for her to understand what I meant. "So, I need a way to do the drop offs. And I was thinking, if you're going to be coming and going..."

She winked at me. "You got it."

That evening was the first time in a long time I felt alive. Farrah, despite being younger, bonded well with my friends and was reluctant to leave for dinner at her parent's house. The walls echoed our nonsensical chatter. Sumayyah held my hand and Halima's shoulder was my resting place when I was laughing so hard I needed to muffle it.

"Can we have a house tour?" Rani asked.

I had a feeling she wanted a private moment away from Shazia. They had seen the ground floor when they came for Karim's party. I only showed the boys' room and my own.

I smiled at Idris. "The girls wanted a look around."

After clashing with both Sumayyah and Rani prior, he didn't acknowledge any of my friends. He carried his laptop out of the room.

Rani shut the door with an eye roll. "Does he ever smile?"

"Believe it or not, he actually does."

"Are your sister-in-laws out? We haven't seen them since we got here," Sumayyah said.

"They're in their rooms, as always." Not wanting to dampen my mood, I sat on my bed and change the subject. "This is my room."

"This is almost the same size as my flat," Halima exaggerated.

"Changing your sheets must be such a chore," Rani said, eying the bed. "And with the way you two are at it, you must have to change them every day."

"Rani," Sumayyah groaned.

She flopped onto it. "These are definitely clean because she's closed the gates to her vagina."

Halima stifled her giggle while Sumayyah looked even more uncomfortable. "Can we talk about something else?"

But one of Rani's favourite pass times was making Sumayyah squirm with embarrassment. She winked at me. "I bet he likes it best when you're on your knees serving him. Are you a spit or swallow type of woman?"

"Do not answer that!" Sumayyah said, pointing at me. "That is not an answer or image I need in my head."

Rani wasn't done. "How has his thing not fallen off from how much he uses it?"

Nothing could have contained the roar that came out of me and Halima.

"How big is it? I bet he's packing *heat* in his pants. Just give us a rough number."

I shook my head. "Okay, that's enough. Sumayyah might burst if you push her any further."

Her devilish grin was directed at our friend. "How about Yousef? Are we talking party sausage or a meatier one that leaves you feeling *stuffed?*"

She threw a pillow at her. "Shut up."

"Ravi's got the perfect girth and length to hit the right spot ... if you know what I mean." Halima was her next victim. "I bet Nazir is feral. It's always the nice ones that know how to throw a woman around in bed."

Halima waved her hands in surrender. "Okay. Let's stop before one of us has to call Yousef and tell him his wife went into cardiac arrest."

I caught my breath and stared at my friends with gratitude. "Thank you for coming. I didn't realise how much I needed this. When Rani said she was meeting you guys, I was gutted."

"They only came so they could see this before we gave it to you." She handed me an envelope from her bag. "We're really sorry you felt like you couldn't tell us when you lost the baby."

The tears brimming in my eyes were instantaneous. "It wasn't because of you guys. I..."

"We know," Rani smiled. "It was something you felt you had to do on your own. We totally respect that, but we wanted you to know that you are never alone. Even when it feels like the world is dark, there will always be light while you exist. Because *you* are the epitome of light. You have always dreamed brighter than any of us. You were always the one that wished upon a shooting star."

Sumayyah wiped my tears. "Rani mentioned you spend a lot of time drawing when the sun goes down. So, we wanted to make sure you always had company. We know you never got the chance to name your baby. And while we wanted to commemorate his existence, we also thought you deserved a reminder of who you are and the strength we envy and admire in you."

"When you sit in that chair and dream of the life you know you deserve, look up at the sky and remember all you have achieved." Rani's cryptic words were only meant for me, and I appreciated them more than I could vocalise.

I opened the envelope and revealed the star they bought for me. My breath hitched when I read the name.

Zoya's strength.

"You guys..."

"We know it's been hard, but you've always found the strength to pull through." Halima held my hand.

"You have always survived." Sumayyah held the other one.

Rani completed the circle by taking their hands. "Now it's time to *live.*"

CHAPTER THIRTY-THREE

IDRIS TOOK HIS FOCUS off the road to glance at me. "This is breaking the rules."

"You said you would take me out when I wanted. So, *technically* no rules have been broken." I smirked at his irritation. "If your will is breaking, you know what you have to do."

"I went twenty-five years without having sex," he argued.

"Thirteen of those you didn't have the tools. And the other twelve you had no idea what you were missing out on," I laughed.

His hand was on my thigh. "Come on, Zoya. You've had your fun."

"If you're that desperate after only four weeks, you could just take care of it yourself."

He parked outside Halima's flat but locked the car doors before I could escape. His horrified expression was directed at me. "Is that what you do? You pleasure yourself instead of coming to me for that?"

"The fact that you think I have the *time* for that is hilarious. And *why* would I need to do that? How many days have we gone in our marriage where we haven't had sex?" I cut in when he opened his mouth. "My period and postpartum bleeding days don't count. Neither do the times you've been in Pakistan."

"I won't feel ashamed for wanting my wife." He squeezed my thigh tight. "I would have sex with you right now, here in this car."

Thankfully, the boys were at home with their grandparents and not in earshot of our conversation. Pushing his hand off me, I said, "I told you what the deal was. My freedom for your satisfied libido."

His jaw clenched as he avoided looking at me. "Is there no part of you that misses the intimacy?"

A scoff passed over my lips before I could stop it. "*No.* I've quite enjoyed the break."

"You don't enjoy having sex with me?"

How was this news to him?

It wasn't the *worst* thing, but I wasn't exactly jumping his bones every chance I got. Idris was as rough and selfish between the sheets as he was in every other part of our marriage. But I couldn't exactly say that to him.

"That's not what I said."

"Your tone said it."

"This is stupid. Let's go; we're already late."

"What don't you enjoy?"

"I don't even know how I'm supposed to answer that."

"Is it me? If it was another man, would you enjoy it?"

My head fell against the headrest. "How would I even know that? It's not like I have anything to compare it to." I instantly felt regret. "Not that I want to compare it," I blurted out.

His silence was choking me. Idris continued to stare at me and I felt compelled to ease his bruised male ego.

"It's not you. I've just never understood why people obsess over it. It feels alright but nothing to write home about."

"So you've never..."

I was internally dying from the awkwardness. "Can we not have this conversation right now?"

"It's a yes or no question."

"Yes, I have. Happy? Can we go now?" When he didn't budge, I groaned. "You must have known that I barely ever orgasm. The times that I did were only because I was pregnant and that feels like sex on crack. It's not a big deal because most women don't. As long as you've had your fix, I don't really care."

He said nothing.

The doors were unlocked and I could finally breathe when we exited and walked towards Halima's block of flats. When she welcomed us in, I was relieved to escape his broody mood. I hugged my friends and greeted their husbands. Leaving the men to chat, we stood in her kitchen.

"What were you doing in the car? We saw you park up five minutes ago," Halima said as she plated the starters.

I let out an exasperated sigh. "He started asking me why I don't orgasm."

Rani's drink spluttered everywhere as she failed to contain her laugh. "He *what*?"

"Keep your voice down!"

"What did you say?"

My blank expression only made Rani laugh harder. "I said most women don't."

Her mouth hung open. "So you don't ... *ever*?"

"We are not talking about this when our husbands are in the other room. In fact," Sumayyah's eyes narrowed, "We aren't talking about this at all."

Ignoring her flustered expression, I answered Rani's question. "I have a few times, but most of the time I'm just hoping he hurries up so I can go to sleep. He's like a freaking jackhammer."

This time her drink sprayed over herself. Her laugh travelled behind her as she left the kitchen to touch up her makeup.

"How does that even come up in conversation?" Halima asked.

"I brought it upon myself when I said it was nice having a break from sex. I can't be the only one, right?"

"I get it. Jannah is an early bird. After spending my day running after her, most nights I'm too tired and asleep before Naz comes to bed. That doesn't stop him from waking me up sometimes."

"He doesn't even try to make me enjoy it," I admitted.

"That's because the sex is for him," Halima remarked. "They don't understand that we also have needs."

The conversation was cut short when Rani rejoined us. "Jannah is so precious!"

"She's a sweet girl. Shall we break up the football talk?"

Helping her, we each carried the plates to the living room and placed them on the coffee table.

Ravi stood up. "Zoya, come and sit here. You're pregnant."

I felt Idris' gaze on me and shook my head. "No. It's okay. I'm alright here."

"Don't be ridiculous. You can't sit on the floor. I insist."

Our conversation had him in a bad mood, and I knew accepting Ravi's offer would have pushed him over the edge. I shook my head again and tried to break the tension I felt. "The stench of you men would make me gag. I'd rather stay on this side of the room."

"Fair enough. How are you doing? How long do you have left?"

It was mother's instinct when my hands rubbed my bump. "We're okay. We've got just over four months to go."

"Do you know what you're having?" Halima asked.

"Not yet. We find out next week."

My scan was in a week, and the party was two days later. I had been instructed to hand the envelope to Emaan, who was tasked with buying the cannon. My mother-in-law insisted that we cooked all the food at home, even though Idris' restaurant could have done the catering. The guest list had been extended to my family, as well as Farrah's in-laws. I was already dreading the cooking and cleaning that had to be done.

Yousef smiled at me. "What are you hoping for? You've got two boys, so hopefully it's a girl."

I was sick and tired of people saying that to me.

"I'd be happy with another boy."

Halima's mouth dropped open. "No! You want a girl because it's the best having a little version of you to play dress up with."

To my surprise, it was Rani who agreed with her. "O-M-G! Right? Boys are so boring."

"You don't want either."

For a second, I was taken aback by Ravi's hostile tone. But one recollection of their argument months ago reminded me there was another side to him.

Unlike that day, Rani didn't give in and throw a snide comment back. Instead, she turned in the opposite direction and surprised me when she asked, "What do you want, Idris?"

"A father never wants a daughter because she's only ours for a short time. Before you know it, you give her away to someone else."

I didn't know if he was trying to hurt me after I bruised his ego in the car. But after all that spiel about wanting a mini version of me, he finally gave a truthful answer. And it only confirmed what I already knew. *A daughter would live the same fate as me.*

Nazir shook his head. "Not me. No man is ever touching my little girl."

"I had this discussion with a colleague of mine," Yousef started. "She said she wants four children; all boys because she'll have the best of both worlds once they get married. She'll get to keep her sons with her, but she'll also get four daughters without going through the struggle of raising moody teenagers."

No matter what happened, I promised to never make another woman suffer like I did. "Not me. Once my boys are married, I'm forcing them out of the house. Let them go and live their new lives. They don't need to be running around after me."

Rani high-fived me. "Preach sister! Our culture is the only one that forces the woman to live with her in-laws. The normal thing is to get your own space."

There was the Rani I knew. There was no way she was going to let Ravi have the last word with his earlier indirect.

Before Ravi could argue, Yousef did it on his behalf. "Our culture reinforces an environment of family. It's hard to cultivate that when you hardly see them. There's nothing wrong with living with your husband's family."

"Easy to say when you're a man," Sumayyah snapped back with an attitude. "At the end of the day, it's your family. For the woman, it's different."

I expected Idris to have something to say, but he remained silent. I almost thanked him for not instigating an argument with my friends.

Instead, it was Ravi who spoke. "How's that?"

"It never feels like your own home. It's our husband's home. Having one room in an entire house doesn't equal having your own space and privacy."

My mental praise for Idris came a few seconds too early.

He laughed. "What do you need privacy for?"

Sumayyah shot a sarcastic smile at him. "Did you get your wife pregnant in front of your parents?"

Like Halima, my mouth hung open. I couldn't believe it was her to snap back with something so direct. Their glaring match continued despite my silent plea.

Eventually, Idris said, "I got her pregnant without moving out. That invalidates your argument."

Rani scoffed. "No, it just means you can't make your woman scream."

My eyes widened at Rani. *Why would she say that?* She knew it was a sore subject, especially tonight. And the murderous look Idris shot me made it abundantly clear he knew I had told them about our conversation.

"Okay. Let's move this along before there's bloodshed in my apartment."

I tried to follow Nazir's direction by changing the subject. "These are delicious." I wasn't even sure *what* I was eating.

"I found the recipe on this website..."

Idris' thunderous voice cut Halima off. He intentionally went over Rani's head to Ravi to belittle her. "Your wife owes me an apology for speaking so crudely."

When she looked at me in disbelief, I met it with a pleading stare to drop it. But Rani would not take the disrespect quietly. As though Idris were below her, she snapped her fingers to get his attention. "If you want to ask for an apology, then ask *me*. My husband doesn't answer for me."

"Your husband should put you on a leash," he snarled.

"If he ever wants one, I'm sure he'll ask you because you're a pro at that."

Her words hurt no one but *me*. Her dig didn't degrade Idris. She was calling *me* his lapdog and that hurt because, of everyone in that room, *she* knew how hard I had it. I opened up to Rani about my struggles and had I known she would throw that in my face to one-up Idris, I never would have told her.

But what hurt the most was she knew it would be *me* that faced the consequences of her words. Because I had to go home with him. His pride was already bruised, and her comment just made it bleed.

"Rani. *Stop*." I recoiled from her betrayed look.

"He just called me a dog." She was practically telling me to defend her.

But I couldn't because I remembered what happened the last time they argued. "And then you referred to me as one."

"That isn't what I meant. I was trying to say he's always trying to control you."

Sensing another argument, Ravi stood. "Okay. Maybe we should just leave."

Halima spoke to us as you do to children. "Come on, guys. I've spent all morning cooking us a nice meal. Let's all apologise and forget about it."

We all muttered a weak *sorry*, but I knew it wasn't the end with Idris. More importantly, I wanted a genuine apology from Rani for what was going to come when I got home.

⤜⤜⤜⤜

Idris controlled his temper throughout our drive home. He stormed straight to our bedroom while I checked in on the boys. They were fast asleep, and I wished they were awake so I could avoid the impending argument.

"You are *not* talking to that girl anymore," he declared the second the door shut. "She has no respect. What woman speaks so crudely in front of other men like that?"

My friendship with Rani wasn't the hill I wanted to die on that night. "Fine. Are you going to shower?"

"How could you talk about our sex life with *them*?" He referred to my friends as if they were dirt beneath his shoe.

"I didn't."

"Don't lie to me! She could have only made that comment if you told her! And clearly it's true, no?"

"I'm not lying. I'm also not going to argue with you about this."

He grabbed my arm and pulled me against him. One arm wrapped around my waist while the other pushed my hair to one side. "You want to scream?" He held me tighter and his lips rested on my ears. "I'll give you something to scream about."

"Idris ... no. Don't do this."

He released me. "Take your clothes off."

"We had a deal."

"I don't care."

The ice in his voice made it clear we were going to have sex, whether or not I wanted to. My clothes pooled at my feet and I stepped over them. Idris slowly unclasped my bra and pulled my underwear down my legs. We stared at one another. I swallowed hard.

He bent me over the edge of the bed and rubbed the lube over me before taking what he wanted. His fingers dug into my hips as he quenched his thirst for sex. "How does it feel?"

It wasn't a question he had ever asked me. I didn't know if I was supposed to answer until he repeated himself. "It feels good?"

"Then why can't I hear you?"

Oh god. This wasn't going to end until he proved a point and made me climax. After the long evening of tension and small talk, that wasn't going to happen. So, I did what most women do; *I faked it.* My eyes closed, and I forced a few moans. When I could no longer tolerate his brashness, I pretended to orgasm.

Idris pulled out of me. "Do you think I'm fucking stupid?"

I sat on the bed and sighed. "What do you want me to do, Idris?"

"I want you to be present! How can you enjoy this when you're never living in the moment? Your head is always somewhere else! Just *want* me. Why can't you crave *me*?"

"I'm having sex with you, aren't I?"

"Not that! I want *you*."

"What do you want me to do?" I snapped, feeling exasperated.

His chest rose and fell as he stared at me. Then, with a small shake of his head, he resigned and said, "Nothing. I have never been worthy enough to get any part of you. Even as your husband, you won't give me the one intimacy that belongs to me. You won't look at me. You won't kiss me. You won't touch me." He shook his head. "I'm going to shower."

I felt guilty at the hurt expression he wore because he was right. In my defense, I never needed to instigate the sex because he was always all over me. Even in a room full of people, he always found a subtle way to touch me.

I walked until we were facing one another. Reaching up on my tiptoes, I cupped his face and kissed him slow. My fingers snaked through his hair as he met my passion.

His muscles relaxed under my touch. He pulled me closer and kissed me like his life depended on it. Goosebumps littered my skin everywhere he touched me. Needing air, he broke the kiss and lightly nibbled along my neck.

A gasp left me as his fingers curled inside me. "Idris, slow down." I could feel my arousal slipping away as he rammed them inside me. I stilled his hand. "Slow. Down. You're not digging for gold."

He led us to the bed. "I want you on your back."

His obsession with missionary was something I never understood, but I did as he asked. Being nearly five months pregnant, I knew this wasn't going to get me anything but uncomfortable pain. Yet, I spread my legs and listened to his throaty moan at claiming me.

His filthy tongue did nothing for me because of the pressure on my bump. Idris noticed it too because after a few minutes, he stilled. "Why are you making that face?"

"I'm carrying a baby inside me and right now gravity isn't doing me any favours. Plus, you're pressing on my bump."

"Then what do you want?"

Pulling myself up with a groan, I pointed at the headboard. "Take a seat, Mr Qadir."

Doing as I asked, he stopped me when I faced away from him. "I want you to look at me."

Turning around, I eased myself onto him. Giving myself a second to adjust, I started to move and nothing could have prepared me for the sound that came out of us. My eyes screwed shut as my head fell back.

Idris held my face. "Look at me, Zoya." The fire in his eyes was electrifying. Never had he looked so aroused before. He moved my hands from the headboard and placed them on his chest. "Touch me."

Now that I was in control, everything felt visceral. Every nerve in my body was on high alert to the sensation rippling through me. My nails dug into his shoulders as a tingle shot through me.

His hand covered my mouth. "You're going to wake everyone up."

Taking his hands, I placed them on my bump. "That's better," I moaned now that he was bearing the weight. It allowed me to move in ways he'd never let me before.

"You look so good like this." His gaze travelled from where our bodies met, up my torso to my face. "Just looking at you is going to make me..."

"Not yet," I begged. I could feel it and was desperate to get to the end. I buried my head into his neck to muffle the sounds coming out of me. My toes curled when he ran his hands over my skin.

"What's wrong?" he asked when I froze. "Are you okay?"

"My legs are tired," I laughed. "Give me a second to catch my breath."

His body shook with mine. "Hold on to me." Then he held my hips and resumed control. "Is that okay?" Idris watched me like there was nothing else worthy of his attention. His praise fueled my arousal and tightened my core. "You look so perfect like this."

I couldn't see anything beyond the stars floating in front of me. "Idris..." I don't know what I was begging for.

His arms weaved around me and pulled me as close as my bump allowed. "Say it again."

My fingers tugged at his hair. "*Idris.*"

His name was a plea and prayer as it slipped off my tongue like a mantra. It only stopped when pure pleasure tore through me and every muscle in my body locked and spasmed. My mouth opened but was incapable of producing any sound.

And only seconds later, Idris met me in oblivion. His movements went from sharp to sloppy as he called upon me like I was being worshipped.

My body collapsed against his from a satiated exhaustion. "I feel like I've run a marathon."

He was as breathless as me. Pushing my hair out of my face, he kissed below my ear. "I need more of that."

"You're getting nothing else from me tonight."

He moaned. "You're still..."

"I know. Give me a second before you move."

"Take your time." His fingers ran up and down my back as I tried to fight my sleep. Idris didn't seem to mind me half-dozing off on him. He held my naked body against his. A gentle sigh passed his lips and every few minutes, he would place a kiss on my shoulder.

The minutes ticked by as we stayed immobile like that. My breathing evened, and I found a sense of comfort in his arms. I closed my eyes and prayed for this version of Idris to never leave. Because this was the man who promised to never become my father. This was the husband who brought me back to London. This was the Idris who held me when I was mourning for a baby I never got to hold.

Idris thought I had fallen asleep. In an almost silent whisper, he said, "I wonder what you're going to dream about. Can I meet you there?" He let out a resigned sigh. "Will I ever become part of your dream?"

CHAPTER THIRTY-FOUR

THE HOUSE OVERFLOWED WITH people. We weren't expecting everyone to accept the invite, but with it being Christmas day, nobody was working. My arms protected my bump from being elbowed as I brushed past our guests.

I finally got the chance to relax and enjoy myself now that everyone had eaten. My feet were aching from all the cooking, cleaning, and serving. Despite that, Shazia kept giving me one order after another; and I followed through because I didn't want to add any fuel to my husband's bad mood. I didn't know why he was walking around with a glare, but every time I caught his gaze, it only intensified.

The morning after Halima's dinner party, Idris declared that our agreement was still intact. There had been no more slip-ups, and it seemed that night offered him enough satisfaction because he kept his hands completely off me.

Uncle Farhan gave his seat up when I walked in. "This is a very nice party."

"It was all your daughter. I don't want to know how much Farrah spent on decor."

She cradled her bump. "I'm allowed. It's my first baby and seeing as you've never even had a baby shower, you deserve it."

Emaan shook her head. "I still can't believe you're only two weeks apart."

"God always finds a way to strengthen the bond of sisters," Uncle Farhan said. He placed a kiss at the top of my head before resting his hand on it. "You have always been a good role model to my daughter, and now she gets to learn how to be a mother in step with you. I truly believe Allah knew she couldn't get through this without you."

My heart warmed at the love in his eyes. "She's going to be an amazing parent because *you* and Aunty Jahan set a perfect example."

Farrah hugged her dad before she pulled me into it, too. "I love you guys," she breathed.

I relished in his fatherly love until I felt Idris' stare. Pulling away, I looked away from him. "Shall we get to the main event?"

"Can you just check on Umaiza for me?" Emaan put her daughter to sleep in our bedroom as it was the only space free from our guests. "I'd go but..."

I didn't need her to explain because everyone knew Idris didn't allow anyone to enter there. With a promise to be right back, I climbed up the stairs. Umaiza was still sound asleep in the middle of my bed. I smiled at how cute she looked before turning around.

I jumped in surprise. "What the hell, Idris? Don't scare me like that."

He closed the door and leaned against it. "Change your clothes."
I looked down at my dress. "Why?"

"I can see the entire shape of your breasts and bump. Why would you wear that, knowing you represent me? Don't you have any respect for the elders of my family?"

He said nothing about my clothes when I dressed in front of him before. He also wasn't in a bad mood then. As always, he was pissed off about something else and I was getting the brunt of it.

"And why did you hug him? Why did you let him kiss you?"

My brow arched. "Are you actually pissed off because of that? He's old enough to be my dad!"

"I don't care! And if you had any respect for yourself or our marriage, you wouldn't allow it."

I immediately understood which version of Idris I faced. Today he was the ruthless one who would say anything to hurt me. This side of him craved an argument that resulted in me crying.

"You always do this," I said. "Whenever there are other people around and you see me happy, you make sure to take it away. This is *your* family that I'm making an effort with. You should be grateful that I care for them as my own. If anything, I go out of my way for them."

"Why should I be grateful for you ignoring my presence when they're fucking here? I *hate* when they're around you. I *hate* how they call you *our Zoya*. I *hate* when they talk to you or make you laugh. And when they touch you, I want to kill them."

Is that why he was in such a bad mood? Because I wasn't following him around like a lost puppy?

"What do you want from me? I run around being the perfect host and you have a problem with it. If I stayed glued to your side, you'd shout at me for not helping mum. There's no winning with you."

The door opening caused him to withdraw. His icy stare landed on Emaan, who looked terrified.

"Sorry, I thought she'd woken up and..."

Idris gave me one last look before exiting.

"I'm so sorry," she squeaked. "I had no idea he was in here."

"It's fine. She's still asleep and looking adorable while doing it."

She got lost in her thoughts as she stared at her child. "I wish I could keep her like this forever because it's a scary world out there for women."

"With a mum like you, who has so much knowledge about all that, she's in safe hands."

"Is she?" She looked at me. "I can read every book about the signs to her, but love makes us blind, and this culture teaches us to stay and make it work, no matter the cost. Even outside of our culture, people hear abuse and they think of bruises and getting slapped around. But there are a million ways to abuse someone." It was unlike her to wear such a forlorn expression.

"Is everything okay? You look like you have a lot on your mind."

"It's been a tough week at work." She sighed. "We had this woman come in. She is beautiful and so incredibly intelligent. She has a good job and a sweet little girl, no older than two. They live a comfortable life in this stunning house. Her life seemed practically perfect, so I asked her why she came to us."

"What did she say?"

"She said she had intrusive thoughts about killing herself."

I flinched in surprise. "Why was she feeling like that?"

"At first, I couldn't figure it out. She had a great work-life balance. Her child was healthy and happy. So I asked if there was anything her husband was doing to support her. And the more she spoke about him, I understood. He took this strong woman and slowly crumbled her until she saw herself as worthless. He constantly spoke down to her. It's *always* his way or the highway. I mean, he's a complete control freak. Over the years, he's conditioned her to his will. When she abided by his rules, he was loving and sweet, but the minute she did something he didn't like, he was cruel. He would *never* hit her, but he was vicious with his words. And because he never put his hands on her, she couldn't accept it when I labelled him as abusive."

She was describing my life without realising. And it felt like I stopped breathing. The years of my marriage flashed through my mind and it was a chaos made up of my sobs and Idris' harsh words. I never viewed Idris as abusive, either. Only twice had he put his hands on me and both times I had written it off as momentary anger.

"What happened?"

"The hardest part of my job is when I want to shake reality into them. But these men dig their claws in so deep. She kept telling me he's a good man that loves her and wants her to be the best version of herself. But if that was true, why would he point out every minor mistake she's made? Why wouldn't he celebrate her promotion instead of telling her it was a dead-end job? It's a cycle that never ends. She does something that irrationally enrages him, he lashes out, she appeases him and then he's the perfect husband until the cycle begins again."

I swallowed hard. "How do you break the cycle?"

Emaan shrugged. "I can't. She has to find the strength to say enough is enough. But men that are psychologically abusive are some of the hardest to shake because they *know* how to get what they want. They make you feel like you can't live without them."

I didn't process anything past *psychologically abusive.* Is that was Idris was? Everything Emaan described fit him perfectly. And like that woman, I couldn't accept that I was that type of victim. I couldn't be a victim of abuse because where were my scars?

But at that moment, my heart clenched, reminding me of the wounds nobody could see.

With a shake of her head, she said, "I'm sorry. It's a party and I'm here talking about work. What time are your friends getting here?"

I didn't invite them after the fiasco at Halima's. Rani was yet to message me, which meant she believed *I* owed the apology. But I wasn't at fault.

And you know Idris would lose his shit if he knew you were speaking to her again.

It killed me, especially after the conversation I just had to admit it was true. I didn't want to disrupt the calm that had somewhat settled between us. This party would have been the best excuse to see my friends again. But no matter how upset I was with Rani, I didn't have the heart to invite the others and not her.

"I thought best to keep it just family," I answered.

The second we rejoined the party, Farrah grabbed my hand. "Come on! Pictures!"

We stood in front of the backdrop with wide smiles and posed for the cameras and crowd. I could barely contain my laughter as Farrah made us do the silliest poses.

"Why don't you take some with Masoud and then we can pop the cannons?" I stood amongst the crowd and admired their excitement at becoming parents.

When it was our turn, Idris stood beside me and surprised me when his arm wrapped around my waist. I smiled at the camera before calling the boys to join us.

One picture turned into many more. Asma welled up as we took our picture. Idris' sisters told me they had prayed I got the chance to experience this once again after my loss. My mum looked at me like I had won the lottery.

"I would hug you, but I'd like to keep my arms," Rizwan muttered as we smiled at the camera.

A giggle broke free. "That's a smart idea."

"Thank you for being the best big sister, even though you're technically younger than me. You've always taken such good care of me, Farrah, and Emaan. That's why your children are so lucky to have you."

I stared at him, warmth filling me. "I barely did anything."

"Give yourself some credit. You were only eighteen and thrust into this crazy world I call my family. You went from being just a sister and daughter to becoming a million other things. And you did it with such grace."

"Come on, Rizwan!" His mum gave him a pointed expression. "Your conversation with your favourite Bhabhi can wait until later. I want to know if I'm getting a grandson or granddaughter!"

Everyone laughed, but a buzz filled the room. I wasn't excited, though. My heart hammered in my chest because what if it was a girl? How would I stop her from becoming me? *How would I save her from Idris' abuse?*

"What was that about?" he asked the second he reached me.

"Nothing."

"Why were you looking at him like that?"

I smiled ahead. "There's people right next to us. Can you not do this right now?"

Whatever he said was drowned out by the cheers. Farrah jumped into Masoud's arms as pink confetti showered over them. Everyone took a minute to celebrate with them before it was our turn.

"Three!"

I felt sick.

"Two!"

Please don't be a girl.

"One!"

Everything moved in slow motion. The roar of happiness was muffled by the ringing in my ears. Farrah's excitement doubled, and she squeezed me tight. Karim and Nadim pouted as the pink confetti landed on the floor before us.

It's a girl.

I'm having a daughter.

And the realisation made me want to burst into tears. I couldn't move. I couldn't even pretend to be happy. I waited for Emaan to say she made a mistake and my one was supposed to be blue. But she was joining in with the celebrations. Nobody had noticed I was frozen with fear.

Nobody but Idris.

His green eyes locked onto my brown ones. I became lost in the vibrant green depths. Would our daughter adopt them as our sons did?

I knew she wouldn't.

She would never inherit his wealth, nor his status. She would never sit at the head of the table. She would never be anything more than he allowed. She would be confined by his belief that a woman is nothing without a man.

She was destined to live my merciless fate.

Our daughter was going to have my brown eyes. Ones that would look at Idris, hoping to decipher which version of him she was going to get.

Our daughter was going to have my brown eyes. Ones that would be unable to see a way out of the cycle.

Our daughter was going to have my brown eyes.

And like me, only when she closed them would she be able to see her dreams come to life.

A dream where freedom was hers.

CHAPTER THIRTY-FIVE

ANOTHER WEEKEND MEANT PLAYING hostess again. This time it was for Idris' paternal family after they threw a hissy fit because they weren't invited to the gender reveal party. Shazia tried to explain her family was only invited because it was also a party for Farrah, but that didn't smooth the hump they had. So, to appease his family, Abbas invited them for dinner.

"What are you doing here?" I asked when Farrah entered the kitchen.

"Remember that thing I was supposed to pick up?"

"Oh, I wasn't aware you were coming today."

There were still orders that needed to get to our customers, but my friendship with Rani was still hanging the air. She hadn't reached out to me, which told me she still wasn't sorry for what she said.

"She said she would be in the flat today." She looked at me with apprehension. "Has something happened between you guys?" She listened intently as I recounted what had happened. "Be honest with me. Are you still mad at her, or are you just trying to keep your husband happy?"

"She called me a dog."

"I don't think she was. It probably wasn't the best choice of words from her side, but she was talking about *his* behaviour. Not yours."

"She didn't need to make that comment in the first place. It's like she enjoys riling him up, knowing it's *me* that has to answer for it."

"I'm not taking her side, but I don't think that was her intention. She was trying to defend you." Farrah let out a sigh. "You've always said she's like your sister, and maybe I'm wrong, but sisters fight. They mis-communicate and misunderstand. I know it's unfair you're torn between your husband and sister, but you shouldn't have to choose one or the other. You love both, and if they truly loved you, they wouldn't ask you to."

But Idris was asking me to choose while deciding for me. I knew there would be consequences if I chose my friendship and I didn't have the courage to face those.

I missed Rani more than I could explain. I missed her snarky tongue and ability to make me laugh even when I didn't want to. It was the longest we had gone without speaking since we'd met, bar my trip to Pakistan all those years ago. Deep down I knew I wasn't angry anymore, but her silence made me wonder if she wanted to rekindle our friendship. Perhaps she had realised that her life was no different with or without me.

Rani weighed on my mind for the rest of the morning. I ticked everything off my mental to-do list before showering. In the solitude of my bedroom, my finger hovered over the call button.

"Are my clothes ready?" Idris asked, making me jump.

"Yes. They're hung up."

He eyed me with suspicion. "What were you doing?"

I locked my phone and stood up. "Nothing."

"Is there a reason you're sitting there naked?"

"I just came out of the shower."

I waited for him to make an advance, but he simply nodded with a look that said he didn't believe me.

❦ ❦ ❦ ❦

If there was one thing I never took personally in my marriage, it was Idris' lack of words. We rarely had conversations that were outside of him needing something. Perhaps that was because we had little to talk about. But it was mostly because Idris hardly spoke to anyone. It didn't matter who it was. He wore a blank expression and didn't speak unless he was spoken to. Even then, it was a miracle to get more than a few words from him.

The only exception to that was Sanam. At family gatherings, they somehow found themselves hidden away, sharing private words. She was only two years younger than him, so I always put their close relationship down to growing up together. But I also knew my husband and his traditional views on mingling with the opposite sex. He had other cousins, both male and female, he grew up with, yet did not speak to them as much as he spoke to her. Sanam had also never been married. *Was that because Idris refused to share her?*

I watched from across the room as they stood in a corner, invested in one another. He stared at her intently as they continued their hushed conversation. It had been fifteen minutes since I clocked them and not once had Idris searched for me as he normally did. And something about that triggered my woman's instinct.

When they discreetly slipped out of the room and up the stairs, I tried telling myself it was nothing. But subconsciously I started a timer. Exactly seventeen minutes later, when they were yet to return, I was climbing upstairs. I checked every room and couldn't find them until I stood outside my closed bedroom door and heard their voices. Bracing myself for the worst, I flung the door open and stared at them.

They weren't naked nor on the bed. They stood in the middle of my bedroom with a look of secrecy amongst them.

"I'm sorry for intruding. Please continue." My sarcastic tone irked Idris.

He stared at me. "Sanam, get out."

Avoiding my harsh glare, she scurried out of the room and shut the door behind her.

"Are you screwing her?" I asked before he could speak.

"*What*?"

I experienced a rage unlike any I'd known. The edges of my vision blurred, and all I wanted to do was slap him. "Are you *fucking* her, Idris?"

His nostrils flared as his eyes darkened. "Speak to me like that again. I *dare* you."

"You *hypocrite*," I spat at him. "After all the grief you have given me about any man that has looked at me, *this* is what you have been doing behind my back?" I stepped back, laughing. "That explains why you haven't even flinched from the lack of sex. Is that what you've been doing when I think you're at work?"

Amusement danced on his features. "Are you jealous, Zoya?" He was enjoying this, and that hurt more than anything. There was no remorse in him. He didn't deny it or try to apologise after being caught.

I wanted to scream. I wanted to cry, but I wouldn't give him that satisfaction. I squared my shoulders and stood tall. Every trace of emotion was wiped from my face and tone. "Is it good?"

"Is what good?"

"Her pussy."

That drained the humour from his face. "I'm giving you one chance to take that back."

I shrugged. "It must be a pleasant break from me. I mean, after two kids, there's probably hardly anything left for you to enjoy. Is that when this started? Or were you fucking her before you married me?"

"If you know what's good for you, you're going to shut your mouth and *never* say that to me again."

And there was the reason he held no remorse or panic because he believed I wouldn't leave. I had let him think he could treat me however he saw fit and I would tolerate it; because I had tolerated it. I kept my mouth shut and became his doormat. But his infidelity wasn't something I could forgive.

"Me and you are *done*. After everything I have given you, you chose the worst way to disrespect me and this marriage. Marriage is not a game. It is a vow before God."

Idris recognised those words from a lifetime ago. How could he not when they were his own? "This has never been a marriage to you."

"This marriage has become who I am! It was *you* that never saw it as a marriage. I have always been a toy you bought. A machine to cook and clean for you. A vagina and womb to give you children. And I did it! I did it all! Yet, nothing was enough to gain your respect. So, I'm done." With one last look at him, I left the room.

I wanted to hit him where I knew it would hurt the most. As I climbed down the stairs, my plan was to be overtly friendly to every man in this house. I wanted to sit and laugh with them so loud until it concealed just how much my heart was breaking.

But I couldn't.

Not because I was scared.

But because I valued my marriage too much. I couldn't break the vow I was forced to take because somewhere along the way, it started to mean something. Refusing to lower myself to his level, I blinked away my tears and forced a smile onto my face.

"Come back upstairs," he muttered into my ear. He grabbed my hand when I tried to walk away. "Our conversation wasn't over."

I looked up at him. "It's over, Idris."

His throat constricted. "Don't say that. Come back to our bedroom."

"I am never stepping foot in there again."

"Zoya," he warned. Panic turned his eyes wide. "Please?"

"Let go of me before people notice."

"I'm not having an affair."

"Said every man who's had an affair. I don't want to do this with you right now. So I am asking you to let go before you hurt me more than you already are."

319

The rest of the evening dragged by. I was forced to smile and pretend everything was fine; all the while, I felt like I was crumbling on the inside. Shazia shot me a look of worry when Idris' voice boomed when he couldn't find me. He'd only lost visuals on me for a few minutes while I heated the food. When an aunt said I was in the kitchen, he practically ran and visibly relaxed once he had sight of me.

After the guests left, I cleaned up, showered and climbed into bed with the boys. It was a tight squeeze, but I'd rather have that than have to sleep next to him. I wanted to be asleep before he got back from taking some relatives home.

But the front door slammed shut, and his voice boomed. "Where is she?"

"What is wrong with you today?" his mum asked.

"Zoya?" he called. "Zoya!"

"She's gone to bed."

His footsteps were loud as he ran up the stairs and past the boys' bedroom. I heard our door open and him walking around. He called for me again. He checked our bathroom and then he was coming straight towards me.

The darkness broke when the door opened. Rage contorted Idris's features as he peered into the room. "What are you doing in here?"

"They're going to wake up. Close the door on your way out."

He stepped inside and barely contained his anger. "Come back to our bed before I turn this house upside down."

"Do whatever you want; you always do."

"Zoya!" he screamed.

I ran my fingers through Nadim's hair when he jumped. "It's okay, baba. I'm right here." My heart eased as his eyes fluttered closed again.

"Get up." He was looking down at me. "You're not sleeping in here."

"Just go away, Idris."

Grabbing my arm, he pulled me up. "I'll drag you back to our bed if I have to."

"Let go! You're hurting me!" I snatched my arm out of his hold. "I am never sleeping in that bed again!"

"I'm not having an affair!" he snapped. "If I was, do you really think I would bring her to *our* bed while you were downstairs?"

"You love finding new ways to hurt me."

He held my face before he rested his forehead against mine. "I wouldn't do that," he whispered in desperation. "Not to you or our marriage. Please, just come back to our bed."

When he tried to kiss me, I turned away. "Shut the door on your way out."

"Even when you won't be mine, I have only ever been yours. Tell me you believe that." My silence hurt him. He held my hand and kissed my knuckles. "Please, Zoya?"

Blinking the emotion out of my eyes, I cleared my throat. "I've had a long day and I'm tired."

A look of defeat came over him. "If I leave, do you promise to still be here tomorrow?"

"You have given me a million reasons to leave. Every tear I've cried at your hands is enough to wash myself clean of you. But I keep hoping that you'll give me one good reason to stay."

He silently released me and took his leave. He stood outside the door for a few moments before he retreated to our bedroom.

Sleep never came. Instead, I quietly cried. Knowing there was only one person who could make me forget, I dialled her number. Before I could fill my head with doubts about her answering, the ringing stopped.

"Hey."

"Hi," I whispered.

"Are you okay? You never call me this late."

"I just missed you."

Rani went mute. "I missed you too."

"I'm sorry," we blurted out simultaneously.

"I overreacted and took what you said completely out of context."

"No, Zoya. I shouldn't have said what I did. The whole comment about making you scream was uncalled for. I knew he was feeling temperamental, and I only egged it on. I really hope he wasn't too horrible to you because of me."

An empty laugh filled the silence. "It got me an orgasm."

I could imagine her mouth dropping open. "I guess you owe me." She sighed. "I really loved the clothes, by the way. Especially the orange one. Where did you get that fabric from?"

"It's one Idris bought me from Pakistan a few years ago." The line went silent again. "You have no idea how many times I wanted to call or text you. I missed you so much."

"I missed you too. My plan was to call you the next day, but things over here have been..." She didn't finish her sentence to clarify what she meant.

"Idris was so pissed off and I didn't want to poke the bear. He forbade me from speaking to you."

"That doesn't surprise me. How are you talking to me now? Is he still at work?"

"I'm sleeping next to the boys."

"How come?" She listened intently as I relayed the events of the day.

"I guess you were right," I said to conclude.

"That was a joke! I can't believe … Are you sure they're banging? What were they doing when you walked in?"

"Standing in the middle of the room."

"Maybe they were just talking?"

"They were definitely hiding something. They were standing very close to one another. This is the same man that won't even look at another woman."

"That's exactly my point. I just can't imagine him doing that."

My eyebrows furrowed, and I felt hurt at her defense. "Since when were you Team Idris?"

"I'm not! I can barely stand the man, but if there is one thing I know, it is that he is *obsessed* with you; the type of obsession that gets people locked away in a prison or insane asylum. When the two of you are in the same room, he literally cannot look away from you. His eyes are locked on you like nothing else in the room is worthy of his attention. If he wasn't such a misogynistic pig, he would worship the ground you walk on. He's not conventional; I'm not even saying that it's healthy, but it is true. And a man that obsessed wouldn't cheat because nothing holds a candle to their obsession."

Her speech cast a doubt on my suspicions. If it had been any of the other girls, I would have assumed they were just attempting to cheer me up. But while Rani was always blunt, she was also always honest.

Plus, not even a fortune would buy a kind word about Idris from her.

323

"That makes it worse," I said. "Because he was okay to let me think it was true. He didn't deny it. There was a sick look of happiness when he saw how hurt I was."

"Maybe that's because he was happy."

"What do you mean?"

"You've never really given him any indication that you *want* to be married to him. You've always made it clear you couldn't care less if he fucked around because he means nothing to you. Perhaps he was happy you were hurting because it proved to him you cared. It gave him the validation that, no matter how small, you felt something other than hatred for him."

CHAPTER THIRTY-SIX

IT WAS BACK TO the early days of my marriage, where everything set Idris off. Over the last two weeks, his patience and pleading had worn thin when he realised nothing was getting me back into his bed. He was happy to pick a fight with me every chance he got about the stupidest things.

At that moment, he was screaming about the mess in the living room as he made his way to the kitchen. "Before I throw every single toy in the bin, go and pick them off the floor!"

I didn't flinch at his raised voice. I continued to chop the onions without acknowledging him.

"Did you hear me? I am sick and tired of this house always being a mess!"

"I cleaned it up in the morning, but there are children that live here. It's going to get messy."

"It was a mess before I left to go shopping and it's still a mess now. A good mother cleans up after her children. What are you doing all day?"

I slammed the knife down and turned towards him with a scowl. "I'm doing everything else; on top of being nearly six months pregnant! Why don't *you* pick it up if it bothers you so much? Or better yet, get your sister-in-laws to clean up after their children! I am not the fucking maid!"

"You've stopped being a wife, so you may as well be a maid."

Normally I wouldn't have risen to his bait, but I was exhausted of him bullying me into submission. He knew if he kept pushing me, I would give in because nothing was worth suffering his verbal abuse.

"You should ask your mistress to help loosen those knots that have you all wound up," I said sweetly, before picking up my knife and resuming my task.

He grabbed the knife out of my hand. "Go and clean that fucking mess before I leave for work."

"Is it really work if she's giving it up for nothing?" I almost smirked when his eye twitched.

"You think I don't have ways to fix that smart mouth of yours?"

"Are you scared I'm going to tell your parents that you're a dirty cheat?"

He stepped closer. "I will not tell you again."

"What's in it for her?" This time I couldn't hide my grin as I hit him where I knew it would hurt. "Or, unlike me, does she actually get an orgasm?"

His eye twitched. "Get the fuck out of my face and clean that room!"

"Will you two stop shouting? The children are getting scared," Shazia said.

"Who was talking to you?" he snapped. "I was dealing with my wife."

She looked disheartened at his harshness. Her head jerked towards the living room. "Go. I'll finish cutting the vegetables."

"Where are the other two? Why can't they clean it? Why is it always me?"

"Idris!" She held her son back as he reached for me. "She'll clean it. You go get ready for work." Her pleading stare turned to me. "Just go."

"Fucking prick," I muttered under my breath as I walked past him. But I wasn't quiet enough.

"What did you say?" He shook her hold off him. "What kind of wife swears at her husband?"

"And what kind of son speaks to his mother as you do to yours?" I fired back. "Respect isn't given. It's *earned*. But who the hell am I to you when you have no respect for the woman who carried, birthed, and raised you?"

"Zoya," she pleaded. "That's enough."

Without sparing him another glance, I went to clean a mess that wasn't mine. *The story of my life.*

"Give me a cup of tea," he demanded when he returned fifteen minutes later.

Shazia glanced at me when I didn't move from the stove. We both knew he was talking to me, but I was set on acting like he didn't exist.

His glare bore into me as she brewed the drink for him. "Did you pack my lunch?"

"It's in the fridge," she answered for me.

My smugness only grew the more irritated he got. Ignoring him was the only control I had in this marriage, and it worked because it made Idris *burn*. Not wanting to suffocate on the tension in the room, Shazia excused herself and left us alone.

"What are you looking for? Let me get it," he offered when I stooped to search the cupboard. This was the guilt that always followed when he treated me like that. It was the vice he used to force me to forgive him.

"I don't need you to do anything for me." Grabbing the saucepan, I pulled myself up.

His hand rested on my back when I wobbled. "I told you to let me get it."

"I'm the maid, remember? It's my job to bend over backwards for you and your family."

Realising it was another word he'd permanently etched into my skin, he let go. "Don't cook dinner. Karim asked for food from Balti, so I'll send it for everyone. What would you like? The chef's special tonight is *nihari*. That's your favourite."

It was a lie. Idris thought relieving me of dinner duties would make up for what he said.

"I'll make my own food."

Panic was alive in him. He couldn't conceal the rapid rise and fall of his chest. "You liked the *biriyani* last time. Do you want that again?"

"I said I don't want anything."

"Do you want food from somewhere else? I'll leave work early and pick something up for us on the way. Maybe we can have a late dinner, just the two of us."

"No."

"Or do you want to go out and eat? I'll take you anywhere you want."

I sighed. "Just go away, Idris."

He stood immobile while I tended to my curries. "You are still going to be here when I get back from work?" He stepped closer when I didn't offer any reassurance. "Zoya? Look at me."

With a blank expression, I stared at him. "What?"

"Tell me you're still going to be here when I get back." He held my face. "Say it or I swear I'm going to chain you to these walls. Tell me you will not leave."

"Where would I go? I have no respite or a home."

It wasn't the answer he wanted, but was forced to accept because my mother-in-law rejoined us. With a lingering look in my direction, he took his leave.

"You know how he is," she started, when the front door slammed shut. "Why do you argue with him about small things?"

I really didn't want a fight with her. But I was done being the only one held accountable. "It's not small things. Why am I responsible for everyone in this house? Why are Amal and Anisa never asked to help? They woke up hours after me and haven't helped with anything."

"You are the eldest daughter-in-law. That means you shoulder most of the responsibility."

"Why? We all live in this house. When they were pregnant, nobody asked them for anything. Yet, I'm expected to do everything."

She went silent as she stirred the pot. "Do you think your father-in-law was always the man he is today?" Her eyes latched onto mine. "When we first married, he was very demanding. Bilal and Hamza have always been more relaxed. But not my Idris. Being the eldest, his father made sure he understood that one day he would be the man of the house and family. I had a hard time with my husband. Everything had to be exactly how he liked it, and when I got it wrong, he made sure I knew it. My hands and feet were cracked from taking care of him. My body would ache every day. Once I complained about being tired and he said generations of women before me used to walk miles to bring fresh water for their husbands."

"That was how many years ago? Was he expecting you to fetch water for him? The times had changed."

She shook her head. "The duties of a wife never change. Whether that is getting water, cooking or picking up toys; our job is to take care of our husband. I suffered then because I knew relief would come later in life."

Her entire belief was moronic. Where was her relief? By allowing Idris to see her husband treat her that way meant he thought he had a right to be the same towards her. Idris thought being a man gave him a higher standing over his own mother. Of course, her husband was content with life because he was free of his daughters. He'd taught his son to step into his shoes and he had an obedient wife. To him, nothing could make life sweeter. But her life was still the same.

"What am I supposed to do, Ammi? How much more of him am I supposed to tolerate?"

"My mother used to always say the easiest life is one where your husband is happy."

"There's my problem. My husband is never happy."

❀❀❀❀

As I hugged my friends, I couldn't believe my lie worked. I told Idris I was going to visit my mum as she was unwell. His fear was alive because he thought I was using it as an excuse to leave. But his guilt from earlier didn't let him shut me down completely. He said I had to be home before dinner and I was to leave the boys at home. I knew the latter was his reassurance of my return.

"All is right in the world again."

The hug disbanded, but Rani held onto me. "I've missed you."

"It's forgotten."

"It feels like your bump has grown overnight," Sumayyah said.

The doctors reassured me she is a healthy weight, but I agreed with her. It felt like I had gained weight in places not possible. My bump was already making daily tasks feel impossible.

I got comfortable on the sofa with a groan. "I don't know what it is about this pregnancy, but I am really feeling it. Maybe it's my age because my body can barely keep up."

"Don't say that! You're making me question if we should carry on trying."

Rani turned to Halima with wide eyes. "You're trying again?"

Her cheeks turned red, and she gave us a timid smile. "Yeah. We only decided a few weeks ago. Jannah is in school, so it feels like the right time."

"The jump from one to two is a *nightmare*. Jannah is nearly five, so you should have it easier than I did. But she's going to get extremely clingy when there's another one."

"Is Nazir excited?" Sumayyah asked.

"Yeah. He really wants a boy."

"Aw! That would be perfect. A mini Halima and a mini Nazir," Rani gushed.

Halima's excitement turned to me. "What are you having? Do you know yet?"

As if she knew we were talking about her, she fluttered in my stomach. "A girl."

Rani fist bumped the air. "Women for the win! Isn't it crazy that she's all tucked inside her mum, unaware of the love that awaits her?"

We all looked at her in surprise, but it was Sumayyah who spoke. "Has someone changed their mind about children?"

A look of horror came about her. "No. I just think it's crazy that she's in there, getting ready for the big, wide world. Who knows what she's going to become or who she will meet in her life? The world is at her feet and we get to see her take her first step."

A laugh broke out when Halima reached over to check Rani for a temperature. "Are you okay?"

Rani's eyes twinkled as she smiled at me. "I guess I'm just feeling grateful for you girls. When we met, we were just children and now we're all settled into our lives. We're on completely different paths but still tied together. How many people are that lucky?"

Tears brimmed in Sumayyah's eyes. "You're right. We are the lucky few to have a friendship that turned into sisterhood."

My chest filled with a love I had never received from anyone in my life. The three women surrounding me were the only ones who saw me for who I was and loved me, regardless of my flaws. They picked me up when I didn't have the strength to keep going.

I willed my own tears to stay back. "My hormones run my body and you guys are making me cry. I love you guys. My baby girl is so lucky to have you guys as her aunts. She will look up to you. You are going to be the best role models for her."

Rani frowned. "So will you. Her mum is so strong."

What part of my life had I been strong enough to lead? I had kept my head bowed and followed everyone else's direction.

"No, I'm not. I've spent my whole life letting others tell me what to do, and I've never found the strength to push back. I never want my little girl to see me as a role model."

Halima shuffled until she was sitting on the floor before me. She gripped my knee when I didn't look up from the ground. "Never sell yourself short. She is so lucky to have you as her mum. None of us are perfect. We all have our shortfalls. It's down to us to make our children learn from our mistakes. We teach them what we were never taught. We build them to be stronger than us."

Sumayyah nodded in agreement. "If we look back at our lives, none of us can say we did it all right. Mistakes are part of life. We just have to learn from them. We need to promise ourselves to never make the same mistake twice."

"You speak like you don't have a story worth telling. But you do. Your story is filled with equal parts struggle and strength. Look at the life you have built. You were forced to write a story with characters and a setting you didn't want. But you made it work and one day when your little girl comes and asks for advice, you'll know exactly what chapter to turn to guide her. Isn't that what motherhood is about?"

Only I understood what Rani was trying to say, and she was right. Despite all the limitations Idris and his expectations placed on me, I had achieved what I could. I honed my sewing skills and built a business that was turning over enough money for both Rani and me to be comfortable. And I did all that without failing the only people I owed myself to: *my children.*

Feeling a little better, I wiped my tears away. "I love that. A story worth telling."

Rani held her hand out to me, which I took, and the other girls followed suit. For a moment, I saw the young girls we were in school. Our eyes met as our shoulders squared, prepared to face any challenge together.

Halima broke the silence. "We all have a story, and we all deserve a happy ending."

I couldn't wait until Idris was happy to find my happiness. I deserved to be happy. "We will get the ending we deserve."

Rani dabbed under her eyes. "Great, now I'm crying. I love it. The story of the four *bous*. The four women that are going to break tradition."

"The four wives that are going to live for themselves," Sumayyah added.

I smiled. "The four daughter-in-laws that will stand up for themselves."

Halima shook her head, and when she spoke, her fierceness filled the room. "*Wrong*. We're the four *bows*. We are those young girls who, at sixteen, were forced into the world. We were beaten, bruised and forced to live for our families. Not anymore. We're not just a *bou*. We are *women*. We forged a bond with those ribbons. We tied the knot with our own hands. Our stories are not the ones where we belong to *them*. Why should our story be tied to them? Our lives started long before them. It started when we were sixteen and tied the only bond that never let us down. We're The Bows: intertwined, strong and forever-lasting."

Chapter Thirty-Seven

RANI CHECKED THE COAST was clear before she shuffled closer to me. "Have you thought about the business name?"

I fell against the pillows. "I can't think of anything original."

"I really liked *Regal Designs*."

My grimace was uncontrollable. "That sounds like we're trying too hard. I want something short and sweet, but also defines us. Most designers just use their name."

"Why don't you do that?"

"Really?" I asked sarcastically. A wide grin took over my lips as an idea came to me. "But we could use yours."

She shook her head. "Absolutely not! This is *your* designs."

"But it's *our* business. Rani is such a powerful name and literally embodies how we want our customers to feel in our clothes."

"If anyone's name is going on the label, it will be yours. Everything we have achieved is because of *you*. Anyone can source fabric and find a base to work from, but to have your skill to make the clothes is rare."

There was no way I could use my name. "Well, I'm on maternity leave now, so we have time to think of something."

Rani shot me a sheepish smile. "I was thinking..."

I groaned and covered my face. "That never leads to anything good."

"What if we opened a shop?"

My blank stare gave her my answer. "Are you out of your mind?"

"Okay!" She put her hands up in surrender. "Not a shop, but more like a boutique? Super small and low key, but luxurious. Once our custom fabrics come in, we can display them to give customers a chance to get a look and feel in real life. We stop making clothes with fabric from other places and only use ours. It's a one-stop shopping experience for our customers. We could even start those family collections we've spoken about. I was thinking of putting in a workshop for you in the back."

"It's official. You have gone mad," I declared. "How would I explain that to my husband?"

"You're going to have to tell him eventually, Zoya. How long are you going to hide this from him? He'll have to suck it up and deal with it."

"He won't do that. He's going to come into the business with a bulldozer and put an end to it."

"What if he doesn't? You could come to an agreement where you're *both* happy."

"If I thought it was a possibility, I would tell him." But I remembered our trip to Bali, where he made his stance clear. "I'm three months away from giving birth and I can't deal with him being more difficult that he's already going to be. I'm sorry."

"This has the potential to be something so much bigger." She handed her phone to me. "We received an invitation to speak at an event they are hosting for South Asian women in business. We've been asked to sit on the panel and tell our story in hopes of encouraging and empowering other women to start their own venture."

I reread the email three times because I couldn't fathom it. I stared at her in confusion. "Why us?"

"Because you're damn good at what you do. Have you any idea how big you've become? You wouldn't believe the number of requests I have to reject because of capacity. I'll post a picture of a new piece and ten minutes later it's sold. People not only love your work, but they trust in it. They believe in your vision. And they don't even know your name."

I couldn't comprehend the level of success she was talking about. My role in the business was solely on production, and I never gave much thought to the social media element. Before I could comment, the tension increased in tenfold when Idris appeared in the doorway.

Pretending that Rani wasn't there, he turned to me. "Come upstairs."

Rani rolled her eyes before she stood. "I better get going. Devi wants to go dress shopping." She hugged me tight. "Happy birthday. I love you," she whispered and then kissed my cheek.

"I love you too." I walked her to the door before I climbed the stairs behind Idris to our bedroom. Nerves swarmed me because what if he heard what we were talking about?

"Why was she in my house?" he asked when our bedroom door shut.

"She was here for less than an hour and only came to wish me happy birthday."

"I forbade you from ever speaking to her."

"Rani is one of my best friends. I'm sorry you don't like each other, but I can't cut her off. She's been part of my life for twenty-one years. She's important to me."

"And I'm not?"

My hands rubbed my face as I let out a groan of frustration. "I never said that. But the same way I can't leave you, I won't leave her."

"*Can't* leave me?" His hard expression stayed on me. "Do you want to leave me?"

"I'm still here, aren't I?"

"That wasn't my question."

"Sometimes I want to run and never look back," I answered honestly. "Other times I get glimpses of the husband I've wanted. It's that version that keeps me hostage because I keep hoping he won't leave. Maybe, just maybe, I'm enough for him to stay."

"I'm here. It's you that has left. It's been a *month* since you've slept in our bed."

I maintained the distance between us when he stepped forward. "What difference does it make? We still have an agreement in place."

"That's not why I need you to come back. Please, Zoya?" He reeked of despair. Then, in a desperate whisper, he said, "I can't sleep without you."

I knew this was true. Every night, after he thought I was sleeping, he'd sneak into the boys' room. The first night, when his hands ran over my body, I thought he was going to have sex with me. But after reassuring himself that I was real, he settled into a peaceful quiet. I always pretended to sleep until slumber overcame me while counting his breaths.

"Fine. I'll sleep in this room again." Almost in an act of defiance, the baby gave a sharp kick. I stifled my giggle as I placed my hands on my stomach.

"Is she moving? Can I feel?" He never cared in any of my other pregnancies. In fact, Idris had felt none of the kicks, not even when Nadim would keep me up all night with his movements. He closed the distance between us and placed his hands above mine.

I snatched my hands away like they had been electrocuted. He was so close to me I held my breath and only exhaled when she cause another flutter inside me.

Idris let out a soft laugh. "She's very strong."

"If you don't need anything, I'm going to—"

Now that he finally had me in his embrace, he wasn't going to let go. One hand cupped my face while the other held my hip. "Happy birthday." His green eyes were filled with an emotion I couldn't face. They darted down to my lips. "I'm going to kiss you."

"Don't."

"Please," he begged. "Nothing else, but I want to kiss my wife."

Unable to meet his burning stare, I lowered my gaze. "That's not fair. You don't get to act like nothing happened."

"Look at me." He forced my focus back to him. "You know I never had an affair. If you still doubted me, you would have gone by now. But you know I would never do that to our marriage." He swallowed hard. "Just one kiss. I want nothing else. But I need to feel you."

That's why he asked to feel the baby kick. He didn't care about her; he only wanted an excuse to get close to me and knew I wouldn't refuse him his fatherly right. Knowing that only made me stand firm in my decision.

"I said no."

"You said me and her are equal; yet she kisses you and I can't?"

"That was different and you know it."

"Because you love her?"

"Because *she* loves *me*."

Idris released me, retreating. "Last year, on your birthday, he asked if you loved me. You never answered him. But now I'm asking you the same question."

I shook my head. "It doesn't matter. Love was not listed as a requirement in our marriage contract. It was you who said you needed a wife, not love."

"It's a yes or no answer. Do you love me?"

"Love has to be equal. There is no room for it to exist in my reality."

"What have you ever understood about love? How could you distinguish between the reality and dream of being loved when you can't even look at it when it's standing before you?"

Chapter Thirty-Eight

I sat cross-legged on the bed and watched Idris button his shirt. Sumayyah asked us to meet her at a random address this afternoon. When we asked questions, she said she would explain when we got there. A bad feeling was running down my spine, and I knew I had to be there. I had one problem: *Idris*.

"Can I go to Sumayyah's in the afternoon?"

He stopped fiddling with his tie. "What for?"

"I haven't seen them in ages," I lied. "And you're all going to this wedding."

"Hashim's mum repeatedly asked me to bring you along to her daughter's wedding. The only reason I declined was because you said you weren't feeling well."

That was a half-lie. My feet were starting to swell, and the fatigue was hitting me hard. But truthfully, I didn't feel like dressing up to make small talk with strangers.

"I'll only be gone for two hours. One of them will pick me up and drop me off way before you get home."

"That's not part of our deal."

I climbed off the bed and fixed his tie for him. My hands rested on his chest as I stood as close to him as I could. "I'll share my location with you, so if I'm rushed off to the hospital you'd know. *Please?*"

He looked less than impressed. "I know what you're doing," he said, peering down at my hands. "One hour."

My arms flung around his neck, and I hugged him from excitement. "Thank you!"

Once Halima confirmed she'd pick me up, I got the boys dressed and ready to go. They swatted me away when I fawned over how adorable they looked. I got in one more kiss before they were driven away.

Halima and I spent the entire drive trying to guess what Sumayyah's surprise was. Halima was confident it was a pregnancy announcement, and I hoped it was true. Nobody deserved to be a mother more than Sumayyah. Rani parked up outside the block of flats at the same time as us.

"This new-build is so *nice*," she complimented as we pressed the buzzer. "I bet she's surprising us with a housewarming party. Her and Yousef probably moved out."

The Sumayyah that opened the door looked like a ghost of the one we knew. Under her eyes were hollow and her cheeks looked sullen. "Thanks for coming."

There was definitely no party. Moving boxes filled the small apartment. We all shared a look as we followed her to the living room. I tried not to gawk at the mess.

Sumayyah moved a few boxes, so we had room to sit on the sofa. She stood in front of us and forced a smile. "Welcome to my new home."

"I knew it!" Rani shrieked. "How did you get Yousef to move out? I'm going to need some tips to get Ravi's ass to follow in his footsteps."

Her fingers twisted together. "I..." She looked away, but we saw the tears.

Halima sat forward. "Sumayyah?"

She swallowed hard. "Yousef didn't move out with me."

We all knew what that meant, but the shock rendered us mute.

It was Halima that stood and hugged our friend. "I'm so sorry," she whispered.

"Thanks. I'm sorry I didn't tell you guys, but I needed time to process everything and find somewhere to live and I..." She brushed her tears away. "I can't believe this is my life."

Halima led her to the sofa and handed her a pack of tissues from her bag. "What happened?"

Rani still looked pale. "Who's ass do I need to fucking kick?"

Somehow, she managed a smile. That smile vanished as she told us the reality of her life for the past seven years. We cried with her when she did. We raged with her when she did.

My heart ached with hers. I couldn't comprehend this was all happening, and we had no idea. Aside from her struggle with fertility, from the outside Sumayyah's marriage and life seemed close to perfect. But the walls of her married home told a different story. They saw a woman filled with love and hope be torn apart. They heard the volatile words her mother-in-law hurled at her. They listened to the silence of Yousef's incompetence as a husband. They witnessed her anguished cries as she fell apart.

"What about your parents?" Rani asked. "They must have made Yousef and his family answer for all this."

I didn't think it was possible, but her sadness deepened. "They blamed me. They said I had done this to myself by working and not giving him a baby. Even when I begged them to stand by me, they turned their backs on me. My parents disowned me because I wanted a divorce and they didn't want to be associated with the shame."

Our friends couldn't understand the pain of being disowned by the people who are meant to love us unconditionally. But I did. "I'm so sorry," I whispered.

"My dad called me Maya from the day I was born. He literally called me *love* my whole life and threw it away when I needed him most."

"I'm sure he still loves you," Rani reassured.

Her words tangled with her cries until she took a few breaths to calm herself. "My whole life I did everything they wanted. I became a doctor because that's what my dad wanted. I wanted to earn the name he gave me. And I thought I did that, but the dream wasn't complete. *Education, career, marriage, and children.* I so badly wanted it all. But then I threw my career down the drain for a marriage that was empty. How stupid that I dreamt about giving birth to a daughter and naming her Maya?" She shook her head. "But today, in failing to complete Yousef's dream, I also shattered my father's."

"Who cares about what they want?" Rani asked. "You couldn't stay in that marriage."

Sumayyah didn't register her words. "All I have is an education. No parents. No husband. No children. Just an education."

The three of us shared a look of despair as she stared at the ground with tears streaming down her face. None of us knew what we could say to make her heartbreak disappear.

"I know we hate him, but what is Yousef saying about all this?" I asked.

Her scoff came out with a dry laugh. "He's refusing to go ahead with the divorce."

"He should have thought about that before he..." Rani's snappy tone subsided when Sumayyah flinched. "He's an absolute dick-head."

"The worst part is, I miss him. This wasn't supposed to be my life," she sobbed again. "I did everything right. I tried so hard to make it work. I begged God to fix my body so I could give us a baby. I loved him so much. Why wasn't I enough?"

"You were," Rani reassured. "You *are* enough and it's his loss that he realised that too late."

"I couldn't do it anymore. I had forgiven him time and time again. I gave up *everything* for my marriage, but that final lie just pushed me over the edge. It wasn't even the truth that hurt. It was that he knew how much the infertility was killing me, and he let me die. He chose himself while I was bleeding out for him."

Holding her hand, I gave it a tight squeeze. "That is why you made the right choice by getting out before he could take anymore from you."

Rani's burning gaze practically screamed *hypocrite* at me. "This culture makes us feel guilty for choosing ourselves. We are expected to give ourselves up and become our husband's shadow. But we are our own person. We have a name that deserves to echo across the globe."

Halima brought the conversation back to reassuring Sumayyah. "Remember what we said about our lives being a story? This is just a chapter that is hard to write. But one day you're going to read back on it and it won't hurt as much. You'll realise why it had to happen this way in order for you to survive."

"Your story is not over," Rani added. "There's still so much life you have to write about. There are so many characters that are going to come into your life that need you. Not forgetting the three standing alongside you." She grinned. "Metaphorically, of course; because we're technically sitting right now."

She locked her fingers and sighed. "I really wanted a happily ever after."

"We're running with the book analogy, huh?" I joked, earning weak chuckles.

"Let's hope not, because I would have to title it *The Broken Bou*," Sumayyah remarked.

I rubbed her back. "Your heart may be broken, but *you* aren't. Time does wonders in healing things. Let yourself grieve and grow from this, but don't give it the power to change who you are. You've let them control the narrative, but don't let this culture label you. Snatch that pen back because you are free to write whatever ending you want. You don't need a husband to write a happily ever after. You are not the broken *bou*. Like Halima said, we're *The Bows*. You are a woman who is no longer confined by the boxes of this toxic culture. And now that you're free, I hope you learn to see yourself as we see you. You are the *perfect* bow."

🎀🎀🎀🎀

My eyebrows furrowed. "Why is Idris already home? They left less than two hours ago."

Halima parked the car and shrugged. "Maybe they left early?"

"Before food was served? I doubt it." I grabbed my bag. "Thank you for the ride."

She blew me a kiss and drove away.

Anxiety found a home in the pit of my stomach. I unlocked the door and stepped inside. "Hello?"

It seemed only Idris had returned early as the house was silent except for the havoc he was wreaking. The loud noises from upstairs propelled my feet forward.

"Idris?" I asked at the top of the landing. "What are you doing home?"

Our bedroom had been turned upside down. All the clothes from our closet were strewn all over the floor. The contents from the bedside draw was tossed on the bed. If I hadn't seen his car parked outside, I would have thought someone had broken in to burgle us.

"What the hell are you doing?" I asked.

His jaw clenched tight, and his eyes housed a fury I had never seen in him. "Where is it?"

"What are you talking about?"

"Don't fucking come any closer to me!" He held his hands up when I stepped forward. "I don't know what I'm going to do if I get my hands on you."

I felt sick with fear. *What happened between him leaving for the wedding to now?* His next question gave me an inkling of what caused him to trash everything we own.

"What did you do with the fabric I bought you from Pakistan?"

Dread filled me. Trying to keep my tone light, I said, "You saw me make outfits with them."

His arms bulged as he crossed them over his chest. "Show me."

The lump in my throat made it hard to swallow. "How am I supposed to find anything in this mess?"

"Find them!" he bellowed so loud it echoed. "Show me every single fabric I bought."

To keep him from suspecting anything, I used some to make myself clothes. My knees wobbled and my fingers trembled as I weaved through the heaps of clothes. I found a few pieces and placed them on the bed.

He watched me with calculating eyes. "That's not all of them," he said once I stood still. "I bought fifteen different designs. This is only six. Where are the others? Because I've searched this entire room for them and they're nowhere to be seen."

"I used some to make clothes for Farrah."

He pulled his phone out. "Okay. Let me call her and tell her to bring them to me."

"They weren't all for her," I blurted.

Panic was an understatement. I was certain he knew something, but couldn't understand how he found out. The customers didn't even know my name. I only met a few if I was in Rani's old flat; and that was rare.

"Who were they for?"

"Her friends and in-laws."

"Don't lie to me," he snarled. His chest was rising and falling at a dangerous speed. He could barely hold himself back as he spoke. He pointed at my sketch book laid on the bed. "I always wondered why you spent so much time drawing in that *fucking* book. When I asked you, you fed me some bullshit about the miscarriage. I kept questioning how you had any space in your wardrobe when you were constantly fucking sewing. Now I know."

"Idris—"

"Don't fucking speak to me." He stepped closer. "Don't even say my name."

My teeth ground together as I forced my sobs from bursting out. The betrayal in his eyes was making it hard to breathe. The truth rested on my tongue, but I lacked the courage to let them free. I swallowed hard when Idris walked towards me. Unable to look away, I was forced to face his heartache.

"Say it, Zoya," he ordered.

"What are you going to do to me?" I cried.

"Look at me." His hands reached out for me, but he recoiled. "Tell me I've got this wrong. Tell me you wouldn't do this to me."

He already knows. Just say it.

But I was too scared; not only for myself, but for our daughter, too. I knew what he was capable of and knew I wasn't strong enough to fight him off.

He retreated when I remained silent. He took a deep breath. He spoke again, devoid of emotion. "Did you know Hashim has two sisters?"

I nodded. His wife had mentioned it one of the few times she had come over with her husband.

"Marwa came to our table and thanked us for attending her sister's wedding. She asked about you. She probably wanted to thank you."

"I—"

"She was wearing orange and Ammi just *loved* her outfit. I barely glanced at it, but I couldn't help but feel like I'd seen it before. Mum took a picture of it to show you when she comes home. She didn't need to do that though because I found the original." He tore a page out of my sketchbook and held it up. "This is it, no?"

"Those are just drawings of outfits I've seen."

Idris ignored me. "Marwa kept bragging about how it was custom made. Her husband happily paid a tidy sum for the clothes because it was her only sister's wedding and the value went up as it was hand-made." His laugh was dark and menacing. "And then it clicked where I recognised that material from."

I undeniably felt terrified. I couldn't get myself to admit the truth because that would also mean admitting to lying to him for all these years. It felt easier to uphold the lie.

I shook my head. "She wasn't talking about me. It's just a coinci-dence that her outfit is similar to what I drew. She could have bought that fabric from anywhere."

"All of my hotels have the same upholstery because I like everything to look uniform. I exclusively get everything, from the cushion covers to bedding, made in a factory. It's all designed and manufactured in the same place because my contract states that they cannot reproduce my designs for anyone else."

My eyebrows furrowed. "What does that have to do with…"

I knew the answer to my incomplete question before he answered.

"She can't have bought that from anywhere because the only roll to exist is the one that I designed and bought for you." He stood tall. "So now tell me Zoya, what should I do with you?"

Chapter Thirty-Nine

He was going to kill me. Nothing I could have said would have eased the rage swirling in his orbs. His hands were trembling as he stared me down, daring me to lie to him again.

"It's not how you think. It was never meant to turn into this," I cried.

After three years, I confessed. I told him about the course I completed and how we came up with the business idea. His anger only amplified when Rani was mentioned and doubled when I explained how Farrah delivered them to her when he stopped me from doing the school run. I would have kept them out of it, but I knew he would not rest until he uncovered every lie. I hoped including how much I had achieved would make him understand why I went behind his back, but he only grew more repulsed.

"Everything just kept growing, and it got to a point where I didn't know how to tell you. I knew you would get angry and I—"

"What were you expecting? You lied to me for years. You worked even though I told you I don't allow it. You hid money from me, even though I have always taken care of you."

I shook my head. "It wasn't like that, Idris!"

"*Don't* say my name!" he roared. His chest rose and fell, a slow, painful rhythm mirroring the despair etched onto his face. His voice cracked, each syllable piercing my heart. "How dare you lie in my bed when you've been going behind my back? How could you *dishonour* me by acting like I can't take care of my family?"

"It wasn't about the money! I've never even spent a penny of it. If you want it, you can have it."

He stepped back. His tone brought a chill to the room. "You think I need your money?"

"Then what do you need? What will make this all stop and go away?" I tried to hold my sob in, but it broke out.

Idris was barely holding himself together. I had enough experience to survive his anger. But his heartbreak was killing me. He was putting all his energy to rid himself of the tears in his eyes. "I have never been dishonest with you. That first day when you told me the truth to ward me off, I appreciated the honesty. I thought no matter what, I could trust you to always remain truthful with me. But you have continuously lied to me. I am your husband. Does that mean nothing to you?" He shook his head. "*How* could you lie to me?"

"Because you never would have understood! I needed something more than cooking and cleaning. I needed something for myself!"

"You had me!"

"It wasn't enough!" I screamed. "Designing gives me a sense of freedom. I love doing it. I love that something I do is good enough. Because I was never enough for you. No matter how hard I tried, you made sure I knew I was failing. But this was something I didn't fail at. I made something of myself! I was finally in control of something and I felt free."

He stood taller and his face became a blank slate. "If you value your life, this stops now. You are going to throw everything away and if I ever see a needle in your hand, *nothing* will save you."

"Why? Make me understand, Idris," I begged. "You never suspected a thing because I did everything you needed from me."

"No, Zoya. I never suspected you because I couldn't have ever dreamed of you betraying me like this."

"What betrayal?" I screamed in frustration. "I never sacrificed my duties as a mother, wife, or daughter-in-law. I did both parts of my life well, so why does it need to stop? Why can't I put them together and just be me?"

"Even after fourteen years and two children, you haven't understood the role of a woman."

"A woman can be more than just a wife and mother. And I'm proof of that."

He laughed at me. "What proof? You sewed some material together and think you're a businesswoman now?"

A wave of despair washed over me, leaving me feeling utterly hopeless. The dream I had been chasing dissolved like mist, leaving me to accept my reality.

"So, that's it? I do as you ask and forget everything I've worked towards? We go back to silently tolerating one another? Because I can't do that."

His lip curled into a scowl. "If you hoped I would divorce you, then you were mistaken."

"Why are you doing this? You don't want me; so do us both a favour and end it. You keep clinging to this marriage like it's worth saving.

What for? Is it to punish me? Are you trying to hurt me by keeping me here?"

He pointed at me. "That is your problem. You've always had one foot out the door. You have never tried to make this work."

My mouth hung open. "Not tried? What have the last fourteen years of my life been? I did everything you asked of me. Now that I'm asking for something, you can't get over your pride to give me that. A woman's success is not something to fear. Especially in this culture, because she's had to fight tooth and nail to make a name for herself. Don't you think I wanted to share my success with you? I *wished* you could be happy for me."

"Then you should have given me the chance!"

"I tried, and you shot me down in Bali! You made it clear that I had no business in the real world."

He couldn't defend himself. "We are not divorcing. That is final."

"I can't live like this anymore. We can't keep pretending that we're happy. I want a husband that can celebrate my wins with me."

"And I want a wife that loves me back!"

We stood frozen on opposite sides of the room, tears welling in our eyes, the silence heavy with unspoken emotion.

He masked his pain with anger. "Is that what you need to hear for you to understand why I need this marriage to work? Because if that is what it takes, then hear me loud and clear. I *love* you, Zoya. I love you so deeply that I cannot be without you; even if it means forcing you to stay. You are the *worst* thing to have ever happened to me because my mind and heart cannot escape you. No matter how hard I try, I cannot stop the control you have over me. I love you so much. It's that love that has driven me to insanity. It's why today, when I can't stomach your betrayal, I've held myself back and not laid a hand on you. Even though you have hurt me more than I can explain, I would rather live with you tolerating me than be without you. I have loved you enough for a thousand lifetimes. Yet you cannot love me even in this one."

I dreamed of swooning love confessions as a young girl. I wanted love that you could only find in movies and books. But standing before me was a desperate man who was far from an ideal love interest. He was angry. He was hurt. He was pleading with me.

"Then love *me*, Idris," I cried softly. "*All* of me. Love the real me; not the one you broke to your will. Love the part of me that stands up for herself. Love the part of me that wants more than this life you've given. Love the part of me that has dreams beyond your wildest imagination." I held up the clothes I made and repeated the words he had said to me throughout our marriage. "Look at me."

"You're the only thing I have seen since we met."

Whatever remained of my heart broke at his tears. "This is me. My name is Zoya Iqbal and I have two beautiful sons and a baby girl on the way. My name is Zoya Iqbal and I own a business. My name is Zoya Iqbal and I want to be loved for being me."

$$\text{🎀🎀🎀🎀}$$

Before everyone returned, I cleaned the mess and began making dinner. Idris remained in our room with his laptop open; he wasn't really working, but blankly staring at the screen. Shazia asked Idris why he abruptly left and he brushed her off with an excuse about work. Idris and I slept with as much distance between us as possible. I couldn't sleep and at six o'clock I got out of bed and began my day.

Neither of us mentioned his love declaration. In fact, we never spoke to each other at all. Any vulnerability he showed vanished, and I wondered if it was just an illusion. But his harrowed tone echoed in my mind. I wished he would give me something other than the cold shoulder. If he truly loved me, then maybe we could reach a mutual agreement where we were both happy.

"Where did you go the other day?"

I turned the vacuum off and faced him. "Which day?"

Instead of answering, he said, "Was it a business trip? Because I spoke to your mother and she said she hasn't seen you in weeks."

"I went to see Halima."

He pursed his lips. "You're banned from leaving the house. I don't care if your mother is on her deathbed, you aren't allowed to go."

"That's a bit extreme."

"No, it isn't. Not when I can't trust a word that comes out of you." He stepped closer. "And just so we're both abundantly clear on the rules; unless we are hosting a family gathering, nobody is allowed inside this house to visit you either."

After last night, I already felt like I couldn't breathe. Now the walls were closing in on me and I was completely alone.

"Why can't they come here?"

When he spoke, it was a matter of fact. "I said no, and that makes it final. If you so much as take a step outside, I'll take your phone. And if you try again, I'll ban you from going to family gatherings. And if you dare to try after that, I'll ban *everyone* from coming here altogether. I'll keep taking until you learn your lesson. Say you understand."

I swallowed hard and nodded my head. "I understand." I waited for him to finish getting dressed for work before I resumed cleaning.

He's angry right now. This is going to blow over and things will go back to normal.

But even my normal wasn't enough. And I knew Idris would never let this go. It was going to hang over my head until I died.

Bending down, I picked up the scan picture. It must have slipped under the bed during his ransacking. I sat on the bed and stared at her. "I'm sorry," I whispered. "Please forgive me for bringing you into this life. If I knew how to save you, I would."

A younger Zoya sat opposite me. *"You can save her. You know what you have to do."*

In my other ear, I could hear my mother's sadness from the day they found out about Adeel.

"One day, if you are unfortunate enough to have a daughter, you will understand the lengths a mother would go to protect her child."

But she didn't protect me. She left me to the wolves and stayed silent because that was what a good woman does. She bows her head and doesn't speak unless instructed to.

I didn't have to be that type of mother. I *couldn't* be that type of mother. If I stayed, she would be forced to live in my footsteps. Idris would constrict her to this house and his unbearable rules. One day, she would be in my position and ask me why I didn't do everything in my power to save her.

I called the one person who found the strength to do what I needed.

"Hey," Sumayyah said.

"Hey. How are you?"

"My back is aching. I just finished putting all my clothes away. Is everything okay?"

No. But I need to know that you are. I need you to reassure me that if I do this, I'll be fine.

"Yeah. I just wanted to make sure you were okay."

"I'm okay." Her vague answer wasn't enough for me.

"Are you really okay? I mean … do you have any regrets?"

Her silence momentarily choked me and then she came through, reassured. "No. When you know you've given it your all, and you tried your hardest, there's no room for regret. I didn't fall at the first hurdle. I picked myself up and tried to make do with what I had. It wasn't enough. I deserved better."

Nobody could say that I hadn't tried. My suffering had spanned over fourteen years and I couldn't do it anymore. I had to show my daughter that she deserved more.

I cradled my growing belly as my throat tightened. "How did you do it? How did you leave?"

Sumayyah fell silent. I heard the fear in her voice as she asked, "Why are you asking?"

I stared at the scan once again, my heart aching. I blinked back my tears, having no room to be weak. "I'm having a daughter. I already know the life that has been written for her and I don't want this for her. Unless I get her out, she'll be exactly like me. They'll mould her to be weak and obedient."

She went mute again. The only sound was her heavy breathing. "What are you saying?"

I held my breath. The sound of his keys echoed as he locked the front door. With one last look at the four walls of my prison, my eyes hardened and determination flowed through my veins. "I need to protect her. I need to get out of this prison."

"But your children..."

"Are exactly why I need to get out," I finished for her. "I can take him to court and fight for custody. But I can't stay here any longer."

"You'll need a lot of money for that. Where will you live? You can't rent anywhere without a substantial income."

"What if I had that? What if I had enough money to buy a house?"

"Please don't tell me you've robbed him."

I managed a laugh. "I don't need his money when I've been running my own business for years."

She spluttered. "What are you talking about?" Her side of the line went quiet as I told her about the business. "*Wow*. That's amazing. Why didn't you tell us?"

"Because I was scared of failing. But I didn't, Sumayyah. I got to live my dream, and that's why I can't give it up. Not only for myself, but also for my little girl. I need her to know a woman can dream just as much as a man can. Why should she have to watch her brothers live a life she wants? Why should her brothers get to step into the real world while she's smothered in this culture's version of protection? I need her to know she can be more than this culture will allow. I need to stand up for her because I can't let her down; not the way I let myself down. I didn't fight for my dream and look at what I allowed myself to become."

Her smile was palpable, even over the phone. "Then we'll fight."

My cry got lodged in my chest. "You'll help me?"

"I will *always* stand with you. Between my hope and your strength, they won't know what hit them. We'll fight until you're dreaming with your eyes wide open."

CHAPTER FORTY

I HALTED AS I stepped into the living room. My eyes dragged from Idris to a sullen Yousef. It took biting down on my cheek to stop myself from hurling every foul word I knew at him. I wondered whether he told the whole truth to Idris or just the parts that painted Sumayyah as the villain. Knowing my husband, he probably believed Yousef had every right to treat her like scum because she couldn't fulfil her *duties* by giving him a baby.

"Make tea for us," he ordered.

Yousef's pathetic puppy eyes were on me. "How is she?"

I smiled. "Absolutely *perfect*. Would you like sugar in your tea?" My sweet tone made Idris' eyes narrow.

"Can you tell her to pick up my calls?"

"No."

"I'm really trying. I want to fix this."

I stared down at him. "You mean you're trying to fix her? She was always too good for you, and you knew it. So, you took a woman who trusted you and stomped all over her heart."

He shook his head. "That isn't true. You've only heard her side of the story."

I laughed in his face. "Me and the generations of women before me have heard your story. All men do is complain about how miserable they are and find someone to blame it on. Your predecessors have made a living stealing our voice. But we're done listening to your breed droning on about how *hard* life is for you."

"Zoya!" Idris snapped.

Yousef held his hand up to calm him down. "It's okay. She's going to defend her friend."

"Thank you," I said with a sarcastic smile. "Had you defended her, you wouldn't be sitting in my house crying about your failure to be a good husband."

"She's still my wife. I'm going to prove to her we'll make it through this."

I covered my mouth to hide my laugh. "And *he's* going to help you do that?" I asked, pointing at Idris. "This is a man that can't even make his own wife happy. Do yourself a favour; don't take any advice from him. He hasn't a clue about proving his worth to a woman."

I hoped if I pushed the right buttons, Idris would kick me out. There was a plan in motion for when that happened. Sumayyah was leading on part one, as I wasn't allowed to leave the house and Idris hadn't been to work all week. Once she completed phase one, the next part was on me and simple. I pack a bag, grab my children, and never look back.

Yousef thanked me when I served his tea. Idris glared at me as I left them to it.

My phone lit up with Sumayyah's name. I pressed the phone to my ear. "Hey."

"I can see his car parked in the drive. Come to the door and get the key."

"Did you also see Yousef's car parked on the street?" I hissed.

When she went silent, I assumed she was trying to locate it. "What is he doing here?"

I rolled my eyes. "He's sharing his sorrows with the only person who would defend him."

"Okay." She sighed. "I'm already here. Just come and take the key."

"Are you sure? I don't want to put you in that position. You can drop it off another time."

"I'm working back-to-back over the next few days. It will be fine."

I hung up and crept down the hallway before opening the door as slowly as I could. "Thank you," I whispered as I tucked the key into my bra. "How is she?" I asked.

"She's doing okay. She's Rani, you know?"

"Did you tell her I wanted to come but…" I sighed. "I can't imagine how she's feeling. I wish I could give her a tight hug and let her know that she'll get through this."

"She's got her family and knows we're only a phone call away. I better get going. Myra invited me over for lunch, and I wanted to pick up some baked treats for her boys."

My name echoed behind me, followed by his heavy footsteps. "What are you doing?" Idris snapped.

"Enjoying some fresh air," I retorted sarcastically.

His eyes narrowed at my friend. "Have you come to fill her head with the same ideas that ruined a good man's life?"

Sumayyah laughed. "A good man?" she echoed. "And who would that be?"

"Have you no shame? How does a woman walk out of her husband's home?"

"And how does a husband trample on the sanctity of marriage? Don't stand there and judge me on something you have no knowledge about."

He wasn't going to back down. "I know what is expected of a wife and you failed in those."

She flinched at his harshness. Just when I thought she would walk away with her tail between her legs, she stood tall. "When you lack both the anatomy and courage to be a woman in this culture, I would greatly appreciate you keeping your *opinion* to yourself." Her sweet tone was cutthroat and made me smile in pride.

He laughed at her. "Where are you going to go? You have no father. No husband. You should be falling at his feet, trying to make it work."

Her brow arched. "I would rather die than ever bow to serve a man again. It is not our job to worship you." She mocked a look of concern. "If I were you, I'd learn from your friend's mistakes. Once you push a woman far enough, there is no getting her back."

Worried she'd let off more than she intended, I said, "Sumayyah, that's enough."

Her name being a beacon, Yousef's rushed steps were heading our way. "Sumayyah?" Yousef gasped. He pushed past me and stared at her. "What are you doing here?"

I expected her to panic or burst into tears, but she stood strong. "I don't answer to you anymore."

He pointed at his wedding ring. "We're still married. I've been trying to call you, but it doesn't go through."

"Because I changed my number," she stated bleakly.

"Let's talk this out."

"There's nothing left to say." She waved at me. "I'll call you later."

He held onto her. "Please? I'll do whatever you want. We can be happy, just the two of us. I love you, Sumayyah."

She looked at him with pity. "It's just words."

Just to dig the knife in deeper, I said. "Tell Ibrahim I said hello."

She shot me a look of disapproval and left him standing on my doorstep with broken hope.

A smile crept onto my face as I watched her sway back to her car. This was the same woman who loved her husband enough to die for him. There was no hesitation in her decision to walk away. She never looked back once and her strength empowered me.

I left them at the front door and headed upstairs. Now that I had the key to the flat, nothing was stopping me. I only need an opportunity to grab my children and run.

Our bedroom door slammed shut. "What the hell were you playing at?"

If I was going to do this, I needed to have the same strength as Sumayyah. "Has your friend gone? He didn't even drink his tea."

Idris spun me around so I was forced to face his anger. "It's like you want to piss me off."

"No. I want a divorce!"

"Well, you can get that idea out of your head because I will not give you that!"

"Then give me a reason to stay! Look at the way you have treated me the past week; why wouldn't I want to leave? Prove to me that this marriage is worth the sacrifice I've had to make!"

"Why would I need to prove anything to a woman that is worthless?" he spat at me.

"There's my husband," I goaded as I stepped back. "The man who only knows how to reduce me to filth. You say you love me, but we both know that isn't true. You can only love me when I'm on my knees serving you."

He held his hand out. "Give me your phone. I told you what the rules and consequences are."

"I didn't break any of your precious rules. I never stepped outside, and she never came in."

"Give it to me! Or when I find it, I'm going to smash it into fucking pieces."

"How long are you going to keep doing this? Aren't you exhausted? Because I am. I get you're angry, but this isn't fair. You can't keep doing this to me. I'm not asking for the impossible, Idris. I'm asking you to treat me like a human."

He looked at me incredulously. "You *lied* to me for years and are yet to apologise."

"I've spent our whole marriage apologising to you! I apologised when *you* put your hands on me. I apologised when *you* misunderstood and tried to throw me out. I apologised even when I did nothing wrong! I can't keep giving when I get nothing back."

"What haven't I given you, Zoya? I've kept a roof over your head. I've put food on the table. I've provided two sons. What more do you want?"

I stared at my husband, who was blind to my tears. He watched me with nothing but disbelief in his eyes. And maybe part of him had a right to feel like that because he believed that was his sole job. To

Idris, he had done his part in this marriage. But his frustration also highlighted something I already knew.

The daughter I was carrying was not his. *I've provided two sons.* He failed to acknowledge the other child he forced inside me because a daughter is not her father's. She is only borrowed property.

The ghosts of my childhood played in front of my eyes. I heard my father's abuse. *Stupid. Useless. Lazy. Shameless. Dirty. Used. Dishonourable. Filthy. Immoral. Worthless.* I felt the sting of his assault. And then I was looking at the future. I saw a little girl who mirrored me. Her tearful eyes held the same pain I did as Idris labelled her the same way. I heard her begging me to save her as I once pleaded with my mother.

Holding back my sobs, I stepped back, but taller. "My freedom."

My mother couldn't break the cycle with her daughters. *But I had to.* No matter what it cost. So, pulling on whatever strength remained, I turned away and began gathering my hospital notes and paperwork. Remembering what he said the night of Rani's engagement party, I didn't pack any clothes.

"What are you doing?"

"I can't do this anymore. Do whatever you have to do, but I'm done."

"You think just because you have a little money, you'll make it out there?"

I turned on my heels and stared him down. "I survived this marriage, didn't I? Nothing out there could be as cruel as the fate you've made me suffer. Even if I have to live on the street with my kids, it has to be better than this prison!"

He chuckled. "You think I'm going to let you take my children? My blood doesn't belong on the street."

The chain he always held onto was pulling me back into the fold. I closed my eyes and saw Sumayyah's determination. I felt my friends' words of encouragement etch themselves onto my skin, rewriting the abuse my father and Idris marked me with.

"Okay," I breathed. My heart was shattering inside me, but my voice came out strong. "Keep your children. Maybe you'll understand how hard it is to be a mother and maintain a home. Live in my shoes and see if you can last longer than a day."

His face drained of colour. He wasn't expecting me to agree with him and now that I had; he was failing to conceal his panic. "What kind of mother leaves her children behind?"

"One that is forced to choose between life and death. I have died for my children, but I realise they need me alive. I don't want to just survive anymore. I need to live."

"I'll make sure they never know who you are."

I lugged my bag over my shoulder. "Then at least promise you'll love them for me. And give them a version of you that is worthy of their love." A cry slipped past me. "Ask me again."

"Ask you what?"

"The question I never answered."

"I don't need to. I have my answer."

I shook my head as I cried. "You said I couldn't love you even in this lifetime. But that was untrue. I couldn't understand why or how it happened. I told myself that somehow you tricked me into feeling this. There's no denying it anymore. I love you, Idris. You said your love drove you to insanity? Then what has mine done to me? Because it was the one reason I stayed when you gave me a million to leave. You weren't the love story I dreamed, but it was enough for me. I knew you were trying to love me as much as you could. I understood that your love was angry and imperfect. I learned to love every version of you. But I need to leave because it's time I learned to love myself more."

CHAPTER
FORTY-ONE

THE SILENT FLAT ECHOED what I felt inside. I missed my children and not a minute had gone by the past two days where I wasn't crying for them. I'd lost count of how many times I grabbed my phone to call Idris and check if they were okay. But that was all the ammunition he needed to trap me. He needed to know I was serious and could survive without them. *Even if it was false.*

I was expecting either Idris or his parents to call me the evening I left, but no one did. *Had Idris warned them of consequences if they spoke to me?*

I suddenly understood why Sumayyah missed Yousef after everything he put her through. Because no sane person in my shoes would feel sad at being served divorce papers. I should have been jumping for joy at finally being free of him. Instead, I was laying in bed and only eating because my body was growing a baby.

After everything he said, Idris wasn't even fighting for me and our marriage. He hadn't reached out once to fix things. He was happy to pretend I had never existed.

When my mum called for the third time, I put her out of her misery. "Hello." I braced myself for her lecture about how I disgraced the family name.

"Where are you? He said you'd be here by now and your sons won't stop crying for you."

My eyebrows furrowed as I tried to make sense of what she was saying. "He dropped the boys off to you?"

"How long will it take for you to get here?"

Something felt off. It was unlike Idris to leave the boys at my parent's house; especially since his house had people to watch over them. "Why can't I hear them crying?"

"Zain took them to the shop. Get here quickly." She hung up.

As I got dressed, I knew I was walking into a trap because Idris would have rather lost his pride and given them to me than lose face with my parents. But he also wasn't the type to ask my parents for help in our marriage. No matter what it was, I was desperate to see my children, so I called a taxi.

The boys ran to me before I could step over the threshold. My heart felt alive again at seeing their faces and hearing their joy. "I missed you guys!"

"Are you feeling better? Baba said you had to go to the hospital because the baby wasn't well," Karim said.

I peered into the living room before following them to the dining room. "Is your Baba here?"

Nadim shook his head. "He went to work. Are you coming home today?"

His sadness felt like a knife to my chest. I didn't know how to lie to him. More importantly, I didn't want to. "I don't think so." I looked around at the empty room and an idea hit me. "But you can come and stay with me. Where are your bags?"

"You just got here. Are you already leaving?" my mum asked as she entered the room.

"He said he wants me home."

"Stay for a cup of tea."

I stood. "I'll have tea another day. Boys, put your shoes on." I was almost at the door when my dad blocked my escape route.

Unlike my mother, he couldn't hide his anger. The scowl on his face made it clear he knew what had transpired and confirmed I had walked into their trap. "You're not going anywhere."

I stepped to him. "Who's going to stop me? I am not your problem anymore."

"Who gave you the right to walk out of your husband's house? Can you understand the shame I felt when he called to tell me what you had done? What answer was I supposed to give?" he shouted. "I did everything I could to save me from this and today you tore it all apart."

"I hope your heart is bigger than mine and you can forgive me in ways I could never forgive you. But if you're expecting me to say sorry, you're going to be very disappointed. The same way you never apologise for ruining my life, I won't apologise for saving myself."

"You are going to sit down and wait for him to take you home."

"I'm not going back there. I'm taking my children and leaving. You won't ever hear from me again. To save face with the community, you can tell them I died. Tell my siblings to mourn for me and then you all move on with your life."

He didn't budge. We stayed locked in a staring match until the doorbell rang.

Like me, Idris looked like he hadn't slept since that night. His heavy gaze never left my face. They scanned every inch of me as if he thought I was an imposter standing before him.

"Is this how low you've stooped? You came to *him* to finish me?"

Karim looked between me and his father and tugged my hand. "Ammi?"

I crouched down to his level. My lips pressed against his cheek. "Take Nadim upstairs and play together nicely. The adults need to have a conversation and then we're going to our new home."

My dad and Idris walked into the living room and the door was shut once I joined them. For the first time, they stood shoulder-to-shoulder on their side of the battlefield. I stood opposite them, ready to fight on my own.

"Unless you're coming home with us, you are not taking my sons anywhere," Idris stated.

I laughed at him. "You made that threat already and only lasted two days. This time, I won't leave them with someone so incapable of being a parent."

"You wouldn't have come if I called you home."

"Because this is a trap to get me within your walls again?"

He grit his teeth together. "You either come home or—"

"Or *what*?" I spat. "You two are going to kill me?"

"Zoya!" my father bellowed. "You are going to apologise to him and go back home."

"I'm not doing that and no one can make me."

He stepped towards me. "I won't say it again. For once in your life, do as you're told!"

"I'm not a little girl anymore. You don't get to decide what I do." Anger thrummed in my veins as I looked at them. "If you don't like it, then you can *fuck* off."

One second my dad was walking towards me. The next he was falling backward. In the few seconds it took to realise it was me that pushed him to protect myself, he regained his balance and slapped me.

My cheek stung, as did my eyes. Their faces blurred as I stood there in momentary shock. I looked at Idris as if he would protect me, but he stood immobile.

"I hate you," I whispered, unknowing who it was directed at. I blinked my pain away. "I *hate* you," I spat. "I hate you!" I screamed so loud my throat felt hoarse.

His hands were trembling. "How dare you hit your father?"

My sharp gaze landed on him. "What kind of father are you? What father beats his daughter until blood fills her mouth? What kind of father teaches his daughter fear, not love?"

Idris stepped towards me with guilt written over his face. "Let's go home."

"Don't touch me," I sobbed when he reached for me. "How could you let him do that to me? How could you bring me here knowing what he is? Why do you keep finding ways to hurt me?"

He grabbed my fists before they could reach his chest. "Tell me you'll come home and you'll never have to come back here."

Idris was asking me to choose between a life and death sentence. But I wanted freedom.

Before I could reach the door, a hand dragged me back by my hair. My scream was cut off when a hand wrapped around my throat and squeezed tight.

I was seventeen again. I believed him as he promised to kill me. I couldn't breathe.

One hand clawed at his arms. The other held my bump.

I would not wait for someone to save me.

A bloodcurdling scream ripped through the room as I shoved him with all my might. I shoved Idris away when he reached out to steady me. A coughing fit seized me, my nails raking across my throat in a desperate attempt to ease the burning. My breaths hitched in my throat, each gasp a ragged sob that stole the air from my lungs. Leaning my forehead against the wall, I fought to regain my composure.

Idris' arms wrapped around me. "Zoya?"

Pushing off the wall, I put as much distance as I could between me and them. I stared at Idris. "Is this what you wanted? Is this what you brought me here for?"

"I pulled him off you! I told you, let's go home!"

"No! Why would I go there? So you can do the same thing?"

My dad held his hands up in prayer as he cried up at the ceiling. "What did I do to deserve such a curse? Why is this girl trying to kill me?"

Wiping my tears, rage consumed me. "Aside from being born a woman, what did I do to deserve such hatred? The two men that should have protected me hurt me more than anyone."

My father turned to Idris and put his hands up in a begging motion. "Forgive me. I gave you a ruined woman for a wife. Save your honour and leave her to the streets. Clean your hands of her as I have done."

His righteousness pissed me off. "You're so blinded by your own male ego, you can't even accept responsibility for your failures."

His eyes bulged out of their sockets. "*My* failures? I have three other children that are happy and settled in life. It is only you that brings trouble to my door, as you've always done."

"Because I never conformed to your dictatorship. Ask any of your other children if they love you. Ask if any of them respect you; because I can guarantee they don't. I was punished for having dreams because in your world, a woman doesn't have a place to dream. I dreamed of love and happiness, and that was unacceptable. So you did everything to make me live a nightmare. But I won't let my daughter experience that."

There was a knock at the door and my mum entered timidly. "The children are getting scared."

My dad pointed at her. "This is on you. Had you raised her right, she never would have become insolent. You got lazy with her and she ran amuck. A mother controls her children and raises them to be good people."

Like a deer in headlights, she feared for her life in the face of his rage. "She's going to fix this."

"What wrong did I do? Why is it my duty to fix this? Why is nobody telling him to be a better husband?"

"It wasn't me that lied," Idris said. "I said you can't work, and you still went behind my back."

"Why is it such a sin for a woman to earn a living?"

My dad braced his shoulders back. "Because God said so. A woman doesn't work."

"Don't twist the religion to suit your agenda," I snapped back. "A woman can work if it maintains her modesty and is within the home." I turned to Idris. "I asked for that."

He met my harsh stare. "And I told you it is my duty to provide as your husband."

"And what about all your other duties? What about *my rights* as a wife?"

"Which of those haven't I honoured, Zoya?"

I looked between them and let out a laugh. "You're both so pathetic and ignorant. How funny is that men pick which marital rights and laws they wish to abide? You're all quick to remind women that intimacy is your right, but lack knowledge in how to truly respect your wife."

Idris's gaze was solely on me. "I will not ask you again. Which of your rights have I not honoured?"

"A husband is to provide financial security for his wife." I turned to my father. "She is entitled to spending money. When have you ever given my mother a penny? How many times have we had to belittle ourselves to ask for a few pounds to buy something for ourselves?"

"Have I ever denied you anything you've wanted?" Idris fired back.

"A wife has the right to be treated with kindness, love, and respect. A wife is entitled to her emotional needs being met." I looked at my mother. "Does that describe your husband? Because mine would threat to burn the house if I ever cried."

She shook her head. "That's enough."

"For too long we've let them twist religion with culture so they can keep power and control. If we must fulfil our duties, then we are also entitled to our rights as women."

She pleaded with me. "Go home with your husband. This world is unkind to women."

"You once said I'd understand the lengths a mother would go to protect her children." I wrapped her hand in mine. "Tell me, if you knew what my life would become; if you knew how many tears I would weep, would you have brought me into this world?"

She wiped my falling tears. "A mother cannot survive without her children. The moment that cord attaches them, a bond is formed and cannot be broken."

I held our hands against my chest. "They are the only reason my heart is still beating. You knew I would come running for my children; that's why you used them as bait today."

"For their sake, forgive him and go home. You aren't the first woman to suffer at the hands of her husband. I, too, died for my children."

I shook my head. "We shouldn't have to die for their happiness. We have to break the cycle, Ammi. I tried so hard to be you. I became a wife and daughter-in-law. I took care of his parents and loved them as my own. I cooked and cleaned. I raised my children. I fulfilled my duties as the eldest *bou* of his family. I did what the generations before me did and I'm tired." I fell to the floor at her feet. "I'm so sorry, Ammi. But I can't do it anymore. I can't cry tears for a man that doesn't see them. I can't forgive a man that isn't sorry."

She knelt on the floor and rubbed my back. "Don't cry so much. The baby will get distressed." No matter how much she begged me to get up, I had no strength left in me.

"I can't do this anymore. Why didn't you let him kill me? Why did you bring me into this world knowing what he is?"

"Zoya, the baby..." she pleaded. "You're hurting her."

"Get up," Idris ordered. His footsteps were drowned by my sobs. His fingers hooked around my arm as he tried to ply me off the floor. "I said stand up, Zoya!" he screamed. His hard expression stayed on me as I refused to move.

"Sit. Stand. Serve. Speak. Silence." I looked up at Idris. "That has been the mantra of my existence. An observer into my own life, letting everyone decide who I should be. I've always known I was worth more than this culture could ever value. But you broke me until I felt worthless. A daughter is not a curse. She is not borrowed property to her father. She is not here to serve her husband. Our happiness is not a luck of the draw. We deserve to see our dreams, no matter how big or small, come to fruition. We are our own person. I waited for permission to speak. But no more." I pulled myself off the floor and stared them down. "This is me. See me. Hear me. This is not love or respect. I was only doing what generations of women have been taught. But we now know how powerful we can be. We will no longer be obedient."

I was lost and directionless. My feet took me to my children, who looked at me with worry. I hugged them both tight and promised them that everything was going to be alright.

My gaze landed on the spot where I had died. I could still see me laying there, tolerating his assault. She looked at me and silently begged me to free her. I gave her a nod of reassurance.

With their shoes still on, I called a taxi and only took them downstairs when it was a minute away.

"Zoya?" He was walking towards us. "Zoya." He was panicking as I put my shoes on. "Zoya!" He grabbed me before I could open the door. "Where are you going?"

I looked past him at my mum. "I finally understand the lengths a mother would go. I followed your footsteps in everything else, but I cannot let her endure this pain. I would rather lose everything than sacrifice her happiness."

"No." Idris forced me to look at him. "No. No! Don't go. Zoya, look at me. Don't do this."

"You're going to scare them."

"You can't leave me. Please let's go home." He held my face and whispered, "I love you. Please don't do this."

I escaped his embrace and opened the door while ignoring Idris' yells. With both of their hands in mine, I turned my back on the guards and slipped through the bars. I stepped out into the world and alongside me, so did the Zoya who died in this house. She gave me a nod of encouragement as pride shone in her eyes.

Free of our chains, we could finally breathe.

Idris blocked my way when the taxi pulled up. "We can fix this. I'll give you anything you want. All you have to do is ask."

I wiped his stray tear before stepping back. "I'm done asking for permission."

CHAPTER FORTY-TWO

I ALMOST DROPPED THE cup when Karim ran past me. I yelled at the boys to stop running around before settling onto the sofa with Rani.

"Thank you," she muttered. The shadows under her eyes showcased her sleepless nights. She lost herself in her thoughts as she stared into her cup.

"You okay? If you want, we can talk about it?"

She shook her head. "I'll be alright." She arched her brow. "The hair is very new and different."

I ran my fingers through the short locks. "It was a spur-of-the-moment decision. Once when Idris was in Pakistan, I cut my hair and when he came back, he *forbade* me from ever doing it again."

Her laugh filled me with warmth. "So it was a *fuck you* haircut?"

"Sort of. I don't think I like it though," I chuckled.

"I think you look great; like a *sexy* momma bear." Her smile faded, and she sighed. "It's been a shit few weeks for us, hasn't it?"

I looked around the messy flat that had become my new home. "You can say that again."

"Now that we've got the keys to the shop, when did you want to start renovations? You're only a few weeks away from your due date."

"You know what the vision is. I'm going to be out of commission for at least a few months, especially now that I'm on my own."

As of yesterday, Idris had finally stopped calling me; I guess he finally got the hint when I ignored every call and message. The boys missed their dad, so I answered his call on two occasions and handed them the phone. He tried to speak to me afterwards, but I hung up.

It would be a lie to say I didn't miss him, but I made sure to never ask about him the few times I spoke to my mother-in-law. Our conversations were brief and after ensuring her I was doing okay, she would only ask about her three grandchildren and hang up. She never pried for information or begged me to come back. Perhaps she understood I had reached my limit.

"You're never on your own. Me and the girls will be here every step of the way." She sipped on her hot drink. "Do you know what you want to do?"

I hadn't filed for divorce yet. Islamically, we couldn't be divorced while I was pregnant. It was the perfect excuse because it wasn't a step I was ready to take. Now that I'd admitted my feelings out loud, they felt real, and I couldn't deny that I loved him. After dreaming about love, I never could have imagined how vicious the reality of it was. It was knowing the thorns would hurt but being unable to let go.

Needing to change the subject, I held up the leaflet, advertising my name as a guest speaker. "I want to finish writing the speech for next week's event. Can you imagine if my waters break while I'm sitting on the panel?"

Rani burst into laughter. "That would be disgusting, but hilarious. You don't need a speech; they're only going to ask you a few questions."

"That I have to answer in front of a couple hundred people. Don't you remember our Drama lessons in school? I clam up from nerves. Why can't you do all the talking?"

"Because it's *your* business! I'll be next to you for moral support. Are you definitely happy with the samples because I'm going to finalise the order with the factory when I head to India next month?"

I shook my head. "There's no rush. You're going there to see your family, not for work."

"It's fine. Devi has asked me to shop for some of her wedding pieces while I'm there." She couldn't register the shock on my face because there was a knock at the door. "*Finally!* Food."

What the boys enjoyed most about their new home was the exciting array of takeout food. I still cooked most days, but we weren't limited to traditional Pakistani dishes anymore. They loved trying new cuisines, but their favourite was ordering in.

I rummaged through my bag as I shouted, "Let me get this one! You can't keep wasting your money..." My voice faltered.

Idris looked too large for the room. His hair and beard were unkept and outgrown. His hands were shoved deep inside his coat pocket as he watched at me.

"What are you doing here?" Before he could answer, I asked a more imperative question. "How did you even find me?"

His deep voice reached the pit of my stomach. "You never stopped sharing your location the day you met your friends."

Dammit. I forgot about that.

"I would have come earlier, but I thought best to give you space to calm down."

"You think calling and texting me a hundred times a day is giving me space?"

"I miss you."

The boys gasped at the sight of their father and wrapped their arms around his legs. Idris blinked back his tears and forced a smile onto his face.

I looked at Rani, who stood behind them in the doorway. She mouthed *I'm sorry*, and I shook my head, hoping to reassure her she did nothing wrong. The boys' presence prevented her from unleashing her anger and slamming the door on him. She knew I didn't want them to get caught in the crossfire and witness their parents hurling abuse at one another. Regardless of what happened between us, I was still their mum and he was their dad. Children should never have to choose a side; our failure is not their burden to bear.

"We're going to wait for the delivery man downstairs and have pizza in the car!" she said excitedly.

Karim grinned at me. "Then we're going to go on a drive and eat ice cream."

I gasped. "Without me?"

"The baby is too small to have ice cream, remember?" Rani said. "Sorry, but you're going to have to miss out on the fun tonight." She got them to put their jackets and shoes on before closing the door behind them.

Idris' longing stare didn't waver from me. "You cut your hair," he stated. "It looks nice," he added lamely, when I never responded.

"You need to leave."

He ran his hands through his hair. "What was I supposed to do? You won't come home. You won't talk to me on the phone. You won't reply to my messages."

"Because I don't want to talk to you!"

"How else are we going to fix this?"

"There's nothing to fix."

"Yes, there is!" he shouted. "Because this isn't over. *We* are not finished. I love you."

"That isn't enough!" I turned away from him and covered my face. He'd only been here for a few minutes and I already felt exhausted. It was hard to hate him when he was looking at me like that.

"Then what will be enough?" He circled me and pulled my hands from my face. "What do you want? I'll give you anything you want, just don't leave me. Tell me what I have to do, and I will do it. I'll give up everything in this world, but not *you*." His hands held my face until I was forced to face his tears.

"That's not fair, Idris!" I cried. "You don't get to waltz in here and feed me false promises. How many times have I begged you for something only for you to shut me down?"

"This is different."

I stepped away from him. "Why?"

"Because these two weeks without you made me realise nothing matters to me more than you, our marriage, and family. Every day away from you has been killing me."

"Then you finally understand how every day in that house slowly killed me. You've only been dying for fourteen *days*. I have spent fourteen *years* taking care of your family. Who was taking care of me? Keeping a roof over my head, clothes on my back and food on the table isn't taking care of me. That is basic human rights, and it was your *duty* as a husband. Everything I did for you was not my duty, but I did it to make you and your family happy. I did it to sustain my marriage."

"It will be different this time."

I couldn't help but laugh. "No, it won't!"

"I promise it will."

"I'll still be the maid, cooking and cleaning for everyone because I was unlucky enough to be the eldest daughter-in-law."

He shook his head. "They're my parents. I can't kick them out."

"I'm not asking you to. But why am I taking care of your brothers and their families? They get a free pass to do nothing, while I have to slave over the cooker and clean up after their children. They never tell their wives to help, but are quick to ask me to bend over backwards for them. They all eat and leave their plates. They fill the laundry basket and never think to actually put the wash on. They all shit and piss, but never clean the toilet. That's for me to do because I'm the maid."

Idris paced around the room as he took in my argument. "I'll have a word with them."

Was that all I got from him? Was that his version of doing anything for me?

"It won't change anything because you've let them get comfortable for far too long. They'll make an effort for a day or two; then it'll go back to normal. I am *your* wife; not theirs. I am Karim and Nadim's mother; not theirs or their children's. They are grown men who still live off you. It is *your* house; yet your wife can't eat or drink anything without offering it away. Your sons can't watch TV because they hog it. Your daughter doesn't have a space to sleep because they refuse to get off their ass and move out. But why would they do that when you have me catering to their every need?"

Even though I stepped back, Idris made his way over to me. He held my shoulders and smiled with hope. "This is good. Come back home and we can talk about it. We can find a middle ground."

I wanted to believe him. I wanted to believe that life would be different, but this is what he did. He dangled a thread of hope in front of me and then bound my wrist with it once I gave in.

For that reason, I stood my ground. "I want you to leave."

"No," he snapped. "I'm not fucking leaving unless you're coming with me. I don't care if I have to drag you."

I pushed him away. "This is the problem, Idris! Whenever you don't get your way, you use force to break my will! And I always give in because you have a temper you can't control and I don't want to cover a bruise!"

"I haven't done that in years!"

"No, you just use sex to punish me. You won't raise your hand on me, but you'll grab my jaw too tight. You won't strangle me, but you'll choke me in bed. You won't slap me, but you'll pin me on your mattress and use my body because it's yours."

His eyes hardened. "What else was I supposed to do? Your body was all you offered."

Stepping away from him, my tears stopped falling. "We both know I never offered it. You *took* it."

"If you gave me any other part of you, I wouldn't have been that way. But you were so closed off and I was *desperate* for some part of you. You wouldn't talk to me. You couldn't even *look* at me, Zoya!"

"That didn't give you the right to do that to me!" I screamed. "I was seventeen and *scared*. I asked you for some time to get to know one another, but you weren't interested. You just needed somewhere to stick it and satisfy yourself."

"We were husband and wife."

"We were strangers, and you forced me to give that part of myself to you." I had pushed our wedding night out of my head for so long, but the fear and anxiety hit me all over again. "I said no," I whispered. "And you still did it."

Idris went stiff. His head shook slowly as his mouth opened, but no sound came out. My accusation hung heavy in the air. "A husband cannot rape his wife," he whispered.

"The vows of marriage do not override the importance of consent. You knew when I didn't want to have sex, but you still stripped me down. And this culture made me believe if I didn't follow through, I was failing as a wife. It taught me that sex belongs to a man. But our bodies do not belong to you. It is not yours to take."

Still in denial, he stammered over his words. "But you ... you... you wrapped your arms around me and you became aroused."

"Because I couldn't let myself become that type of victim."

He stumbled back, seeming sick. Unable to breathe, Idris yanked his jacket off. When that wasn't enough, he barely got the window open before he stuck his head out and gulped the air in. His knuckles turned white from how hard he was gripping the window pane.

When he turned towards me, his face was ashen and his eyes bloodshot. "I knew it was bad when you took away sex as your bargaining chip. The fact that you thought that was the best way to hurt me made me realise how little you thought of me. That's why, apart from that one night, I never touched you because I needed you to believe what I felt was more than lust. I wanted you to know it wasn't just sex to me."

"But that is all it was to me. It was just another daily chore because that was what you made it become. I *hated* it because you never gave me a chance to love it. That first time stole any chance of it being an act of love."

His steps were slow towards me. He put his hands up before saying, "I'm going to touch you. Not in that way. Can I..." He hesitantly held my face in both hands.

"What are you doing?"

"I want you to look at me when I say this because I need you to believe me." For the first time in our marriage, Idris accepted blame and took accountability. "I'm sorry." It wasn't a quiet whisper. He spoke with clarity and honesty. His sorrowful eyes held my gaze. "I can't change the mistakes I've made, nor erase the pain I've put you through. I know an apology won't do that either, but it's the start to being a better man for you. If you give me the chance, I promise to be a better husband. I won't get it right a hundred percent of the time, but I promise to learn. Just one more chance; that is all I am begging you for. Let me prove to you I can love you the way you deserve."

I held his wrists. "There's more to marriage than housework and sex."

"Like what? Tell me what it will take for me to fix this because I'm not going down without a fight. I'll do *anything*. I love you so much."

"Then *show* me that every day. It doesn't have to be big gestures. It could be buying me flowers or rubbing my feet after a long day. Make time for me that doesn't include having sex. Be a space for me to find comfort. How do you expect this marriage to work when I can't even talk to you because I'm scared?"

"You don't have to be scared of me."

I pushed his hands off me. "Yes, I do! Because the smallest of things set you off. Even if you won't put your hands on me, I'm scared you might. But that doesn't compare to the wrath of your tongue. When you're angry, you say whatever it takes to make me cry and then get angry because I'm crying."

"Zoya, please! Do you want me to get on my knees and beg? Because I'll do it. I will give you whatever you want; just come home with me. I'll be different. I'll be good. I'll be whatever you want me to be as long as I'm still your husband. I'm sorry I did it all wrong, but give me a chance to prove I can be better; because I will. I'll do it right this time."

Standing in front of me was a man who was devoted to honour his word. I felt his desperation as deeply as I felt the emotional wounds he inflicted. Halima once said an apology is just words, but so was *I love you*. So, why did we give the latter more power? Ultimately, the value of words depended on the intention behind them, and I did truly believe Idris was sorry. I believed he wanted to be better for me, but I couldn't just think about my happiness.

"Your children deserve a father who teaches them love. Our daughter deserves a father who is her first love. She deserves a father to set an example of how she should be treated."

"I'll do that," he pleaded. "You cannot say you have questioned my love for our children."

It would be a lie to say Idris and I had no good moments in our marriage. We had phases of being content with what we shared. But they didn't last long enough for me to feel reassured. The good times ended when Idris no longer found contentment with me. I had only ever seen his rage rise to that level with me. Nobody else warranted such harsh reactions from him. Before anyone else, including myself, I had to think about protecting my children, and the thing they needed most protection from was their father's anger. I never wanted them to witness, let alone be subject to, his abuse. There was only one thing, *one person*, to take out of the equation to ensure their lives totaled peace.

I nodded my head as I made my decision. "I know you will when you see them on weekends and school holidays."

A string of *no* slipped past his lips. He fell to his knees at my feet. "Please don't do this. Don't leave me, Zoya. We took a vow of forever. I love you."

"We're not good for each other. I bring out the worst in you." I tried not to cry, but he was falling apart at my feet as he begged me for a chance. "There is nobody in the world I love more than my children. A mother's vow always supersedes ones of a wife. When I brought them into this world, it was a silent promise to protect them at any cost. The cost I must pay is my marriage."

"Stop it! Stop saying that! We are not getting a divorce. Before anything else, you are *my* wife."

I shook my head. "I'm sorry, but that's not true. I am first a woman and then a mother." Grabbing the event leaflet, I crouched down. "This was never about making money. It was never a statement about your ability to provide. All I ever craved was freedom to be anything I wanted in life. I wanted to make a name for myself. I've done that. And now I want our daughter to know freedom is hers. I can't do that in this marriage."

"What if you can? Run your business. Run five hundred businesses if you want; just don't give up on us." He grabbed my hands and kissed all over them. "I'll stay at home and look after them. Is that enough?"

My mind reminded me of Sumayyah. She was forced to choose between her marriage and career. She had poured a lifetime of hard work and determination into becoming a doctor. It was her dream for as long as I had known her. Yet, she sacrificed it all to placate her husband's need for the perfect wife who catered for him as his family. Yousef and his mother couldn't accept she could be both a *bou* and doctor. So, she was forced to become only one. She hoped by doing that she'd be loved by Yousef and find happiness. Somehow, she still ended up on the losing side.

"How unfortunate that in this culture, a woman must sacrifice so much for an ounce of happiness? It is unacceptable for her to be more than just a housewife. If she wishes to be more, it comes at a cost." As I held his face, the dam broke one more time. I was grateful my tears blurred the heartbreak written on his face. "Fourteen years of actions cannot be rewritten by desperate promises. This Idris, the one before me today, is only a flash of a dream. He disappears as quick as he comes. I'm tired of living a nightmare. The handcuffs you've held onto have cut into my wrists, and if I don't find the strength to walk away, I'll bleed out."

CHAPTER FORTY-THREE

THE LARGE HALL WAS filled with people. Every seat was occupied by women from a range of cultures. I was surprised by the few men that were intently listening to the panel of women sharing their experiences.

My sons eagerly waved at me from the front row. Jannah imitated them, which made Sumayyah and Halima silently giggle. I offered a wave back to them before turning my attention back to the current speaker.

When she wrapped up, Rani clapped louder than anyone. She leaned closer to me, covered her microphone and whispered, "She's such a boss. I think I'm in love with her."

Layla, the host, thanked her before smiling at the crowd. "Last, but certainly not the least, we have the dynamic duo behind the online fashion brand. In just a few years, they have built a bespoke retail experience that takes tailoring to another level. Please welcome Rani Batra and Zoya Iqbal!"

There was a round of applause that pounded alongside my heart. Now that it was our turn, my palms began to sweat.

"Thank you for having us," Rani said. "It's been amazing hearing all these women share their experiences in the world of business. While we've faced some of the same challenges, our journey has been unique with hurdles of their own." She was a natural at doing this, and I wanted to run off the stage and leave her to it.

"Where did your journey start?"

"2003 in secondary school. I had just moved to London from Manchester over the summer. On the first day of school, I was seated next to Zoya in form class. When she offered a seat with her and her friends at lunch, I greedily accepted it." She pointed at them with a laugh and waved. "There are our biggest supporters."

Layla also waved at our friends, who were now blushing from the unwanted attention. "A friendship that blossomed into a business partnership. How has it been navigating that?"

Rani waited to see if I would answer, but when I didn't, she answered on our behalf. "It's made this experience more fun. It's been amazing to grow our business the same way we have done as people. Together, we're experiencing the highs and lows of business as we have in life. There is nobody else I want to do this with."

"What led you to the world of fashion?"

"I believe the designer is the best person to answer this."

With all eyes on me, I forgot how to speak. I cleared my throat. "I never expected to end up in this sector. My love for sewing started when my mother-in-law showed me how to make small fixes on my husband's clothes. Being a housewife, I was bored with the same routine and textiles gave me something to think about. It forced me to be creative, and I craved the freedom in that. I started with making a few basic outfits for myself and I had people praising my handiwork.

I used to think they were just being polite; and after all these years of practice and progress, I *know* they were being polite."

My chuckle was drowned out by the round of laughter. Something about the noise calmed my nerves, and I sat taller.

"It all changed for me after I had my first son. My body felt disproportionate and nothing quite fit right. Western clothes were okay, but traditional Pakistani suits made me feel ugly and uncomfortable. We all know what I'm talking about," I said, addressing the crowd. "The waist is non-existent and so is the chest, because this culture is afraid of big-breasted women. To get our heads through, we have practically to decapitate ourselves. The sleeves pinch our arm fat and god forbid if you don't have slender shoulders. Unless you are a model-sized woman with the perfect proportions, nothing looks as good as it does on the mannequin. I was tired of feeling like that. I didn't want to feel ugly in the clothes I wore. So, I began making clothes built for my body that had grown and birthed a baby."

"Speaking of which…" She gestured to my large bump. "Congratulations! Do you know what you're having?"

I cradled my bump and with a proud smile I said, "A baby girl."

The room broke out into cheers and I hoped she could feel the empowerment we were surrounded by. Everyone listened as Rani and I spoke about our achievements and how we organically grew the business. My nerves had completely vanished, and it felt like a conversation between friends. Every few minutes I would glance at the boys and my heart warmed as they watched me in awe.

My attention was stolen from them when the door opened. Like a magnet pulling me to him, I watched as Idris took a seat in the back. I looked away from him before he could catch me staring at him.

"What are your next steps?"

Rani was practically bursting out of her seat. "We're getting ready to roll out our own custom designed fabrics, which will then be available in our family sets. We have so many exciting launches upcoming, including opening our first boutique."

"With a newborn on the way, how will you manage such a large step?"

"I understand that as the mother, there are certain expectations. But we would never ask a man that," I retaliated. "If anything, my daughter is my motivation. I want her to see that a woman can have it all."

"Agreed! Will you be getting dad to do the feeds and nappy changes?" she joked, after thinking she offended me.

It took everything in me to not look at him, especially when I felt his stare. "I'll do it all. I'll breastfeed her while I sketch. I'll change her nappy in the middle of a work call. I'll cradle her in my arms as I give orders."

This time the applause was for me.

"Your husband is a lucky man to have such a strong-willed wife. And you are lucky to have a husband who supports you. In our culture, that is not a luxury most women have."

I didn't want to slate Idris, but I also didn't want to give the women present a false version of reality. "My husband did not support this dream. In fact, up until recently he did not know about the business. Admittedly, it was wrong of me, but I kept it a secret from him. This culture taught him and many others that a woman should not work because that is the man's job. For some, that is enough and there is no shame in that. I respect all the women who stay home and take care of their families. That was once me, and it was the hardest job I have ever done."

"What pushed you to go against his wishes?"

"Because once upon a time I had wishes too. I had a dream to be more than this culture could ever allow. I always wanted marriage and children, but equally I wanted a version of me outside that. I wanted a life where I wasn't required to lean on a man to survive. As a child, I witnessed the struggles my mother faced. She was no one without my father. If he dropped dead, she wouldn't have survived. And I knew I couldn't allow myself to be that version. My children deserved a mother who could stand against the world."

She looked out into the crowd. "What an inspiring story from our final panel guests. If you had any advice to give our audience, what would it be?"

Rani went first. "Do it; whatever that may be, just do it. You'll make mistakes and fail; that's okay. Whatever the journey may be, make it your own. Be the best version of yourself because nobody can do that better than you. Most importantly, never let a man say *you have that because of me*. You make sure when your name goes up in the hall of fame, it's your victory."

I clapped for her before smiling. "Chase your dream, even if the world is telling you it's far-fetched. Who says we can't have the best of both worlds? If I could run a business while also being a mother, wife, and daughter-in-law, why can't you? We shouldn't have to choose one or the other. We can craft dreams with stitches of heritage. We can dream in colour while dressing in culture. Before I make one last announcement, I'd like to share one last thing, if that's okay?"

Layla nodded.

"My parents named me Zoya. For those who don't know, my name means loving, caring, joyous and alive. I've always found that ironic because I loved those near to me, but was never good enough to be loved. I cared for my family, but was never cared for. I spread joy, but wasn't always given it back. I was alive, but not truly living. I let those around me dictate who I was going to be. I became the Zoya they needed. Until I found the strength to stand up for myself. It's taken me a long time to wake up and now I'm ready to dream in reality. I have finally reclaimed my name."

Rani took my hand and squeezed tight. Her eyes brimmed with pride as she gave me a nod of encouragement.

"My name is Zoya Iqbal and I am the co-owner of a business I founded. My name is Zoya Iqbal and I am a designer. My name is Zoya Iqbal and I am proud to announce our new official business name." I turned to Rani. "Shall we?"

"This one is all you," she whispered.

Gripping her hand tight, I took a deep breath. "No matter your size or skin colour, we will create pieces that make you feel your best. Whatever your dream outfit may be, we will bring it to life. We want you to *love* your clothes. We *care* about true inclusivity. We want to be part of creating memories for every *joyous* occasion. We aspire to create timeless classics with a modern touch that will be *alive* for our children to love. We are more than a business. We are the voice of many women who also have a dream to share. So, I welcome you to *Zoya*, where every stitch tells a dream."

CHAPTER
FORTY-FOUR

THE DOOR FLYING OPEN put an abrupt end to my breathing exercises. Sumayyah held her hand up as she tried to catch her breath. Her wide eyes told me I was about to receive news I would not like. She confirmed my suspicions with only two words. "He's here!"

Rani abandoned supporting me. "Where?"

"I saw him at the reception desk."

Rani looked at me in panic. "How does he know you went into labour?"

I stopped sharing my location, so that wasn't a possibility. I couldn't give any more thought to it as a strangled scream passed through my lips. I snapped my fingers at Sumayyah. "Can you check if this baby is ready to come out? I can't take this anymore."

This was by far my hardest labour and I wanted to kill everyone who said it gets easier the more kids you have. A string of profanities filled the room as another contraction hit me.

For the second time in minutes, the door flew open. Idris stormed in and pretended that he couldn't see my friends. "Why didn't you call me?"

We were still separated; not that Idris seemed to remember that. He resumed his daily barrage of calls and texts. For a man that spoke very little to me throughout our marriage, he suddenly had a lot to say. He had also used the boys as an excuse to turn up to the flat. Not wanting to cause too much disruption for them, I allowed him in. Instead of leaving when they were sleeping, he used the time to convince me to take him back.

There were only so many times I could say no. So, just last week it was decided he would pick the boys up on Friday evening and drop them back off on Sunday. He said that would mean he barely got to see them, as those were his busiest days at work. I argued that if he was so desperate to see his children, he would reorganise his priorities. He tried one excuse after another, but he only wanted a reason to keep coming around every day.

"I don't want you here," I said. "Please leave."

"That's my baby! I have a right to be here."

I glanced at my friends, wishing they could fight this battle for me, but they avoided looking at either of us. "I can't do this with you right now."

"Do what?" he snarled. "I'm the father, no?"

My teeth grit together as pain shot through me. "How did you even know I was here?"

"After you had that scare a few months ago and failed to let me know, I called the hospital and told them to notify me if you were admitted again. It's a good thing I did or else you would be alone."

"I'm not alone."

He didn't even look at Rani when speaking about her. "She's not the father and she sure as hell will not be your birthing partner. I'm not letting her see my baby before me."

"Don't make this any more difficult than it already is. Just go."

"No! They can leave, but I'm not going anywhere. You're *my* wife. I don't give a shit if you think we're done, because we're not. If you think I'm going to sign any papers once the pregnancy is over, you've got another thing coming."

Pain and frustration fueled my scream. I pushed him away when he tried to comfort me. "Sumayyah, get her out or give me something to numb the pain!"

Rani pushed my hair away from my face. "Breathe through the pain."

"Get away from her," he said, finally addressing her.

Rani stood tall and blocked me from his view. Her arms crossed over her chest. "She asked you to leave. Don't make me call security."

Idris stepped to her. "Go on. I dare you." He looked over her shoulder at me. "We both know I'm not going to leave. I will smash this hospital to pieces before anyone can force me out."

Sumayyah took a hesitant step forward as Rani and Idris continued their staring match. "Maybe you should leave. She's in a lot of pain and you're making it worse." There was instant regret as Idris turned his thunderous glare to her.

"I am not the problem! This is you putting stuff into her head. Why won't everyone just leave us alone?" he shouted. "We would be fine if everyone stopped trying to steal her from me!"

"Idris—"

He cut me off. "Don't you dare tell me to leave again. I'm not going anywhere."

I was in too much pain to continue arguing with him. When he wanted something, nothing could convince him otherwise. "Fine. Stay," I said, feeling defeated.

Rani looked down at me. "Don't let him intimidate you like that."

"There are other mothers here. The last thing they need is to hear us arguing. Why don't you go into the waiting area and call Halima? Check if the boys are okay and having fun with Jannah."

With a dirty look directed at him, she gave me a kiss and took her leave. Sumayyah, not wanting to witness the explosion about to come, followed right behind her.

Once the door shut, Idris breathed a sigh of relief. He wore a smug smile and settled into the chair next to me. Despite me ignoring him, he repeatedly asked if I needed anything. He tried to take my hand when a contraction came, but I gripped my bed rails instead. No matter what I did, nothing deterred him.

"I spoke to Hashim, and he's agreed to take over some operational work at the restaurant. As I manage my other businesses remotely, that means I can work from home most days. There will be some kinks in the beginning, but I'm confident I've figured out a rota that would work for both of us. I'll still need to visit my businesses from time to time and travel to Pakistan here and there. You'll have some more flexibility with your hours; at least until the shop opens. Monday would be a good day to have as our set day off."

He had lost his mind.

"What are you talking about?"

"We need to agree on a day when we're not working so we can have some time together. Weekends will be too busy for both of us. Any day from Monday to Thursday is good for me. Now that we're both working, we need to make sure someone is home with our children. It would be good if you could work from home too; you know how the boys get if they don't see you enough. How long are you going to be off once she's born?"

I stared at him, feeling perplexed. "Did you hit your head or something? We're separated. The only rota we need to agree on is which weekends and holidays you're going to get."

Idris acted as if I hadn't spoken at all. "You can technically keep designing at home. If you need to overlook the renovations at the shop, I've been looking into those pump things for your milk. I don't know how much milk you can leave with me, but it should be enough for at least a few hours."

"You've lost your mind," I muttered. My hands held my bump as another contraction came.

He dabbed the sweat away from my forehead before saying, "No. I'm trying to show my support. You said desperate promises can't rewrite my actions. So, let my actions do the talking. I'm trying to prove that life will be different; it will be better if you give me one more chance."

"And how long will it be before your work takes priority again?"

He shrugged. "There will be times when I have to travel. I'll give you enough notice to adjust your work schedule and I won't go for longer than necessary."

The small voice inside me asked *what's the harm in trying*? That side of me loved him and was desperate to make my marriage work.

But I knew there were too many hormones flowing through me to make a sensible decision.

Idris took my silence as permission to carry on speaking. "I signed up for anger management classes. I haven't been to one yet, but my first session is next week."

My heart wavered at the vulnerability in his voice. "Why?" I whispered.

He pulled his chair closer and stroked my cheek. "So I never have to make you any type of victim ever again. I don't want you to be scared of me."

My hand held his wrist and tightened when pain rolled through me. He didn't flinch when my nails dug into his skin as my groan filled the room. The words I wanted to say were forgotten as I fell against the bed with a cry.

"I'm really trying, Zoya," he pleaded. "I kicked my brothers and their families out. I can't take away all your duties of a daughter-in-law, but at least you won't have to take care of them. I'm not saying you won't have to cook and clean, but this is better, no?"

I would never expect him to kick his parents out. With his siblings out of the house, that was nine fewer people to cater to. It was a big step for Idris and showed how determined he was to meet my requests.

"Where did they go?" Guilt prompted my question. Their children were stripped of their home because of me.

"They're renting somewhere. I don't really care, as long as you come home. I miss you so much." His thumb brushed over my lips. "Mum and dad said they'll divide their time across all our houses to share the care responsibilities fairly."

I shook my head. "They don't have to do that. That is their home and at their age, they deserve to live in comfort."

The door was knocked, and in came my doctor. "How is mum feeling?"

"I'm exhausted. Is she ready to say hello?"

She snapped her gloves on and measured how much I'd dilated. "You're at six. These last few centimeters will happen quick and the contractions will come fast. Dad, why don't you get behind her and help ease the pain?"

Before I could protest, Idris was on his feet. He was never this invested to help at my other deliveries. He climbed onto the bed once I shuffled forward and positioned himself so I was sitting between his legs. "Is that okay?"

I groaned in agreement as another contraction came. I didn't fight him when he threaded his fingers through mine. All I could focus on was breathing through the pain.

He kissed my shoulder. "Come on. You've got this."

"There's another one," I cried.

Our conversation remained incomplete. It wasn't because he didn't have more to say, but his focus became about making sure I was getting through labour. He tied my hair out of my face. He fed me sips of water. He held me tight when I cried from the pain. He rubbed my back when I was struggling to breathe. He encouraged me every time I wanted to give up. Idris finally became the dream I always wanted.

He never turned away in disgust when it was time to push. He remained behind me as a solid sounding board through one of the most excruciating pains ever known. When I collapsed against him, he sat us both up and channeled energy back into me.

"Come on, Zoya," he said when my head fell against his shoulder. "One last push!"

I shook my head. "I can't. Please don't make me do this anymore."

He kissed my shoulder. "She's almost here. Come on, take my hand."

My fingers thread through his, and a few minutes later, my scream blended with her cry. I collapsed against him and cried with relief.

They held her up. "Congratulations! You have a beautiful baby girl."

My tears meant I could barely make out her face. I watched in a daze as they took her for a wipe down and measurements. Everything happened in a blur, and time only slowed down once they placed her on my chest.

"Hi," I breathed. "You're so perfect."

Idris wrapped his arms around us and whispered the call to prayer in her ears. "You were amazing," he praised as he kissed my temple. "I love you. Thank you for giving me another piece of you to love."

I'm sure if someone snapped a picture of that moment, they would have called it *wholesome*. But they couldn't have possibly known the fight and sacrifice it took to get to here. They wouldn't see a mother clinging her onto her lifeline; nor a father who was beginning to understand how fragile a life begins.

"She's so small," I laughed. "Does she have all of her fingers and toes?"

Idris counted each one to confirm. "Are you looking at your Ammi?" His thumb brushed gently over her cheek. "She has the most beautiful eyes," he said in a daze.

I held her close against me. "Thank you for choosing me to be your mum. I love you so much." I closed my eyes as I leaned into Idris. "Thank you for giving me a daughter. Thank you for making me a mum again."

He kissed the top of my head and wiped my tears. "Let me hold her while they clean you up." He froze as I burst into a loud cry.

"I should have four. She should have been my fourth." A wave of grief hit me as I remembered the baby I never got to hold. "What if something happens to her and she leaves me?"

"Nothing will happen to her." Idris wrapped his arms around me. "I won't leave your sight. We'll be standing right next to you and once they're done, she'll be back in your arms."

I reluctantly agreed, but never took my eyes off her. She looked even smaller in his embrace. To my surprise, Idris took on the midwife's recommendation and had skin-to-skin contact with her. Everything about him that day was a complete one-eighty from our boys.

He held her close, already in protection mode. He only looked away when my pain caused me to wince. Worry filled his eyes before he'd relax and go back to doting on our daughter.

"You look just like your mum," he whispered. "Everything about you is perfect." When his voice cracked, I couldn't hold back my tears. "I promise I won't let anyone hurt you. I promise you won't ever yearn for anything while I'm alive. I'm going to be a real father. I'm going to teach you what love is supposed to be. I'm going to be better for you." He looked at me. "For *both* of you," he promised.

CHAPTER
FORTY-FIVE

I COULDN'T STOP LOOKING at her. She exceeded my wildest dreams. Her small lips settled into a pout as she slept soundly. My fingers slowly ran through her full head of hair as I sighed with content. It was our first full day at home and I didn't want to do anything except watch her.

Our first night at home was daunting with just me and my three children. After refuting his offer to take us home, Idris insisted on spending the night. When I reassured him I'd be fine, he offered to take the boys, but they didn't want to leave their baby sister. With a forlorn expression, he left at two in the morning. The encroaching loneliness tempted me to invite him back. But I had to stay strong until I decided what I was going to do.

Having a newborn left me with no time to ponder about the future of my marriage. My mind was overwhelmed, and I just wanted to savor the precious first days with her. She was a quiet baby until she was hungry. At that point, it was hell and havoc until she was latched onto my breast.

"Ammi," Nadim whispered. "When can we play with her?" He peeked over her crib with disappointment.

Karim's head popped up next to him. "Why is she always sleeping?"

My heart filled with a calm at the love in their eyes. "Because she's a baby and they sleep a lot."

Nadim held up a toy car. "I got this for her to play with. She can keep it; it's pink." His nose scrunched in disgust.

I squeezed his cheeks. "That's so kind of you, baba. Did you finish your breakfast?"

They nodded. "When is she going to eat?"

"She already ate. Babies can only drink milk because they have no teeth."

That earned me a giggle from Nadim. "Shall I get her more milk?"

"She has a special milk Ammi makes." I was grateful when he didn't ask questions about where the milk came from. I tore my gaze from the three of them when my phone rang. "Hello?"

"Were you sleeping? Did I wake you up?"

"No. Is everything okay?"

"Mum was asking what you wanted to eat for lunch?"

"I don't mind."

"Did you need anything? I'm going shopping before I come to you. Nappies or wipes?" he offered.

I smiled down at them. "I've got everything I need."

🎀🎀🎀🎀

"I'm feeding!" I shouted when the door handle turned.

"It's me." The aromatic scent of spices wafted in behind Idris. He closed the door behind him and watched us. "Don't do that," he said when I draped her muslin over my chest. "I'm your husband; you don't need to cover in front of me."

I rocked her when she cried. Peeking under the cloth, I tried to get her to latch again. "If you're hungry, why did you let go?" After only a few more pulls, she cried again, and I huffed.

Idris pulled the muslin away. "I got you pregnant. I've seen all this and more. I might be wrong, but being able to see her should make it easier, no?"

As she stared up at me, I realised it was her that wanted to see me. I looked up at Idris. "Why are you standing like that?"

He wore a flustered look as one hand was hidden behind his back. "I wanted to give you something." A tinge of pink covered his cheeks as he revealed the present.

My eyebrows furrowed. "Roses?"

"Nineteen roses, to be exact. Fourteen for the years we've shared, each one a testament to our vows. One for my love for you. One for each of the children you've given me. And this one," he said softly, as he touched the single delicate white rose, "this one is for the little one running free in heaven."

"Idris—"

"You have carried *four* of my children therefore, you are a mother of four."

I didn't know how to thank him for the gift. Aside from the fabrics he bought me from Pakistan, Idris had never shown me such thoughtfulness. My throat constricted and made it hard to breathe.

Blinking away my tears, I let out a soft laugh. "I don't know how you've made it this far in business when you can't count. There's twenty roses there."

He smiled and picked out the sole pink rose. "This one is not for you. It's for my daughter. I wanted to be the first man who ever bought her flowers."

If it was physiologically possible, my heart would have burst at the gesture. I looked down at her, only to see she was asleep. "You'll have to wait until she wakes up to give it to her."

"Let me do that," he offered when I positioned to burp her.

I arched my brow. "Do you know how to?"

"It can't be that hard." He took a seat and followed my directions. "This feels dangerous. Are you sure this is working?" He got his answer when she let out a small burp.

Adjusting myself so I was fully clothed again, I sat up. "Let me help mum."

He jutted his chin towards the pillow. "Why don't you get some sleep? Karim complained that his sister cries a lot at night."

"She wasn't that bad. Newborns wake up frequently for feeds."

"I bought that pump for you. If you came home, we could share the night feeds."

"Your parents are only in the other room. I don't want to get into this right now."

"This isn't fair. I don't want to miss out on time with her."

It was tempting to remind him he never cared with the boys; I did everything on my own and he never batted an eyelid. Idris barely carried them when they were babies. But rehashing the past would not benefit either of us.

"If you're not ready to come home yet, then let me stay here with you. At least you won't have to worry about the boys with me around."

"Everyone will be here soon," I said, avoiding the conversation and him. "If she's asleep, put her down." I didn't leave any room for argument as I left him alone. Once I put the flowers into a vase, I turned to Abbas. "Baba, would you like tea?"

He diverted his gaze from the TV to flash me a smile. He shook his head but couldn't say anything because Karim was warning him he was about to miss the best part of the show.

Leaving them to it, I joined my mother-in-law in the small kitchen. "What can I do?"

She batted me away. "Where is the princess?"

"Sleeping. What's left to do?"

"It's okay. You go and sit."

I wondered whether Idris' attitude change was forced upon everyone.

When I didn't move, she spoke to me in a hushed tone. "I was very angry at you when you first left. I couldn't believe you walked out of your husband's house, let alone that you left your children. I told Idris that he was better off because a good woman would never do that."

Despite speaking regularly on the phone, this was the first time she ever brought it up. I lowered my gaze. "He never let me take them."

"I know. He knew for as long as he had them, you would come back. That is the downfall of being a mother; we always stay for our children."

"I couldn't do it anymore. There was no reprieve from everything. I'm sorry I couldn't be the daughter-in-law you wanted."

"Shall I tell you why I always called you and not the others?"

I nodded my head.

"You are my eldest daughter-in-law. Another part was because I lived with you the longest and trusted you to get the job done well. But it was mostly because I know what my son is. I, too, suffered at the hands of a man like him. I tried my hardest to make sure he never had a reason to get angry with you."

"Then why, in the beginning, did you complain to him about me?"

She stopped stirring for a second. "How did you learn to behave as a daughter-in-law?"

I shrugged. "I don't know. My mum?"

With a hum, she nodded. "We copy what we have seen and experienced. You adopted the behaviour you saw your in your mother as a daughter-in-law because that is all you know. Nobody teaches you how to be a mother-in-law. All you know is what you experienced; and my mother-in-law was harsh and critical. She would complain to my husband about everything I did. She gave me a hard time."

Perhaps it was naïve of me to understand her logic, but I knew all too well how hard it was to break a cycle. "Then why would you do that to another woman? We have it hard enough without making enemies with one another. We need to stand as allies."

"That was a lesson I learned that day. When I saw what he did ... what he was capable of..." She shook her head. "After that day, I never said a bad word about you to him. And he was better to you?"

"Sometimes."

"Then this can be fixed?"

"I don't know," I said with honesty. "Because I'm tired of paying the dues for a man's rage. I shouldn't have left the way I did, and for that I apologise to you all, because I can't imagine how angry he was."

"Angry?" Her sad smile was haunting. "He wasn't angry. He was *broken* without you. He never spoke a word to anyone. He wouldn't eat, even when I made his favourite food. And it was then I understood how much my son loved you. I know he is not always a good man, but at least you have that."

"Is it enough?" I asked. "Does he love me enough to change?"

"Men see a woman for three things: child bearer, intimacy and maid. That has been the case for generations. They are blind to everything else we do and feel. But he saw you even in your absence." She glanced at me. "I should thank you."

"What for? Because of me, your other children and grandchildren were asked to leave. Because of me you feel as if you cannot stay in your home."

In a surprising move, she held my hand. "Because in just one moment you taught him something I couldn't in nearly forty years. You taught him the value of a good woman. As a woman, I cannot ask you to take him back. You endured a lot at his hands." She sniffled. "But as a mother, I am begging you to save my son."

I blinked my tears away when Idris joined us. "Why are you still carrying her?"

"She's awake," he explained.

Shazia dabbed her tears with her dupatta. "Don't spoil her like you did with Karim. Do you remember how he used to be? As soon as you put him down, he would cry," she scolded, but her voice was still thick with emotion. "Farrah is the same. That daughter of hers is always being carried."

Farrah gave birth exactly two weeks before I did. Aliya was adorable and a spitting image of her mum. Farrah said she was a handful and did not settle unless she was being carried. I felt bad that I was yet to meet her, but she understood my circumstance. Idris was still pissed about her helping me and refused to pay a visit to them. While they weren't close, I blamed myself for the breakdown in the relationship.

"I can't wait to meet her," I said, glancing at Idris.

He was too busy studying our daughter to hear me. "Always looking at her mum," he muttered.

I smiled at her. Taking her from him, I peppered kisses over her cheek. "Do you want to learn how to cook? Your Dadi taught me how to cook too."

She laughed. "Not only cooking. I taught your Ammi how to sew." There was a twinkle in her eye as she grinned at me. "And it's a good thing I did."

Everything around us faded as we shared a silent moment of gratitude. I wondered if seventeen-year-old Zoya, who detested her mother-in-law, would believe what that relationship would become. That Zoya was resentful. She never gave herself the chance to accept a mother's love and guidance. Over the years, I learned to respect Shazia and appreciate all she had taught me. She wasn't perfect and also made mistakes; and it took me nearly fifteen years to understand that she was also healing. Perhaps we didn't see eye-to-eye on everything, but she had been a good mother to me. And without her, I wouldn't have attained the success I had. It was her patience and willingness that allowed me to hone my craft.

The doorbell interrupted the moment. Idris let my mum, Zain, and Ilham in, barely greeting them. They rushed over to see her and my mum eagerly stole her from me.

"It's been three days. When are you going to name her?"

I shared a look with Idris. "She has a name, but there's someone I want to share it with first."

As the mothers complained about that, Zain pulled me to the side. "Go easy on mum, okay?"

"Why?"

"He never wanted her to come today," he said, referring to my father.

I made it clear that he was not welcome to join us. The little girl inside me that craved his love begged me to put everything aside; especially as I allowed Idris to be here. But the grown Zoya understood there was a difference between the two. Idris accepted blame and was trying to make amends. My father was yet to admit he hurt me. The one who refuses to face their faults will forever be trapped in a cycle of repeating them, and I didn't want that around my daughter.

My mouth hung open. "She went against him?"

He had a proud smile on his face, too. "For the first time, she stood up to him."

I walked over to my mother and hugged her.

She was surprised and froze. "Kia huwa he?" *What's wrong?*

"Nothing," I whispered. "Everything is finally right."

The unlocked front door signaled the final group's arrival. My friends waltzed in with flower bouquets, balloons, and gift hampers. They all hugged me before showering the baby with attention.

I eyed the masses of gifts. "This is too much!"

"This little princess deserves everything," Sumayyah cooed. "She's so gorgeous!"

"She has the most perfect cartoon brown eyes," Halima gushed.

"How has she changed so much in a few days?" Rani asked.

The flat remained full of business supplies. It got worse last night when we returned home with all the baby stuff. Now that there were so many people here, it felt like there was no space to walk. Not that anybody cared. They were all too busy admiring my daughter.

"Now that everyone is here," I said, calling for their attention, "I'd like to share what we have named her. Picking a name is always so hard, especially when I believe we live up to our names. So, I wanted to make sure my daughter's name gave her something to aspire to. More importantly, I wanted to make sure she had a strong woman to look up to; one that would guide her through any hardship with hope that never falters."

Rani impatiently tapped her foot. "You're going to kill us with the suspense."

"Fauzia Maya Qadir." I stared at Sumayyah. "Victorious. Love. Powerful." My arms wrapped around her when she stepped into my embrace.

"That means a lot," Sumayyah said.

I wiped her tears. "I can't do anything to change your circumstances, but now you will *always* have a daughter named after you. And just as you did with me, your love and hope will guide her through the darkest of times to happiness."

Halima rubbed Rani's back as she jokingly said, "Don't worry. If I ever have another daughter, I'll name her after you and leave these two out."

I rolled my eyes and pulled them into a hug. "I love you guys."

We were huddled on the street outside the block of flats. Everyone had taken their leave, with my friends the last to bid me goodbye. Wanting a moment alone with them, I left Idris upstairs with our children.

I turned to Sumayyah. "Can I ask you a question?"

"Anything."

"How did you know it was time to leave Yousef? I mean…" I struggled to find the right words. "In the end he was ready to give you everything you wanted, but something told you it wasn't enough."

Halima hugged Jannah close to her. "Do you want to take him back?"

I looked across their faces for judgement. "Does that make me stupid?"

"If it's about saving face with the community, then yes," Rani said bluntly. "But if it's because you believe it can work this time, then no."

"He's making all these promises and putting these changes into practice. I can see how much he's trying. But what if it's all a ploy and once I go back, it goes back to normal?"

"Then you leave for good," Rani advised. "You've already done it once, so you know you can do it again."

"Do you love him?" Sumayyah asked.

"Yes," I admitted. "Maybe not all the time, but is love constant? How many of us love our spouses every minute of every day? But that's part of the battle, right? It's choosing to stay because you know it will get better."

Sumayyah nodded. "It is a choice. It's choosing to be the best for them even when it's easier to turn the other way. It's choosing to stand by them and holding them up when they're falling. But they must also choose you too. You asked how I knew it was time to leave? It was because *I* couldn't love him anymore. The difference between them is that Yousef could only love me when I fit his ideal, and Idris loves you despite you being the opposite of his. Yousef took and took and even at that last hurdle, he couldn't give anything back. In the end, his promises were as empty as I felt."

I thanked my friends and headed back upstairs. I took her from a pacing Idris and kissed the top of her head.

"She's only three days old and already won't settle without you. I've been trying to make her stop that crying for ten minutes and you did it in ten seconds," he grumbled.

"That's because you don't have boobs," I laughed. "She's hungry."

"It would be a lot easier if she could just tell me that."

I held her head up a little. "Did your Baba show you the flower he bought you?" Her response was another wail. "Okay. Let's get some milk in you."

Idris watched as I settled on the sofa with her. "Does it hurt?"

"A little, but nothing too bad. Where are the boys?"

"In the bedroom playing a game." He took the seat next to me and tucked my hair behind my ear.

"Please, don't," I said, when he tried to kiss me. "I don't want to complicate things anymore than they are."

"What's so complicated about me kissing my wife and the mother of my children?"

"You know what I mean."

"This is so stupid, Zoya. Today was a good day because we were together. This is what life could be if you just came home."

"I need some more time, Idris. I don't know what I want."

"What is there to think about? Look at us. Our boys are playing together while you nurse our baby. How can you not want this?"

"Of course it's what I want. But our children aren't the problem; our marriage is."

"This is what Sanam and I were talking about that day. She was helping me buy this." He shifted and pulled something out of his back pocket. He opened the small velvet box and revealed a diamond ring and wedding band. "You once said this was your dream wedding ring."

It was absolutely beautiful. The lights reflected off its perfect shine and I could tell it cost him a lot of money. But he couldn't buy his way out of this one.

"A ring won't fix our problems."

"I know, and that's why it's not just a ring. It's a token of my promise to be a better husband. It's a symbol of our new understanding. This is our chance to start fresh without erasing the past fourteen years. Those years gave us our children, but more importantly, without those years, we never would have learned. We have both made mistakes and hurt each other. The biggest mistake I made was saying I need a wife, not love. That set off a motion of events I cannot change, but I can stop. I don't want us to tolerate each other anymore. I don't want the marriage we've been living." He got down on one knee and stared at me with desperate hope. "So, I'm asking you to marry me, Zoya. Not out of force, obligation, or fear, but love."

I wiped my tears with my free hand. I so badly wanted to fall into his arms and disappear into a fantasy. I wanted the happily ever after the movies ended with. But the credits wouldn't roll once I said yes. I had to live out the consequences of my decision.

"I'm not saying no," I whispered. "I'm just asking for some time."

His lip quivered. "I have worked hard my whole life because I knew that one day I would have a wife and family to take care of. There isn't anything I can't give you. With my wealth, neither you nor our children will ever yearn for anything. But if I don't have you, none of that means anything to me. Without you, I'm the poorest man in this world. I will give it all up for just one chance to prove myself to you. You asked me to give you a reason to stay, and this is it: I love you. Nothing else I can give you will mount to how much I love you. I have loved you enough for a thousand lifetimes and I promise to love you in every lifetime that comes after."

CHAPTER FORTY-SIX

I DIDN'T WANT TO be back here and was tempted to tell my mum to throw my old belongings away. But I knew there were things from my school days I wanted to keep. It would have remained in black bags if Zain wasn't already in dad mode. Ilham was only six weeks into her pregnancy, but Zain was eager to build a nursery. He asked us sisters if we were okay with it; to which I encouraged him to knock that entire room down because of the horrors it had witnessed.

Taking a deep breath, I knocked on the door. The boys let out a scream as they pushed past my mum and straight for the cupboard with the sweets.

"Come in before she catches a cold."

I almost reminded her we were on the doorstep of May, where the light breeze wasn't enough to make her sick, but I remained mute. My plan was to grab what I needed and head back as soon as I could. "We're not sitting for long. Their dad wants to see them later."

"Is he coming to the flat again?" A critical tone colored her voice.

Omitting parts of the truth, I said, "It's his weekend to see them."

"And the baby?"

"She's going to stay with me." I looked around the room. "Where is he?" I didn't need to clarify who I was talking about.

"Please don't fight with him. When he comes, say hello and show him the baby."

My arms wrapped around the carrier, which held a sleeping Fauzia against my chest. "Why should I do that? Have you forgotten what he did to me last time? He slapped and then choked me."

"He was angry after what he heard."

"I'm not obligated to accept his anger. My whole life, he's treated me this way. What have I done to deserve that?"

It wasn't her that answered me. He came into my line of sight wearing the same rage-filled expression he always paraded. "Ever since you were a baby, you have given me a headache."

I stared him down. "How would you know what I was like as a baby? Were you ever there? What hand did you have in raising me except the one you raised on me?"

"Who paid the bills and kept a roof over your head?"

"You were repaid for your efforts when my husband paid the price you put over my head. I paid your burden of having a daughter with my happiness. I owe you *nothing*."

He stared at me in disbelief. "You have a daughter now. If she followed in your footsteps, would you allow it?"

"I would be proud of her because I know how hard I fought to get here. Even after everything I went through, I came out on the other side. I made something of myself."

"You made a mockery of yourself. It's not you that has to hear what people are saying. I have to hide in shame because the world knows you walked out of your husband's house!"

Fauzia jumped at his raised voice. Her eyes fluttered open before they closed back into slumber. As much as I wanted to scream back at him, I didn't because there was no point wasting my breath on someone who was unwilling to listen.

"Why do you care what people say? In this community, in this *culture*, someone always has something to say. Somehow, no matter what we women do, it's always wrong. We kill ourselves following their orders, in the name of what? We're not birds you can keep caged. If you let us spread our wings, you'd see how beautiful the world could be."

Everything I said fell on deaf ears. I could have argued endlessly, but his belief in male superiority would never have changed.

I shook my head at my mum as his rant continued. "I can't do this."

He pointed his finger at me. "Don't you dare speak over me!"

"Why? Because you understand a daughter won't tolerate your abuse as a wife does? Or is it because you finally understand how powerful the roar of a woman is?"

My mum held her hands up. "That's enough."

"You would be so much happier if you just told him to go. What has he ever done for you? What happiness or peace has he ever given you? You have killed yourself to meet his expectations, and it still wasn't enough."

Blocking her from my view, he stood in front of me. "If I never came to this country, what would you have? You would have lived like a pauper in Pakistan! I worked hard to give you the life you have today."

"What life? The only life I saw was inside these four walls! You came to this country in hopes to give your children a better life. But you still caged us within backdated cultural rules. You wanted the status of a western citizen but were unwilling to learn and change by their norms."

"This is *my* house, and you will show me some respect."

I laughed at him. "Have your castle. Sit on your throne and feed your pathetic ego because one day you're going to wake up and you'll realise you have nothing. You have washed your feet in a river of our tears. You built your kingdom on our broken hearts."

"Get out and don't ever come back!" he snarled. "You are not my daughter!"

I stared at him; and while part of me felt broken by the lack of remorse, the other realised I deserved better. "I used to be so scared of you. It was always head down and mouth shut when you were home. That day you said I was a failure. You were wrong. The failure was you. You failed as a father. You failed as a man. But I thank you because growth and pain are one and the same. Had you not let me down, I wouldn't have learned how to crawl from the depths of hell. I got out and taught myself to stand on my two feet. Now stand back and watch me pave the path for the next generation."

❦❦❦❦

Abbas welcomed me and the children into the house. It was Fauzia's first time in her father's home and she wasn't awake to experience their joy.

"I would have picked you up," Idris said as he shut the door behind us.

"I had to go to my mum's house first to pick some stuff up and then drop it home before coming here."

"Stop calling that place home. *This* is your home." He stepped forward. "Let me take her."

"I was hoping we could talk."

Placing a kiss on her cheek, he climbed the stairs as I passed her to Shazia.

The vacant bedrooms proved that Bilal and Hamza had moved out. Our bedroom remained exactly as it was, except the bed was unmade and a few of his clothes littered the floor. After years of cleaning up after him, I had to fight my instinct to clear the clutter away.

"Sit down," he said, when I pressed myself against the closed door.

"I don't trust those sheets have been changed since I left," I teased.

He smiled. "They haven't."

"Because you don't know how to change them?"

"Because it still smells like you." He tilted his head. "What do you want to talk about?"

Walking towards him, I held my hand out. "Can I have your wedding ring?"

Panic filled him. "I told you we are not getting divorced."

"Idris, please give me your ring."

"No! And even if you forcefully take it, that won't stop me from being your husband. I am not signing any fucking divorce papers, Zoya! We are going to make this marriage work and be a family! If you think I'm going to let you *move on*, then you don't know me. I will never stop fighting for us." His rant only stopped when I pulled a small box out of my bag. "What's that?"

"I once said that I would never love you. That set off a motion of events I cannot change, but I can stop." Opening the box, I revealed a wedding band. "This is a token of my promise to love you. It's a symbol of our new understanding. If we find a way past this, I don't want it to be tied to my father. This is *my* choice and I want you to wear a ring that was chosen and bought by *me*. I want our marriage to start with my love, not my father's duty."

He slid his band off his finger and placed it next to him. "You don't want a divorce?"

Taking a deep breath, I mentally went through all the points I gathered. "I really appreciate the Idris you've been the past few weeks. As much as I hate you for not being him since the beginning, I'm grateful you're making a change. Marriage is a partnership. It's equal pull and push. So as much as I have loved you being at my beck and call, that is not a power I want to hold. I don't want to exact revenge and become a version of you."

"Where does that leave us?"

"In a space where we can *talk*. No screaming. No violence. A conversation where we *both* have a voice. I've given a lot of thought about what I want and if you're willing to discuss them, I would like a chance to make our marriage work."

He let out a breath of relief. His shoulders sagged and he couldn't hide his smile. "Okay."

"Let's take it in turns. You can go first," I offered.

"I still want you to help around the house and with taking care of the children."

I was expecting this to be on his list. I nodded in agreement. "I never intended to stop helping mum. If I have set days off and start later in the day to help with the cooking, are you happy with that?"

"I also don't want you working into stupid hours of the night."

Holding my hand up, I sighed. "That isn't how a conversation works, Idris. One thing at a time and before you can bring another request, let me put in one of my own."

"Okay, sorry. Yes, I am happy with that. Will you adjust your working days to accommodate family gatherings?"

"Where possible, yes, I will. But if I have deadlines that cannot be moved, work will be a priority. It may mean I join later on, but it also may mean I won't attend some." I waited for him to agree before laying down my first request. "No more babies."

"Can I ask why?"

I stared at him. "Because I don't want to have anymore."

He wasn't expecting the abrupt answer. Perhaps he was waiting for me to talk about my age, business or argue that we already had three. But if I didn't want more kids, then none of that mattered.

"No more children," he declared with a little too much force.

"I'm going to get my tubes tied."

Blood drained from his face. "What if you change your mind and want more children?"

"I won't," I stated. "Your turn."

"No working late nights. I want you home no later than nine o'clock. If you must bring your work home, I don't expect it to interrupt our time together."

I almost reminded him he rarely made it home for dinner and worked until after midnight. But that would not be helpful, nor a fair comparison based on what our businesses involved.

With my agreement, I moved on to one that held great importance to me. "You cannot interfere in my friendships with the girls."

His eyes narrowed at their mention. "Those women interfered in my marriage."

I crossed my arms over my chest. "No, they stood by me; there's a difference. I love them. Sometimes more than I love you because they've held my hand through every storm I've had to face. Even when they don't agree with me, they have never turned their back on me. I would love if you could get on with them, but you're different people and that's fine. They are hardly your biggest fan, but they try to be civil with you."

"Civil?" he scoffed. "You've heard what they've said to me."

"Because you rile them up by passing judgement." I took a deep breath. "I'm not saying they are always in the right, but they're my best friends. You don't have to agree with them. Hell, you don't even have to like them. But I need you to respect my bond with them."

His jaw clenched, but he muttered a half-hearted, "Okay. Is that one done because I have another?" He waited for me to nod. "Just because you're working doesn't mean I need your help to pay the bills. I am still your husband and their father. I can take care of you."

We spent the next hour going back and forth. One of us would present an item and the other would either agree or provide a counteroffer until there was a mutual agreement. Perhaps it wasn't the most romantic way to solve our issues, but we'd have been fools to believe that love would have solved all our problems. The biggest hurdle we could never overcome was communication because we grew comfortable in silence. My childhood home taught me silence was better than violence. But it didn't have to be one or the other. And Idris and I were finally on the path to teach our children that.

Most issues were settled, leaving one key aspect of our marriage unspoken. I clasped my hands together. "Our sex life..."

Idris blanched as he stood up. He shook his head. "I'm sorry Zoya, but that is a part of our marriage I cannot give up. That is an intimacy that belongs between a husband and wife."

"That isn't what I was going to say. But before I make my point, explain to me why it's such a vital part to you."

"That's a stupid question," he remarked. "What do you expect me to say?"

I shrugged. "What is it that makes you want to have sex practically every night? Is it your sex drive?"

His eyes narrowed. "*No.* I'm not a horny teenager."

"Then what is it, Idris? The visceral reaction you just had clearly tells me you need to have sex."

"It's not the sex that I need." His jaw tightened. "It's been nearly six months since you took sex off the table. It's been five months since we actually had sex, or any form of intimacy, for that matter. If all I wanted was *sex*, I could have got that from anywhere. If I really wanted, I could have had one or multiple women satisfy me during my visits to Pakistan. But I never strayed. You could fill this room with a hundred naked women and I could guarantee that none of them would even remotely arouse me. It's not about the orgasm."

"You still haven't answered my question."

"I want *you*." His eyes hardened as he stared at me. "If you offered yourself to me right now, I would have you. You don't even have to try, and I want you. Especially when you look at me like you can actually see me. It's the one part of you I do not have to share."

A deep sigh passed my lips. "This obsession you have about sharing with me has got to stop. You're right, that part of me is just for you. But you can't use that as a weapon when you get jealous. You have to accept that I have platonic and familial relationships outside of our marriage."

"Why?" he snapped. "Why do you need them when you have me? I don't want you to talk to them. I don't want you to laugh with them. You're mine."

"I'm not something you own. There are parts of me that others get, the same way there are parts only you get."

"When I see you with anyone else, I feel sick with rage. Do you have any idea what it makes me want to do? I want to set everything on fire and when that's not enough, I want to scream at the top of my lungs and throw my fist into a wall."

I shook my head. "That's not normal."

"I don't care, Zoya! I'm not fucking sharing you!"

As I took in his frenzied expression and trembling hands, I realised nothing good was going to happen if this conversation continued. "Okay, I think it's best if we stopped here."

He held onto my arm. "Where are you going?"

"Look at the state of you. I'm not talking to you while you're being like this."

"I'm sorry." He held my face. "I'm sorry. I won't shout again."

"Let's just take a break—"

"No. I said I'm sorry. Don't go," he begged. "I won't shout again. Please, don't go. We were doing so well. Please, don't leave me." His features contorted into panic. "I've been waiting for you to come home. I'm really trying," he pleaded.

It terrified me how much control I had over him. His chest was rising and plunging as he struggled to breathe through his fear of me walking out on him again.

I placed my hand on his chest. "This isn't healthy. You can't expect me to never speak to another person. I need more in life than just you."

"Why do they get a side of you I'm not allowed?"

Trying to understand him, I asked, "What do you want, Idris?"

"I want you," he begged. "I want you to laugh with me. I want you to talk to me. I want you to look at me."

And I finally understood what he meant when he said he didn't want sex. He wanted intimacy and not just the physical kind.

I nodded. "Okay. I can give you that, but you need to learn to accept that I have other people I love in my life. You can't get angry and hurt me because you're jealous."

He swallowed hard and let go of me. "I won't hurt you."

With him calmed down, I brought it back to my original point. "I want the sex to be on my terms."

"What does that mean?"

"If I don't want to have sex, then we don't have sex. If we're in the middle of having sex, and I want to stop, then we stop. Sex does not belong to a man. I am not a toy for you to use. I don't want it to feel like a chore."

"I want you to want me. When we share our bed, I want you to do more than lie there. I want you to touch me."

"Then uncuff me, Idris."

The double meaning wasn't lost on him. "What if you leave me?"

"Don't give me a reason to leave."

"I can't promise that I will always get it right."

"Neither can I, but we'll learn from each other. I'm not expecting perfection, but I deserve happiness. For too long, I lived under the weight of rules that were imposed by those who never understood my worth. But I found the strength to break free. Now that I know the power of freedom, there's no turning back. I choose my path, and I will never be confined again."

His lips pressed against my forehead before he wrapped his arms around me. Every muscle in his body loosened and he let out a soft breath. "I'm going to love you right this time," he promised.

My arms reached around him, and I smiled into his chest. "I don't believe there is a *right* way to love. We have spent too many years running from this emotion, so we're still learning how to love each other properly. But that's the beauty of it. We get to keep learning because life will bring changes we never thought possible."

"I've lost count of how many nights I've watched you dream and wished I was part of it. But now all I want is to be part of your reality. I want to celebrate your wins alongside you. I want to see you fall in love with our children a little more every time you see them. I want to wake up beside you and still feel like I'm dreaming. I want you to love me even when I haven't given you a reason to that day. I won't be perfect, but I promise, even on the hardest days, to give you the best version of me."

My whole life I dreamed of a love that was worthy of the books and movies. But in that moment, I understood that love, the kind that's patient, imperfect, and ever-evolving, is enough.

CHAPTER
FORTY-SEVEN

I ADDED THE LAST of the labels to the boxes and dragged myself up from the floor with a groan. "I think that's everything."

Rani did a final scan of the room before nodding in agreement. "I didn't realise how much stuff we kept here."

Before I could respond, my phone was ringing. With a sigh, I answered and pressed it against my ear. "Hello."

"What are you doing?"

This was the third time Idris had called me since I left this morning. It had been six weeks since I returned home and it was a bigger adjustment than I expected. The boys were happy to be living with both parents again and my parent-in-laws were overjoyed to have me and Fauzia home. While it was frustrating having Shazia comment on how I cared for my daughter, I had a newfound appreciation for her support. She was always willing to watch over her so I could shower, eat, sleep, and play with the boys.

It also helped that Idris was home most days. After a while, he would get frustrated and hand her back to me, but I reminded myself it was about baby steps. I let him do the night feeds, though I could have done them faster. I needed to give him the chance to prove it wasn't all false promises.

"We just finished packing everything. What are the kids doing?"

"The boys are doing homework and she's sleeping." He fell silent. "I miss you. When are you coming home?"

The one thing I hadn't prepared for was his clinginess. *It was worse than any of our children.* The few times I had been out, he inundated me with calls.

I sighed. "I told you I'll be home once the van drops everything to the shop."

"I can come and help you."

While the paperwork for the shop was being completed, I put all the business needs to one side. It meant I could relish the last few weeks with my family. But the renovations were underway, and it meant my time and focus had to be split. Idris hadn't expected how difficult that was going to be for him; and as a result, he was constantly offering to help. It ranged from his opinion on the interior to putting us in contact with his fabric supplier. While helpful, this was something I wanted to do on my own. I was ready to make mistakes and learn along the way.

"Someone needs to be home with our children. And anyway, the movers are going to do all the heavy lifting."

He was sulking, like a child. "Fine."

I shook my head at Rani when she raised her eyebrow. I gestured for her to give me a minute and stalked out of the room. With the bedroom door shut, I continued our conversation. "What's wrong, Idris?"

"We've barely seen you all week."

"We talked about this. Right now, things are busy and that means I won't be home as much. But once things fall into place, we'll settle into a routine."

"We also agreed to having one evening together a week. You've been coming home and spending all your time with the kids."

I couldn't argue my case because he was right. "Okay, I hear you. I need to pop into the shop later. I'll take Fauzia with me so you can have a break. We should be back within an hour, and once we're home, I'll feed her and put her to sleep. And then I'm all yours. We can do whatever you want."

"That's going to last all of one hour because she'll start crying."

"Then let's go out. I'm sure mum would be happy to watch her for a few hours."

"Say it, Zoya," he ordered softly. "I miss you and need to hear it."

"I love you."

He sighed with content. "Not as much as I love you."

A small smile played on my lips as I ended the call. Those three words were slipping off my tongue with ease the more I said them. With my phone tucked into my back pocket, I rejoined Rani. "Sorry about that."

"Is everything okay?"

"Yeah, he was just checking in."

"Checking to make sure you didn't lose that *enormous* diamond ring?" she joked.

I held my hand out and admired my rings. While it took a few days to adapt to the extra weight, it now felt completely natural. A school-girl giggle filled the room. "It is big and sparkly, isn't it?"

She laughed at my childishness. "How are things between you two?"

"Better," I said honestly.

"Does that include the sex?" she teased.

"Believe it or not, we've only had sex once. Now that he's also getting up to feed Fauzia, he's too tired to do anything," I laughed.

"Has he learned how to put a nappy on yet?"

"Well, her wee leaked out the other day. So, I'm going to say *no*. But he's really trying, and that is all I can ask for."

"I'm glad it's all working out for you."

I took a moment to absorb her words. Warmth spread through me until I was safe in its embrace. "I never would have got here without you."

She rolled her eyes. "What did I do? This was all you. You worked until your fingers bled. You fought even when the odds were against you."

"And who reminded me I had the strength to fight?" I arched my brow. "I believe we were standing in this exact room when you told me to find a way to make my dream come true. *You* brought out the fighter in me. You believed in my dream even when I saw nothing but darkness. You stood up for me even when it wasn't your fight. You practically built my backbone so I could stand up for myself. Because that's the friend you are. That is who you are. You are loud and confident because you know what you bring to the table. You have never let anyone cast a shadow on your sunny day. The Rani I am so lucky to know and love isn't afraid to fight the fight. You are strong-willed, determined and unapologetically yourself. Don't you forget that."

Her chest caved as she let out a gentle cry. "Thank you."

"What for?"

"For reminding me who the hell I am and the courage I posses." She swallowed hard and dabbed her tears away. "Are we done here?"

"Yes?" I answered as she gathered her things. "Where are you going?"

"I gave him and his family all of me. Instead of loving me, they tore me to pieces until I couldn't recognise the woman I saw in the mirror. But I am *done* bleeding on the shards I never broke."

Afraid she was going to do something she regretted, I blocked the door. "Okay. Let's sit down and talk about this."

She shook her head. "I can't do it anymore, Zoya. I learned and practiced all their customs, traditions, and rites of passages. But it wasn't enough."

The tortured look in her eyes broke my heart. "What have they done to you?"

Wiping her tears, she said, "They never wanted me. It was a crime that I married for love and I've been punished enough. I couldn't win being the traditional *bou* they wanted. So, I'm done. I'm going to show them the courage of a modern *woman*." Her back stiffened as she stared me down. "If you could do it, then so can I."

"What are you going to do, exactly?"

"I'm going to give Ravi an ultimatum. He either accepts me for who I am or I leave for good."

I stood back and smiled at the sign. My name was large, centred and illuminated by a deep green light. When Fauzia let out a soft whimper, I tightened her blanket around her and stroked her cheek. "This is all for you," I whispered.

I walk into the vacant shop. With most of the paint job complete, the vision is coming together. The boxes from Rani's flat cover most of the floor, and I have the tiresome job of sorting through them. Hoping something might get my creative juices flowing again, I open the bags I picked up from my mum's house. It's mostly old outfits gifted by relatives in Pakistan. Just as I'm about to give up, a familiar fabric catches my attention.

My laugh echoes as I hold my prom dress up. Fauzia is hypnotised by the glimmering gems. "I bet you're wondering how your mum ever squeezed into this. Maybe one day you can wear it to your prom. Hopefully, like me, you'll have the best night ever; not because a silly boy tells you that you look beautiful. But because you'll have three friends who remind you that the world is yours if you want it."

I hug the dress as memories of that night come rushing back. I chuckle to myself as I remember winding Sumayyah up with a ridiculous business idea. I wonder what that Zoya would say if I told her where we ended up. I'd like to think she's proud of me.

I notice something on the ground. The second my fingers touch the silk fabric, a surge of strength passes through me. That night I had so many anxieties about the future I knew was planned for me and I was desperate to escape. But even then, I didn't panic because I knew I was never alone.

I tie the silk ribbon loosely around Fauzia's wrist. "You are protected by the sacred bond of friendship. I wish I could promise that life will be easy. I wish I could protect you from heartbreak, but that is impossible. But I promise to guide you through it. Just like the generations before me, I will teach you how to cook and clean. If you're up for it, I'll teach you how to sew and run a business. But above all that, I am going to teach you how powerful a woman is because it is the heaviest title one can be trusted with. It is hard to be a woman in this culture. We must be tolerant. We must be resilient. We must be worthy. We must be obedient. We are treated like puppets for their pleasure and if we fail to conform to their orders, we are told we are not good enough. But being a woman extends far beyond that. We are more than just a daughter, wife and mother. A woman is fierce. A woman is strong. A woman is visionary."

Her brown eyes reflect mine as she stares at me in wonder. The innocence in her eyes brings tears to mine. I can't help but wonder who she's going to be and what achievements she's going to call her own. Did my mum ever envision my life becoming what it is when she looked at me?

"I won't pretend that this is the exact dream I wanted. It took a lot of sacrifice to end up here and along the way I realised ultimately my dream called for one thing: *love*. Not love from a man, but love from myself. They made me believe I was the defected one because I wanted more from life. They branded me unlovable and shameless because the small corner of life they showed me wasn't enough. The hardest thing a woman can do is love herself, because this culture makes being a woman feel like a burden. They tell us a woman does not have a place to dream. But why? Who set that rule? Who said a woman can't have it all? Who said a woman who works is less of a mother? Who determined we aren't worthy of freedom? Because we are, and once you learn that, victory will be yours."

I stroke the ribbon once more and smile. Her little fingers wrap around my single one and I kiss them.

"You have the power to become anything you want in this life. I don't care what it is, as long as it's your dream. I will be by your side every step of the way, reminding you of your worth, strength, and how deeply you are loved. I will never let a man take that away from you. When you feel like giving up, I'll be there to remind you of the strength within. We are breaking free from this generational cycle; because in a life meant for happiness and freedom, there is no room to be *obedient*."

The end.

Sumayyah, Zoya, Rani and Halima will return.

Upcoming books in *The Bow Series:*
The Modern Bow
The Silent Bow

Other books in *The Bow Series:*
The Perfect Bow
The Obedient Bow

AFTERWORD

I cannot believe this book is now out there in the world. There is a selfish part of me that wants to keep this one to myself. It has consumed my mind since 2022 and it is all I have lived and breathed the past one year. I really hope you love this one just as much as I do. And before I get the comments about how much you have cried, I'm sorry!

Of all my published works, this book is the one I am most proud of. While writing Zoya's story has been painful at times, it holds a special place in my heart. As I write this note to you all, my heart aches knowing that I will never write as Zoya and Idris like this again. Just as they did, I laughed, cried, and fell in love while authoring this novel. Of the books within this series, this is the one I was most excited to write. I believe that every book I publish is a little part of my heart and soul. But this book is a slightly larger part of me because I see so much of myself in Zoya.

One year ago when I published *The Perfect Bow*, I never could have predicted what the future held. I wrote Sumayyah's story of revived hope in a fight for happiness on my own, but it is your voices that have made corners of the world roar with women's empowerment. It is your determination and strength from which *The Obedient Bow* derives. If you have been here before, this may sound familiar: I never started this journey to make money. I have always wished to create stories that my readers can connect with. So, in publishing this book, I am not chasing the same monetary success *The Perfect Bow* generated. I only hope that at least one person can resonate with Zoya's story and know they are not alone.

There is a recurring theme of 'love and dreams' throughout the book. We see how Zoya's perception of these adapts as she progresses through her arc. While I was determined to give her a happy ending, I felt compelled to write a 'realistic' conclusion to her story. Frequently, I'm asked if my books have happy endings. My answer will always be yes. I understand the innate desire as a reader to want the characters to run off into the sunset, having got everything they wanted. And this certainly isn't the case for Zoya, as she is still bound by her duties as a mother, wife, and daughter-in-law. But we cannot deny that her ending is one of happiness. She can run her business while also having her family by her side. Her ultimate strength comes from setting the rules of her life and marriage. Most importantly, we leave Zoya at a point where she understands her worth, loves herself and has gained the freedom to be the woman she wants to be.

I know many of you are going to be disappointed she didn't leave Idris, but Zoya deserved to have an iteration of her childhood dream. Writing Idris has been a challenge. In planning this series, I always knew that Idris would have good intentions but struggle to act on them in a healthy and safe manner. Since the beginning, I have repeatedly said that this series is not a hate campaign against men or the culture. It is simply to highlight the injustices we face daily as women. With that being said, it would be ignorant if I was to disregard that there are good men out there or that some men are willing to learn and be better. That was the foundation of Idris' arc. In the end, we saw how desperate he was to make his marriage work for no other reason than his love for Zoya.

As an author, I feel a responsibility to ensure I am not promoting anything that could put you at risk. It was important to me that both Zoya and Idris understood that his behaviour was abusive. Her choice to give her marriage another chance was only on the condition that Idris works to correct his unhealthy behaviours. I've always strived for realism in my characters, believing they should be flawed — Zoya included. Idris is not the 'villain' in this book. All the characters have done things that we all would collectively agree are wrong. But there is not necessarily a right or wrong side in this story. We cannot deny that, while it may not be the same level, Zoya also hurt Idris. In the end, they realise they both have progress to make, but are ready to do it together.

I know there will be questions about if Idris has truly changed. I'd like to believe he has. But also, if he hasn't, we know Zoya has the strength to leave. As we end this book in the present tense, we leave her at a point where her life truly begins. She is the one leading the decisions and I can't wait for you all to see her post *The Obedient Bow* through the remaining books.

The Bow Series is an interconnected series that runs along the same timeline. While vastly different people, their journeys are ones of women's empowerment and breaking tradition. I hope you see yourself in at least one of our female leads because they each harbour a characteristic that deserves to be celebrated.

Like Zoya, I have spent my life judging my worth against the labels others have put against me. I have spent too many years holding out for love and acceptance. During my childhood, I was either engrossed in books or lost in daydreams about a life that always felt too vast. I believed people when they told me I would never get there. I let their discouragement silence me and the stories I wanted to tell. But I found the strength to break free of the handcuffs this culture put on me. I often think about a younger Samirah and wonder what she would say if she saw me living her dream. I'd like to think she's proud of me, because I know I am.

Details for upcoming books in the series will be shared via Instagram (*@szaman.author*) and TikTok (*@samirahzamanauthor*).

Acknowledgements

I would first like to extend my thanks to all the women who shared their stories and experiences with me. Reading your submissions never gets easier and breaks me in ways I wish it didn't. It takes courage to share your vulnerabilities with anyone, let alone a stranger. I hope in reading this story; it reflects the strength I saw in all of you.

A special thank you to my cover designer @_brints who did such a phenomenal job on this cover. I still remember seeing the first sketch of Zoya and Idris and being in awe of how well you depicted their dynamics. This cover will go down as one of, if not my number one, favourite. I don't know how you're going to top this one! Your patience and dedication are unquestionable. Thank you for all your hard work.

To Bushra — the one this entire book is dedicated to. How fitting that a book about dreams and strength is dedicated to you? You have always brought out the fighter in me, always pushing me to strive for all the crazy dreams and ideas I concoct. Nothing I have achieved would have been possible if you didn't believe in me from the beginning. No number of dedications or acknowledgements will ever be enough to express how grateful I am to you and your sisterhood. But I hope you know and feel it, always and forever.

My real-life Masuma ... my Bhabhi... Thank you for taking the time to share your honest experiences of marriage and its trials. Without those frank conversations, I would not have navigated Zoya's arc accurately. And also a special thank you for all the TMI conversations we've had ... you know which ones.

Ammara, thank you for supporting me since my Wattpad days. I find it surreal that we're discussing my books when, once upon a time, we sat in school laughing about the dumbest of things. Thank you for educating me on the Pakistani culture and never getting annoyed at the multitude of questions I asked. I know this is one you were excited for, and I hope I did it justice and it healed a small part of you.

My blurb fairy, I don't know how many of these I can write while keeping it original. Your skill to co-write these blurbs without knowing the story is something you should charge me for. Aside from that, you deserve a public acknowledgement for your unwavering support and belief in me.

Last, but never the least, my readers. There aren't enough words to explain how grateful I am to you all. I often say 'publishing *The Perfect Bow* changed my life'. But that is inaccurate. It is you that has changed my life. I published that book truly believing nobody would want to read it. And then I found all of you. While I am proud that I have done these stories justice, it equally kills me when I hear how accurate these are to real life. The anticipation and excitement for this book has been positively overwhelming. I hope it was worth the year-long wait. Your faith in me as an author astounds me and every comment, message, and review means the world to me. I will always be eternally grateful because without you, I wouldn't be living my dream. Thank you for trusting me to be our voice.